The Queen's Intelligencer: Book Two

The Shadow of the Tower

A Robert Poley Novel

Peter Tonkin

For

Cham

Guy and Cat

Mark and Lana

With love,

as always.

Table of Contents

Scotland. 1570

1

James Stewart, Earl of Moray, sits astride his finest stallion at the head of a cavalcade trotting through the heart of Linlithgow, some twenty miles west and a little north of Edinburgh, whither he is bound. Like everyone else in the group, the earl is heavily cloaked, gauntleted and hatted, though he disdains to wear a hood. If he allowed himself the sin of pride, he would be proud of his red beard and the golden hair that the tartan bonnet cannot quite contain. Beneath the cloak he is wearing a cuirass and back-plate. His arms and legs are also well-armoured. This might be the heart of the land he rules on behalf of the child-king but it can still be lawless on occasion. The weather is cold even for January. The clouds hang low and grey. There is a wind coming south off the Firth of Forth that moans like a sickly infant and the sleety drizzle it carries freezes on contact with whatever it touches. Despite this, the earl is in fine fettle. He is forty years old, fit, healthy, powerful and wealthy. As regent to King James VI, currently only three and a half years old, he is effective ruler of everything he surveys. It is less than two years since he defeated Queen Mary's larger force at the battle of Langside, cementing his power as successor to the French regent Mary of Guise, becoming regent himself and forcing the French educated Catholic queen to run south into England where she is currently imprisoned while Queen Elizabeth decides precisely what to do with her unwelcome guest.

Although he has earned the title of 'The Gude Regent', Moray is well aware that he rules a divided kingdom. There are still those who support the Queen Mary of Scots, despite her foreign education, marriage and religion. Dumbarton Castle is held by such men who stand against him and his reforms on the Queen of Scots' behalf. But under him, the true Church's Protestant grip is tightening on the land and even now he is on his way to a meeting in Edinburgh which should resolve many of his problems. He has ambitions to bring the restless lairds – each with his own great castle and band of men under arms – to heel. To settle the differences – endless and bloody – between the lowlanders like the Balfours and the Burns and the tartan-clad highlanders like the MacGregors and MacBeths with their claymores and their great kilts. Perhaps even to settle the running sore which is the Debatable Land - that swathe of utter lawlessness along the English border. Yes. It is just as well he is still so young and fit. He has years of work ahead of him.

Moray looks up, pulling himself out of his brown study. He glances around, craning his neck, orienting himself. He is in the heart of the town, just coming past the Archbishop's house. The sun comes out for an instant, making his hair shine like a flame in the dull grey scene, and glittering on the green glass of upper windows in the Archbishop's house. James Stewart notices that one window stands wide, despite the weather. He lifts his chin, the better to see what is going on. Something gleams in the shadows behind the open window. A bright flare, the colour of a daffodil flowering three months early. The moaning of the restless wind is broken by a flat *bang!* The bullet takes him in the red-bearded throat. It breaks his jaw and rips away everything between that and the high steel collar of his armour. He is thrown sideways with sufficient force to unseat him and he crashes onto the cobbles of Linlithgow's main street with stunning force. He has no time for last thoughts. Not even the realisation that his golden hair and bright red beard have made such an excellent target. But as he lies there, surrounded by the shuffling feet of the horrified crowd, he observes with a shock of surprise, a huge lake of steaming redness washing across the road. Who would have thought, he muses as he dies, that a man could have so much blood in him.

King James never really comprehends the fate of this regent he hardly remembers, even when it is repeated to him time and again through childhood. But fourteen years later, when James is rising eighteen, William the Silent, Prince of Orange, Stadtholder of Holland and Friesland, is also assassinated, shot dead at his palace, the Prinsenhof in Delft. And James, like every other ruler in Europe, comes fully alive to the dangers of this brand new, disturbingly effective, method of killing kings.

2

1600

James Stuart walks unsteadily across the cobbled courtyard of Falkland Palace, steps up onto a grey stone mounting block and, refusing the aid of the groom at the horse's head, swings easily up into the saddle. The simple act transforms the man. On foot, he almost gives the impression of being crippled. His legs dominate. They are short, bandy, thin and twisted; obviously weak, despite the thigh-boots with their high, spurred heels. And despite the galligaskins supported by a thick belt with a huge silver buckle, from which hang his sword and dagger. The whole of his body is ruled by them. The result of a birth that nearly killed his mother, they cause him to walk with a stoop, almost a hunch, and a slightly rolling gait, like a drunkard or a sailor recently come ashore. They make his shoulders move uneasily out of line, his arms swing automatically, ape-like, as he fights to maintain his balance. Because of them, his head bobs and sways, seemingly too big for the body it crowns. His breath comes in uneven gasps, clouding on the cool morning air despite the fact it is high summer.

But the instant his feet are in the stirrups and his seat in the saddle secure, he changes almost beyond recognition. Now the solid, muscular torso above the thick belt predominates, filling his silk-slashed doublet until the silver buttons strain. Broad shoulders sit squarely atop a barrel of a chest; a short, thick neck above them holds a regal head high. Eyes like those of a roosting hawk glance all around the stable and the courtyard. One deep breath and the breathing becomes light and easy; that of a confident man very much in his element. Long, muscular arms end in broad, steady hands. For a moment the gloved fists rest on the hilt of the dagger on his right hip and the basket-hilt of his brutal highland claymore on his left. Then thick gauntlets grasp the reins decisively, turning the great stallion's head even as the spurs on his heels rake his hunter's ribs and he canters out through the castle gate with a group of his closest companions hard on his heels.

James Stuart is thirty-four years old and has been a king for more than thirty-two of those years. He is a successful husband to a loving wife, Anne, and father to a growing family. He has a fine son, rising six, whose name, Henry, shows that James has an interest in the throne of his royal neighbours to the south, whose line of succession is coming to an end with the life of a barren queen. He has a four-year old daughter – Elizabeth of course – and although Anne had lost a year-old baby daughter, Margaret, less than six months since, she is pregnant again and due to come to term with their third child in three months or so. The wise women tell her it will be a boy. James is toying with the name of Charles for the bairn.

James thinks of himself as a fine scholar and a cunning politician, expert on everything from statecraft to witchcraft. But he is sufficiently aware of his handicaps to keep them under review if not always under complete mastery. His tongue sometimes seems too big for his mouth and ill-controlled, making the Scottish accent with which he speaks even more impenetrable to strangers. More than that, his lips behave as though they are palsied though he has long stopped worrying about the wine that escapes from the corners of his mouth when he drinks, running down into his straggly brown beard. His legs and the way they dictate his gait always give a negative first impression to any stranger seeing him walk. So it is that he prefers to communicate through his writing or through the mouths of others who understand him well and can pass on his observations clearly. Particularly if they are young and well-favoured. He prefers to meet strangers – and he has to meet many strangers – sitting down. Or, best of all, as now, in the saddle of a good strong horse. He is a bruising rider, capable of covering more than thirty miles in an afternoon if his horse stays strong. He is famously always at the forefront of any hunt – first over a hedge or stream, first through a gap be it never so narrow. Today, the men accompanying him – most of whom are his elders – exchange a look of mild resignation and wry amusement; like the parents of a beloved but wilful child. His reputation is such that even better horsemen on stronger mounts – few and far-between though they are – will always yield the lead to him. He is, after all, James, by the grace of God, King of Scotland.

Apart from the gillie and his men, the beaters and the dog-handlers, James Stuart is accompanied by several of his closest friends and advisors, all of them a good deal older than he is. These men are Ludovic Stewart, the Duke of Lennox, John Erskine the Earl of Mar and his brother Thomas who is Captain of the King's Guard, Sir John Ramsay, Edward Bruce and the King's Physician Dr Hugh Herries. Herries often accompanies the hunts because James is so fearless, well aware of the dangers which this presents, independently of the added risks that arise from the prey turning and fighting back. Something that today's quarry, a massive stag, might well choose to do. But further to that, the gillie has reported that there is a pack of enormous wolves running wild between here and the city of Perth some fifteen miles, perhaps two hours' hard riding, to the north. It is northward that the band of huntsmen are planning to go, for the country there is hilly, with a combination of forest and heath which the gillie says is home to the stag. If they cross the stag's trace first, they will hunt it for their own amusement. If they cross the wolves', they will hunt them for the good of the local farmers. And so they set out bravely, in blissful ignorance of the fact that before the day is out it will be James who will be the prey in a different, treasonous and murderous, hunt.

They stop for lunch at the crossroads of Aberargie, half way to Perth, still without having met either the stag or the wolves. This is disappointing because the hilly, forested terrain is perfect cover for either of the animals they are hunting and, led by the hounds, they have explored many hopeful-looking thickets on either side of the road they are following. The gillie for once seems to have let them down. It never occurs to James that the huntsman might be leading them along a prearranged path for purposes other than finding their quarry. But they have to rest the horses after an exhausting if unrewarding morning. Fortunately, the attendants have come well-supplied with cold meats, bread and wine. At James's insistence there is also a supply of uskebeagh, though he himself is a modest drinker. The inn at the crossroads has been happy to supply water and beer as well as hot pies for those desirous of something warm, even though the day is overcast and increasingly muggy. Thunder rumbles somewhere in the distance, over the peak of Moncreiff Hill immediately ahead of them, perhaps, or over the broad estuarine valley of the river Tay which lies beyond it.

All the preparation of food and drink comes to nothing, however, for as they are washing in preparation for the meal, a horseman approaches down the road from the north. As the rider with his companions draws near, James recognises young Alexander, Lord Ruthven, brother to John Ruthven, the current Earl of Gowrie. Both, despite their titles and responsibilities, are young men. Alexander is only six months past his twentieth birthday and his elder brother John, the Earl, is little more than twenty-three. Lord Alexander is accompanied by a personal servant and a small group of followers. He reins to a stop beside James and his companions, apparently unsurprised at the coincidence of finding them here. 'Sir,' says Alexander, 'my brother has sent me to summon you. He has, at Gowrie House in Perth, a stranger who was arrested at the river dock trying to evade our authorities and smuggle himself into the kingdom without any papers or authorisations.'

James is at first disinclined to pay much attention to the young man, whose family he neither likes or trusts. Especially as Alexander Ruthven is looking down on him from the height of his saddle while James is dismounted and stiffly afoot. Besides, he is parched and starving after his exhaustingly frustrating morning. 'What is this to me?' he demands, eyeing the table set in the tavern's garden, laden with food and drink. 'Let Lord Gowrie resolve the matter.'

'But my brother sent me to warn you,' repeats Alexander anxiously, wide-eyed, his face a picture of innocence, 'for he believes the matter to be too great for him to deal with alone. The anonymous stranger has about him a great fortune in gold. It is French by the look of it, but perhaps Dutch or even Spanish. It is certainly foreign.'

'Gold, you say?' demands James, the luncheon immediately forgotten.

'Indeed, sir: a great chest of gold. And it is my brother's opinion that, as the stranger will vouchsafe neither his name nor his standing, the fortune might well be confiscated and revert to the Crown as treasure trove.'

James glances around the companions at his shoulder. 'Gillie, take your men and your hounds back to Falkland Palace,' he orders. 'The rest of you, pack this food away and follow him. It seems that we are done hunting for today.' With every sign of relief – and no surprise at all – the gillie obeys. As he organises his men and the hounds, James continues speaking, 'Ludovic, John and Thomas, John Ramsay, Edward Bruce and Dr Hugh, be so good as to accompany me. It seems that we are off to Perth.'

As James says this, Alexander Ruthven turns to his nearest follower, a massive man in a great kilt of highland tartan, carrying a claymore even larger than the king's, with a hooded cloak on his shoulders. 'Henderson,' he says. 'Ride on ahead and tell the Earl what's toward.' Henderson obediently pulls his horse's head round and vanishes up the road.

Back in the saddle, James is once more confident and commanding. He and his companions trot along the uphill road after Alexander Ruthven and the group of riders accompanying him until they reach the peak of Moncreiff Hill, where they pause to let their horses catch their breath before the final four miles down to the granite city of Perth which crouches across the river Tay in the distance like some great grey animal drinking. The view across the river and its estuary is breath-taking, but James's head is full of golden visions. He is poor in terms of ready money and circumscribed by the demands of the various powers he is forced to deal with, most particularly the hierarchy of the Church or Kirk – and the restless, sometimes rebellious nobles who align themselves with the powerful churchmen. What James sees as modest generosity, they see as wicked profligacy; what he believes are the simple necessities of a man in his position, they see as sinful spendthrift. They hold the purse-strings, in marked difference to the way such matters are handled in England where Queen Elizabeth can spend as much as she wants on whatever she likes; or so it appears to James. At every turn, it seems, the self-righteous zealots of the Kirk keep him cabined, cribbed, confined.

A fortune in gold is, therefore, an almost irresistible temptation. But the fact that it is Gowrie who has discovered it and who now, apparently, holds both the man and the fortune locked up in Gowrie House, cannot fail to raise suspicions in James's mind. He and the Ruthven family have been at war almost since the day he was born. Before that, in fact: the first earl tried to seduce James's mother the Queen of Scots when she was in his charge, despite his standing as an upright, Godfearing man. Then he held a dagger to her pregnant belly mere months before James's birth while his father Henry Stuart, Lord Darnley, murdered her companion, David Rizzio. Then Ruthven, who replaced the Earl of Moray as regent, held James himself captive for several months when he was a lad of sixteen. More than just a lad, of course: a young king. And, as such, a helpless pawn in the power-games being played out by the ruthless nobles with which Scotland was all-too well supplied. But that Earl of Gowrie had offended more men than merely his monarch – and had been executed two years later when James was eighteen and when the canny young king finally organised a group of nobles more ruthless and powerful than the hated earl. Amongst the many charges brought against him was one of Witchcraft, not least because his issue included five strong sons. His successor, his eldest son James, only survived him by four years.

The current earl, his second-eldest, John Ruthven, lately returned from some years travelling and studying on the continent seems to be too wise to follow in his family's treasonous footsteps; as is young Alexander. William and Patrick are mere schoolboys and of no account at all. Moreover, Gowrie House is not Castle Ruthven, where he was imprisoned in his youth, James reasons now. The earl and his brother are both untried young men in their early twenties. He has trusted friends with him. And a fortune in gold is a fortune in gold after all. It seems to James that the prize clearly outweighs the risks.

3

Gowrie House stands just inside Perth's solid city walls where the wide roadways of Speygate and Watergate meet, its gardens opening onto the river Tay. It presents to the broad, cobbled city streets, a forbidding grey wall with a narrow gate opening into the courtyard which is guarded by a pair of turrets whose narrow windows look over the courtyard and out into the street. Like many of the more substantial houses here, it is almost a castle in design and the purpose of the turrets is to guard the gate. James glances up at these as he and his companions follow Alexander and his men into the courtyard, then he turns his attention to the matters in hand. The stranger and the gold are still his main priority, but bodily needs take precedence. The hunters have been riding all day. It is nearly two hours since they left the inn. James needs to relieve himself and assumes the others will need to do so too. Because they followed Alexander instead of eating or drinking, they are all parched and extremely sharp-set. The stranger and the gold are clearly not going anywhere if John Ruthven has them securely under lock and key. A visit to the jakes followed by food and drink are, for the moment, far more important even than a fortune in foreign gold.

James limps clumsily into Gowrie House, his treacherous legs even worse than usual, for they are stiff from riding. He is met a little way inside the door by Alexander's elder brother John who gives every evidence of surprise at seeing his clearly unexpected guests, despite the presence of Alexander's messenger Henderson at his shoulder.

'Your Majesty, my Lords, gentlemen, what is it I can do for you?' John Gowrie asks as he and James confront each other in the reception hall, each surrounded by their attendants and companions. It is only now, standing face to face with them that James registers how tall and powerfully formed the Ruthven brothers are. Like their servant, the messenger Henderson, they tower over him.

'Privy, food and drink,' answers James, speaking for them all. He glances around the stark room, noting the inner door that leads through to what looks like a great hall, and a set of stairs in a shadowy corner leading upwards as though they are in a tower rather than a good-sized room in a well-set house.

'Why, of course, of course,' says the earl. 'Alexander, send one of your men to alert the kitchen.' He turns back to James, his face pale and his hands clasped as though in prayer. 'It may take a little time, sir, we were unprepared…'

James frowns. This was not the impression young Alexander had given or that the messenger's presence suggests. But perhaps the earl is merely surprised at the speed with which his message has been answered. He shrugs.

'Henderson,' says Alexander to his messenger, breaking into James's thoughts. 'Please do what the earl requests.'

'Aye, sir. Food for His Majesty and his companions.' Henderson shrugs off his cloak and gives it to the man standing behind him. As he straightens, James studies him more closely. He looks old enough to be the boys' father. He is easily twice their age and every bit as tall and powerful-looking as they are. He seems to be different to the others of the Gowrie household. Not least because he is wearing highland tartan and that great claymore at his belt. 'Will you and the earl be joining them My Lord?' Henderson asks.

'No,' answers Alexander. Then he turns to James, 'But, Your Majesty, if I may, I will conduct you to the privies and arrange water for washing.'

Henderson vanishes into the great hall and Alexander leads the way to the privy that overlooks the garden. It is perhaps fortunate, thinks James as he relieves himself, that the threat of a thunderstorm has receded – or he and his companions would have been pissed on as they pissed.

14

Side-tracked into preparing a set of witty observations to be tried on his companions in due course, James loses track of time. He will never be quite certain how long the ablutions took, but it seems to him that it is more than half an hour before he and his men are conducted back to the dining hall where the Ruthven brothers are waiting nervously with water, beer and wine. Then, by the time everyone has refreshed themselves and food arrives, it must be coming up to an hour since they rode through the gate beneath the baleful gaze of the guard turrets.

Despite the impression that his various infirmities and his liking for ribald wit seem to give, James is no fool. As he settles to his makeshift meal, he finds himself feeling that he has somehow arrived in the middle of a play. That he and his hunting friends are unwitting performers in a drama that the Ruthven brothers and their household are improvising; as though this were one of the masques that Anne so loves. His experiences in Ruthven Castle keep recurring ever more forcefully. But if this is a trap, he has put his head into it willingly enough. He and the others with him are likely outnumbered by the Gowrie household – but not by much unless the earl has arranged for more men to be hiding about the place. On the other hand, like James, the hunters all rode well-armed and could likely stand anything short of a full assault either by soldiers or by guns. And, he keeps reminding himself, when all is said and done, he is only facing a couple of lads.

James has reached this far in his reasoning by the time he finished the scant meal of river fish, fowl, porridge and rough bread which the earl's kitchen has managed to supply. His priorities re-ordered, he draws breath to ask about the incarcerated stranger with his hoard of foreign gold. But young Alexander prevents him. 'Your Majesty, now that you have eaten, may I conduct you to the room where we have our prisoner under lock and key?'

'You may indeed,' says James expansively as he wipes his wine-wet beard. He stands, leaning against the edge of the table until his legs steady. Several of his friends stand as well, but James gestures them to be seated. He is keen to see where this charade is leading and besides, he is armed with a dagger more than a foot in length and a basket hilted claymore. Young Alexander is carrying no obvious weapons at all except for a bunch of keys, though he has kept his cloak on and James can see nothing of what he is wearing beneath it.

James follows Alexander to a broad, formal staircase which they mount to the house's upper level. Here, behind a broad landing, stands a solid-looking door. The young lord fusses with the keys. It takes him a while to find the one which unlocks it. He turns the key then the handle and ushers James through into a long gallery, the upper reflection of the reception room and great hall below. He pauses to lock the door once more then leads James along the bright chamber to another door. He walks slowly, apparently taking courteous note of the fact that James is still limping and in a little discomfort. Because he noticed the cramped little spiral staircase downstairs, James is not surprised to see it opening in a dark corner of this room too, but his attention is soon distracted by the noise of Alexander unlocking another door. Again, the process is slow and time-consuming.

This door opens into a small room with circular walls, brightly lit by windows facing two ways. At the far side of this room stands a man wearing a cloak with the hood up, with his back to the door, who appears to be staring out at the courtyard below. Alexander ushers James into the room – clearly a turret room – and turns to lock the door once more. James is not yet disturbed. This must be the mysterious smuggler after all. His heartbeat speeds up. He looks around the floor for the chest of gold the stranger has brought with him.

But then, in an instant, everything changes. The man in the turret room turns and James recognises not a stranger or a smuggler but Alexander's massive servant Henderson. James takes a step back. His first reaction is disappointment: there is clearly no gold. Then anger: he has allowed himself to be tricked. It has not yet occurred to him that he is in fact trapped. But then he sees the truth. At first, he is vexed but then he realises what is going on. And, if Alexander has no weapons about him, Henderson is almost as well-armed as James himself. Not to mention the fact that he and his lord are both nearly twice as big as their victim. James turns to Alexander. The young man has caught up a steel bonnet from a stool behind the door and put it on. His raised arms open his cloak to reveal a solid-looking breastplate. James realises with at tingle of shock that although the boy is not armed, he is nevertheless fully armoured now; proof against the dagger and the claymore unless they are very expertly wielded.

'What…' James reaches across his breast, right hand to left hip, planning to draw his claymore. But Alexander's hand closes down on his fist, holding the sword in its sheath and making it impossible for James to reach across his right arm pinioned on his chest to reach the dagger at his right hip with his left hand. He is, for the moment, helpless. 'What are you about, boy?' he demands, spitting into Alexander's face as he says '*Boy*'.

'Revenging our father!' spits Alexander in reply. He looks past James to the servant standing by the window 'Henderson!' he calls.

But Henderson does nothing. Either he does not understand what Alexander wants or he is unwilling to do it. To stab his king in the back, obviously. Or to reach around and slit his throat. Suddenly desperate, James wrestles free. He turns, tugging at his claymore. 'Your father was duly condemned by a jury of his peers after a fair trial,' he says as he wrestles with the sword. 'And besides, I have shown the Ruthven family many benefits since I came into my rightful power.'

He stops there, sword half-drawn for Alexander is pushing the tip of Henderson's dagger through the cut silk of his doublet and into the skin immediately above his heart.

'If you open the window, call out or try to escape, you are a dead man,' hisses the young lord, and then he is gone through the door back out into the upper gallery.

Henderson steps forward, blocking the doorway. 'He's gone to talk with the earl, like as not,' says the servant.

'To talk about what? Killing me in revenge for their father?'

'I do not know, Your Majesty,' answers Henderson. 'But if that is what they determine, they will have to do the deed themselves. I'm no' going to kill a king. Not even for them.'

'Then let me go,' says James. 'If you hold me here until they return then you are as guilty as they are.'

'Mayhap,' shrugs Henderson. 'But still, it'll no be my hand as holds the mortal blade.'

There is a short silence which is broken by the sound of bustle down in the courtyard. James looks out of the window and Alexander's threat suddenly makes more sense. James's companions are preparing to leave. The Ruthven brothers must somehow have convinced them that James has left already. The final part of the situation falls into place in his mind. They have not dared kill him while so many of his friends and followers were nearby. But as soon as he is alone, he is almost certain to die.

James leaps at the window and begins to wrestle it open but the catch is stiff. Henderson is on him in a moment, pulling him back as the first of his friends mount up and walk their horses out through the gate. Then Alexander is back. He takes over from Henderson and tries to bind James's hands. But James struggles free once more – only to be betrayed by his legs. As he limps across the room, Alexander takes his feet out from beneath him with a brutal kick at his ankles which comes near to breaking them. James falls forward into the window embrasure. His head and left shoulder hit the frame, and the window at last yields, swinging wide to slam against the outer wall with a sound of breaking glass. Everyone in both courtyard and street looks up at the sound. James's head is thrust through. John Erskine, the Earl of Mar, is still mounting his horse close below with Edward Bruce beside him. 'John!' shouts the frantic man. 'Help! Treachery! Murder!

The Earl of Mar looks up into his king's desperate face. 'Lennox!' he yells to Ludovic Stewart who has just ridden into the street, 'Here's treason! Be quick!'

All of James's friends turn and come riding or running back into Gowrie House. Alexander pays no attention to all of this – he is still concentrating on tying James's hands, his face a mask of desperation. Henderson, however, sees which way the wind is blowing and stands well back, though he still blocks the doorway. In surprisingly little time, James hears the sound of his friends beating on the great door at the top of the main staircase. But the door is locked. With a howl of frustration, James tears his wrists free from Alexander's grasp. He reaches for his sword but pauses. The great blade is far too unwieldy for this close-quarters fighting and in any case is nearly useless against a man in full armour. He grabs for his dagger instead. But before he can draw it, Henderson is pushed aside as the turret door bursts open. Sir John Ramsay erupts into the little room, clearly having seen – like James himself – that there is a small spiral staircase in the corner of the reception room which leads almost directly to the turret. Edward Bruce is close behind him.

Alexander turns and seems almost to throw himself onto the blade of Sir John's dagger which avoids the steel breastplate and buries itself deep in the young lord's right side, just below his arm pit. The two men stagger out into the gallery, Sir John shouting, 'Thomas Erskine! To me! To me!' Edward Bruce grabs young Alexander and his dagger does on the left side what Sir John's did on the right. James runs after them, just in time to see Alexander, gushing blood, stumble down the shadowy staircase and disappear. Sir John runs down

19

behind the falling man, still calling for Erskine. James and Bruce are hard on his heels. Half way down the staircase they find Alexander sprawled on his back while Thomas Erskine and Dr Herries finish the work that Sir John and Bruce have just begun. Alexander's throat is slit and his forehead chopped open. The courtiers lug the young man's corpse on down the stairs into the reception room below.

Alexander's body crashes onto the flags of the floor just as his brother the earl comes running in from the courtyard to see what all the commotion is about. He is followed by a stable hand who is followed in turn by Ludovic Stewart, Duke of Lennox, and John Erskine, Earl of Mar. They are armed and have their swords drawn as they have been trying to break down the great door at the top of the main staircase. In spite of the allegiance of the men surrounding him, despite of the fact that they are all holding naked blades, in spite of everything, the Earl of Gowrie hurls himself over the lifeless body of his young brother at the man he blames for his death as well as for the death of their father. James steps back up onto the lower steps of the staircase, reaching for his dagger once more. But long before John Ruthven can come anywhere near James, he has joined his brother Alexander in a pool of blood on the cold stone flags of the floor, chopped almost into pieced by the heavy highland swords wielded by Lennox and Mar. Edward Bruce leans down and puts an end to the matter with a dagger through the dying Earl's throat.

James looks at his companions as they wipe the blades of their swords and daggers, shocked into silence by the sudden brutality of what has just happened. 'This was none of my doing,' says James. 'I did not look for this!' He is speaking not only to his own followers but to the household of the late earl who are gathered at each of the doorways, frozen with shock and horror. He comes down off the final step and staggers a little, his legs damaged from Alexander's brutal kicking. 'We hunted a stag and a pack of wolves,' he observes at last. 'But it seems we have killed a pair of traitors instead.'

***

When Lady Audrey Walsingham brought word of this adventure south from the court of Queen Anne in Edinburgh and told it to her husband Sir Thomas, he passed it straight to Robert Cecil, Secretary to Her Majesty's Council.

Master Secretary Cecil summoned a pair of his closest confidents to discuss the news with them. These men were the forger and code-master Thomas Phelippes and his chief intelligencer Robert Poley. The three of them were currently engaged in plotting the downfall of the Earl of Essex whose popularity was putting Cecil's standing and prospects under immediate and dangerous threat, despite Essex's misfortunes in Ireland to the west. But they turned aside to look at matters to the north. 'I see two ways of assessing this,' said Cecil. 'Either King James was tricked into an attempt to kill him and fought his way free, killing the men who had hatched the plot. In which he has proved himself quick-thinking, decisive and by no means afraid of facing hard choices – strengths to be admired in a king. Or he plotted the entire situation in order to rid himself of powerful men who wished him ill and who would do their best to destroy him in due course. In which case he has proved himself devious, decisive and by no means afraid of facing hard choices…'

'Strengths to be admired a king,' said Poley. 'And particularly, perhaps, in a king of England.'

'But,' said Phelippes after a moment more, 'how will this news affect the queen and her thoughts on the succession?'

'A good question,' admitted Cecil. 'But I believe I have a way to obtain an answer. Poley. I will put you in contact with my eyes and ears among the Ladies of the Privy Chamber. You and she will begin to meet each other regularly but in secret. Her name is Lady Janet Percy.

England. Three Years Later

1

When Lady Janet Percy was ejected from the most senior group of Ladies in Waiting to Her Majesty, the Ladies of the Privy Chamber, forbidden the Royal Presence, barred from the Court entirely and exiled to the Scottish borders with her cousins Charles and Jocelyn Percy because of her involvement in the downfall of the Earl of Essex, no-one could have predicted the impact this would have on Robert Poley. Least of all Poley himself. Until he started to suspect the cause of the pain he began to feel soon after she left. It was an ache of the spirit, such as he might have expected were he condemned to Purgatory after Judgement Day rather than to the Everlasting Bonfire he was certain awaited him.

It was a purgatorial pain which seemed to grow more intense the longer Lady Janet lay beyond his reach; effectively, indeed, dead to him. This was a situation compounded by the fact that he seemed to catch glimpses of her with her flame red hair and sparkling eyes in the corners of his vision; to hear echoes of her voice with its lilting accent from the Scottish borders at the edges of his hearing. By the fact that she moved so regularly through his dreams, always distant and unattainable. Oddly, it was the living who haunted him rather than all the dead, like the Queen of Scots and her unfortunate followers Thomas Babington and the rest; Christopher Marlowe; Robert Devereux, the Earl of Essex; Sir Christopher Blount, Sir Gelly Meyrick and Sir Henry Cuffe, all of whose terrible deaths lay directly at his door. Eventually it took a great deal of willpower not to let Lady Janet's all-too lively spectre distract him from the day-to-day demands of his work. For that work was of supreme importance. Having secretly overseen the downfall of the greatest of Master Secretary Cecil's rivals, he was now commissioned to ensure - to engineer if need-be - the downfall of the next, while working to ensure that James Stuart would succeed Elizabeth Tudor to the throne of England.

It was not as if he had ever stood more than the faintest chance of engaging Lady Janet's affections as she passed to him secret instructions from Robert Cecil, spiced with gossip from the increasingly elderly and capricious queen's most intimate circle, an activity that allowed an unusual level of intimacy between the pair of them, which in itself had given him a kind of hope. Like secret lovers, they had held clandestine meetings in secluded pews of St Clement Danes church, in her private carriage and – once – in the intimacy of her bed-chamber when she was visiting Essex House. All, always carefully chaperoned by Agnes her maid. But he allowed himself some modest optimism. Mere months older than the Queen's 45-year reign, Poley was still lean, muscular and fit, features he had inherited, perhaps, from his mother, Mary Blount. Lady Lettice Knollys, widow of both the Earl of Leicester and the First Earl of Essex, mother to Robert Devereux the Second Earl, had often remarked on Poley's striking similarity to Sir Christopher Blount, her third husband and his maternal relative. Sir Christopher was generally reckoned to have been extremely well formed in proportion of both body and limb - and striking in the manly beauty of his looks. Or so he was before his face was torn open during the fatal confrontation at Lud Gate during the Essex uprising as he fought to support his step-son's ill-conceived attempt to capture Queen Elizabeth and make her change both her policies and the membership of her Privy Council, as though this were Scotland and such political games were possible. The Blount blood had given Poley an excess of black hair with a virile tendency to curl, dark hued skin and piercing blue eyes. Yet, strangely enough, when he contrived to veil those eyes, lower that dark head and round those square shoulders, he had the ability to become so unremarkable as to be almost invisible. It was a facility he found far more useful, given his profession, than any amount of noble blood.

However, Lady Janet was of aristocratic stock, first cousin to Henry Percy, the ninth Earl of Northumberland, who was husband to the late Earl of Essex's elder sister Dorothy. Henry Percy also had a legitimate claim to the throne of England via his descent from Plantagenet King Henry III's son, King Edward I's brother Edmund Crouchback, Earl of Lancaster. But Northumberland was only one name on the list of possible successors to the ancient and sickly queen. A list she steadfastly refused to consider; a succession she refused to admit must come, and come all too soon. Soon perhaps but still far too far in the future for a disturbing number of desperate or impatient men and women.

Poley was only distantly related to Sir Christopher Blount, perhaps fortunately in the end. Sir Christopher's social standing was sufficient to ensure that he merited beheading on Tower Hill for his part in the uprising led by his step-son the desperate and impatient Earl of Essex. Poley had been lucky to escape hanging, drawing and quartering, the fate he had seen enacted on Sir Gelly Meyrick and Sir Henry Cuffe, Essex's close friends and advisors; knights of the realm perhaps, but meeting the terrible fate of common traitors found guilty of High Treason. His involvement as *agent provocateur* in the uprising would have been fatal for Poley himself had not Cecil let it be known that Poley had been working for him all along. It was a commonplace in Poley's world that espials and intelligencers were often tarred with the same brush as the men and women they were spying on. And all-too-often shared the terrible fate of the people they had betrayed. Only Poley's close association with Robert Cecil, the most powerful man in Queen Elizabeth's realm, had saved his neck. Even though the price of Poley's safety had been his unmasking as the council's chief intelligencer. And Lady Janet's banishment; something else that weighed heavily on his overburdened soul as well as allowing her to haunt his waking and sleeping hours.

But then, Poley was married and had mounted a mistress; both potent barriers against a further liaison even had Lady Janet been close-by and willing. But as the end of Elizabeth's reign drew lingeringly onward, sodden summer and starving autumn after freezing winter and mud-boltered spring, several changes overcame Poley and his situation. His mistress's husband, Master Yeomans the cutler and silversmith, in whose house on Hog Lane he had rented rooms, betrayed him to the Court of Star Chamber in revenge for being cuckolded, condemning him to a term of incarceration in the Fleet Prison. For more than a year after his release, he had been a member of Essex's household working on Cecil's orders – now, with many others, cast out of Essex House. Almost all of the beheaded Earl's followers found themselves on the unwelcoming streets of a London which was well past its golden age. Those without patronage went in search of employment and accommodation; many becoming whoremongers – a profession that solved both problems at once as well as offering some side-benefits as long as the pox could be avoided. Poley himself, though, was fortunate not to be as destitute and debt-ridden as most of the rest of the dead Earl's supporters; those, at any rate, lucky enough to have avoided both axe and gallows and escaped imprisonment in the Tower alongside the Earl of Southampton amongst many others - or the crippling fines that reduced the lordly houses of Rutland, Monteagle, Sandys and Cromwell to near penury.

Then there was the Plague. Although its visitations were not sufficient to label the first years of the new century as plague years, nevertheless it visited, working its way north from Greenwich, Deptford and the riverside docks where the European trade-ships sent their goods ashore. Their goods and their rats. And in this case, it visited the area of London bounded by Bow Lane and Bishopsgate. It did so while Poley was absent from home - working undercover in Essex House. After the Earl's downfall, he returned to the property belonging to his parents-in-law on Bow Lane to discover that he was a widower. Not only that, he found himself sharing a sizable inheritance with his brother-in law, Thomas Watson, which arose from the late Lambert Watson's thriving business as a senior member of the Worshipful Company of Mercers supported by very successful investments in the piratical adventures of the corsair William Piers. Poley and Thomas Watson might well have been enemies, especially given the way Poley had treated his wife, Thomas's sister. But Watson had fallen out with both his Puritan sibling and his grim, tight-fisted parent long ago. The sharing of their inheritance brought the brothers-in-law, if anything, closer. As did the fact that Thomas Watson wished to make his way as an intelligencer; an ambition Poley was well placed to assist him in. Even split in half, the inheritance was sufficient to make Poley's friend Sir Francis Bacon envious, especially as Sir Francis' sickly elder brother Anthony, sometime the Earl of Essex's chief intelligencer, had just died - leaving the impoverished lawyer yet more debts to take care of.

Finally, there was Poley's relationship with the council and Master Secretary Cecil, who, with Essex's execution and Anthony Bacon's death, was now the unrivalled head of the most effective English spy network since the glory days of Sir Francis Walsingham. And, after the success of the secret mission to destroy Essex, Cecil had chosen to keep the intelligencer Robert Poley at the heart of it. Poley was the man who sent the secret agents abroad, who assessed the information they brought back, who sifted it so that only the nuggets of purest gold were presented to the ever-industrious but increasingly overwhelmed Master Secretary. And, in keeping with his position and responsibilities, Robert Poley rented rooms on King Street above the tavern at the sign of the Lion, hard by Westminster and Whitehall with other senior courtiers and important officials, and shared an office with the code-master Thomas Phelippes in Salisbury House - which had been completed by Cecil just in time to entertain the queen late last year. Shared an office with Phelippes and a regular stipend into the bargain.

So, by the third week in March 1603, the Fates had contrived to position Poley as a man of some substance, standing, responsibility and reputation. A man who might indeed be worthy of Lady Janet Percy were she to return his regard. Were she not the length of the realm distant, and far beyond his reach in oh so many ways. And, as his experience with the Earl of Essex had proved beyond any doubt, as long as the man whose patronage protected him remained standing high in royal favour, no matter who sat on the throne. If Robert Cecil ever fell from grace, then all those who depended on him would fall along with him, just as Essex's desperate, destitute supporters had.

Which only went to emphasise how utterly crucial it was to ensure that the king of Scotland, who had so ruthlessly destroyed the Earl of Gowrie and the rest of the hated Ruthven family, came to sit firmly on the English throne in the full and certain knowledge that he owed his position to Robert Cecil and no-one else.

These were the thoughts that occupied Poley as he sat in unaccustomed reflective idleness in his office at Salisbury House. Opposite him sat Thomas Phelippes, hard at work translating a report from their man in the embassy at the Archduke's court in Brussels into clear English. On the table in front of Poley was a pile of letters and reports which he had scanned with eyes that were hardly focussed. Still with his mind far removed from the present, he piled all these together and was in the act of slipping them into his leather satchel when Robert Cecil himself came bustling in, big with news. 'I have just had word from Richmond Palace,' he said. 'It is all-but over. She hasn't spoken for more than a week and remains silent even now. Unwilling or unable to give voice at all. Her doctors say she has scant days to live;

perhaps mere hours. And she has still not settled the question of who she wishes to succeed her.' His slightly protuberant brown eyes raked across the faces of his two most senior intelligencers. 'We must go thither,' he said. 'The three of us. At once.'

2

'I wish you to accompany me,' said Robert Cecil, raising his voice above the sound of oars slapping water and fixing Poley with a penetrating stare of those bulbous brown eyes which the intelligencer found frankly unsettling, 'because I want you there at the end. Both of you.' The gaze switched to Phelippes who shifted uncomfortably on the thwart they were both using as a seat while Cecil sat facing them on cushions beneath an awning in the broad, square stern. All three were heavily cloaked, hatted and hooded against the icy weather of yet another drearily unpromising spring. Poley's satchel sat securely on his lap, protected by the layers of oiled wool which comprised his cloak – though the leather was robust and sufficiently proof against water to keep the vital contents safe. 'Both as witnesses, as messengers if need-be,' Cecil continued. 'And as code-masters should the message need to be made absolutely private.' He paused for a heartbeat. 'By *there* I mean in my private chambers at the palace where you will watch and work under my orders. But to reach my chambers you will have to get past the Queen's Guard, though the Captain of the Guard, Sir Walter Raleigh, is in Plymouth at the moment about some business in his position as Governor of Jersey. Ignorant, I understand, about how rapidly her majesty's situation is worsening.' Just the way he said it confirmed Poley's suspicion that Master Secretary had had a hand in Sir Walter's uncharacteristic absence at the moment of greatest crisis. 'And you will only get past the guards if you are in company with me. Even so, expect your satchel to be searched, Poley. *Faster*, damn you!' This last remark was addressed to the four wherrymen who each held an oar as they rowed upstream as fast as possible, aided by an incoming tide. Fortunately so - Richmond was an hour's journey upriver from Salisbury House.

The Thames was bustling with waterborne business as usual, even though the weather was overcast and icily drizzling. But now that he was out in the open, surrounded by the sounds of lively riverine commerce, Poley realised that something was amiss. Something was missing, in fact. It took him a moment to realise what it was. The bells were silent. London was a city famous for its bells. He had lived for more than a year in Essex House opposite the great old church of St Clement Danes and knew the reality of the child's rhyme, 'Oranges and lemons say the bells of St Clements...' as it listed many of the famous peals that regularly rang out from London's bell-towers. But suddenly, strikingly, they were all silent now. He shivered with something deeper and more disturbing than the cold. He wondered briefly whether he should make a remark to Cecil. But forbore to do so – the man was clearly on edge as it was.

And understandably so, thought Poley. He appreciated very well why his employer might be tense but he had never seen the calm and self-possessed courtier as worried as this. It was almost frightening. The intelligencer found his heart was pounding and his breath short. Conditions which only worsened when the full impact of what he and Phelippes were about to do finally gripped him. Unless he was very much mistaken, the only men other than the royal physicians in close attendance where they were going would be senior members of her majesty's Privy Council, whose one single mission now must be to discover who the queen wished to occupy her throne when she was forced by age, infirmity and death to vacate it. Something mere hours away now, apparently. Poley had been born when Bloody Mary sat on the throne but he had no memory of any sovereign other than Elizabeth and the prospect of her passing was deeply unsettling. But not as unsettling as the realization that unless she nominated a successor, the country might be utterly

33

leaderless until power eventually passed to another monarch. The intoning of the time-honoured phrase, 'The King is dead: long live the King.' was more than mere ritual. For everyone who held an office did so at the order of the monarch, therefore if one occupant of the throne was not followed immediately by another, while the throne remained vacant, they were technically without office, title or power. No king, no council, no civil authorities; no admirals or generals commanding in the field or on the foam. Anarchy, in fact, as the realm stood helpless in the face of civil disorder or foreign invasion – both of which, as Poley knew all too well, were most potent threats. There were eyes just beyond the Channel and many more closer to home, watching for the chance to turn England back to a Catholic country, ruled by the heirs of the Plantagenet dynasty whose last king died on Bosworth Field; a dynasty whose offspring now had branches in almost every ruling house in Europe. In fact, several of the letters and reports packed in the satchel on his lap had such men, such women and such dangers as their subject.

It seemed that Cecil wished his two most senior agents to join the men of the Privy Council awaiting word of the succession, thought Poley, dragging his mind back to the present. And, he realised, the women of the Privy Chamber, whose responsibility it was to ease the queen's passing so that she could die quietly and in peace; preferably in the presence of the Archbishop of Canterbury and the Bishop of London who would be praying for her burdened soul as she passed. A soul weighed down, she made no secret, with an excess of heavy guilt over the executions of another divinely-appointed monarch, her cousin Queen Mary of Scots, and Robert Devereux, her beloved but overreaching Earl of Essex. The gentlewomen's mission, therefore, almost certainly putting them, the Bishop and the Archbishop in direct conflict with the anxious councillors who needed her so urgently to speak of earthly matters before she began to consider heavenly ones. The cause of the conflict lay at the queen's own door, of course. It all turned on her absolute refusal to name a successor.

Well, Poley temporised, perhaps not *all*. There was the potentially fatal element which rested on Cecil's crooked shoulders alone. Master Secretary simply had to ensure that King James of Scotland received the queen's nomination as her successor – because little more than a week ago he had sent Ingram Frizer, who worked for Sir Thomas Walsingham and was absolutely trusted by Cecil, riding hot-foot to Scotland with a copy of the speech he had prepared to give immediately after the queen's death. A speech informing the country that she had nominated as her successor the son of her cousin Mary, Queen of Scots.

And it was now, quite clearly, Cecil's mission to ensure that she did just that; otherwise he was lost and might well end up in the Tower himself. But the plan was not without its dangers. Cecil had to ensure James's succession without making his manipulation of the dying monarch too obvious, especially not to courtiers keen to supersede or even replace him. Courtiers like Sir Walter Raleigh, Henry Brooke Lord Cobham, Cobham's brother George Lord Brooke, Sir Griffin Markham, the headstrong young Lord Grey de Wilton and a good number of their friends, relatives and associates; all worried about losing power to Master Secretary in the new dispensation. All, to one degree or another, desirous of manipulating whoever came to the throne after Elizabeth. Among the reports in Poley's satchel was one suggesting that Raleigh proposed that whoever won the throne – whether it was his favoured candidate Lady Arbella Stuart or not – should only be offered conditional authority. Only allowed to sit in the seat of power if they agreed to a long list of demands. Raleigh was Governor of Jersey and Cobham was Lord Warden of the Cinque Ports – a match worthy of Machiavelli himself. Not to mention that Cobham's brother Lord George, seemed to have his fingers deep in another treasonous movement. One that sought to manipulate the succession – and the new monarch – for religious rather than political reasons. Especially if James was to succeed – after all, kidnapping kings was a popular sport in Scotland.

'Call at the Privy Steps! The Privy Steps damn you!' snarled Cecil, jerking Poley out of his reverie as the wherry swept towards Whitehall Palace and Westminster beyond it. Surprised, the boatmen began to pull towards the north shore. They were really only minutes into the hour it would take to reach their final destination, Poley realised, but were slowing and approaching the shore in order to pick up another passenger. Poley too was sufficiently surprised at Cecil's order to look closely at the figure waiting on the stage at the foot of the Privy Steps. Only as the stranger prepared to step aboard did Poley recognise him. It was Sir Thomas Wilson, Member of Parliament, occasional agent in Cecil's service and one of the greatest living experts on the matter of the queen's succession. The intelligencer was not particularly surprised, therefore, when Cecil said, as the wherry pulled back into the mid-stream, 'I wish to discuss your report on the succession, Sir Thomas. I need to have all the contenders and their sponsors clear in my mind by the time we get to Richmond.' Sir Thomas eased himself on the pillows at Cecil's side. 'Start with the Catholics and their European supporters,' ordered Master Secretary.

A short silence settled as the constitutional expert cleared his mind and ordered his thoughts. Poley had read many of the tracts published – and banned – in recent years and felt that he knew the main contenders well enough, but he was keen to hear the thoughts of such a widely acknowledged expert in the field.

'You know Henry Percy, the Earl of Northumberland has ruled himself out,' Sir Thomas began.

'Yes,' answered Cecil. 'He is wise to have done so. He may be a Protestant like his father but – also like his father - he is too close to Catholic conspirators like Charles Paget and the edges of the Babington Conspiracy, or what is left of it, as

Poley here knows only too well. And he's a close friend of Raleigh's. Not to mention being married to the late Earl of Essex's sister. One wrong move from him and it's a choice between the Tower and the axe.'

Poley thought, *Master Secretary has more than the obvious reason to be glad that Henry Percy is easing out of the running.* He and Cecil were both avid gamblers and as matters currently stood, Cecil owed Percy more than eight hundred pounds lost at cards a few nights since. Were Percy to become serious about gaining the throne, he could use that debt very much to Master Secretary's disadvantage.

Sir Thomas, still thinking about Northumberland's decision to ease out of the succession, nodded his agreement. 'Then there's Ranuccio I Farnese…' he said, 'though his position is weakened since his marriage. And truth to tell he is far too busy with his current responsibilities and the attempts to reclaim Portugal from King Philip the Third of Spain.'

'I agree. He is far too busy ruling Parma to be distracted, though the Spanish and apparently the Pope might support a move on the throne of England,' answered Cecil. 'King Philip might wish it as a distraction from the matter of Portugal, of course. But I have eyes on them both and understand Ranuccio's own thoughts on the matter. Parma is sufficient for his needs and abilities. No. He is no real threat.'

'Philip the Third of Spain himself?' Wondered Sir Thomas.

'Nothing like his father Philip the Second. Too fat and lazy. And his claim through John of Gaunt is too distant to succeed, I believe, through anything but a great deal of money and effort.' Cecil shrugged. 'Oh, he may finance some of the other contenders with what little gold our corsairs allow him to receive from the Americas. He pays me a pension as you know, in the forlorn hope that it might do him some good. But he is nothing to us.'

'The Infanta, then,' said Sir Thomas. 'Popular with King Philip and the Pope alike these five years and more.'

'Isabella Clara Eugenia, Sovereign of the Spanish Netherlands, wife to the Archduke.' Cecil made a meal of her titles as his expression became more thoughtful.

'Also able to assert her right through the Lancastrian claim by descent from John of Gaunt,' emphasised Sir Thomas. 'Which was also the basis of the duke of Westmorland's case before he fled abroad and died in penury.'

'Because the duke, Charles Neville, saw how dangerously possible his case might be. Fatally possible. Yes.' Cecil emphasised the word 'fatally'. 'Not unlike Lord Ferdinando Strange or Queen Mary of Scotland's fatally powerful claim. Eh, Master Poley?'

'So, you accept that the Infanta is a serious contender as I suggested in *The State of England*?' Sir Thomas continued.

'The Earl of Essex thought so,' Poley interrupted, given license, he felt, by Cecil's oblique reference to his part in Mary of Scots' downfall. 'And he believed that those on the council leaning towards the Catholic cause were willing to push her forward, supported as she is by both King Philip and His Holiness. Both, as Master Secretary has observed, willing to part with great sums of money to see their ambitions for her come to fruition. Master Secretary is by no means the only council member in receipt of Catholic gold and there is always the concern that some of those other men are much more open to bribery than Master Secretary is himself. That was why My Lord of Essex contacted King James in Scotland in a desperate attempt to outmanoeuvre them, pleading for direct action by the Earl of Mar. That was why he rose in revolt when King James was too slow to reply.'

'A case of fatal impatience if ever there was one,' said Cecil shortly. 'But we have never treated the Infanta as a serious candidate, no matter how much Catholic gold King Philip and the Pope invest, or how many spies they send with promises of yet more gold, Heavenly salvation, and threats of exposing those recusants in receipt of monies already. All in spite of what poor deluded Essex believed.'

'That leaves the more immediate possibilities, then,' said Sir Thomas. 'The English and Scottish contenders.

'Yes,' nodded Cecil. 'The more dangerous ones. The closer to home, the closer to the throne'

3

'George Hastings, Earl of Huntingdon,' began Sir Thomas. 'From the Plantagenet line, descended from George Plantagenet, Duke of Clarence, brother to Kings Edward the Fourth and Richard the Third, succeeded by Edward, Earl of Warwick who was executed by her majesty's grandfather Henry the Seventh apparently for trying to escape the Tower but probably, like Mary of Scots, for being too great a threat to the Tudor line...'

'Hastings is, what, sixty-two? Sixty-three?' said Cecil, as though he wasn't certain. 'It's a race between him and her majesty who will be meeting St Peter at the gate of Heaven first. No, he's simply too late at the feast, Plantagenet or not.'

'Very well, then,' huffed Sir Thomas. 'Henry Stanley, the Earl of Derby, son of Lady Mary Clifford, a title that passed to his niece, Anne Stanley, daughter of the unfortunate Ferdinando Stanley, Lord Strange...'

'Ferdinando,' Cecil almost purred, 'As we have already observed, subject of an unexpected and as yet unexplained illness. One that carried him away suddenly and violently...'

'When they found his body, I've been told,' observed Poley, 'his vomit had begun to dissolve the fire irons at his feet.'

There was a brief silence. Poley had not been involved in Lord Strange's death, but he had heard rumours about the men who were – and their desire to clear the line of succession, no-matter which minor branches of the Plantagenet and Tudor family trees got lopped off in the process.

'Which goes a long way to explaining, I would suggest, why William Stanley, the sixth Earl of Derby, has travelled so widely abroad,' observed Master Secretary after a while. 'Taking almost no part in English politics at all and employing not only a physician to be in constant attendance but almost as many food-tasters as her majesty. No. His threat to the succession is purely theoretical; as, I would suggest, is the next in his line.'

'I would concur,' said Sir Thomas. 'A paper challenge; no more. There is, however, the matter that you have raised. The position of the Lady Anne Stanley. She has a claim, though it is distant enough, and she has never pressed it to my knowledge.'

'Nor to mine,' nodded Cecil. 'Nor, more importantly, has she ever accrued a circle of traitorous followers as did the Queen of Scots.'

'So, we can take her also off the immediate list,' said Sir Thomas. 'And that covers all the Stanleys, living and dead, though there is notably almost as many of this generation mysteriously dead as there are still living.'

'Well?' demanded Cecil after another brief silence. 'Who is next?'

'Edward Seymour, Lord Beauchamp, whose claim would be made through his mother, Lady Catherine Grey - sister to Lady Jane Grey who was so nearly settled onto the throne before Queen Mary - and lost her head in consequence.'

'The Nine Days Queen,' nodded Cecil. 'But Queen nevertheless, which demonstrates the strength of Seymour's case. And of course, he is a scion of the line most favoured in the old king's will, which passed over the Stuart claimants and, in any case questioned whether anyone could sit on the throne of England who had been born outside the realm.'

'Edward Seymour was born in the Tower,' observed Poley, who had been stationed there and occasionally posed as a captive there and so knew the Tower well. Though the last time he had been within its walls was to observe the beheading of the Earl of Essex two years and one month ago almost to the day. 'It is hard to imagine a place more central to the realm than that.'

41

'True,' allowed Cecil indulgently. 'Seymour's claim might pose a threat, could he ever prove his legitimacy. But there is no proof extant that his parents ever married. Nor, I am certain, will there ever be any. So, all the world knows him for a bastard and bastards do not inherit the throne.'

Poley looked at his employer, his face studiedly expressionless. For Cecil, it seemed, had forgotten that Queen Elizabeth herself had been declared bastard time and again – by the Pope amongst many others including the English Parliament and, indeed, by her own father. Because King Henry's annulment of Queen Catherine's marriage to him was never recognised in Catholic Europe, nor, therefore, was his marriage to Queen Anne. So that its issue was never declared legitimate; a bastardy compounded by the King himself as Queen Anne's head fell and he went on from one marriage to another and another, declaring the offspring of earlier marriages illegitimate as he did so.

'So,' continued Sir Thomas over the top of Poley's cynical thoughts. 'As the Seymour line is discredited, that leaves the Stuart line after all. The relations of Queen Mary of Scotland whom the queen had beheaded. The Stuart line as famously favoured by the Earl of Essex...'

'Whom the queen also had beheaded,' nodded Cecil. 'Just so.'

'Were the old king's will to stand in any point,' said Sir Thomas, 'Then Lady Arbella Stuart's claim might be the stronger. She is great-great-granddaughter in direct line of succession to the old king's father, King Henry the Seventh, founder of the Tudor line.'

'Able to call herself cousin to the queen. And she had the good sense to be born legitimately,' mused Cecil.

'And in England,' added Poley. 'Nor has she ever stirred abroad.'

'Indeed, we keep her close-mewed with Bess, the Countess of Shrewsbury, at Hardwick Hall,' allowed Cecil. 'There is no great gathering of treason around her as there was with her aunt the Queen of Scots.'

'Though she was raised as royalty,' observed Sir Thomas drily, 'and is by no means contented with her lot.'

'The redoubtable Bess of Hardwick keeps me fully apprised of the Lady Arbella's loud disappointment at her treatment,' said Cecil. 'It is a finely balanced approach, for although she is English-born, her Scottish heritage may make her precious in the eyes of her Scottish relations. Particularly King James. So, she will still be royally housed, fed and treated; let her be never so loudly discontented. But not too much so, for her name is mentioned in more than one treatise that states her claim to the throne is the strongest of all.'

'And especially now that Kit Marlowe is no longer available to read to her and soothe her. And observe her even more closely than Bess of Hardwick could.' Poley added pensively. He and Phelippes exchanged a glance, then the intelligencer felt the full weight of Cecil's gaze upon him.

'Marlowe has been dead nigh on ten years past,' said Master Secretary. 'And still the man keeps cropping up.' He was silent for an instant then continued, 'Like the Queen of Scots and the Earl of Essex. All of them dead but not yet at rest.'

'That leaves James, King of Scotland, even though he was born outside England,' said Sir Thomas, refusing to be distracted by Master Secretary's supernatural aside. 'Can the council set aside the old king's will?'

'If the council cannot, then perhaps the commons can,' said Cecil. 'Especially if the queen is clear upon the subject.'

'"*I will that a king succeed me and who but my kinsman the King of Scots.*"' Sir Thomas said, his tone making it clear that he was quoting the words. 'The phrase is spoken all over London and it is supposed that it represents her majesty's final statement on the matter. Has the queen not said this after all?'

'Never in my hearing,' answered Cecil smoothly. 'Nor in the hearing of anyone I know.' He shrugged. 'Her throat is terribly swollen with boils and pustules within and without. She can just manage to swallow water, can hardly breathe and certainly is in no way capable of speech. Especially not such measured and considered phrases as you have just mouthed.'

'Then how in the name of Heaven did the rumour that she had said it get started?' Sir Thomas wondered. 'Indeed, once started, how did it get put about so widely and so swiftly?'

'I have no idea,' said Cecil quietly, his face a picture of innocent ignorance. 'No idea at all.'

4

'James is of course not only by far the most realistic contender - which is why I allowed the rumours Sir Thomas has talked about to circulate, despite the queen's trenchant silence on the matter,' said Cecil pensively, his gaze distant. 'Though both she and I have been in contact with him at Holyrood.' His rushed speech explaining his tumbling thoughts on the matter, thought Poley. And also explaining why he should be telling the men who wrote and encoded the letters and helped fashion the announcement of James's succession which had gone North with Ingram Frizer. But, realised the intelligencer, Master Secretary was not really talking to them at all. 'Especially since the Earl of Essex could no longer lead the 'Friends of King James' faction at the English court,' Cecil continued. 'But his majesty is also by far the most dangerous.'

Master Secretary hardly needed to add that James was the most dangerous *to him*, whether he had sent letters to Holyrood or not, thought Poley. Though, to be fair, there was a strong possibility that James would be fatally dangerous to Poley as well – and to several others he had worked with to bring about the downfall and death of not only the king's mother but also his strongest supporter in the English court.

It was well over an hour later. Phelippes and Poley sat opposite Cecil at the table in his private rooms at Richmond Palace. The Secretary to the Privy Council was finally able to speak his mind freely to his two senior intelligencers for they were at last alone. The remains of a simple meal stood between them but the flagon of watered wine had been moved aside so the three conspirators could see each-other across the remains of the baked carp, the roasted capon and the eel pie they had just finished eating in company with the recently departed Sir Thomas Wilson and the servants who had been dismissed after him. Their cloaks and hats hung from hooks on the door, as did Poley's precious satchel. 'On the one hand we must ensure his smooth and trouble-free succession,' Cecil continued pensively. 'He must progress through the dangerously restless Catholic strongholds of the North after all.' At Cecil's mention of the Catholic North, Poley glanced at his satchel. He must go through the papers it contained in rather more detail than he had managed so far. But Cecil continued speaking. 'On the other hand, even if we are able to ensure that he can do so, it must never be revealed to him - or even faintly suspected by him - that we were instrumental in the execution of his mother or the downfall of his most ardent English supporter.'

'Or that we were involved in the death of his cousin Arbella's favourite tutor, Christopher Marlow, who regularly came all the way up from London to be with her,' added Poley.

'Twelve hours' hard riding,' added Phelippes. The suspicion in his tone testifying to his belief that Marlowe was motivated by something other than a desire to educate a lonely orphaned teenager caged in her overpowering grandmother's home. Like a maiden of Arthurian legend incarcerated in a witch's castle.

'Who read plays and wrote poems to her while she grew from a girl aged fourteen to a woman aged seventeen,' continued Poley. 'A dangerous age to be in regular company with a pretty youth.'

'Who was dead within months of stopping his visits.' Phelippes concluded.

'Or of being forced to stop them,' added Poley. He leaned back, sharing Phelippes' suspicions. He thought he knew everything there was to know about the man he had seen murdered in Deptford ten years ago but he had never been certain about Marlowe's dealings with Arbella. She was, after all, the woman who might be queen and who therefore would have had in the past – as in the present – the spymaster's keenest eyes upon her. Only Master Secretary Cecil or Marlowe's patron, spymaster Sir Thomas Walsingham would have been fully informed about those. Unless Sir Thomas's uncle, spymaster supreme Sir Francis Walsingham, had had a finger in that particular pie as well - until his death in 1590 at any rate.

There was a brief, pensive silence.

'That's a lot to keep hidden,' observed Phelippes at last.

'Then it is fortunate,' snapped Cecil, 'that we are past masters at keeping secrets.'

'It would seem' said Poley after a few more moments of silence, 'that the best way forward is the one that serves us best; and you, My Lord, best of all.'

'And that is?' demanded Cecil.

'Arrange matters so that any blame and much suspicion passes onto someone else's shoulders,' said Poley simply.

'Whose?' demanded Cecil.

'Why, My Lord, onto the broad, square shoulders of the next man we must ensure can never come between you and King James. The Captain of the Queen's Guard, Sir Walter Raleigh.'

'Raleigh is Captain of the *Queen*'s Guard because Her Majesty had an eye for a man with dash and swagger. But Captain of the *King*'s Guard?...' Cecil let the question hang.

'My Lord,' said Poley, 'my acquaintance with King James can never be called intimate, but I know the man for he has received me as messenger from the council on several occasions. And I must observe that King James, too, has favourites. And many of these favourites are to be found amongst handsome men with dash and swagger. Sir John Ramsay, Sir James Hay and Sir Philip Herbert spring to mind. I should also observe that King James is famous for his learning and his love of disputation...'

'I know this,' Cecil interrupted. 'Come to the point.'

'The point is, My Lord, that Sir Walter is one of the most widely travelled and deeply learned men in Her Majesty's court as well as being, if I may so phrase it, famously well-formed in body and limb, and an epitome of manly beauty, despite his advancing years – he is as you know nearing fifty-five. Despite his silver hair, he is in many ways the very personification of the type of man King James is closest to. There is a very potent danger that, should they meet under propitious circumstances, every likelihood exists that Raleigh will make as deep and lasting an impression on King James as he has made upon Queen Elizabeth.'

'Hmmm.' Cecil narrowed his eyes as though considering Poley's words – but the intelligencer was pretty sure Master Secretary had already considered this danger – along with all the others they were preparing to face. Cecil opened his mouth to speak, but his words were stopped by an urgent tapping on the door.

'Come!' ordered Cecil and a young man entered. He was a stranger to Poley, though clearly from his attire a servant to one of the most powerful men on the council. 'The Lord Admiral,' he began, revealing which power he owed his position to. Then he stopped, clearly torn between the need to deliver Admiral Howard's message and his nervousness of the man he was to deliver it to.

'Well?' prompted Cecil.

'The Lord Admiral has sent me with an urgent summons Master Secretary. Something within Her Majesty's throat has burst and…'

'What in the name of Heaven…' snarled Cecil, almost leaping to his feet. 'Where is Lord Howard?'

'In the royal bedchamber…'

'Very well. Tell him I'm coming at once. Poley, Phelippes, you will accompany me.'

The young messenger turned and vanished obediently, though Poley had a feeling that he had not delivered Lord Admiral Howard's entire message. Cecil bustled urgently out

48

of the door with Phelippes close behind. Poley paused to pull a wax tablet and a stylus out of his satchel and noted that Phelippes had done the same. Well, he thought, two sets of records could hardly be gainsaid. As long as they agreed, of course. As he exited behind the other two, Cecil's servants appeared in the room almost by magic and began to tidy up. Poley shook his head. They had been watching and waiting, unobserved but observing. That was why, as well as overseeing networks of agents and couriers, he kept a servant on fee in as many questionable and equivocal households as Cecil and his purse would permit.

5

The passageways between Cecil's rooms and the Royal Apartments were brightly lit and increasingly well manned. Captain of the Guard Sir Walter Raleigh might have been tricked into visiting Portsmouth on duty as Governor of Jersey with his friend Henry Brooke Lord Cobham, Warden of the Cinque Ports, at this critical time, but his men were all in position, well-armed and alert. And this was no surprise, thought Poley grimly. Even at this late stage, Her Majesty might still be at risk. Not only had the Earl of Essex planned to kidnap the queen little more than two years ago, but the King of Scotland himself had been the subject of kidnap and attempted murder by John Ruthven, Earl of Gowrie, also little more than two years since. But who on earth would want to kidnap the ailing monarch now, and spirit her away from her deathbed? A surprising number of malcontents, he thought; and some of them sufficiently powerful to do it if the Guards' guard was dropped.

'Is that what the Admiral's message means?' wondered Poley aloud. 'That whatever has burst in Her Majesty's throat signals the end at last?'

'She has hardly been able to breathe, let alone eat or drink,' said Cecil, still clearly distracted. 'Speech has been all-but impossible. The last thing I heard her say – and that in a croaking whisper - was that she felt as though there was a chain around her throat, choking her.' There was a brief silence as the three of them strode onwards. Then Cecil added, 'Whether this occurrence will be good or bad I have no way of knowing. Let us hurry to find out!' And he suited the words with action, pulling ahead even though his legs were a good deal shorter than those of his two tall intelligencers.

'Moreover,' puffed Cecil after a few moments more, clearly trying to lessen his worries by sharing them. 'She seems to have lost the will to live since some fool obeyed her demand to bring her a mirror. She saw herself with her own eyes for the first time in I don't know how long. With her own eyes instead of through those of her flattering courtiers,' he emphasised. 'I'm told she hardly recognised the raddled, toothless, balding hag she saw in that mirror and the shock came near to killing her on the spot. I pray to God that whatever has burst in her throat does not signal the end. By word - or by gesture if she still cannot speak – she must name her successor!'

And that successor must be King James, no matter what the dangers, added Poley silently.

They were met at the door into Her Majesty's chamber by several Ladies in Waiting, led by Lady Philadelphia Scrope, raven-hair threaded with silver, tall and vigorous in her mid-forties. The ladies were accompanied by the two most senior men of her Privy Council – Lord Admiral Howard and Edward Somerset, Earl of Worcester. Both, like Lady Scrope, were straight-backed and square-shouldered, despite their grey beards and thinning hair. Admiral Howard was well into his sixty-sixth year and Worcester was fifty-three. Neither man was surrendering mentally to their advancing years – any more than they were surrendering physically; though, in Poley's opinion, neither quite matched Lady Philadelpia's sharp acuity. 'Whatever has burst in her throat – does it signal the end?' demanded Cecil breathlessly, addressing the four of them.

'Apparently not,' answered Lady Philadelphia. 'Although the process itself was painful and no doubt distasteful, once Her Majesty had spat much of the poison out into a bowl, her throat seemed to clear somewhat. She breathes easier, sips water, is able to consider a little soup. And she can, it seems, speak.'

'A little, at least,' added Worcester. 'She won't be giving any lengthy speeches, but I believe her doctors are confident she can answer questions.'

'Such as who she wishes to succeed her,' suggested Cecil. 'I have brought my clerks here to note down every word...'

'In case the collective memory of the Privy Council is not sufficient for the task?' asked the Earl of Worcester ironically, turning to lead the little group back into the Privy Chamber. Poley followed them into the queen's bedchamber, last of the little crowd of men and women. He paused at the door, overcome for a moment by the enormity of being allowed into the private chamber of Gloriana the Faery Queene herself; and by the rank stench of the place. It was an odour compounded of unwashed bodies, human waste, foul breath, sickness – and the putrid-smelling medicines to treat it – and ultimately, he supposed, of death itself.

Just as he had suspected, the occupants of the room fell into two – no doubt conflicting – main groups, with a third whose interest was medical rather than personal or political. The Ladies of the Privy Chamber were gathered to one side, those nearest the bed holding cups of water and bowls of soup together with cloths and napkins. On the other side of the bed, the queen's physicians were gathered, their leader holding a large vessel into which the queen occasionally spat thick, greenish phlegm after seeming to heave it up from the depth of the stomach. Behind the doctor were several colleagues, each holding various medicaments; all, obviously, of limited effect. And around the foot of the bed itself, stood the men of the Privy Council. They were all held in a collective hush, half fearful, half expectant, all on edge. All seemingly in outer shadows looking in at the brightness of a great four-poster bed festooned with curtains of velvet and brocade held up with ropes of silk which were threaded with gold and silver, tasselled with carbuncles and pearls. What there was not, thought Poley wryly, was any flat surface on which he could rest his tablet to make his notes.

But there, at the heart of it all lay the dying woman, propped on pillows until she was almost sitting upright, clothed in a magnificent bed-gown with a ruff high enough to conceal the pendant wattles below her chin, but soft enough by the look of things, to coddle the swellings both within and without that sorely infected throat. Queen Elizabeth's face was made up; not fully so, as he had seen it - distantly to be sure – at royal occasions, but sufficiently for a vain woman surrounded by a bevy of younger ladies and a modest crowd of men. Her night-cap covered her head almost to her eyebrows – such as they were – and to her ears. It was loosely tied beneath her chin. Some strands of hair escaped it, however, the contrast with her make-up bringing out the faintest lingering redness in the fine white strands. Poley found himself thinking of Lady Janet. Her hair was flame red still, as the queen's had been in her youth. Dear God, but he missed Lady Janet.

Beneath the ornate weight of the tapestried bed-coverings, Queen Elizabeth's body seemed to be smaller than that of a starving child. Her hands lay on the coverlet, the twisted claws of her fingers with their swollen knuckles all covered in rings – except for the livid scar on her wedding finger where the ring with which she had married her country and its people so famously long ago had recently had to be sawn off as it was growing into her flesh. It had been an experience that had upset her almost as much as that glance at a mirror had done.

Cecil pushed anxiously to the front of the council, until he was brought to a standstill by the bed-foot. 'Your Majesty,' he began. 'About the pressing matter of your succession…'

Suddenly the queen's face was pointing at him. The effect was most unsettling, thought Poley. Her countenance was little more than a mask as pale as bleached bone with red-painted lips and red-arched eyebrows vivid against the dead white make-up. The eyes between them looked black and fathomless. Bottomless pools fit to duck witches; a pastime apparently favoured by her probable successor. The queen

53

tilted her head to Lady Philadelphia as senior Lady in Waiting. Lady Philadelphia leaned forward. The queen's lips moved but Poley heard no words coming from them. Lady Philadelphia straightened. 'Her Majesty is not strong enough to survey all the contenders and choose,' she said. 'But she will signal her preference if you list them to her. Either by word or gesture.'

Master Secretary Cecil had foreseen this very moment, Poley realised. Without hesitation, Cecil began, slowly and clearly, to list from memory all the names he had discussed with Sir Thomas Wilson earlier in the afternoon.

'Henry Percy, Earl of Northumberland has withdrawn any claim he might have had Ma'm,' he began smoothly. 'So let us begin with Ranuccio Farnese, Duke of Parma...'

Poley made notes in simple shorthand he and Phelippes had taught themselves from Willis's *Arte of Stenography* which had been published the year before, though he was grateful for pauses and hesitations, which not only gave him a chance to catch up but also to check on Phelippes and how busy his stylus was.

The right claw hand waved in the air while Cecil was still speaking, a gesture clearly demanding he dismiss the pretentions of the Duke of Parma and proceed to the next contender. The jewels glittered in the candle-light as the Duke of Parma was discharged.

'King Philip the Third of Spain...'

The Queen choked on a laugh. The hand waved. The jewels glistered. The King of Spain was dismissed.

'The Infanta, Isabella Clara Eugenia, Archduchess of Austria and regent of the Spanish Netherlands by order of her father the late King Philip the Second...'

This time there was a subtle difference to the royal gesture. Cecil hesitated, frowning. 'Well, your Majesty, let us put the Infanta to one side for the moment then...'

Poley scribbled furiously. There was, blessedly, a short silence. Cecil glanced around the rest of the council. Poley could almost see him wondering whether they would have been happy to put the Infanta on one side if Sir Walter Raleigh or Lord Cobham had been here.

Then the amanuensis's attention shifted across to the Ladies in Waiting. These were by no means powerless aristocratic servants, Poley knew. Lady Janet had been one of them and she had described in some detail the manner in which the Ladies of the Privy Chamber mixed the interests of their husbands and their families with the interests of their Sovereign. Lady Philadelphia Scrope, christened Philadelphia Carey, for instance, was almost as politically active as Audrey Walsingham, Sir Thomas Walsingham's wife, christened Audrey Shelton. Lady Philadelphia reputedly had secreted about herself a ring sent down from Holyrood by King James – which might indeed have been brought south by Lady Audrey who was a frequent visitor to Edinburgh and a close friend of Scottish Queen Anne. Or by Sir Robert Carey, Lady Philadelphia's brother, who was also a frequent visitor to the court of King James. But Lady Philadelphia held it, of course, because of all the people at or near the Court, she was destined to be at the Queen's side at the instant of her death. The only person equally likely to be there was the Archbishop of Canterbury and there was no way he would ever agree to send a ring northward at the critical instant. Nor, unlike Lady Philadelphia, did he have a fleet-footed messenger immediately to hand. The instant the old queen breathed her last, the ring was to be returned to James as a signal that the final stage of his assault on the English throne had begun; and Sir Robert Carey would be the ring-bearer.

Sir Robert was a regular visitor to Her Majesty's sick-room and had been for the last few days. He had taken rooms at The White Hart immediately outside Richmond Castle, clearly ready to take the ring north with all possible dispatch, the moment Elizabeth breathed her last. And, unknown to either Sir Robert or Lady Philadelphia, Thomas Watson, Poley's brother-in-law and would-be intelligencer, was waiting for Sir Robert to take horse, ready to race him the length of England with the news and with Master Secretary's personal letters of boundless congratulation and undying support, written by Thomas Phelippes in the same code that King James and the Earl of Essex had used for their most private correspondence and then – such was the delicacy of their contents - locked. Only someone very well practised in such matters could open them without destroying their contents – which only an equally experienced code-breaker could translate. It was young Tom's first mission after all – better safe than sorry.

6

Cecil cleared his throat, his attention shifting towards that skull-like face, those fathomless black eyes as he moved onto the English contenders. 'Henry Stanley, Earl of Huntingdon,' he said. Poley started scribbling again, the tip of his stylus raising little curls of wax like watch-springs.

'Dead,' whispered the Queen. 'Too many of the Stanleys died early…'

'Indeed, Majesty, but through his brother Ferdiando, also deceased, we have Anne Stanley, who you may recall was going to marry one of the Tsar of Muscovy's sons as was proposed some time since. The marriage came to nothing, however, and Lady Anne, therefore, by the terms of your father's will, has a notable claim to succeed.'

Poley disregarded most of the discussion and focused on the still-living Lord William and the Lady Anne. The Tsar of Muscovy and his sons were set aside.

'Though the Lady Anne has never pressed it,' Lady Philadelphia pointed out, giving Cecil's amanuensis still more time to make his notes. 'Which may be the reason that she, of all the Stanleys in line to succeed and resident here in England, is still alive.'

'True,' allowed Cecil. 'And given the fates of her father and her uncle, we can quite clearly see why she remains so carefully unambitious. But, to proceed…'

Poley took a deep breath. The stylus hovered over the wax tablet like a harrier over a hencoop.

The queen held up her hand and Cecil fell silent. She hawked something distasteful up from the back of her throat, grimacing at the effort. Then she turned to the left and her doctor held the bowl convenient to allow her to spit yet more emerald phlegm into it. This time the green slime was laced with a thick web of blood. When she had finished, she turned to her right and Lady Philadelphia gently wiped her mouth then offered her a cup of water, which the Queen sipped before raising her hand once more, signalling Cecil to continue. A hand, noted Poley, which shook like a leaf in a storm. Getting rid of that mouthful of poison had weakened her considerably. It occurred to him that the bloody poison she had managed to spit out might well be a good deal less than the amount she had swallowed. And, he noticed, the cloth that had wiped her lips and which was hurriedly being put away was also bright with smears of blood.

'Edward Seymour, Lord Beauchamp,' persisted Cecil, clearly seeing how weak she was becoming and therefore keen to press on before she fell asleep – or worse. 'Son to the sister of Lady Jane Grey, and sharing her strong case to succeed to the throne. Again, under the terms of your father's will which passed over the heirs of his elder sister Lady Margaret Tudor in favour of the heirs of his favourite younger sister Lady Mary, should his own direct line of succession end for any reason.'

'Given only,' added Lord Admiral Howard, 'that any heir proposed be born in England.'

'And Seymour was born in the Tower,' added Warwick. 'Under the terms of the old king's will, his only strong contender would be Lady Anne Stanley.'

'But there have been moves afoot,' added Cecil, 'to strengthen his claim through a divorce of his current wife the Lady Honora and a marriage of convenience to the Lady Arbella Stuart, thus joining the lines of succession of both of the Tudor sisters Margaret and Mary.'

Queen Elizabeth's hand went up. There was instant silence. 'I will have no rascal's son in my seat,' croaked the Queen in a broken whisper, albeit a fierce one, 'but one worthy to be a king!'

This short pronouncement seemed to exhaust the dying woman even further. It was followed by a lengthy, racking cough which robbed her of breath and left her choking as she tried to breathe once more. Time enough for Poley to record her pronouncement, word for word before he glanced up again. Even though she had not sat up in order to make her statement or in the convulsions of her coughing fit, nevertheless, noted the intelligencer, she seemed to shrink back further into her pillows as she finished speaking, coughing and choking. The white make-up on her face was beaded and blistered with sweat. The red-painted arches of her eyebrows were beginning to run. His heart twisted with sympathy for her, not as subject and monarch but as one living soul to another. Especially to another slowly dying. He caught his breath on the thought and paused. For the queen's soul was not dying, of course; only her body was dying. Her soul was immortal and bound elsewhere – freighted as it was with sin and guilt – some of which was of Poley's making. For an icy moment he thought about how she would confront him terribly on Judgement Day when the Lord God would bring to light the hidden things of darkness, and make manifest the secret counsels of all hearts. On Judgement Day the queen would learn how much responsibility he bore for the destruction of her cousin the Queen of Scots and her beloved boy the Earl of Essex. That knowledge disturbed him more than the thought of the hellfire he would be doomed to suffer for all his other deadly sins.

'Then we must leave Lord Beauchamp aside, together with your father's will,' said Cecil breaking into Poley's thoughts so abruptly that he jumped, stabbing his stylus deep into the wax. 'Something I am informed by your Queen's Councillor Extraordinary Sir Francis Bacon that we can do by an Act of Parliament. And, that being the case, we must next suggest Lady Arbella Stuart. Lady Arbella is the most powerful contender of Margaret Tudor's line, as she was born in England and is living in England.'

The queen's hand waved, weakly, as though the weight of jewelled rings on her fingers was becoming too much for her to bear. Cecil took the gesture, such as it was, as a direction to rule the Lady Arbella out and hurry up. And he was by no means loth to do so. For his preferred candidate was next. Last. And he wanted the matter settled before the clearly weakening monarch became too exhausted or too close to death to give a clear decision. 'That leaves the senior contender of the Stuart line,' he said, raising his voice in hopes of rousing the drooping queen, and yet fearful of speaking too fast for Poley to keep up with his notes. 'James Stuart, King of Scotland. Nearly ten years older than his cousin Lady Arbella, sole male offspring of Mary Queen of Scots and Henry Stuart, Lord Darnley, both great grandchildren of King Henry the Seventh; King James being, therefore a great-great grandson in direct line from your father's father. Though he was born beyond the borders of your realm, Majesty, in the foreign country of Scotland...'

Elizabeth's hand rose fractionally from the coverlet and waved languidly, then fell back like a dying bird.

'Your Majesty,' said Cecil, speaking slowly and distinctly. 'Can you clarify? Did that gesture mean you have chosen King James of Scotland as your successor?' The tension in the room was taut as a drawn bow-string.

The trembling hand raised an inch or two, then fell back onto the coverlet once more and remained there. The eyes in that white mask were closed, the eyelids strangely dark where the make-up had cracked and fallen away. The jaw sagged. The mouth opened and Lady Philadelphia leaned forward with a clean napkin to clear a line of pink drool from Her Majesty's lip. The queen appeared to have sunk into an exhausted slumber. A slumber disturbingly close to death by the look of things, thought Poley. His stylus hovered and his heart raced, awaiting the most crucial note of all.

Lady Philadelphia glanced back at the maid of honour closest to her, young Elizabeth Southwell, then turned decisively and said, 'You have your answer, My Lords. I am

60

now about to summon the Archbishop, for I fear the end is nigh.'

Cecil turned to the others. Poley had never seen him so decisive and commanding. 'We have our answer indeed, My Lords,' he said. 'And you all saw it. Her Majesty chose King James of Scotland to be her successor. Without a shadow of a doubt.'

Poley was surprised to discover that he had been holding his breath. He breathed out gently, fighting to keep his hands steady, and began to write once more.

7

'So,' said Poley. 'Everything is settled and nothing is settled.'

Phelippes nodded his agreement. 'We know who will succeed – according to the council at least – and yet nothing can be done about it until Her Majesty finally dies. Then Sir Robert Carey can take to his horse and spirit King James's ring to Edinburgh along with the news.'

'And with me hard on his heels, bearing secret letters from Master Secretary' added young Thomas Watson in a whisper, clearly excited at the prospect of his first major assignment.

'If Lady Philadelphia can find a way to smuggle the ring to him,' added Poley pensively.

'Why would that be so difficult?' Thomas frowned.

'At the first word of Her Majesty's death, Richmond Palace is like to be closed up tighter than the Tower,' Poley explained. 'If Carey is inside the walls, he won't be allowed out. If he's outside, he'll never be allowed in. The palace will be double-guarded until the queen's corpse and her mourners in the council can be moved to Whitehall and Westminster. That too will be conducted amid absolute security. Even on the river, there will be no chance to pass the ring between sister and brother.'

'Unless he and Lady Philadelphia have a plan in place,' suggested Phelippes.

'But why?' Thomas still didn't quite understand.

Poley leaned close to his brother-in –law and dropped his voice still further. 'There will be no communication with the wider world until the council have decided on the precise form of words that will on the one hand inform the people of her passing in a manner that avoids the unrest or rioting they most fear; and on the other hand ensure – as far as they are able – that when King James eventually does come to London, they will all have been confirmed in their current positions, powers and possessions.'

'Except of course,' said Phelippes, 'for the fact that Master Secretary has already written the Privy Council's announcement and sent it north.'

'Do the rest of the council know about that?' asked Thomas.

'No,' said Poley. 'Nor must they do so until King James is securely on the throne and Master Secretary is equally securely at his side. But it seems to me that the time between the queen's death, which may happen later tonight, and the formal coronation of King James, is the most dangerous time of all. I have even heard it said that while the throne is empty, no matter who is named in the succession, it will be impossible to commit high treason, no matter what the act.'

'How so?' asked Tom, his frown deepening.

'High treason is an act performed by any subject directly against his sovereign,' explained Poley, with the authority of a man who had discussed these matters with Sir Francis Bacon, Councillor Extraordinary to the queen. 'Between the death of one and the coronation of the next, there is no sovereign – therefore no act can be called high treason. Not even an attempt to kidnap or kill King James.'

'Unless the act is committed in Scotland, where he still reigns, I would guess,' added Phelippes.

'Indeed,' agreed Poley. 'But once he crosses the border into England, where he is not sovereign until he is crowned, he is in many ways just another wayfarer travelling down to London – and therefore fair game.'

'So, Master Poley,' concluded Phelippes, 'it is just as well that you have your eyes on so many would-be traitors and your fingers in so many treasonous pies.'

The mention of pies, thought Poley, was by no means coincidental. The three men were grouped round a table at the back of the taproom in the White Hart tavern immediately outside the grounds of Richmond Palace. The table in front of them contained a jug of small beer and another of sweet sack. They were filling – and emptying – their goblets circumspectly, for they had not yet eaten. There were pies, chops, sausages and fish on offer, under the aegis of the innkeeper's wife, but they were waiting for the centrepiece of the ordinary to be ready, and while they waited, they talked.

Poley and Phelippes were in rooms reserved for them at Master Secretary's command; Poley content to share his accommodation with his brother-in-law. By no coincidence whatsoever, the White Hart was also the tavern where Sir Robert Carey, lately Warden of the Middle March on the Scottish borders and brother to Her Majesty's chief Lady in Waiting, was accommodated. Though he was, as far as Poley knew, still in the Palace, near the bedside of his dying sovereign. Close to his sister and King James's ring.

Master Secretary Cecil had dismissed Poley and Phelippes as soon as they had finished writing out what they had both noted on their waxen tablets augmented by what Master Secretary also remembered of his discussions with the queen. Particularly her unequivocal dismissal of any claim by Edward Seymour, the Earl of Beauchamp and her final acceptance of King James the Sixth of Scotland.

'I neither like nor trust Edward Seymour,' Master Secretary had observed as the notes were still being written up. 'And I joy at Her Majesty's firm words. Without which I might fear that Beauchamp could lead an army in revolt. The French might support such a move merely to make trouble.'

'I have eyes on all the Seymours, Master Secretary,' Poley assured him, patting his satchel full of reports while Phelippes beside him translated their waxen annotations into his fair round hand then transliterated them into code. The clear records were for Master Secretary, the encoded ones would be locked and given to Tom for transport to Edinburgh together with several other of Cecil's letters. 'As well as on all the others. As, I believe, does King James. There is a deal of the Scottish brogue being whispered in shadowy corridors and dark corners close at hand. However, if you should fear anyone, I would suggest The North. That is where to look for danger and unrest. Even the so-called appellant secular priests are restless. Their appeal to the authorities for gentler treatment of Catholics is still under review – and must stay so until the new monarch makes a decision. By no means all their seditious colleagues are caged in Wisbech castle in the Cambridge Fens either. There are Jesuits and secular clergy still in large numbers working to rouse all those of the Old Religion – and the North is full of such men and women – waiting and plotting in the hope that they can force King James to dispense with recusant payments – at the least – should he assume the throne. And, indeed, to treat all Catholics with a measure of indulgence.'

'I agree,' said Master Secretary. 'His Majesty's habit of appearing to guarantee anything to everyman sows dangerous seeds which will come to bitter harvest when people begin to realise he cannot keep all his conflicting promises. And that harvest will ripen soon after he crosses the border into England. Not only does he come into a situation full of risk as he leaves his sovereign kingdom, the men who hold the most dangerous assurances will soon begin to realise he has no intention of keeping his royal word. I will send my brother Lord Burghley north at once with orders to prepare to meet and overcome any restlessness no matter where it comes from. It is as well, I believe, that we have eyes on all of them; or at least as many of them as appear to be the most dangerous.' He paused, clearly deep in thought, his eyes focused on Poley's satchel. 'In the mean-time, I want you to leave the palace. I have reserved rooms for you at the White Hart. I would suggest that you are safer out than in tonight. Were the queen to die, the Palace would be shut up tighter than the Fleet Prison, with no-one passing in or out without the council's specific license.'

The three intelligencers were still deep in conversation an hour after Cecil dismissed them from the palace, when Sir

Robert Carey came into the White Hart. He glanced around the tap room and summoned the tapster. Neither man bothered to lower his voice so that Poley and the others had no trouble in overhearing their conversation.

'I am expecting a message from the palace,' said Sir Robert. 'I must be awakened as soon as it arrives. Awakened without fail.'

'Of course, Sir Robert. Perkin here will keep good watch all night if need-be and will guarantee to wake you as soon as your messenger arrives.'

Perkin was a gangling, tow-haired, beardless youth. He was currently rotating the handle that turned the spit on which a solid-looking mutton was impaled and roasting. Its odour filled the room and was the main reason Poley and his companions had eschewed the pies and the other lesser alternatives on offer so far. Sir Robert glanced at him, nodded at mine host and vanished upstairs – no doubt to his room. The inn-keeper crossed to Perkin and exchanged a few words with him, then returned to his duties behind the bar. Poley pulled himself to his feet and strolled over to the sweating boy. 'How much longer do you judge we must wait for the mutton?' he asked, his tone one of light enquiry.

'Mere minutes, master,' answered Perkin. 'He glanced at the inn-keeper and at his wife – who was in charge of the pies, the sausages and the chops. They both nodded in agreement with his assessment. Poley's stomach rumbled. He leaned forward as though checking more closely for himself. 'Perkin,' he said in little more than a whisper, 'when you awaken Sir Robert, I would like you to waken me too. There is a silver sixpenny for you if you do not fail.'

8

Poley sprang awake. Tom, at his side on the truckle bed, stirred but stayed asleep. Perkin's anxious face stared down at the intelligencer, lit from beneath his pink, pointed chin by the flickering flame of the candle he held.

There was no need for explanation – indeed, for any words at all. Poley rolled out of bed and caught up his doublet, sword and hangar and rummaged in his purse for the sixpence which he handed to the messenger. Perkin turned and made to leave as soon as the coin was in his hand. 'Wait,' said Poley. He lifted the candle that had lit Tom and his way to bed and stayed bright enough to let him examine the satchel's contents in more detail before he snuffed it at last. Now he used the flame on Perkin's to reignite it. Then Perkin left as silently as he had come. Tom stirred, woken either by the light or by the sudden cold he felt as his companion got out of bed.

'What?' he whispered, sitting up.

'Carey's on the move. Her Majesty must be dead. I can still hear him dressing so you have time to do the same. Follow him when he leaves and don't let him out of your sight.'

Tom froze, eyes and mouth wide as he fought to come to terms with the news – even though they had been expecting it. 'Dead,' he whispered. 'Queen Elizabeth dead. What are we going to do?'

Poley understood well enough that this was a question more of general philosophy than immediate concern but he still gave a practical answer. 'You dress and follow Carey,' he repeated. 'Keep good watch on him and stay as close as you can. I have my satchel; you take yours and keep it with you at all times until you render the letters into King James's hands. Phelippes and I will head back to London. There's no point in staying here any longer and we have work to do there. One or the other of us will be at my lodgings at the sign of the Lion on King Street, convenient to Whitehall, Westminster and Charing Cross. The other will be at Salisbury House. Or, if not, we will make certain that someone at each place knows exactly where we are, should you need us. The Privy Council will almost certainly want to thrash out the final details of the announcement in Westminster after they have moved Her Majesty's body to Whitehall Palace and make their first announcement at Charing Cross, before they repeat it at Paul's Churchyard. I would calculate that Carey may well wait for their blessing before he takes to the Great North Road – whether he has the ring or not – so we will be well placed should you be waiting with him.'

'I see little likelihood of needing your further advice,' said the young messenger confidently. 'The horses are ready at each stage of the ride north. The stages are ten miles apart. I have my groats to rent the horses and like you, I will need no-one to guide me…'

'It is a journey I have done time out of mind,' nodded Poley. 'Indeed, I have gained some notoriety for my speed between here and Holyrood. Say you are my man at the taverns and staging posts along the Great North Road and you will be given the best horseflesh they can supply. I could make the journey within three days when I was your age. I'm sure that Carey and you could be in Edinburgh by Saturday afternoon, depending only on how long you have to linger here waiting for the Council.'

Poley saw young Thomas out hard on Carey's heels, then went to wake Phelippes. 'Where will you go?' asked the code-breaker after they had exchanged their thoughts on the news and the situation they now found themselves in.

'Fulham Palace,' answered Poley.

'Why there?'

'The Bishop of London Richard Bancroft has offered sanctuary to a man I wish to talk with. He is at the Bishop's Palace there. It is time I reacquainted myself with the secular priests, particularly, William Watson. They have a list of the Jesuits in the North I wish to discuss in some detail. I need to get close to the Jesuit leaders – in spirit if not in the flesh. Watson hates the Jesuits as only the recently converted can hate men who have followed a parallel but different path.'

'One Catholic faction betraying another. Bishop Bancroft has done well in this,' nodded Phelippes.

'He is a man to be reckoned with indeed. It was the bishop and Master Secretary's brother Lord Burghley who first put troops in the streets of London to thwart the Earl of Essex's plans to raise the City against the queen, remember.'

'But he won't be there himself, will he? I understood he's in the Chapel at Richmond Palace, waiting with Archbishop Whitgift to offer Her Majesty the last rites.'

'You're right. But it's not Bishop Bancroft I want to talk to. As I said, it's one of his less savoury guests.'

This conversation was sufficient to allow both men to finish dressing and prepare to follow Robert Carey and Thomas Watson out into the icy darkness. When they did so at last, a link boy with a flaming torch guided them to the Richmond steps and hailed a wherry to take them *Eastward Ho*. They both had the council's passes in case they were challenged but it was clear that all of Sir Walter Raleigh's men were on double duty in Richmond Palace as the queen breathed her last even with their captain still in Portsmouth. The secret agents sat wordlessly in the wherry, bundled in hats and hooded cloaks well-oiled against the rain, too stunned by events to give further voice to their thoughts and fears. Poley found himself echoing Master Secretary's technique by going through lists of the men he planned to deal with next. The so-called recusants who preferred to pay often ruinous fines in order to follow their Catholic faith in this grimly Protestant country.

69

The list fell naturally into three columns, as though he was writing in his tablets: the Jesuits led by Fathers Garnet, Gerrard and Persons, though Persons was still in Rome. Then there were the followers of the Archpriest Blackwell, who were close to the Jesuits, but lacking in many ways their missionary zeal. And, finally, the seminary priests, the so-called Appellants. These men hated and mistrusted the Jesuits and held no great love for Blackwell and his followers either. It was the most restless of these men, William Watson, that Poley planned on cross-examining next. For one of the items in his precious satchel promised to put a cat among the pigeons there.

Having surveyed his list and made a rough outline of his immediate actions, Poley sat back, glancing across at Phelippes as he did so. They each had plans for the next few hours, days and weeks but beyond that, the year stretched out before them, the political climate as threatening as the real winter weather. Though, as they swept silently downriver, the latter began to ease. The rain stopped and the clouds started to break up.

The Bishop of London's Palace at Fulham stood half way between Richmond and Westminster and by the time the wherry eased across towards the blazing torches that illuminated the Fulham Palace steps, the cloud had broken up sufficiently to reveal a vast sky liberally sprinkled with low stars as crystalline as ice and a three-quarter moon just beginning to settle towards the southern horizon. Poley climbed ashore and waved to Phelippes as the wherry turned back into the stream, then he turned and used the moonlight to guide him along the short walk to the rear of the palace itself. In truth, he hardly needed the moonlight, for the palace was well lit and little more than thirty yards from the river.

'Matins,' said Poley to himself, realising why the place was so bright so early in the day. He hurried forward like a doomed moth towards the brilliance, too entranced to wonder whether the recusant celebrants were taking advantage of the bishop's absence. With luck, he might arrive before the end of the service and do his overburdened soul a little good, he thought. What he really longed for was confession – but the rite was not likely to be allowed in the palace of the Protestant bishop, even though he allowed his Catholic guests a good deal of freedom in their worship. But confession was only of use, he temporised, if it led to absolution. And that required penance - and he hardly dared imagine what penance would atone for all his sins. Unless, of course, the Lord had already arranged his penance through Master Secretary and the banishment of Lady Janet. Besides, he thought grimly, his musings darkening further, what good would either the ritual, the confession, the absolution or the penance do to the soul of a man ready to take the celebrant to the Tower if need-be and let Rackmaster Topcliffe tear him limb from limb?

9

The secular priest William Watson was not a prepossessing man. He was squat and ill-formed, though by no means as slight and effeminate as his companion Anthony Copley, who it seemed had been the main recipient of the Matins service. They were rapidly clearing away the paraphernalia of a formal Catholic Mass. If they had done so under the eyes of anyone else, they would likely have been bound for the Clink, the Fleet or the Tower. Poley could still scarcely believe that such practises could be permitted in the Bishop of London's palace. Watson had been formally resident here a couple of years ago but was more usually found in the Clink Prison these days. Poley could see the wisdom, however, of bringing the secular priest back to Fulham Palace under the current circumstances, the better to keep eyes on a man who might well be very dangerous. Both Watson and Copley were soon sitting opposite Poley in a small chamber adjacent to the chapel.

Poley tried to meet Watson's eye but he knew from past experience that this was no easy task. The secular priest had a severe cast in one eye which made it almost impossible to guess where his gaze was fixed. Unless he was trying to read or do close work – in which case whatever he was dealing with was pushed so close to his face that it often touched his nose. In Poley's experience, Watson was enormously sensitive about his eyes. He had been known to challenge someone who looked askance at him to a duel – despite the danger such an act would add to his already dangerous situation as a Catholic priest in a land where such men could all too easily end up hanging on the gallows or burning at the stake.

Poley pulled the reason for his visit out of his satchel and laid it on the table between the two men. It was a slim pamphlet the clarity of whose lettering and pristine nature of whose condition made it clear that it was newly printed. 'Master Copley,' he said quietly, his hand still resting on the pamphlet, hiding it from the two men's eager gaze. 'I believe you have published various works attacking not just the Jesuits in general but their leader Robert Persons.

'Under license of the Bishop,' said Copley, defensively. 'Indeed, at his instigation. It is little enough in all conscience against men who would bring such evil into the realm. The Inquisition…'

'Jesuits are black hearted bastards the lot of them,' snarled Watson. 'Black robed; black hearted. Ready to stop at nothing. Merely an arm of the Spanish state as well as the Inquisition – a precursor to invasion indeed. And the Pope has been tricked into supporting them while passing over us when he appointed the Archpriest Blackwell. But Blackwell is as bad as the worst of them. The Jesuits see our country as a godless place needing missions to bring us nearer heaven as though we were the ignorant savages of America! And we note from their dealings there that where the Jesuits go, the Inquisition and the army follow close on their heels. And Archpriest Blackwell, as appointed by the Pope himself to oversee the secular priests and the graduates of the English College, is nothing but a puffed-up bubble of self-importance, all too happy to bow and scrape to the Jesuits!'

'Certainly, none of them have any idea of the true worth of your tireless work here as you seek to bring an amicable arrangement between your recusant flock and the sovereign, no matter who that sovereign might be,' said Poley.

Watson frowned. His mouth opened. Poley knew what his next question was likely to be. So, he spoke first, and forcefully. 'But this, I believe, may change the game somewhat.' He lifted his hand. 'It is a pamphlet that does not come from Blackwell or any of his men. It has come from Robert Persons, the Jesuit leader in Rome.'

Watson took the pamphlet and jammed it hard against his nose. His lips moved silently as he read. 'Printed by Thomas Creede,' he said after a while.

'But penned by…' prompted Poley.

'Ah I see it. Robert Persons.'

Copley strained to see past Watson's ear and cheek. '*Manifestation of Great Folly and Bad Spirit,*' he read.

'*Of Certain in England calling themselves secular priests,*' Watson concluded, his voice thick with suspicion. Of all the secular priests in England, he was most likely to be Persons's target. And so it proved, much to Poley's secret satisfaction.

'*Watson looks nine ways at once,*' the secular priest read aloud his voice trembling with mounting outrage. And, the unkindest cut of all, '*he can discern nothing that touches not his eye!*' He pushed the pamphlet away in outrage and disgust, but almost immediately pulled it back against the tip of his nose. '*He is a very creature of clumsiness and stupidity,*' he continued, almost choking on the words. '*And it is well known that when he arrived in Rheims to study there, he was so poor that he licked clean the dishes that other men had emptied.* This is lies, all lies. Oh, that I could…' He threw the pamphlet down at last.

Copley caught it up and continued, '*and as for his companion Copley that consorts with him, he is nothing more than a little, wanton, idle-headed boy!*'

'Consorts!' snarled Watson. 'What does he make us out to be minstrels, piping with one another's flutes?'

'Did you not accuse him of begetting bastard twins on the body of his sister?' asked Poley.

Watson puffed himself up like a toad, full of righteous outrage. 'But, see here,' he shouted, flourishing the pamphlet. What is to be done about this? How can we strike back?'

'I would suggest,' said Poley, his voice a conspiratorial whisper, 'that you present yourself at Charing Cross later this morning, dressed for travel. And arrange to have well within your reach, a fleet-footed horse and the money needed to hire more. Together with such victuals as you might need to see you through a three-day ride up the Great North Road.'

Watson gaped at him but Copley leaned forward. 'Is she dead then?' he whispered. 'And the succession fallen on the King of Scots?'

'If that were true,' said Poley without raising his voice, his gaze fixed on Watson, whose eye was wandering madly as his mind raced, 'think of what the first man of the secular priesthood to reach King James might achieve before Blackwell or his Jesuit friends here or in Rome got to know of it.'

10

Poley's brother-in-law Tom, cloak tight about his slim person, hood pulled well forward and satchel firmly under his right arm, its strap over his left shoulder for extra security, followed Sir Robert Carey and the messenger back towards the palace. It was not hard to do so as the messenger carried a flaming torch to light their way. The flame blattered and guttered in the restless wind, beams of golden brightness illuminating the thinning drizzle. Tom just had to be careful not to trip or cause any sound as he followed in the shadows as close behind them as he dared. Fortunately, the road they were all following ran through the parkland surrounding the palace. The road itself was gravel and noisy beneath boot-heels, therefore, but on either side of it there was well-tended lawn punctuated with tall, broad-topped oaks. Tom stayed on the silent grass, therefore, and tried to get as much protection as the spring-budded trees with their frail green leaves could offer. As they neared the palace, the brightness streaming from the building itself helped him move confidently as well as silently. In the stillness of the night, the bustle filling the building was carried to his keen hearing by a chilly breeze. Bustle disturbingly punctuated by the sound of women wailing. His excitement at being involved in his first real assignment as an intelligencer was not quite proof against the superstitious shivers that the desolate cries caused to run down his spine.

But then the brightness and the sound were all that were left to him as Sir Robert and his guide vanished through one of the main gates and into the palace itself. Tom stopped dead, his mind racing, as he offered a prayer to the Almighty that Sir Robert would come out of the same gate when he completed the mission he had been called to perform. Then

Tom's heart sank further. What if Sir Robert came out through the same gate – but came out mounted? Tom's divine imprecations expanded to include the hope that Sir Robert's horse, like his own, was stabled at the White Hart. Or that, like Phelippes and Poley, Sir Robert would head for London on a wherry. In either case, as advised by his brother-in-law, Tom had made provision to follow as closely as possible.

As Tom stood shivering and awaiting events, he took the opportunity to study the gate his quarry had vanished through. The portal itself rose to a pointed arch, like the doorway into the church Tom frequented on Sundays. It was far bigger than the church-door however. It was closed by two massive wooden gates, though one of them had a smaller doorway in it – which the men he was following had just used. At the point of the arch, it was possible to see the downward spikes of a portcullis, and above these, the windows of the guard-room from which the portcullis could be lowered. As the palace was not currently under attack, these windows were dark. But, thought Tom, they were just about the only windows in the place that seemed to be so.

As he waited in the shelter of a parkland tree, beneath that slowly clearing sky, feeling the temperature begin to drop as the clouds broke and the moon joined the stars scattered across the icy heaven, Tom distracted himself from the cold by making plans and holding mental conversations – with Sir Robert, with Phelippes, with the King of Scotland if, like Poley, he was granted access to deliver the missives in his satchel in person. But most of all with Poley himself. Tom held his brother-in-law in awe. Poley's treatment of Tom's sister and whether or not he mounted a mistress while still married to her didn't matter a jot. He saw in Poley a man who talked with kings and queens, who walked with giants of government, who had held the fate of England in his hands more than once, and who had never let his grasp weaken. On the stormy seas of secret politics, whipped up further by religious differences, uncontrolled ambition and the death of monarchs, Poley was, as far as Tom could see, a Drake, a Hawkins, a Lord Admiral Howard; perhaps even a Walter Raleigh. If Cecil was captain, Poley was the steady hand at the tiller of the ship of state.

Tom was so deep in these thoughts that he didn't even see the small gate open once more. It was the movement of the figure silhouetted briefly against the brightness within that caught his attention and the dull gold square of the doorway remained open for long enough so that Tom could identify Sir Robert. Then darkness returned as the knight was shut out of the palace. The bang of the door was followed by the scraping of wood or metal. Bolts being drawn, thought Tom, or a drawbar sliding down into place. Sir Robert, like the rest of the world – other than any remaining Privy Council members – was firmly shut out, as the secret of the queen's death was shut in. But was King James's ring shut out along with him or was it, like the queen's corpse, still within those forbidding walls?

Scarcely distinguishable from the shadows along the wall even in the faint promise of dawn, Sir Robert lingered restlessly. Just as Tom convinced himself that the knight had failed in his mission to retrieve the ring from his sister, a glimmer of light appeared in one of the windows above the portcullis. A lamp-flame illuminated the pale oval of a face. It was too distant for Tom to make out much about it but the head dress revealed it to be a woman. She leaned forward and opened the window. Sir Robert moved decisively until he was standing beneath it. The woman threw something down and the knight caught it deftly then raised his fist in triumph before turning and beginning to make his way back. Lady Philadelphia Scrope – calculated Tom – closed the window and vanished, her part of the task completed. The ring was safely out of the palace. The signal was on its way north. And the intelligencer was hot on the heels of the man who carried it.

11

Tom waited until Sir Robert was in the saddle and walking his horse out onto the river road before he asked the stable-lad to prepare his own horse. The lad was quick and Tom was in the saddle himself within five minutes so it was easy enough for him to follow his target keeping far enough back to avoid suspicion. Though it seemed to Tom that the knight was so focussed on his own mission that his follower could have been accompanied by the French cavalry from the battle of Agincourt and Sir Robert wouldn't have noticed. Instead, maintaining a steady canter, the two horsemen followed the road, keeping the river on their left, out of Richmond, through the hamlet of Mortlake and into the village of Putney. Things were busier here because the sun was just below the horizon and the villagers were up and about. Sir Robert went up to the dock where the Putney ferry berthed, but he arrived just in time to see it pulling away, leaving a queue of impatient passengers waiting for its return. The messenger stopped, clearly calculating his fastest way to proceed. He paused for long enough to allow Tom to recall another incident featuring a royal ring that had happened here. When the late queen's father had dismissed Cardinal Wolsey, the disgraced prelate had come south across the ferry here believing all was lost - only to be caught by the king's messenger who passed over the king's ring, and with it the proof of the king's continuing trust and affection. The cardinal knelt on these very stones, thought Tom, and thanked the Lord for His protection – and begged a long, happy life for his overpowering monarch.

Sir Robert ran out of patience, pulled his horse's head round and trotted off once more. Putney gave way to marshy fields through which the road ran, little more than a muddy track. The road hardly improved as it passed through the huts and hovels of Battersea, then came the better tended grounds around Fox Hall which in turn yielded to the increasingly urban village of Lambeth with the Archbishop of Canterbury's palace at its heart. But before they reached the palace, Sir Robert swung left onto the broad dock of the horse ferry. The horse ferry was altogether larger than the Putney ferry and, as its name implied, was designed to carry a range of passengers with four legs as well as two. The bustle of stirring commerce which had become so obvious at Putney, had intensified so that Tom and his quarry were merely two in a fair-sized crowd who eventually packed onto the ferry, each rider at his horse's head, holding the animal still and controlled.

The ferry pulled across the current until it finally reached the dock on the north bank which stood at the edge of Tothill Fields, where the buildings of Westminster School rose from the marshy ground with its reeds and rushes, flocks of snipe and plague pits. The Abbey itself towered behind the school which had been founded more than sixty years ago by Queen Elizabeth's father. Everyone, like Sir Robert and his shadow, turned right and set their faces towards Westminster, Whitehall, and, beyond them, Charing Cross, The Strand and London Wall at Lud Gate, where London itself began. The leading group of horsemen trotted past the palaces and the Cross into the distant Strand and on towards Lud Gate, most of them, obviously, having business within the city. But, much to Tom's surprise, Sir Robert did not join them. Instead of heading into the heart of London, or turning north at Charing Cross, he rode a little way up the road immediately in front of him then abruptly turned right into one of the largest houses on the street. He was challenged at the gate but after exchanging a few words, he vanished into what was clearly a stable yard behind the building.

Tom stopped, his mind racing. He looked around, abruptly at a loss. He had no idea why Sir Robert had gone into the house nor when he would be coming out again. He had no idea, therefore, what he himself should do under these unexpected and worrying circumstances. But then a ray of hope gleamed. The thoroughfare he was sitting on was King Street. The house that Sir Robert was in lay at the far end, nearest Whitehall Palace and Charing Cross beyond it. And Poley lived on King Street. Tom racked his brains trying to remember what Poley had told him about his lodgings, but he hardly needed to batter his memory, for his eyes told him all he needed to know. There, immediately in front of him, almost exactly opposite Westminster's main gate, there hung a tavern sign whose motif, figured in red paint. was a lion.

12

'Master Poley?' said the innkeeper. 'Yuss I reckon he's in. Recently arrived. Is your horse being seen to?'

'It's with the ostler in the stable yard.'

'Good enough. We'll settle for that later. In the meantime, take the stair beside the door there and rouse him with my blessing.'

As it turned out, Poley did not need rousing. At Tom's first hesitant knock he called 'Come!' and the young man entered. Poley was seated in the first of the two rooms he rented. The inner room, visible through a half-open door, was a spacious bed chamber, scrupulously neat and tidy; its bed, of course had not been slept in. The outer chamber boasted a good-sized table and chairs, and a settle. The wall on Tom's left was dominated by a long window which not only rendered excellent illumination but also gave a good view of the main entrance into Westminster Palace. Indeed, from this elevation it was just possible to catch a glimpse of what little was left of the privy sections in the middle which had housed the royal family when Westminster had been a true palace – until they were destroyed by fire and King Henry the Eighth had moved his household into York House, Thomas Wolsey's property, next-door, and rechristened it Whitehall Palace. Then, thought Tom, he divided his time between Whitehall and Wolsey's other great property, Hampton Court Palace. Wolsey's prayers at Putney did not seem to have been answered in the way the cardinal might have hoped.

The young intelligencer shook his head and allowed himself to harbour a seditious thought. King by divine right and Defender of the Faith, Henry effectively owned almost everything in his kingdom and – with only the guiding hand of parliament – could give and take whatever he wanted. Something his daughter had been more reluctant than Bluff King Hal to do. Even so, men could still rise on a royal whim and fall on a regal impulse – as Thomas Wolsey had proved all too clearly in his time and the Earl of Essex had clearly demonstrated more recently.

While Tom was lost in thought, Poley finished reading one of the letters from his satchel and made a note. Then he leaned back in his chair, pushing the satchel and the pile of its contents aside. 'So, he's gone into one of the nearby houses, has he?'

'Mere moments since,' said Tom. 'The large one up towards Charing Cross. He has the ring with him. What's to do now?'

'Wait,' said Poley. 'Wait and watch.'

'But whose house is it?' wondered Thomas.

'The largest house you say? Closest to Charing Cross? That is the London dwelling of Sir Thomas Gerard the Knight Marshal. He was one of the Earl of Essex's followers but he was wise enough to split away from the earl before the uprising. Now he is an influential member of parliament and courtier on the edges of the council. More importantly, perhaps, he is a good friend to Sir Robert Carey. I would calculate that Sir Robert will be asking the Knight Marshal to approach the council as soon as they arrive, to discover whether they have any further messages for him to carry north.'

'But why not simply ask them himself?'

'They did not choose him,' Poley explained. 'They might well have an alternative messenger in mind for this absolutely crucial mission. Consider. Each of them wishes to establish himself in King James's good graces or risk losing everything at one royal word. Each of them, therefore, will wish to send his own man to plead his own case at this most propitious moment. No. If Sir Robert ventures into Westminster, he is unlikely to come out again within the week.'

'But it is safe for the Knight Marshal to do so?'

Poley gave a ghost of a smile. 'The Knight Marshal, under the Earl Marshal, is responsible for keeping order in the court. In parallel you might say to the Captain of the Guard whose yeomen are responsible for the personal safety of the sovereign. Anyone thinking of calling for the Knight Marshal to be restrained is likely to be restrained himself – by the Knight Marshal's bailiffs.'

This discussion was brought to an abrupt end by the arrival of a group of horsemen closely followed by a line of coaches, all of which swung into the gate of Westminster. As Tom gaped down on them, the clock in a nearby steeple sounded the hour of nine and a group of men from the Knight Marshal's house joined the crowd jostling to gain entry. 'The Privy Council have arrived,' said Poley. 'That was quick.'

'What will they do next?' asked Tom.

'Agree the form of words then announce the queen's death at Charing Cross and then at St Paul's, sending messengers with copies of the pronouncements to all the major cities in the kingdom as well as a further formal notification to King James.'

'It shouldn't take them long to agree the form of words if Master Secretary has written them already.'

'True. Let us look lively, therefore. I want to be at Charing Cross to witness this.'

The two men ran nimbly down the stairs and out into King Street. The bustle had momentarily eased as the last of the council entered Westminster. Poley turned decisively and began to stride towards Whitehall and, beyond it, Charing Cross. But as he did so, a mounted man came out of the Knight Marshal's house at the end of the road and began to trot towards the palace.

Poley's breath hissed in, just as Tom observed, 'That's Sir Robert Carey. Off to report to the council after all, I'd wager.'

The knight trotted forward, seemingly oblivious to those few other horsemen and pedestrians still in the road, all moving in the opposite direction. Or he was until Poley stepped in front of his horse and reached up to take hold of its bridle. The look of disbelief on Sir Robert's face was succeeded at once by one of outrage – and then, much to Tom's surprise – recognition.

'You know me, Sir Robert?'

'I know you, Master Poley. What business do you have with me?'

'This. If you venture into Westminster, the council will hold you, as certain as Judgement Day. Hold you and replace you with their own man to carry your message north.'

It seemed to the awe-struck Tom that Sir Robert's recognition of the man holding his horse's bridle encompassed unquestioning belief that what he said must be true. He didn't even question how Poley knew so much about his business or his plans. 'So?' he said.

'So, Sir Robert, I would advise you to take firm hold of King James's ring and ride for Edinburgh with the greatest despatch. Don't even wait for Master Secretary to read out the Council's proclamation. You know well enough what it will say.'

'And why are you so busy about my business, Master Poley?'

'Because Master Secretary would have it so, Sir Robert.'

'Very well. You and your master have my thanks.' Sir Robert turned his horse's head and trotted towards Charing Cross. But as he neared the Cross itself, his horse slowed to a walk and was soon surrounded by a great and growing crowd, all anxiously waiting for more news.

'Get your horse,' said Poley to Tom, 'and continue to follow him.'

'But why? If Master Secretary has…'

'I may have over-stated Master Secretary's involvement,' said Poley. 'And I want eyes on Sir Robert. Careful eyes. Eyes that are wise to possible dangers.'

'Dangers?'

Poley turned to face his young brother-in-law and co-conspirator, the ghost of a smile crinkling the corners of his eyes. 'There is someone else on the road north. They will be just ahead of Sir Robert if my calculations are correct. I advised this other man to wait for the council's pronouncement but like Sir Robert, it seems likely he will disregard my advice. He guesses clearly enough what that announcement will say. And he will be far too impatient to wait at Charing Cross. Someone on the same mission, to inform King James of Her Majesty's death but, further, to make use of any goodwill his news engenders, to plead for relaxation of the laws governing recusant Catholics. He is, in a way, on a crusade, one might say, and thank the Lord I have been careful to keep eyes on him too.'

'A crusade?'

'A mission for the good of his Church and his fellow celebrants at least. But you need to bear in mind that such men, feeling themselves working directly under divine authority, will on occasion think nothing of breaking the laws of mankind.'

Tom was silent for a moment as the implications of Poley's words sank in.

'And how should I know this man who might think nothing of breaking the laws of mankind?'

'His name is William Watson and he is about my age, squat and square of figure, but most strikingly he has a squint in his eye which renders him at once nearly blind to things near at hand and almost impossible to mistake.'

13

William Watson's eyesight and lack of patience were both letting him down again and he knew it. A man of weaker spirit would have prayed for divine assistance, especially given the nature of his mission, but the situation was nothing new. Watson was content to rely on any assistance Heaven deigned to lend him without begging for it. Men like him did not beg not even for the favour of God. It did not occur to the self-righteous prelate that this was the sin of Pride – Satan's sin and the most dangerous of all. And it happened, moreover, that such assistance was in short supply this morning. The ostler at the stables on St Martin's Lane was not a godly soul. He saw in the purblind customer a chance to ask a high price for a swayback nag with broken wind and spavined hocks which he had been unable to fob off on anyone else. Besides, the way the customer observed him with those weird and wandering eyes made him wonder whether the man had recently escaped from the Bethlehem Hospital up by Bishopsgate which was popularly named Bedlam.

The stirrup straps groaned as Watson hoisted himself into the saddle and the horse itself seemed to groan as his broad buttocks settled into the leather seat. Watson drove his heels into the horse's ribs with a force augmented by his frustration at the near-certainty that he had been cheated, and the mount ambled out into the early morning. Watson turned its head northward against the incoming traffic and tried for a trot at least. He was well aware that Poley expected him to be waiting for the formal announcement of the old queen's death and the new king's succession but he had no intention of wasting a single moment. He had come to the stables at the earliest opportunity and spent no time negotiating at all before he mounted up and set out. He was, after all, about God's work.

Nick Skeres watched Watson ambling northward, a steady point in the tide of travellers pulling to one side or the other in order to avoid him. 'Blind as a bat,' he said. 'It's ironic that Master Poley called us to keep *eyes* on a blind man!'

'But it'll make him all the easier for you to track,' observed Will Udall who was recently returned from travelling around Europe at Poley's command and had yet to settle into the new reality that the Tudor dynasty had come to an end.

'True,' agreed Skeres, looking down at his friend and one-time cellmate at both Newgate and Bridewell prisons in the grim days after their lord and master the Earl of Essex met his end - before Poley had secured their release. For the price of their service; almost of their souls. He leaned down from the saddle and lowered his voice. 'But Poley said that he reckons he'll only rely on stables and post horses to begin with. He'll be heading to recusant houses and relying on the good offices of his fellow Catholics to speed him on his way, especially when they find out what his mission is. The further north he gets, the more friendly houses he's likely to find.'

'Which will be at least part of the reason Poley wants him followed,' nodded Udall. 'But it's not as if Master Poley doesn't know who the most dangerous recusants, appellants, secular priests and Jesuits are already.'

'True, friend Will. As he and Master Secretary have long established, and poured into the queen's ear no doubt. But think. If Watson is riding north with news of her death and of King James's succession, then they will have to start all over again will they not? For they'll have a brand-new monarch to inform of the identities and the dangers such men, women and their households might present. A new monarch that might require more solid proof than the old one did.'

'I had not thought of that,' said Udall.

'Which is why you linger here by Charing Cross awaiting the council's word, Will, while I take my wits north in the wake of this impatient and dangerous priest.'

Poley's plans to apprise King James of the dangerous men and women waiting for a chance to control him, kidnap or outright kill him, occupied Skeres as he set off in pursuit of Watson. As did Poley's need to do so in a way that enhanced Master Secretary in the eyes of the new king, upon whose patronage they all depended now. Skeres knew the price of supporting the wrong man better than most. Too many of his friends from the Essex household had joined him in Bridewell and remained there, mouldering, long after Poley pulled him and Udall out, sending Udall on brief forays abroad but keeping Nick Skeres closer at hand. These thoughts took Skeres past the Royal Mews, along St Martin's Lane leading out across the fields to Tottenham Court Road which led to the manor of Tottenham Court north of London. Here his thoughts were distracted once again by the enormity of the news he carried. Tottenham Court had been leased by the queen, which lease had expired, of course, with Her Majesty.

The road leading past it and the parish of St Pancras, eventually joined the Great North Road itself, whose southern end, therefore, was effectively Charing Cross; whose northern end was generally agreed to be at the Mercat Cross in Edinburgh. While considering all this, and St Pancras's less than salubrious reputation as a haunt of hedge priests and runaway lovers, Nick Skeres paced his mount carefully, fearful that he would catch up with Watson before they had properly started out.

'*Will he never start out?*' wondered Tom, afire with frustration.

Sir Robert stood at his horse's head, calming the beast in the midst of a great and growing crowd gathering around Charing Cross and the green close beside it. The Privy Council were assembling on the green, keeping apart from their eager audience. Even as Tom's mind filled with that one, frustrated question, the slight, hunched figure of Master Secretary stepped forward. He was dressed in his accustomed colour – fabulously expensive black. It was as though his whole wardrobe had been purchased in preparation for this moment. He raised his hand and the crowd fell into a fearful silence.

'Forasmuch,' he began, his voice grating like a rusted hinge. He paused, cleared his throat, tried again, his voice louder and more confident. Commanding, thought Tom. 'Forasmuch as it has pleased Almighty God to call to his mercy out of this transitory life our Sovereign lady, the High and Mighty Prince, Elizabeth, late Queen of England, France and Ireland by whose death and dissolution the Imperial crown of these realms aforesaid are now absolutely and solely come to the high and mighty prince James the Sixth of Scotland...'

There it was, thought Tom. The truth of the matter, almost unbelievable though it seemed. He did not listen to the rest as Master Secretary Cecil spoke on, reading the announcement he had already sent to Scotland with the messenger Ingram Frizer if brother-in-law Robert could be believed. And if Robert Poley could not be believed, then who could?

The phrases 'Lords spiritual and temporal...' 'Her late Majesty's Privy Council...' 'other principal gentlemen...' a list, noted Tom, which did not include the Captain of the Queen's Guard. 'James... is now become our only lawful, lineal and rightful Liege James the First, King of England, France and Ireland, Defender of the Faith...' It all slid over his consciousness. His prime focus remained on Sir Robert. When in the name of God and all His angels would the bloody man mount up and head north?

It took another hour before Sir Robert freed himself from the wailing citizens and struck out for the Great North Road. But once he was in motion, he moved so fast that Tom was only just able to keep up with him. The Great North Road was one of the most important in the realm. At its southern end it was cobbled, then metalled, then gravelled as it ran through increasingly empty country, studded every ten miles or so with taverns supplying post horses. Paying well and pacing himself carefully, a rider could cover the better part of twenty miles in an hour – on horses that were always fresh and keen to go. Sir Robert knew the road better than any man except, perhaps, Poley. The knight had won a wager in his youth by walking from Berwick to London and had, therefore trodden every inch that he was galloping over now. He stopped for relief and refreshments after the first seventy miles or so in Godmanchester, eating and drinking in the saddle as he thundered on towards Huntingdon. Changing horses every ten miles, he reached Stamford in mid-afternoon and Grantham little more than an hour later. Tom was at once awed and exhausted. The road between London and Grantham was well supplied and well maintained. It became less so further north, and yet Sir Robert, if anything, rode more quickly, charging through Newark as the sun began to set and, making no allowance for the darkness, presenting himself at the toll on St Sepulchre bridge and trotting into Doncaster at moonrise, having covered the better part of two hundred miles in little more than ten hours.

14

In fact, the two messengers and their shadows all spent the night in Doncaster. Watson's earlier start had allowed him to hire a couple of slower horses without losing his lead and the first section of the journey had been an easy one for Nick Skeres. But once they got to Royston, the short-sighted priest, being first to arrive, got the pick of the horses and their speed quickened markedly. Watson's sense of urgency was every bit as powerful as Sir Robert's. And there was an extra element arising from Watson's faith and his almost messianic mission.

Sir Robert, followed discreetly by Tom, took a room at the Bell close by St Sepulchre itself. There was scant food left in the ordinary as they arrived so late and cold comfort in rooms they would never normally have chosen. William Watson, however, knocked gently on the door of a sizeable house and was welcomed into the bosom of the recusant family within – fed, watered and cosseted, all for the price of a mass. Nick Skeres watched the meal - at least – through the window, then he talked his way into the Swan immediately opposite. Not only because it was a convenient look-out but because its name reminded him of one of his favourite brothels in Southwark. And, as chance would have it, this Swan was a pair with the one in Southwark too. He got very little sleep, therefore, spent more coin than he had planned, and was lucky on two more points than he realised. He was neither robbed nor murdered. In fact, his companion for the night was able to give him details of the family who lived in the house Watson was visiting, which he was happy to commit to memory, unlike the trull's name. And because his bed-mate had domestic duties around the tavern as well as sportive ones above it, he was wakened early. Just in time, in fact, to see the man he was following departing in the pre-dawn. The door of the house he had stayed in overnight remained open as someone – presumably his recusant host – watched him depart. Watson was just turning away from this unremarkable scene when he froze. He recognised that man and realised he was as much of a stranger here as Watson. It was Sir Griffin Markham, the Catholic owner of Beskwood Park away on the far side of Nottingham.

Tom and Sir Robert enjoyed a much more comfortable and salubrious night but they were awakened later than Watson and Skeres who therefore had the better part of an hour's start on them once more. As he rode behind Watson, unaware that Sir Robert and Tom were stirring some five miles behind him, Skeres was deep in thought. This was not just a way of distracting him from his rumbling belly, light purse and itching loins, but he was well aware that he was entertaining the sin of envy to accompany that of lust. The priest was so much more fortunate than he deserved to be. The recusant family who entertained Watson last night had supplied him with a good strong horse. Not only that, he discovered, turning envy to naked jealousy, they had given the recusant priest a kerchief heavy with food and drink for his journey. Not only that, but someone last night had given him a weighty purse to match the heavy kerchief. Watson's new riches ensured every staging post on the northern road supplied him with the best horse they had available. Which, taken all together, meant that Skeres found it harder and harder to keep up with his quarry. However, they reached Darnton, which some men were calling Darlington these days, six hours later, soon after noon, with Nick Skeres and his current mount almost dead for want of breath, drink and sustenance.

Tom and Sir Robert were not as far behind as might be supposed. Although they set out later and the quality of their horseflesh was never quite as strong as Watson's, the messenger-knight was clearer sighted and just as well-motivated as the prelate. He might not have been moving in the service of the Lord, but he was planning to secure the fortunes and future of his family, friends and patron. But then another element entered the unsuspected contest for as Watson and the gasping Skeres rode into the centre of Darnton, the bells of St Cuthbert's rang out loud and clear. The bells were calling the faithful of a different faith to Watson's but the simple coincidence of his being here when the service was beginning moved the priest to stop beside a hostelry which gloried in the name The Tun of Lead, give his horse to a lad to watch and disappear to make his own, secret, observances. And then, thought Skeres, to have lunch from that weighty-looking kerchief he had taken with him. There were plenty of secluded spots down by the river near the Bishop's Palace, calculated Skeres as he also gave his horse into the lad's care and glanced around the wide, tree-lined square before he turned and invested some of his diminishing hoard of coin in a quart of ale and a slice of eel pie from the Tun's ordinary, today being a fish day.

Sometime later, Skeres was back outside, lingering in the broad square of the Lead Yard, keeping an eye on Watson's horse as he finished his food and drink, when Sir Robert Carey arrived with Tom close behind. As chance would have it, Sir Robert also stopped here and went into the Tun for relief and sustenance. Skeres did not recognise Sir Robert, but he knew Tom well enough. Without a second thought, he sucked in a breath to greet the young intelligencer when he was forestalled himself. 'Nick Skeres!' came a great shout that seemed to fill the whole place. 'Well met my bully! What make you here?'

Skeres turned round and gaped with surprise. Ingram Frizer came trotting down the road on a handsome-looking brown horse. 'Much the same as you, I'd wager, Ingram,' he replied. 'Carrying messages. But I'm carrying them from south to north while you're on the opposite path I see.'

Frizer reined to a stop and dismounted, talking all the while. 'Aye. Heading south to London. I'd calculate I know who you're carrying messages *for* but *from* whom and *to* whom?'

Skeres shrugged. 'I carry them for Poley,' he lied, needing a reason to be here when in reality he was stalking another messenger and carrying no messages himself. 'And they are for the attention of King James himself. The main one being the death of the queen.' The falsehood was simple and within easy reach; it was the first that sprang to mind. He was, after all, one of Poley's intelligencers talking to another, for all that Frizer also worked for Sir Thomas Walsingham.

There was a silence as Frizer digested Skeres's news – as did anyone else near enough to hear his unthinking words. Then Nick's easy untruth had unexpected consequences because just as he named his employer, both Sir Robert Carey and William Watson re-entered the Lead Yard square from opposite sides, but both well within earshot. 'Poley?' said Sir Robert. 'Do you both work for Poley?' he glanced around as though suspecting he was surrounded by intelligencers. Which in fact he was. Tom turned away with a guilty start, betrayed by his inexperience. But he was experienced and clear-sighted enough to identify the ill-dressed man with a cast in his eye standing watching in the churchyard.

Watson stood in the shade of a great yew-tree near St Cuthberts and assessed the situation. As with some men, the loss of one sense led to the strengthening of another. He did not see well but he heard acutely. Besides, although his eyes were not reliable when called upon to see anything close-to, they saw well enough in the middle range and in the distance. He saw two men who admitted working for Robert Poley and one man who – at the least – admitted to knowing Robert Poley. And a young man who looked shocked and guilt-ridden at the mention of Poley's name. Years of working to avoid the heretic queen's priest-hunters while labouring in secret for her overthrow had skilled Watson in duplicity. Enacting it and recognising it. In a heartbeat he knew the four he was looking at as his bitter enemies. Indeed, not just enemies to him but also to his church and to his God.

15

Nick Skeres saw his quarry standing suspiciously in the shade of the churchyard yew and knew Ingram Frizer's unthinking words had unmasked him and that his task of following Watson would now be doubly difficult. He would have to dog his footsteps invisibly, keeping constantly aware that Watson might well find some way of trapping, injuring or killing him. They were in Catholic country after all, not to mention that they were fast approaching the Debatable Lands of the lawless Borders and the wily priest probably had ruthless allies here as well as welcoming friends. He was tempted to turn round and ride back south with his long-time colleague but he did not do so for several good reasons. First, he was convinced that now, despite his sudden access to finances, Watson would probably still to rely on his recusant friends and contacts for succour if not for murder – and it was Nick's duty to watch and record. Secondly, he had been commissioned to be there in Edinburgh to see which powers in the Scottish court might also be willing to lean towards Catholic Europe – even after the political disaster of their French Catholic Queen Mary. Thirdly, finally and most importantly, he was simply terrified at the thought of what Poley would do to him if he disobeyed his orders. It had been Frizer who stabbed the loose-tongued, dangerously disobedient Kit Marlowe through the eye ten years ago when he had finally threatened to run out of control, but Skeres had been splattered with thick tears of the playwright's hot blood and he had seen the look on Poley's face as he oversaw the execution. He did not want that face looking at him as his own life-blood splattered someone else. So, taking his life in his hands, he set out after Watson mere moments after the priest climbed into his saddle and galloped off northwards.

Tom watched them go, then, assuming a mask of innocence that he hoped was convincing, he went back into the Tun and bought food and drink – which he was carefully still consuming when Sir Robert also mounted up and set off. Without giving Tom a second glance, thank the Lord. The knight might have looked on the young man with more suspicion had he seen how much of the meal Tom left when he too mounted up and spurred his horse northwards once again.

Darnton had been a little way off the Great North Road itself but was universally accepted as a necessary diversion as the Road ran through the wild and featureless Dales of County Durham, little changed since the wilderness of Yorkshire's North Riding, down into the valley of the river Tees then up onto the Dales once more. But at least it ran straight and true for all that it went up and down increasingly steep inclines. They passed through Durham city itself and Newcastle, both in river valleys, without stopping. Then they climbed back up past the timeless ruins of The Wall onto the wild moors as the afternoon wore on and they found themselves out in the wilderness once more with little else in prospect other than the even wilder border county of Northumberland.

So, it was no great surprise to Tom when Sir Robert left the road once more as the sun began to set. In fact, the Warden of the Middle March – one of Sir Robert's titles – was heading home to Widdrington Castle. Tom, well briefed by Poley, had been expecting this detour and was confident in Poley's assurance that there was a country inn not far removed from Sir Robert's castle – thriving there on the custom of the castle servants, gardeners, suppliers and a considerable military contingent which stood against any Border Reivers coming raiding south out of Scotland. It was called The Widdrington Inn and stood on the only easily passable thoroughfare between the castle and the Great North Road. Poley's information was as accurate in this as in everything else. The intelligencer was noted for his speed and reliability carrying messages between London and Edinburgh himself and knew every step of the way as well as Sir Robert.

Despite a no-doubt warm welcome at his home, and a good deal of work awaiting him there, Sir Robert did not stay long; scarcely longer than from dusk 'til dawn. But he clearly did a good deal of organising in the interim, for when he rode out before sunrise he was at the head of a small troop of mounted men. Fortunately, Tom was up early and so was able to watch his quarry and companions riding past The Widdrington Inn safe in the knowledge that he would be in the saddle and on their trail in a few minutes' time. And so he was, with a kerchief full of food and drink for later tucked in one saddlebag while his precious satchel and a few personal possessions filled the other.

A dull, overcast morning passed without incident, except for the fact that every now and then one of the Warden's companions would take a side-road, no doubt carrying the news of the queen's death and the proposed succession to other points of the Middle March. Then, as noon approached, Sir Robert himself chose to leave the road once more. Berwick lay at the foot of the Tweed Valley dead ahead and the last of his companions spurred down the hillside towards it, but Sir Robert followed a westerly spur along the watershed, out across the moors, with Tom following the lone rider at a careful distance. After a while it became clear that the Warden of the Middle March was heading for Norham castle. He vanished inside the forbidding fortification, leaving Tom to wait – glad of the light lunch the Widdrington Inn had supplied. More organising no doubt. For, thought Tom, the Borders under Sir Robert's watch were already wild and dangerous. What they would become during the interregnum while King James prepared to succeed Queen Elizabeth was anybody's guess. Sir Robert came out of Norham Castle soon enough and he and his shadow took another road – which was little more than a mud track through the heather and the gorse – until they were back on the Great North Road once more.

Suddenly seeming to run out of patience at last Sir Robert spurred into a full gallop. He was on a horse he had picked up at Norham and it was fresh, strong and willing. Tom drove his own mount as fast as it would go but Sir Robert was soon out of sight. Tom told himself not to worry. He knew where Sir Robert was going. He just hoped that there were no more detours planned between here and Edinburgh. Tom never knew precisely when they crossed out of England into Scotland. It might have been when they were riding back from Norham. If not then, it must have been almost immediately after they re-joined the Great North Road a few miles north of Berwick. But the atmosphere changed, as did the landscape. The road down which Sir Robert had charged at full-gallop swung right in a long, shallow curve to run along the coast. There was a sense of the sea, its sound and smell were carried on the easterly wind even though it was only sporadically visible in the occasional bay nestling between headland after headland, mostly cloaked by great bushes of gorse, just coming into yellow flower. The gorse, indeed, pressed hard against the road itself as well as the nearby sea shore. Tom found it all oddly distracting. He was a Londoner born and bred. He had never actually seen the sea before and he had not expected it to be so restless, so grey, so vast. He had heard seagulls calling on occasion – black-headed marsh-gulls downriver from Redriffe, Deptford and Greenwich. But he had never seen great black-backed seagulls and grey herring gulls in numbers like these. They filled the low grey sky as they varied from solid cruciforms riding the roaring blast to tiny dots like black stars against the racing clouds. The numbers and the noise they made were unsettlingly intimidating. Then he suddenly noticed something disquieting. There was a column of the creatures dead ahead, that seemed to be interested in something just beyond the next rise. He spurred his weary but willing horse out of its canter into something of a gallop and crested the rise to see that disaster had struck. Sir Robert's horse was walking uncomfortably towards him, favouring its right foreleg. Sir Robert himself was lying face down in the coarse sea grass between a couple of stands of gorse close beside the road.

Tom dismounted slowly and carefully. Slowly because his mind was racing. Carefully because he did not want to frighten Sir Robert's already uneasy horse. As he did so, he looked round, suddenly suspecting that he was being watched. But beyond the disturbing sensation there was nothing. Taking the reins of his own horse, he walked it towards Sir Robert's and was fortunate that the creature let him take its reins as well. Because he was thinking about the horse rather than its rider at that moment, he crouched to look at the hurt foreleg. There was some twine tangled around it. One-handed, he worked the twine free. There was quite a lot of it and he was surprised to see that there was a pointed wooden peg almost as long as his forearm tied to one end. Once it was free of the horse's leg, he straightened and led both of the horses to a gorse bush that looked strong enough to hitch them to. He put the twine and the peg in his saddle-bag where his lunch had been stored. There was nothing left of it now except the kerchief and a little of the water. Then he went to Sir Robert.

With some difficulty Tom managed to turn the knight's prone body over. He weighed so much that Tom at first thought he must be dead. A supposition strengthened by the obvious fact that he had been kicked in the head. There was a welted black bruise on his forehead that was the shape of a hoof. The bruise stood out so clearly because the face itself was deathly pale. But as Tom knelt there, frankly at a loss as to what he should do, Sir Robert's eyelids flickered. Tom went back to his horse and took the flask of water. There was enough left to give the wounded man a mouthful as he began to regain consciousness with his head cradled in Tom's arm.

101

'What happened?' asked Sir Robert as his wits began to return.

Tom thought about the peg and the twine. There must be another peg somewhere nearby, he reasoned. Strong enough to keep the twine taut across the road just at the right height to make a galloping horse stumble or fall. To pitch their rider out of the saddle in near certainty of breaking his neck. 'I think someone may have tried to kill you, Sir Robert,' he said.

16

It was midnight by the time they got to Edinburgh. 'I had planned to get here mid-afternoon,' said Sir Robert. 'Had it not been for your help I doubt I would have got here at all. I owe you thanks, and I owe Robert Poley thanks for sending you to watch over me.'

'I am as much a messenger as a guard, Sir Robert,' answered Tom, looking around. The road they were following led up a steep hill towards a forbidding castle. Like the buildings surrounding them, the castle was really only visible as a blacker shape in the darkness. The road was lined mostly with shacks and hovels but as they neared the castle, the quality of the buildings improved. Tom spotted an inn with some relief. 'Well, if we cannot get into the castle, at least we can bed down at the Sheep Heid Inn, there,' he said.

Sir Robert gave a weary chuckle. 'I have the ring and the ring has powers to open every door between the main gate and the king's bedroom,' he said. 'We will have no need of the Sheep Heid tonight I promise. You have missives for King James, you say?'

'Locked letters given me by Master Poley direct from the hand of Master Secretary himself,' confirmed Tom.

'Well, I can almost guarantee they will pass straight from your hands into the king's and that he will read them before he sleeps. Unless they are so cunningly locked and encoded that even he cannot open and understand them.'

When they reached the main entrance at the crest of the long straight road they had been following, Sir Robert reined to a stop and so therefore, did Tom. They found themselves hard up against a wide, curving wall with turrets astride a massive pair of wooden doors, lit and obviously guarded. 'Hello the castle,' bellowed the knight. 'Tell the king there is someone from London would speak with him on a matter of the greatest urgency.'

The reply was immediate. One of the full-sized gates swung wide, opening inward like the gates at Richmond Palace, to allow free movement to the huge portcullis that hung above them. 'Who goes there?' demanded a voice in an accent so thick that it took Tom several heartbeats to understand the words.

Not so Sir Robert. 'Sir Robert Carey and his companion. We would speak with His Majesty,' the knight and Warden of the Middle March answered clearly and swiftly.

'Enter, Sir Robert ye're expected. Indeed, ye're waited upon.'

Sir Robert eased his horse through the gate and Tom followed close behind. The young intelligencer had never been to the Tower, which was the closest thing to a proper defensive fortification London had to offer. The intricacies of the building he now entered were a revelation to him therefore. He and Sir Robert did not enter the courtyard he had expected, but a narrow roadway which wound round the side of the main fortification, overlooked by defensive battlements and arrow-slits – all illuminated by flaming torch after flaming torch in black metal sconces. Only at the end of this narrow passage did they find themselves at the castle gate. This was a slightly smaller version of the gate they had just come through and the tower in which it stood blocked all hope of further progress. Or it did so until Sir Robert called out once more, this time adding his titles to his name. And, again, was informed the king was waiting up in hopes of speaking to him and he was admitted at once, with Tom hard on his heels. This time the route they followed was wider. It curved round as it mounted steeply toward the main castle on the hilltop. 'How does King James know to expect you I wonder,' said Tom softly.

'I was puzzling that out myself,' answered Sir Robert. 'It seems hardly possible, but could someone have got here ahead of us?'

Tom said nothing but he found himself wondering about the man Nicholas Skeres had been following. The stranger with the squint who had been eyeing them all so suspiciously in the Lead Yard at Darnton. What was his name? Watson? Yes, that was it: William Watson.

There was the slope – almost a cliff – rising on their left and various buildings on the downward slope to their right. And yet even this seemingly more welcoming way led them simply to yet another gate. As they were invited through this, at last they arrived at the main castle courtyard. Sir Robert guided his mount to the bottom of a set of steps and dismounted as a palace servant came forward to take his horse's reins. Tom did the same, pausing only to pull his satchel from his saddlebag. Then, shoulder to shoulder they entered King James's principal castle.

It was the middle of the night and yet everything was bustling. Sir Robert was led through one brightly-lit reception room after another, each chamber becoming smaller and more intimate until the knight and his young companion arrived in the privy reception chamber whose open inner door revealed the royal bedroom. The bed was unoccupied because the king was waiting for them here, dressed in a gown that might have graced an even more formal occasion. He was seated near a roaring fire on a throne-like chair raised in turn on a dais. He was surrounded by half a dozen or so lordly-looking strangers who could have been castle servants or clan chieftains for all Tom knew of them. The only element that detracted from the formality was the fact that the royal feet were bare and thrust into ornate leather slippers dangling an inch or two above the floor.

'So Sair Rabbie,' said the king – or so his words sounded to Tom's untutored ear. 'Ye've made it to me after all. D'ye ha'it? Ma ring?'

'I do Your Majesty. May I approach?'

'Aye so ye may. Come awa' up tae me, laddie.'

The royal hand was thrust out. Sir Robert stepped up, went onto one knee and laid the king's ring in its owner's hand.'

'So she's deed?'

'Dead indeed, Your Majesty.'

'And I'm named in succession?'

'I heard it done, Your Majesty. And my companion here is carrying letters from Master Secretary Cecil which I believe will further confirm the fact.'

'Weel, weel, we'll look at those in a moment but tell me Sair Rabbie, how came ye by that great bruise?'

'My horse stumbled, Your Majesty, and I was thrown.'

'Stumbled, ye say? Sure, ye're too guid a horseman tae allow sic a thing?'

'There was a length of twine tied across the way, Majesty. My horse tripped on it and I was thrown.'

There was a moment of silence, King James's open countenance folded into a considerable frown. 'Yon's a reiver's trick,' he said. 'Ye were fortunate not tae get yer gullet slit.'

'My young companion here happened by, Your Majesty. If it was reivers trying to rob me, he must have scared them off.'

'Ye're a lucky man, Sair Rabbie. As am I, for they'd like have taken ma ring alongside a' your life.' The king's deep-set, brown eyes turned towards Tom, whose gaze met the king's for a moment – long enough to recognise a fierce intelligence – before he glanced down at the floor.

'And the mission your young saviour was on was tae bring word from Master Secretary ye say?'

A minute gesture from Sir Robert called Tom forward and the practised courtier's actions showed his inexperienced companion what he should do. Two steps forward. One step up. Down on his right knee, offering the satchel to the king. 'I was to bring you these,' Your Majesty.

'Thank'ee laddie. And ye had this from Laird Cecil, ye say?'

'Not directly, Majesty. I had them from Robert Poley on Master Secretary Cecil's order.'

'Frae your mon Poley is it? Well yon's good enough for me. Now, Sair Robert and I have more tae discuss but your work is done.' The King turned to one of the attendants beside him. 'Take the laddie. Feed him and house him. See tae his comfort, mind.'

'With your permission, Your Majesty,' Sir Robert turned to Tom. 'Don't worry, Tom. I will find you tomorrow and we will discuss matters then.'

The man commissioned by the King took Tom in hand then and so, by observation once again, the young intelligencer learned the proper manner in which to leave the Royal Presence – backing away and bowing.

The kitchen was surprisingly small for such a large establishment, thought Tom. And all it had to offer was a thick gruel which his guide called *porage*. When he had eaten, he was taken, via the castle privy to his bed, which was one among several in a dormitory full of other men all fast asleep. The guide led Tom to a bed which was little more than a mound of straw covered in a plaid blanket. The lamp the guide carried gave a little more brightness than was needed to light their way. Enough to reveal the sleepers' faces as they passed down the middle of the dormitory. One face was familiar – and explained everything. For Tom was certain that had the fast-shut eyes been open, one of them would have had a fearsome squint.

17

'Master Secretary wants us both,' said Phelippes, poking his head round the door of the work-room they shared. 'Now.'

'Why?' asked Poley as he tidied his papers and stood.

'He has a visitor. Not a very happy one.'

Poley nodded and walked towards the door. 'Raleigh?' he hazarded. 'I hear he's back.'

'Raleigh,' confirmed Phelippes, turning to let Poley pass him. 'And he hasn't come alone. He has Henry Brooke, Lord Cobham, with him, and Lord Henry's young brother the reverend George Brooke.'

'We'd better hurry, then,' said Poley. 'Raleigh can be quite intimidating enough when he's on his own. Where are they?'

'The library.'

'Master Secretary establishing himself as Raleigh's intellectual equal at least,' said Poley. 'And infinitely more clever than the Brooke brothers. Even so, it isn't all about who is the cleverest, is it?'

The two intelligencers went through the library door shoulder to shoulder. Poley was struck at once by the fact that the atmosphere in the spacious, book-lined room was the very opposite of what the atmosphere in a library should be. Sir Walter Raleigh, nearing fifty years of age, was still tall, straight-backed and lean. His hair and beard were silvering but there was no loss of acuity in those dark, piercing eyes. He towered over everyone there except for Poley who almost matched him in height. The scholar, soldier, sailor and Captain of the Guard had an aura of leadership that put Poley in mind of Burbage playing Henry the Fifth at the Globe. The only other man the intelligencer had seen who had such an air of command was Robert Devereux, the second Earl of Essex. But Essex had begun to lose his grip as he grew older and more desperate. The same could not be said for Raleigh. The Captain of the Guard was dressed in dark velvet, his doublet speckled with pearls, making his broad breast oddly resemble the night sky. His two dowdy companions were effectively eclipsed by their leader, even though one of them was a wealthy Lord and the other a senior churchman. The fact that they were between ten and fifteen years Raleigh's junior went some way to explaining this. And the fact that Raleigh had been one of Lord Grey's captains in Ireland, overseeing the slaughter of six hundred Spanish prisoners who had been unwise enough to surrender at Smerwick, while the Brooke boys were still students at King's College, Cambridge.

Very sensibly in Poley's estimation, Master Secretary Cecil had chosen to sit down. If Raleigh made the avid playgoer think of Henry the Fifth, Cecil was crookbacked Richard the Third – physically at least; and, perhaps, in ruthless political cunning. There was no need to let Raleigh tower over his slight, crookbacked figure and add to his bluster that way. Cecil was seated behind a table piled with a defensive wall of books and Raleigh was leaning on the polished wood, the weight of his upper body on straight arms and closed fists. Lord Cobham and his brother the Prebendary of York stood behind their leader, their faces fixed in frowns of silent support and agreement, the Reverend George shifting uncomfortably on his lame leg.

As Phelippes and Poley entered, Raleigh paused in whatever he was saying and looked up. 'Ah,' he said. 'I see you have called in your hunting hounds. Give you good day masters.' He gave a mocking half-bow. Then he continued, his accent thick with the music of his West Country origins. 'Masters Poley and Phelippes have brought down greater game than me and yet I fear them not.' He turned back to Cecil. 'What was it you said when you addressed the people at Charing Cross and Paul's Cross? *The high and mighty prince James, king of Scotland has now become our only lawful and lineal king?*'

'Even as the Privy Council bid me say,' nodded Cecil, not at all intimidated by Raleigh's bluster. 'Not a word more or less.'

'The council! You know full well that they are but puppets who move at your behest! Could you not have bid them pause? Dear God, man, there is such an opportunity here. Allow James the throne, well enough! But fence him in with conditions and provisos so that he cannot rule by will and whim as did the late queen, God rest her. Make him truly answerable to Parliament. And even to your council if you would have it so. But answerable to *someone*!'

'An interesting point of view, Sir Walter. What a pity you were not present to present it to the council yourself. It was most unfortunate that the Warden of the Cinque Ports summoned you away at the critical moment.' Cecil's gaze shifted toward Lord Cobham.

'I had word out of the Low Countries,' blustered Cobham, Warden of the Cinque Ports. 'Jersey was at risk of invasion. It was imperative I warned the governor.'

'And, of course, you, as governor, had to react, did you not Sir Walter?'

'It was all a fabrication,' spat Sir Walter. 'There was no danger to Jersey.'

'You suspect a ruse to call you away from Westminster at the crucial moment?' asked Cecil quietly.

'I do!'

'A serious accusation. Do you suspect who might do such a thing?'

'Aye. I have suspicions a'plenty!' Raleigh's fulminating gaze rested pointedly on Poley. The intelligencer met the accusing glance with a bland assumption of innocence, though it had been one of his agents, Nick Skeres' friend Will Udall, who had brought the apparently incontrovertible intelligence across the Channel.

'Then you should present them to the Council. Perhaps Lord Admiral Howard…' Cecil continued helpfully.

'In due time. But this is a distraction,' snapped Raleigh. 'I warn you, this new king must be constrained or we will find ourselves with another Henry the Eighth taking palaces and wives, on a whim. As proven by the fate of Cardinal Wolsey. Destroying men and their families for simply disagreeing with him. As evidenced by that of Sir Thomas More. A monster, not a monarch. Defender of the Faith – ruling, therefore, by divine right and answerable only to God Himself! With powers as vast as the ocean and we who try to limit and control him as helpless as King Canute.'

'I'm certain King James wishes his rule to be one of temperance and propriety,' Cecil assured his angry guest. 'What I know of him suggests that he is a modest man of great learning and intellect who is as fascinated by the theory of kingcraft as he is by that of witchcraft.'

'That's as may be,' answered Raleigh. 'But I would hesitate to nail my colours to King James's mast if I were you! You know full well he blames your father and Francis Walsingham for the lopping of his mother's head. And his anger might be visited on their sons and the sons of their sons. He being as close to a divine being himself, like one of the Roman Caesars deified in ancient times.'

'You overstate the case, Sir Walter. His only ambitions are earthly and by no means divine. He simply wishes to assume the throne of England as lawful, lineal and rightful liege and pass it in due course to his son Prince Henry. And, in due course, through the gentle wisdom of his rule, to become as well beloved by his new English subjects as he is by his current Scottish ones.'

'Indeed!' snapped Lord Cobham before Raleigh himself could answer. 'He is so well beloved that they tried to murder him not three years since!'

'Ah. The Gowrie Plot.' Cecil shook his head sadly. 'The final dying spasm of a clash of the clans. What might be called a local difficulty. Such a thing could never, ever happen here.'

111

18

'Three men I do not trust,' said Master Secretary Cecil after Raleigh and the Brooke brothers had gone.

'It is a matter of months, almost – a year at most,' Phelippes observed grimly, 'since I reported Raleigh's involvement at the fringes of the plot to marry Lady Arbella Stuart to Edward Seymour, Lord Beauchamp, and so lay claim to the succession.'

'I remember,' nodded Cecil.

'Aye,' said Poley. 'There's a broth that's still a'simmer. And the French ambassador de Beaumont may have a golden spoon to stir it with and bring it to the boil. Let it boil over into insurrection and invasion indeed. Especially if he believes the Governor of Jersey and the Warden of the Cinque Ports might – at the least – wink at his efforts. Were Beauchamp to take and hold one of the five Cinque Ports or even, God shield us, Plymouth or Portsmouth and manage to marry Arbella Stewart there – as his father secretly married Katherine Grey, would-be Queen Jane Grey's sister – he could open the south coast to an invasion in support of his claim.'

'With Raleigh's blessing,' emphasised Phelippes. 'Though I suspect he'd be equally happy to see the Infanta enthroned – as long as he could confine her powers as he wishes you to confine King James's into some kind of commonwealth. With Raleigh as Lord Protector perhaps.'

'I have eyes on Raleigh, of course,' said Poley. 'And I am heartened by the unconsidered nature of his speech to you, Master Secretary. If he so expresses himself to the Secretary to the Council, you may wager that he expresses himself more fully and forcefully elsewhere. It will be a simple matter I would suggest, to allow him to condemn himself out of his own mouth. He is of course well-beloved by many our English men and women – though not by others, to be fair. But he has to deal now with Scots, to whom he is unknown. And what we have seen and heard suggests that he will find it hard to win anything other than their enmity; and especially that of their king – who is now, of course, *our* king. Or so he will be soon enough.'

'Very well,' said Cecil. 'So it is a matter of timing, then. To choose the most opportune moment that will guarantee the greatest damage to him and his cause – and the greatest good to me and mine.'

'Further to which,' said Poley, 'I will look more closely into Lord Cobham and the Reverend George Brooke. They are weak links too. Breaking them might well lead to a more complete destruction of Raleigh than would otherwise be possible. And, to be fair and clear, the three of them might well contrive to pose a genuine and potent danger to the king, his person, his family and the council in any case. I do not doubt that they are as well aware as Sir Francis Bacon that it is not at the moment possible to commit High Treason – nor will it be possible until King James is duly enthroned. It would be best for the council to advise King James to hurry to Westminster with all despatch, accept the crown and close that door against them.'

'*A month and more!*' spat Poley some days later. Tom Watson and Nick Skeres stood shoulder to shoulder in Poley's lodging above the Lion, taken aback by their chief's frustrated rage. They had only recently returned from Edinburgh and were – frankly – expecting congratulations on jobs well done and intelligence well collected.

'It will take until early April for the Household to get organised and start moving south from Edinburgh,' said Tom warily. 'I had this from Sir Robert Carey who is preferred at the Scottish court for his service in bringing the ring to the king.'

'And the priest William Watson, attending on the king's pleasure in the matter of his demand that Catholics be recognised more fully and the recusancy payments be reduced, has somehow learned that the king and the queen with their children propose to progress the length of their new kingdom of England down the Great North Road, stopping at various great houses on the way to become acquainted in person with the rich and powerful men and women who own them; a process that will probably take a full month. All in all, I warn you Master Poley that the king is therefore not likely to be crowned until sometime in May.'

'May!' Poley repeated. 'And here we are with All Fools yet to arrive with the beginning of April. We'll be *all fools* indeed unless we find a way of speeding the king's progress or ensuring he's guarded against more than thirty days of danger!'

'Dangerous days,' said Nick Skeres with a gloomy nod as the pair of them turned to leave their silently fuming controller. 'Dangerous days.'

Poley chose to lodge above The Lion tavern for several reasons, some of which Tom had understood when he saw the view into Westminster Palace that Poley enjoyed, and the manner in which he could observe the comings and goings through the main gate. Amongst the most important of the others was the identity of the Lion's landlord. His name was Gilbert Gifford. He was a bluff and popular old character. Given his size and nature – not to mention the girth of his fair round belly and the matter of his roving eye - there were those who supposed him the original of the popular character of Sir John Falstaff so beloved of the late queen. Others named Sir John Oldcastle but no-one was absolutely certain. Except, perhaps, for Poley and a close circle of his colleagues. For Falstaff was an old soldier whereas Gifford was an old intelligencer. Poley and Gifford had worked together to bring down Babbington and, through him, the Queen of Scots. Ten years Poley's senior, Gifford was no longer so active in the intelligencer's world. But he had been placed by Cecil's intelligence service behind the bar of the Lion because the Lion not only looked into the heart of Westminster, it also listened to the gossip that emanated from the place. True, the lords of the council all had their London homes and spent any spare time that circumstance allowed in domestic privacy. But their attendants were not always so fortunate. And there were the palace guards, Raleigh's yeomen and the Knight Marshall's bailiffs, the servants, the cooks, the cleaners, the invisible masses who saw to the Lords' comfort and heard what they discussed. These men would often drink in the Lion and discuss what they had overheard, their tongues loosened by liquor.

But Gilbert served Poley as more than a sharp pair of ears. He was also the guardian of the intelligencer's access. No-one got past him or anywhere near Poley's rooms without his approval. But this was not a hindrance – he had been a secret agent for so long that he knew most of the men who came to visit his old friend now. Which was the case early next day with William Udall, lately returned from the Spanish Netherlands where he had been watching the Archdukes' ambassador, the Count of Aremberg, prepare to visit England and her new king. He had returned via the Catholic seminary of the English College at Douai where another of Poley's agents, the more elderly Sir Anthony Standen, had delivered a message from the spymaster to him. Then Udall came straight home via Calais and Dover where he had let word slip out about a proposed invasion of Jersey, which was something demanded by Standen's message. The purpose of the false rumour only obvious when Raleigh was absent for the crucial hours immediately before and after Elizabeth's death. But, after all his recent wanderings, Udall had hopes that, like his friend Nick Skeres, he would stay close to Poley for a while.

'So, Will,' said Poley as both men took their ease at the long table beneath the window overlooking Westminster, each holding an early tankard of Gifford's finest ale. 'Have you any more recent news from the Spanish Netherlands?'

'Other than an imminent invasion of Jersey, you mean?' chuckled Udall. 'I'll wager that rumour put a burr beneath the saddles of both Governor Raleigh and Warden Lord Cobham.'

Poley gave one of his minute smiles – little more than a crinkling of the eye-corners. 'Just so. And have you recollected any further gossip from the English College at Douai?' he asked.

'There will be a full written report forthcoming for you to pass to Master Secretary together with further details of Count Aremberg's arrival and Sir Anthony Standen's further plans. But in the meantime, I heard it whispered at Douai that, together with the Irish and Scottish colleges as well as the other seminaries involved, more than five hundred Jesuit priests have been dispatched on various missions in England at the moment. Looking to push the Catholic cause before the new king is settled too immovably on his throne. Also, of course, in case there is any kind of an uprising planned, which they will be pleased to assist. Or if, so to speak, they would need to follow the Gowrie pattern.'

'The most immediately dangerous ones are still those led by Archpriest Blackwell, and the Apellants Watson and Clark,' nodded Poley. 'Though even they would be mad to try and seize the king. But we need to keep close eyes on John Gerard and Richard Garnet. Murder might not be out of the question – before it becomes regicide.'

''Twould be wise to be alert to such dangers,' nodded Udall.

'William Watson has already been to Edinburgh and made his demands on their behalf,' nodded Poley.

'And what if they fall on deaf ears?' Udall sat back, eyebrows raised.

'It is a question that has occupied me almost to the exclusion of everything else. William Watson waits in hope of an easing of the recusancy laws – a hope that I fear will soon be dashed, which disappointment, I calculate, will lead to some intemperate words – if not actions. Then there are others who wait in hope that the king will grant them other wishes. The Reverend George Brooke, for instance, is in great hopes of becoming Master of the Hospital of Saint Cross as was promised to him by the late queen; a lucrative post that may well mend his fortunes. And his brother Lord Cobham is of course eager to ensure this happens. Which means in turn that – independently of everything else – so is Sir Walter Raleigh. Then there is Sir Griffin Markham, one of the men knighted by the Earl of Essex. Markham hopes to be allowed to return to court - despite his banishment by Elizabeth after the Essex uprising. Nick Skeres tells me he believes Markham may have paid a good sum towards Watson's travels to Edinburgh with news of Queen Elizabeth's death. He would only do so if Watson also carried a message from him to King James as well, hoping to mend *his* fortunes. Important to him particularly because he is burdened with debt and fears he may lose control of the lands round his home of Beskwood Park. Even men like Sir Walter Raleigh and Lord Cobham, leaving the Reverend George aside, hope to retain their old positions and powers, possessions and financial securities under the new administration and may become dangerously desperate if their hopes are dashed.'

'And Master Secretary Cecil,' observed Udall.

'Indeed. He is in like case with all the others. However, it is our duty to ensure a happy outcome for him, even if that means unhappy outcomes for his rivals. You are fortunate in that you have a choice in the matter. I wish you to be my eyes on either William Watson or the Reverend George Brooke.'

'I'll take Watson if it's all the same to you. I can give him news from Douai after all. Twisted, perhaps, into a form likely to appeal to a man who hates – and is hated by – the Jesuits. I believe I can worm my way into his confidence and see what I can turn up. Especially if he finds the new king unwilling to meet his demands as you say.'

117

'Then I will look to George Brooke myself in due time. But in the meantime there is one more player in this tangle to whom I must pay more immediate attention. He is at Hertford House at present which is little more than a stone's throw from here.'

19

Hertford House on Cannon Row on the far side of the palace of Westminster from the Lion, overlooked the river, and in many ways was best accessed from the water. Ever since the young Lord Beauchamp had first been mooted as a possible groom for Arbella Stuart and a ladder, therefore, by which she might climb to the throne, Poley had kept several servants on his payroll in every house the Seymours owned. This one on Cannon Row was the closest, the easiest to contact and, therefore, the hub of his constant vigilance. His eyes there belonged to the most senior – and most expensive – of the spies he personally employed. After Udall went off to begin his watch on William Watson, therefore, Poley followed in his footsteps down into King Street. Here he turned right, walked down towards the Abbey before turning left and strolling past the south end of the Palace, the Great Hall and the Star Chamber through New Palace Yard to the Westminster Stairs. Here he took a small wherry the hundred yards or so to the ladder which led him up the riverbank and into the modest grounds behind Hertford House. He was greeted at the door with the news that, 'The family is not in residence, sir.'

'No matter,' he said easily. 'I am come hither to speak with Master Kinborough.'

'Master Poley!' Kinborough the steward whispered as soon as they were alone. 'You received my message then, thank the Lord.'

'I received no message. What did it say?'

'That Lord Beauchamp is gone down to Netley Abbey. He has taken most of the hale servants with him. He has ridden on ahead leaving orders that he is to be followed by a locksmith, a carpenter, a blacksmith and a gunsmith. Word is that he plans to fortify the Abbey and use it as a base for action. And, they say, before he returned to London, Sir Walter Raleigh left orders that horses be bought. Enough, I hear, to form a regiment of cavalry.'

Poley's mind raced. It seemed clear that one of the possible dangers he most feared was coming into fact already and with breath-taking rapidity. If Lord Beauchamp planned on fortifying the Seymours' recently purchased property, the Abbey at Netley and using Raleigh's troop of horse then he himself must be planning on raising an army. That would take a great deal of money – money available at short notice. Money, therefore, likely to be coming across the Channel, if it was not already here. Enemy money in any case.

These thoughts took him back to the ladder and down to the waterside. Where a wherry skulled him swiftly downriver to Somerset House stairs. He went to Phelippes first. 'Which ambassadors are here waiting to greet the new monarch?' he demanded.

'We await the Count of Aremberg, ambassador from the Archdukes and the Spanish Netherlands, as your man Udall has reported. Also King Henri's ambassador from Paris the Comte de Rosni and, I believe, Ambassador Scaramelli from Venice…'

'Somebody here. Somebody here already,' insisted Poley.

'That would be Ambassador de Beaumont. He hasn't been recalled to Paris since the queen's death though as I say we're expecting another French…'

'De Beaumont. Who do we have who's close to him?'

'Why do you need to get close to Ambassador de Beaumont?' asked a quiet voice from the doorway. The two spies turned round to find their master watching them.

'I believe Lord Beauchamp is trying to raise an army,' answered Poley. 'It may be that de Beaumont will finance him if he can do so. I've been told Beauchamp's fortifying Netley Abbey and that's only a few miles from both Southampton and Portsmouth; indeed, it is almost half way between them. And it may be that Raleigh, on his way back from Plymouth, left orders and coin for a company of horse to aid him.'

'Uprisings cost money,' nodded Cecil. 'Yes, I see your concern. De Beaumont might well seek to finance Lord Beauchamp in the hope that he will seize Portsmouth, marry Arbella Stuart as has long been mooted, and become a puppet king whose strings are pulled by newly Catholic Henri the Fourth in Paris.'

'If he can raise an army and take the port, he will open it to the French who can invade at will, probably with help from Italy and Spain. With Raleigh willing to ease matters for them and – who knows? – Cobham willing to open the Cinque Ports under his control. Then there is every chance that a goodly number of our catholic citizens might rise in support,' said Phelippes.

'There are five hundred Jesuits in the country all ready to back them in any way they can, according to Udall!' Poley looked at the two other men in the room. 'And the queen has been dead for how long?' he said; his tone making it clear that even he was shaken. 'Two days? Three?' His mind raced. The ring, the news, Carey and young Tom must only just have arrived in Edinburgh.

'How quickly can you get to Portsmouth?' demanded Cecil.

'Six hours. Less if the horses are sound and the weather clear. The Portsmouth road is even better maintained than the Great North Road. By sunset at least if I leave soon.'

'Good. You leave from here the moment I have dictated your passes to Phelippes and a message for Lord Mayor Mark James of Portsmouth. There is a regiment of foot in the fort and still more soldiers in Portchester Castle but I cannot recall who commands them. And of course there are the gunners who man the great cannons there as well. The mayor will know who commands, and also know how to raise more men. Phelippes come with me. Poley, send out a servant to get you your first post horse and make any preparations you care to.'

Within half an hour Cecil was back with Phelippes in tow. 'I see your horse awaits you,' he said. 'Here are the commissions you need. They will go in your saddlebag. All save this one – your pass to go from here to Portsmouth without let or hindrance.' As Poley took the documents, Cecil led the little group towards the front door, talking as he walked. 'You also have a letter of authority there, should you find you need it, to speak for me in all matters, including in command of whatever force can be assembled to counter Lord Beauchamp if your information is accurate.'

Poley went out to where the lad was holding his horse. 'To speak for you, Master Secretary?' he asked as he mounted.

'With my voice and with all my authority, should you require it,' the most powerful man in the kingdom confirmed.

20

The Portsmouth Road was the best road in England. It was a little under seventy miles in length and, like the Great North Road, it was studded with taverns and inns – country or town – where a fresh horse could be had every ten miles or so. Unlike young Tom on the ride he had just made up the Great North Road, however, Poley parted with no coin. Master Secretary's pass was enough to ensure he was given the best horse available at every change-over. His first of these was at Kingston little over an hour later, just before he went thundering over the bridge. He rode as fast as he could, but his mind – dangerously – was elsewhere. Mostly it was focussed on what was likely to await him in Portsmouth, how best to organise resistance if Lord Beauchamp was already under arms. What to do, on the other hand, if he was not yet ready to attack. The possibility that Raleigh was involved at the outer edges of the situation was also a distraction, for Sir Walter was Master Secretary's greatest enemy at the moment and Poley had, after all, been commissioned to ensure his downfall. But the Captain of the Guard seemed set on self-destruction instead.

His mind lost in speculation, Poley changed horses once more before stopping below the frowning Norman castle at Guildford to mount his third and guide it over the ford that gave the place its name. By now he was beginning to tire but he was also buoyed by the knowledge that he was almost half way there and was less than three hours into his mission. He swung round the Devil's Punchbowl, keeping a wary eye out for the robbers both on foot and horseback for which the place was notorious, before changing horses once more in Hindhead village. Then it was a straight gallop down to Petersfield and yet another fresh mount – one that got him to

Horndean where his final change of horses took him down to Portsmouth just as the sun was beginning to set.

Breathless messengers on sweat-stained horses were hardly a new experience in Portsmouth and it was easy for Poley to get directions to the mayor's residence at the stable where he left the last post horse. And, once he showed his pass over Cecil's seal in Phelippes's immaculate handwriting, it was equally easy to get to the Lord Mayor himself. Within an hour of his arrival, Poley was in company with the Lord Mayor, the Captain of the City Watch, the Commander of the Castle garrison, the Commanding Officer of artillery and as many captains as could be summoned off the ships anchored close offshore. The great table in the mayor's dining room was spread with maps and charts and the first tentative plans were being laid.

Scouts had been dispatched up the Southampton road towards Netley and, as the group in the Lord Mayor's dining room began to make their plans, reports came filtering back that there was a large body of men encamped around the Abbey. The Abbey itself was being fortified – windows boarded, gates strengthened and walls buttressed. A smithy had been set up and it appeared that the smiths were not only making shoes for the horses supposedly supplied by Sir Walter Raleigh but also seemed to be sharpening swords, daggers, pikes and axes. And, most disturbing of all, beside the blacksmith, the spies were certain there was a gunsmith busily producing bullets – though there was no obvious armoury or storehouse for pistols or muskets. Barrels, no doubt of gunpowder, were being carried carefully up from a barge on Southampton Water. Poley found this all deeply disturbing, particularly because it reminded him so forcefully of what had been going on in Essex House just before the Earl led his ill-fated revolt.

Over the years as intelligencer and messenger to the Privy Council, Poley had visited many battlefields. He had carried vital documents to and from Sir Philip Sidney and his young wife, daughter to Sir Francis Walsingham; to and from the Earl of Leicester, Lord Burghley and the Earl of Essex amongst many others. To and from battlefields in the Low Countries, Spanish Netherlands and Ireland. But he had never taken part in a night action. As the hours ticked by, the returning scouts reported that all the elements of Lord Beauchamp's army were settling down for the evening. There was little in the way of watch-keeping and the watch-fires were being used for cooking. Patrols were lackadaisical and inefficient. Lord Beauchamp's ale was being served by the barrel-full and his men were therefore unlikely to pose a threat before tomorrow morning.

Poley, James and the military men planned their reaction well past midnight then went about the preparations for battle. 'To quote Publius Flavius Renatus,' said one of the more learned captains, *"He who wants peace should prepare for war"*!'

'Which we are doing most effectively, thanks to Master Poley and his timely warning,' nodded the Lord Mayor.

Everything was ready and almost in place an hour or so before dawn. Poley, Mayor James and the other commanders, literary and less so, were escorted out to the stables where they mounted horses whose hooves had been wrapped in cloth to silence them. Silently, guided by the minimum of brightness, Poley and the others trotted along the Southampton road. At Portchester Castle several more horsemen joined them with yet more infantry so in the end Poley found himself accompanied by the mayor and the officers, as well as the soldiers from all the defensive works around the port and shipyards.

The route between Portsmouth and Southampton was packed with men up as far as the bridge over the river Hamble. The force Poley had caused to be assembled overnight was standing on either side of the roadway, allowing the passage of the leaders and the last of the artillery. Lined up in silence – or as near to it as possible – was a

125

regiment of foot soldiers together with several hundred men from each of the forts and castles. They stood six abreast on either side of the road itself – rank after rank of them. Pikemen to the rear, musketeers to the fore. Despite what Poley had heard about Raleigh and horses, there was no real need or ground for cavalry action here. The main battle line was along the bank of the river Hamble where they could defend the bridge. A bend in the river close on their left flank meant on the one hand that it was difficult to deploy the foremost ranks. But, Poley was just able to see, on the other hand the river itself was deep enough to allow several vessels to come here from the harbour, packed with well-armed sailors and as the sun began to rise, and, as the light began to gather, so there were more muffled hoof-beats and the gentle creaking of greased axles as two cannons from the fort were brought to the fore and set in place.

Silence descended, but for the dawn chorus of nearby birds; land-birds in the fields and woods of Swanwick and Holly Hill behind them and of the clamouring gulls along the river beside and before them. Then, over the avian cacophony, Poly was suddenly aware of the beating of distant drums. Then the twitter of pipes became audible and, growing relentlessly nearer, the regular tread of marching feet. Despite the casual way in which Beauchamp had assembled his men the night before, it appeared that they were better organised now. And, with their drums and fifes, ready to give battle and take Portsmouth City.

The officers behind and on either side of Poley called their orders softly, not wishing to spoil the surprise that Beauchamp's force was going to get when it tried to cross the bridge. The pikemen readied their weapons and shuffled sideways to close the road. The musketeers looked to their firelocks and wheellocks, then did the same, allowing room for the two big cannon in the middle of the roadway. The gunners checked their elevations. Lord Mayor James said, 'Ready?'

'Ready,' answered Poley. He nudged his horse forward until he was sitting alone on the very edge of the bridge looking northwards towards Netley and the approaching force. He positioned himself carefully, keeping well clear of the cannons' line of fire. The bridge over the Hamble was old but strong. It would obviously allow Lord Beauchamp's force to cross – but only in ranks of half a dozen at the most. Independently of the cannon, the soldiers behind him were in ranks of twelve and more abreast. And their numbers stretched back as far as Swanwick. At the far side of the bridge, the Southampton road ran up a long incline that ended in a solid crestline. Once they came over this, whoever was approaching would find themselves looking down with an excellent view of the bridge and the army waiting behind it. Unless Beauchamp had managed to season his force with experienced soldiers and officers with a fair sprinkling of mercenaries, he would see at a glance that if he tried to cross the bridge in force he and his men would be slaughtered, thought Poley.

But then again, in much the same situation at Lud Gate in London, the Earl of Essex had led a full-frontal attack. There was a very real chance Lord Beauchamp would do the same. He was playing for even higher stakes than Essex, after all; he was hoping to win the throne. Poley eased his horse forward a few more feet, looking up at the crest of the rise ahead, his pulse racing. He was committed now. If Lord Beauchamp did decide to attack, Poley would be amongst the first to die – killed as likely as not by friendly fire.

The line of the ridge ahead was suddenly forested with the tops of banners and the blades of pikes. The sound of pipes, drums and feet was almost overwhelming. Then, among the waving weapons, the first few heads, armoured with steel helmets. Horsemen, thought Poley, taking the lead like he was. But dressed for battle - as he was most assuredly was not. Half a dozen horsemen came over the crest of the rise with the army boiling into sight behind them – little more than a rabble after all, thought Poley; especially when compared with the soldiers and sailors ranked behind him. Three of the horsemen spurred ahead, cantered down the hill and came onto the bridge. They continued until they were half way across and stopped. The man in the centre held up his hand and the force behind him also stopped on the hillslope. Or the ones at the front did. Those behind pressed forward, unaware of the situation. The heaving to and fro slowly settled. The drums and fifes fell quiet. Except for the screaming of the gulls there was silence.

The central rider dropped his hand and grasped the pommel of his saddle, leaning forward. The face beneath the old-fashioned helmet was familiar – Lord Beauchamp. 'I know you,' he said. 'You're Robert Cecil's man. Poley.'

'You are correct My Lord. I am Master Secretary's man and in this instance I speak with his voice under his commission and that of the Privy Council he leads. And I must ask you, my Lord, what do you mean by this?' Poley's broad gesture took in the rag-tag army hesitating on the hillside.

Beauchamp looked around, as though he was surprised to see the multitude so close behind him. As his lieutenants at his shoulder – and his army, come to that – genuinely were surprised to see the serried ranks standing battle-ready in front of them. 'I... Well, I...' Beauchamp's voice faded away.

There was a brief silence. Poley's gaze lifted from Beauchamp to his followers. The rear ranks nearest the crestline, with the clearest view of what awaited them beyond the bridge were beginning to sidle away, vanishing into the safety of the downslope behind them.

'My Lord, let us be clear,' Poley pressed his advantage as more of Beauchamp's army began to retreat and the noise of their growing panic began to mount. 'It looks to me like you have planned an uprising here. Indeed, that you have undertaken a rebellion against the new King and his Privy Council. And that is what I shall be reporting to His Majesty,

128

Master Secretary and the council. It will mean your head, of course.'

'What? An uprising? No. No.' Lord Beauchamp looked around in rising panic. A feeling obviously shared by his followers, most of whom were in full flight now. Clearly suddenly realising the deadly peril the actions he and they had undertaken so thoughtlessly suddenly placed them in.

'Then I must ask again, my Lord. What are you about?'

'I... ' Beauchamp looked helplessly at the men sitting beside him. Both of whom were staring straight ahead into the gaping mouths of the cannon aimed directly at them. Only pride stopping them from joining the rest of their vanishing army, Poley thought. Neither of them was in any position to offer help or advice. 'Why, I am merely taking this band of fine fellows to announce the passing of Her Majesty and the succession of King James, as your master has read it out at Charing Cross and decreed that it be announced across the land...'

'And where were you planning to do this, My Lord? Mayor James has already performed the task in Portsmouth.'

'Where? Ah... In Bristol. Yes, that's it. In Bristol.'

'In that case I must inform you, My Lord, that Bristol is behind you and the road thither seems to be empty all of a sudden. You are marching further away from Bristol and deeper into deadly danger with every step you take.'

21

'That was his excuse?' said Phelippes, his eyes wide with wonder and disbelief. 'That he was going to Bristol via Portsmouth? With an army? All to help him make an announcement about the succession?'

'It's what he said,' confirmed Poley. 'But I don't think it matters whether anyone actually believes him. It wasn't even worth arresting Beauchamp or any of the few who stood with him in the end. He turned and galloped off as his army simply vanished away like smoke. Master Secretary is convinced that in terms of the succession, the fact that he made any excuse at all and disbanded his troops simply rules him out of the running. He's proven himself too unimportant for anyone to worry about – whether they believe him or not. My man in his household is Kinborough, his steward. I will keep close eyes on the restless Beauchamp. King James might decide to take some action against him…'

'Like a schoolmaster birching a naughty student…'

'But proving him to be a broken reed and exposing his utter inadequacy reduces the threat provided by the Lady Arbella, who will no longer consider him an appropriate husband; so one more route to the throne is closed to her. King James can afford to be a little more indulgent with her. Up to a point, of course. Just because Beauchamp is no longer in the game doesn't mean that there is no-one still plotting to use her.'

'Sir Walter Raleigh you mean? And Lord Cobham?'

Poley was silent for a moment. '*Raleigh*…' he said.

'Did you manage to find out whether he paid for a troop of horse to support Beauchamp?'

'Not while I was at Portsmouth, but I haven't stopped ploughing that furrow yet. Raleigh will be with the Privy Council later today ostensibly to discuss his place and duties in the queen's funeral. But the funeral is the better part of a month away. Master Secretary is planning to use the opportunity to probe Raleigh's actions and intentions further in the mean-time. But I have a way of adding to Master Secretary's fund of knowledge. Raleigh's man of business is called Magnall. He keeps Raleigh's accounts. But Magnall also keeps a mistress with expensive tastes – a situation of which is wife is ignorant. And, since his wife is the one with the money in that family, if she were to discover the truth, she would leave him penniless and destitute. In the unlikely event that she left him alive.'

As Phelippes had observed more than once, Poley had been both a spy and a philanderer himself. Thinking about that later in the day as he waited in Little Drury Lane for Raleigh's man of business Magnall, Poley wryly observed to himself that the two occupations shared much in common. Men and women involved in political duplicity and those involved in sexual deceit tended to behave in similar ways. Poley himself had been reckless on both counts, tempting Fate and probably Heaven both as Walsingham's and Cecil's intelligencer and as Joan Yeomans' lover. He had risked death and exposure in his dealings with Mary of Scotland's murderous associates and with the execution of Kit Marlowe. Similarly, he had found ways to entertain Mistress Yeomans to lavish dinners while working undercover as *agent provocateur* in prisons such as the Clink, the Fleet and the Bridewell. Hence, he admitted wryly, his near-destruction at the hands of her cuckolded husband. And it was only the direct intervention of the Plague that ensured his wife and her Puritan parents remained ignorant to the end. A potent element to the bond between him and his brother-in-law Tom, he reckoned.

Magnall, however, was the soul of regularity – and, therefore, of reliability. On the surface at least. He worked in Durham House, keeping Sir Walter's books as precise and exacting as a man in that line of work should be. Especially given the amount of money the Captain of the Guard had lavished on the place over the years, turning it into something very like a palace. The book-keeper arrived to work at a certain time each morning and left at a certain time each evening, returning to the bosom of his loving wife and family in Blackfriars as the local clocks chimed seven, having hurried straight from Durham House. Or so he let them believe. But he actually left Durham House at five and spent the intervening hours in company with his mistress in Little Drury Lane, and nobody any the wiser. Except Poley.

The chimes of five were just echoing into silence when Magnall appeared, hurrying round the corner from The Strand. Seeing Poley standing at the door he was headed for, his pace slowed and his expression darkened. Poley stepped forward and fell in at his side. 'A moment of your time,' he said brusquely. 'At the New Inn.' The two men turned and moved briskly across the road. As they did so, a stranger detached himself from the shadows and began to follow them. The stranger was some six feet in height, dressed in a great kilt and a bonnet sporting an eagle's feather. A month ago he would have been an object of wonder but London and its outskirts were filling with Scotsmen so rapidly that no-one even gave him a second glance.

The New Inn was nearby and offered a range of secluded tables that made excellent secret meeting places. 'Well?' demanded Magnall truculently as they sat in one of these. The stranger sat, unobserved and unsuspected, in another. Close enough to watch, too fat away to hear the conversation above the bustle of the inn.

'I have heard whispers,' said Poley, leaning forward, 'that Sir Walter left sufficient funds with Lord Beauchamp to purchase the mounts for a troop of cavalry.'

Magnall blinked. His eyes narrowed and his gaze wandered. In Poley's experience these were the actions – unconscious perhaps – of someone preparing to lie. 'A troop of cavalry could number up to one hundred. That would cost well over a thousand pound,' said Magnall, clearly hoping Poley would mistake failure to meet his eyes as a by-product of mental calculation. What Poley noticed most clearly was that Magnall was avoiding giving an answer. 'Sir Walter hardly has a thousand pound in ready coin.' The bookkeeper concluded.

'He could promise it, though,' Poley observed softly. 'He would know where to obtain such sums.'

'He would be mad even to promise it,' countered Magnall. 'When you consider how much he has spent – indeed, is still spending – on Durham House.'

'There is much madness about,' observed Poley. 'Perhaps he caught it from Lord Beauchamp. Like the Plague.'

'Well, if he had then I would know!'

'Precisely. And *do* you know?'

'No!' Magnall, frowning, met Poley's gaze, his expression at its most trustworthy and reliable.

Poley watched Raleigh's bookkeeper hurry out of the New Inn. Was he rushing towards his expectant mistress now he was late? Or was he running away from a powerful man who had caught him in a lie? Poley remained where he was, mulling his suspicions over in his mind and deciding on his next step. A broad-shouldered stranger pushed through the bustle at the door; a tall man in a great kilt. Poley didn't notice – why should he?- because he was too preoccupied. In fact, his next step was obvious enough. Master Magnall needed closer watching. The task should be easy enough. He would assign young Tom as soon as he got back from Edinburgh. In the meantime, he would have a word with the City Watch. They could keep an eye on the Blackfriars house. But who would have jurisdiction here, outside the City walls? He could do worse, he thought, than enquiring of the Knight Marshall who his opposite number outside the Palace of Westminster was. Failing that, of course, Gilbert Gifford as tavern-keeper of the Lion would also have a good idea who enforced the law out here.

It took him little more than twenty minutes to walk from one tavern to the other, and perhaps five minutes more to begin his conversation with Gilbert Gifford. The time, approximate though it was, seemed important in the end because he had just learned the name and location of the man he wanted when a couple of youngsters burst into the Lion, breathless with running and big with news. It took little more than ten minutes for Poley to follow them back to Little Drury Lane and to push through the crowd of onlookers standing horrified at the door. Poley had never been in the love-nest but he followed the impressions he had garnered from his conversations with Magnall and so he ran upstairs and pushed past the men and women craning to see in through the half-open doorway. Magnall and his mistress were both lying naked on a rumpled bed whose coverings were carelessly piled on the floor beside their clothes. Their eyes were wide, their mouths agape and their throats had been cut from one ear to the other. Poley could not recall ever having seen so much blood in his entire life. 'Who would have thought,' he wondered, shocked, 'that a man could have so much blood in him?'

22

'It ought to be the Queen's Crowner I suppose,' said
Phelippes, later that afternoon as he and Poley discussed
matters in their office in Salisbury House. 'The deed was
done well within the verge. Especially now that her body has
been moved to Whitehall. You knew the old crowner Sir
William Danby, of course, who looked into the matter of
Marlowe's death. But he is long-retired now. And our actual
monarch-in-waiting has, I presume, yet to appoint his own
man. Not to mention that he is so far to the north that the
verge does not begin to reach Little Drury Lane. The verge
stretches no more than thirteen miles from the monarch's
person. But I would strongly advise you not to waste your
time by becoming further involved. Quite the opposite, in
fact. Keep well clear of the situation. Allow the civil
authorities in Westminster to do their job.'

'Even though,' said Poley, 'it has got to be to do with Sir
Walter Raleigh and the coin for the horses?'

'Even so,' said Phelippes. 'Not that you have anything more
solid in the matter than airy suppositions. Besides, as you told
me Magnall said, where would even Raleigh get a thousand
pounds and more?'

'The same place Lord Beauchamp was doubtless hoping for
it – Ambassador de Beaumont. Or Count de Rosni when he
arrives from Paris as it is rumoured that he soon will. Or,
failing him, The Count of Aremberg. Or, via the Count's
good offices, from Spain. That is what Master Secretary
suspects and he has asked Lord Admiral Howard to go down
to Portsmouth and look into the matter both with the Lord
Mayor and with Lord Beauchamp himself. I have half a mind
to send Nicholas Skeres to follow his footsteps and tell me

what he discovers now that he and Tom are back from Scotland.'

'But in the meantime, you have other matters pressing on you do you not? His Majesty and his household are about to leave Edinburgh now that we are well into April. They may already have done so, indeed and Master Secretary still has doubts about the Catholic North! Leave this dead man and his mistress alone.'

'Very well. I will do so. But you should remember, should you ever wish to stray from your own wedded bliss, that there is, all of a sudden, an extremely rich widow come available in Blackfriars.'

'You are of course the very pattern of mistress-keeping,' riposted Phelippes. 'You were fortunate your wife died in ignorance of Mistress Yeomans; though I will admit the revenge of Master Yeomans which caused you to be thrown in the Fleet Prison must have smarted!' Realising he had gone a little too far, Phelippes threw his hand up like a swordsman admitting a hit. 'But I know your heart is pure nowadays and it belongs to Lady Janet Percy alone. Which reminds me, I understand King James is likely to be entertained by the Earl of Northumberland on his journey down to London and as you know Lady Janet, being a close relation, is now a part of his household. A part of which, I hear, he is planning to move to the section of Essex House he now rents from the late Earl's mother.'

'And you believe Lady Janet might be among them?' Poley was suddenly breathless at the prospect.

'Did you not tell me that she has slept there in the past? And, indeed, entertained you in her bedroom there – in pursuance of Master Secretary's plans for the unfortunate Earl. In the days before you managed to purify your heart.'

'But you believe there is a good chance she will be coming to London again?'

'I would say it is a certainty,' confirmed Phelippes. 'All you need do is make sure you remain here too, and she will no doubt come to you quite soon.'

Master Secretary Cecil entered the room the moment Phelippes finished speaking. 'Poley,' he said. 'King James is on the way south at last. Prepare to ride north to find him. I will brief you before you leave and give you messages for the king both from myself and from other correspondents.'

The king was not hard for Poley to find. Like many others crowding the Great North Road in hopes of seeing their new monarch he soon discovered King James had indeed left Edinburgh and come south – past Berwick already. The king's moving court numbered more than five hundred and was growing larger every day. News of its current position and impending approach seemed to emanate towards London on the very wind. The intelligencer with his satchel of letters – most of them locked or in code – caught up with the south-bound court at Widdrington Castle, near the coast just north of Newcastle. And, courtesy of Master Secretary's passes, he caught up with the king himself in the castle's blood room. The king and many of the others in Widdrington had spent the afternoon hunting. It was King James's favourite occupation and it provided not only sport but also food for the feast.

Two fine stags were hanging head-down from the ceiling, their antler-points inches from the floor as Sir Roger Aston, the King's master huntsman oversaw their preparation under His Majesty's own supervision. They had already been bled and gralloched. Their blood and guts removed for preparation either as black pudding or umble pies – or as reward for the hounds. The skins were being expertly stripped from the hollowed carcases, starting at the top immediately below the hooves of their hind legs. The loins were already on their way to the castle kitchens. As soon as King James recognised Poley, however, and understood his mission, he commanded, 'Come awa' Master Poley,' and led the way into the castle itself. The great building was so crowded even the king found it hard to discover a place private enough to go through the contents of Poley's satchel. As the increasingly irritable monarch led the search, Poley saw a large number of familiar faces. Lord Cobham was there, no doubt putting Raleigh's case as well as his own. But then so was Lord Henry Howard who Master Secretary had sent north some days ago with orders to stay with James and counter Cobham. Until James reached York, at least, where Cecil planned on meeting the king himself. He also caught a glimpse of William Udall – and his presence here could only mean that the cross-eyed William Watson was still nearby. Udall pointedly turned away when his gaze met Poley's. Whatever he was involved in, he did not wish Poley to be a part of it. Yet. Amongst the others he recognised The Reverend Tobie Matthew, the Bishop of Durham, titular owner of Durham House in London. Which had been purchased from an earlier bishop by an earlier monarch and was now, of course, the London residence of the Captain of the Guard Sir Walter Raleigh.

The sight of the churchman made him think about the recusant Watson with his squinting eye once more and a shiver went down his spine. If Bishop Matthew was here then Watson's hope of help from the new king were bound to die. Perhaps he should send Tom north once more and set him to work on Watson alongside Udall. Then he caught a glimpse of Henry Percy, the Earl of Northumberland and thoughts of Lady Janet came close to overwhelming him, driving all other considerations out of his mind for a moment. However, when the red-headed figure turned, Poley realised it was not the earl after all, but one of his lesser relatives. Perhaps, as Phelippes had suggested, the earl was currently resident in Essex House, and Lady Janet along with the rest of his household.

But in truth, he thought, dragging his attention back to present realities, all these supplicants except Bishop Matthew were kept well away from the king himself. The only English faces in his close circle belonged to the ring-bearer Sir Robert

Carey and that of Edward Somerset the Earl of Worcester who had been a friend of James's since he came north to congratulate the Scottish monarch on his marriage to the Princess of Denmark and on surviving the tempest-tossed voyage home. If Worcester was here, thought Poley, then so must his secretary William Sterrel be. Sterrel, who might or might not be the mysterious double agent who went by the pseudonym of Anthony Rivers. Poley looked for Sterrel in the crowd but gave up in the end without having seen him. Other than Sir Robert and Lord Edward, Ludovic Stewart the Earl of Lennox, John Erskine the Earl of Mar and his brother Thomas Erskine of Grogar Captain of the King's Guard, Sir John Ramsay and of course Doctor Hugh Herries were the men at King James's shoulder, and Poley soon found himself surrounded by them too, until the king courteously shooed them away.

The two men ended up in the castle's modest library. James insisted that they be left alone until he called, then he asked Poley if he had a verbal message from Master Secretary but Poley had none. Cecil had decided that the safest thing would be to think through everything he wanted to communicate at as much length as possible then commit it to well-balanced almost legalistic phrases. The language of his communication was so carefully chosen that even putting it into code might detract from it – or even damage the clarity of its meaning. It was written in plain hand therefore – in Phelippes's clearest and most beautiful. Then Cecil had locked it using the method Poley's man in Venice, Simeon Foxe, habitually used. It was one of the most painstaking – and safest – methods of locking a letter Poley and his network knew.

Phelippes had been careful only to write in certain places on the letter-strength, Kent-made paper. Then he had folded it in a certain, complex manner cutting a long strip from an unwritten section which had a point at one end and a broad base at the other still attached to the page. This was folded back and, when the letter itself was re-folded, it pushed through a cut made for the purpose before being held in place at its base with sealing wax. The point of the strip was pushed through another cut and pulled into place as the letter was folded shut. Then, using a sharp awl, a hole was made in the tightly-closed letter that passed through the now-concealed tip. Using this hole, a needle pulled thread through and through the letter, sewing it tightly closed before the thread was carefully tied off. Then, finally, more sealing wax was applied to the knot and Cecil's seal was pressed into it. Any inexpert attempt to open the missive would simply result in its destruction. And even an expert could not open it without revealing that they had done so. Of all the letters in the courier's pouch, this was clearly the most important but also the most difficult by far to open. James laid it aside, sorted through the rest, then turned to Poley with a rueful expression on his face. 'I cannae open this,' he admitted. 'D'ye ken the trick of it at all?'

'I do, Your Majesty,' answered Poley. 'May I assist Your Highness?'

'Ye may. But away with these *Majesties* and *Highnesses* when we're in private out of the common eye. God-appointed though I am, a simple *Sir* will be quite sufficient, man tae man.'

Poley went to work on Cecil's letter. As he did so, the king continued talking and the intelligencer's quick ear became attuned to the Scottish accent compounded by that slightly lolling tongue. 'Tell me Master Poley, you were a member of the Earl of Essex's household, were you not?'

'I was, sir.'

'And you stood with him in his attempt to make changes to the council when he marched on London. And were near killed at the Lud Gate I hear. Yet you kept your head when the earl lost his and your kinsman Sir Christopher Blount lost his as well.'

'That is true, sir.'

'But now you work for Robert Cecil, the man who brought him down?'

'If you believe that, sir, you have been ill-informed. Master Secretary Cecil was always a good friend to the earl,' said Poley, glancing up to meet his monarch's thoughtful gaze. 'And stood friends to like-minded men like me who gave good advice to the earl whether he heeded it in the end or not. He personally advised patience, forbearance, caution. I believe he hoped that, like himself, the earl would be content to await your eventual succession – which both men were working hard to ensure, as you know.' His attention returned to the delicate matter of unlocking Cecil's letter. 'But of course, there was the matter of Lord Grey de Wilton's attack on the Earl of Southampton, which the Earl of Essex saw as a declaration of war against himself and his followers by his enemies at court and in the council such as Lord Cobham and Sir Walter Raleigh, who, so the earl believed, were working to ensure the succession of your cousin Lady Arbella Stuart or, failing her, the Infanta of Spain. But, I am sad to say, the earl in the end listened to hot-heads such as Sir Gelly Meyrick and Sir Henry Cuffe. Who both met their ends at Tyburn. Hung, drawn and quartered.' Poley finished unfolding the letter and passed it over to King James.

'Thank you,' said the king courteously. 'And thank you for reminding me about the Earl of Southampton. Whatever else I send back to London with you tomorrow, there will be a letter ordering the immediate release of Southampton, if I can discover who to direct it to.'

'That will be to Sir John Peyton, sir,' said Poley. 'He is the current Lieutenant of the Tower of London. Or to his associate Sir William Waad.'

Poley was found a room to sleep in - though he had to share it. He was placed in an honoured seat at table and filled his belly with venison and umble pie. But, in the absence of any contact from the suspiciously silent Udall or directly from Watson, his head remained full of Lady Janet and his last

141

thought before he fell asleep was of her, distant and unattainable though she seemed to be.

23

Lady Janet Percy was thinking about Robert Poley. She often did so, but her thoughts and memories were given fresh impetus by the fact that she was back in the bedroom in Essex House where they had met so soon before the Earl of Essex's fatal uprising of two years ago. She was an analytical person who preferred to see herself, her feelings and relationships in a clear light. She had no patience with self-indulgent men and women who were too easily fooled or led by the nose – often by their own unrecognised wishes and desires. She admitted that she was attracted to Robert Poley, therefore – despite the disparity in their social standing. Despite his reputation with women. Despite the fact that he was a professional deceiver. Such an adept at deception, indeed, that he might well find a congenial home on the stage of the Globe with the men of the Lord Chamberlain's acting troupe who were also past masters at pretending to be who and what they were not. She also saw that he knew himself to be, in some light at least, a lying whoremaster and his conscience was heavily weighted with his past sins. But he would never play the deceiver with her. That was the rub. Poley had never lied to her, would never lie to her and, once he had given his word, be true to her and her alone. Until death. She knew this about him as surely as she knew everything about herself.

But who was she, that he should be true unto death to her? On the one hand her personal position was that she was a single woman of advancing years. A woman in a political position like Lady Audrey, wife to Sir Thomas Walsingham, Cecil's friendly rival in the world of intelligencers, who worked as a spy for both men. Lady Janet had spied and carried messages for Cecil – often to Poley. But in the end, she had been betrayed and used as a method of punishing the intelligencer, who had disobeyed his master's instructions and saved someone who befriended him from the unimaginably awful death Cecil had planned for them. Her expulsion from the Ladies of the Privy Chamber and her exile to the wilds of Northumberland had been Cecil's work, she was sure.

On the other hand, her social position was not unlike that of Lady Arbella Stuart, though Essex House was no Hardwick Hall and her cousin Earl Henry was no termagant like the Lady Bess of Hardwick. She stood a step or two further away from the throne than Lady Arbella and was therefore freer but still tightly bound by society and circumstance. She was less of a political plaything than Lady Arbella but by no means actually at liberty to follow her own dreams and desires. In truth, her part in Essex's downfall had been slight enough, mostly passing messages from Master Secretary Cecil and gossip from the queen's privy rooms, to Master Poley as he worked in Essex House. She had long got over the bitterness she felt at Her Majesty's rejection but she still harboured a grudge against the manipulative Master Secretary. In any case Queen Elizabeth was dead, the Ladies of the Privy Chamber were waiting to meet the new occupant of those rooms – unless they were usurped by her husband King James. In any case, Lady Janet would never be called upon to serve Queen Anne as she had served Elizabeth.

But would she still serve Cecil and because of that service come into company with the enigmatic Poley once more? That would bear careful scrutiny. Not only because of Poley himself but also because everything was upside-down now. She no longer trusted Cecil even if she still trusted Poley, who had been promoted after being punished. Which seemingly was the way of the intelligencer world. Cecil and Poley had schemed to bring about Essex's downfall so Cecil could remain close to the throne, whoever occupied it. But the man who would sit on the throne from the moment of his coronation onwards, saw Essex as a martyr to his cause and would without a second thought destroy the men who had destroyed the earl if he could discover who they were. And where did she, who knew exactly who they were and felt one of them tugging at the strings of her heart, stand in all this deadly tangle?

Lady Janet had reached this point in her thoughts when her servant and companion Agnes came bustling into the room. 'You would swear,' announced Agnes, her voice quivering with outrage, 'that the house was all a'fire! It is bad enough when Sir Walter visits, but he has them all at the tobacco now! Good for their health, they say! I cannot believe a word of it.' Agnes shook her head.

'Sir Walter is here?' Lady Janet asked, her interest piqued.

'Sir Walter, Lord Thomas Grey, Sir Griffin Markham and the reverend George Brook, all in close conference with Lord Henry. All puffing away at their pipes! I cannot begin to imagine how they can breathe!'

'They will open a window, Agnes.' As she said this, something stirred in Lady Janet. A quiver of excitement. The exhilaration she had felt most strongly in this very room, discussing deadly secrets with Robert Poley. Abruptly – uncharacteristically – she was in motion with little idea why she was moving. She picked up a book she had been reading and left Agnes gaping in her wake. It was only as she descended the stairs, trying to remember the nearest way out into the garden that she realised. She was going to spy on her relative and his friends. She was going to find the open window through which the tobacco smoke would be issuing and she was going to listen outside it. Her book was the excuse – she would be looking for a bright and quiet place in which to read it. Should anyone enquire. Her breath shortened at the prospect and her heartbeat speeded.

It proved to be easier than Lady Janet had feared it might. She knew the layout of the house and gardens well. Now that she was officially resident there of course she had access to any area she wished to visit. This included the garden which

145

ran down to the river and Essex House steps. Immediately outside the rear wall of the building there was a paved area which was being prepared for the Summer. There were chairs and benches there which she had used before on dry and clement late-winter days. She was a northern woman, after all. With the exception of the grimmest mid-winter, London's climate held no fears for her.

Book in hand, therefore, crossed the reception hall and went into the servants' quarters, past the kitchens, the store rooms and the two damp chambers which had housed the late Sir Anthony Bacon, Essex's sickly spy-chief, and so out into the garden. The weather conspired to help her. It was a warm, dry afternoon – a promise of spring arriving in early March. The sun was low but warm. The garden was still and utterly untenanted – no servants, no gardeners, no-one at all. There was no breeze so it was easy to see which window opened from the chamber full of smokers. Grey clouds issued sluggishly and hung in the air, a tell-tale banner. Like all of the family day-rooms, this was on the second floor so the window was more than fifteen feet above the flagstones. But there was a bench immediately beneath it. Lady Janet sat on this and settled to read, as though the one-sided romance between Astrophil and Stella held great interest for her. But she soon let the little volume fall onto her lap as she preferred to amuse herself by observing the dazzling show afforded by the river and the various craft upon it. The noise of waterborne commerce was distant. The whole of Essex House garden was as still and silent as the grave.

'… dead in his mistress's bed,' said Walter Raleigh's west-country voice. 'Both with their throats cut. There's a crowner's quest called but no suspects, no witnesses and none any the wiser.'

'Who will you send now?' enquired Lady Janet's kinsman Henry Percy, Earl of Northumberland in his flat, northern tones.

'It is not decided,' answered Raleigh. 'But we need to discuss it.'

'I am in contact with William Watson and William Clark and they are in contact with many others, recusants, apellants, Catholics and Protestants unhappy with the way the wind is blowing...' said a gruff new voice in a forthright, impatient tone.

'I hear you paid Watson's way to Edinburgh, Griffin, on condition that he put your case in the matter of Beskwood Park alongside that of tolerance for Catholics.'

'I did, George. You of all people should know that I could trust a churchman - even one who can look two ways at once!'

This exchange allowed Lady Janet to identify the voices of the old soldier Griffin Markham and Lord Cobham's brother the Reverend George Brook.

So when a new voice joined the discussion, it could only belong to Thomas Grey, Lord Grey de Wilton implacable enemy to the Earl of Essex, who had assaulted the Earl of Southampton – some said ultimately causing Essex to lead his revolt. Ultimately responsible for the Earl's downfall and death, therefore. There was no doubting why he was uneasy at the approach of the king who saw Essex as a martyr to his cause. 'From what I hear,' said Grey, 'none of this is in the hands of the Almighty. It's in the hands of those damnable bloody Scots.'

'Scottish lords advising a Scottish king to take what we have worked for and paid for with our own hard-earned coin, then give it all to them,' said Raleigh bitterly. 'And when we talk of limiting royal power with a commonwealth the men on the council who hope to get close to King James – close, that is, for *English* men – forbid us to discuss it. I have been ordered – *ordered* mind you – to remain here and not approach the king in person. I have, it seems, too many duties attendant upon Her Majesty's funeral.'

147

'God's death,' spat George Brooke in a blasphemy most unbecoming to a churchman, 'could she not have lingered long enough to confirm my appointment to Saint Cross?'

'It is too late to sit and voice recriminations now,' snapped Raleigh. 'We all stand to lose something we value to one Scotsman or another – be he king or lord or mere new knight with his honour purchased cheap. The question must be what will we do about it? Griffin, I do not trust your man William Watson. Besides, he will never travel abroad until the question of the apellants and the recusants is settled. Magnall cannot go now. Who else could we send?'

'And where?' wondered Grey.

'If we are serious about this, there are only two alternatives,' said Raleigh. 'We could send to Brussels. The Archduke Albert and the Infanta Isabella are there.'

'But we might just as well wait for their ambassador the Count of Aremberg,' said Henry Percy. 'Surely that would be safer. And rumour has it that he will be here soon.'

There was a stirring of general agreement.

But then Raleigh spoke up once more. 'He will not even stir from Brussels until he has word that James Stuart is ready to be crowned. And he seems to be taking his own good time in coming down from Scotland. The longer we wait the more we stand to lose. The only swift way forward might well be to send to the Spanish court in Valladolid and ask King Philip for money and troops to support an uprising. And that means we would have to support the claim of his sister Isabella the Infanta of Spain and the Archduchess of Austria and the Spanish Netherlands. I know some among you favour the Lady Arbella Stuart, but the surest way to the Spanish king, his troops and his purse, must surely be through his sister.'

'Surely, then,' persisted Sir Griffin Markham, 'it would be wisest to send to Brussels first and then to Valladolid if no satisfaction can be gained there?'

'A risky undertaking, no-matter the destination,' observed Lord Henry uneasily. 'Especially at a time like this. Look

148

how swiftly poor Lord Beauchamp was outmanoeuvred. I hear the Lord Admiral is in Portsmouth looking into the matter. And he has men perusing the passes of everyone headed away across the Channel.'

'Oh, there's no fear there,' said George Brooke breezily. 'Whoever we send can go through Dover. Or any of the Cinque Ports under my brother Cobham's control.'

'Have you anyone in mind to replace Magnall, Sir Walter?' wondered Grey.

'There is no-one with Magnall's detailed understanding of finances,' said Raleigh. 'But as chance would have it, I interviewed a man to help him with my accounts not long ago. I did not appoint him despite his obvious suitability because he is a Catholic recusant. But now, it seems to me that such a man would be the very one to carry a letter to The Archduke's court in Brussels or to King Phillip's court at Valladolid. His name is Dutton. I will get in contact with him.' His voice dropped. 'Lord Henry, can I look to you for some funds in this matter? Does not Cecil still owe you more than eight hundred pounds? It would be a delicious irony to use some of the money he owes to bring about his downfall!'

There was a stirring of agreement, then Raleigh continued, 'Sir Griffin, close the window. Now, as to the contents of the letter, we should all agree...'

The window creaked closed and the voices became a distant indecipherable hum. Lady Janet stood. Her cheeks were flushed and her heart was racing. She used the unread book to fan herself. It was impossible to overestimate the importance of what she had just heard. Or the danger. She was guilty of treason every second that she did not report what she now knew. And the men who had spoken were all guilty of high treason as far as she could estimate. But who should she tell?

Lady Janet took a deep breath and gave her red head a little shake. She knew the answer to that question even before she posed it to herself. She would tell Robert Poley.

149

24

'So,' concluded King James as he handed Poley his satchel stuffed with letters. 'There are instructions there for the Privy Council, for Master Secretary Cecil, for Sir Robert Peyton at the Tower, and for Sir Edward Bruce, the new-made Lord Kinloss, my main representative in London. There is also a proclamation to be read out in London and all the major cities of the kingdom. It will all go through Lord Cecil and the council of course but I would be grateful if you could deliver the letter to the Lieutenant of the Tower and the other to Lord Kinloss in person.'

'Of course, Your Majesty,' said Poley formally. This time King James had the Earl of Lennox on one side and the Earl of Mar at the other. 'God willing, they will all be safely delivered within three days; perhaps two.'

'That will be fine. Away with you now and God-speed.'

Poley slept that night at the Sun and Bear tavern in Doncaster and was at Charing Cross late the next afternoon. He turned his weary horse's head left into the Strand and soon he was dismounting at Salisbury House. One of Master Secretary's stable lads returned the horse to the nearest post-tavern while Poley went through to Master Secretary with his precious satchel. Cecil was at dinner with his mistress Lady Catherine Howard. He was not best pleased to have his intimate repast disturbed, though Lady Catherine, living up to her reputation, eyed the tall intelligencer as though he was a prize bull she wished to put to her finest cattle. 'The king was at Widdrington when I left him,' Poley reported. 'He should be at Newcastle now and is planning to stay there for a while. Half the kingdom seems set on going to see him but he does not like crowds. I heard tell he left them kneeling in Berwick awaiting some words of pleasure and gratitude at his welcome such as the old queen would have given them. They might have waited fruitlessly all day but the heavens opened and they all went home wet and disappointed. He is all walled about with his Scottish lords and some of the English lords seeking to talk with him are becoming nervous that they cannot claim his ear as their Scottish rivals do. There are papers here for the attention of the Council, of yourself, of the Lieutenant of the Tower and of Lord Kinloss. The latter ones the king has ordered me to deliver in person.'

'Sort through them first, leave anything vital for my perusal immediately after Lady Howard has departed, then take the letter for Sir John Peyton directly to the Tower as His Majesty directed. It is of course the release order for the Earl of Southampton. Leave no-one at the Tower in any doubt that the release has been all my doing, which is why my man is bringing King James's letter. And there's another for Lord Kinloss, you say? Well, that can wait until tomorrow. Report to me betimes and I will direct you whither to take it.'

Poley turned to go, but Cecil added, 'Wait. I wish you to prepare for me as detailed a list as you can of the important lords and ladies attending the king. I would also desire you to make note of any striking elements of accommodation, food or sport that particularly pleased the king.'

Poley went through to the office he shared with Phelippes, pausing on the way to order that some sustenance be brought to him there. Then on a table it shared with half of a cold chicken and some wrinkled winter apples, he laid the satchel and began to sort through its contents. The first thing that struck him was the proclamation. The council was to let it be known through all the land that in celebration of his accession to the throne, King James hereby ordered an amnesty - the release of all prisoners held for petty crimes and debt. The only exceptions to be those being held for murder, treason, witchcraft and recusancy. Murderers, traitors, Devil-worshipers and Catholics. Poley looked at the paper as though he couldn't believe what he was seeing. So far, the

151

king had promised to consider every request – even Watson's appeal for leniency in the matter of religion. But now this. Poley was going to have to get his organisation here in England, in Brussels and Valladolid on double-watch as soon as possible. There were going to be a lot of sorely disappointed Catholics out there. And five hundred Jesuits here in England keen to make mischief amongst them. But he had to go to the Tower first.

He wiped his fingers, finished sorting the letters, putting aside those marked for Master Secretary, then he took the order destined for the Tower and went out into the evening. It was a little over a mile to the Tower, a twenty-minute walk. He gave himself half an hour and went via Tom's lodging. His brother-in-law was in residence and agreed to ride north in the morning to keep an eye on Udall as he watched Watson. 'There's something amiss there already,' Poley warned Tom. 'And that's before Watson and the men he leads learn what will be proclaimed throughout the land tomorrow!'

The last time Poley had visited the Tower was to witness the beheading of the Earl of Essex. Memories of that terrible event were all too fresh in his mind as a yeoman warder guided him across the green with its block and platform to the Lieutenant's quarters in the Queen's House. Like Master Secretary Cecil, Sir John Peyton was at dinner, but unlike Cecil, he was dining with a colleague rather than a mistress. The colleague in question was Sir William Waad. Both men were well known to Poley and recognised him in turn. Also unlike Cecil, Peyton was pleased to see Poley. 'I've been expecting this,' he said as Poley handed him King James's letter.

'Master Secretary has been working tirelessly to bring the king round,' said Poley smoothly.

'Of course, the king knows the late Earl of Essex as one of his firmest supporters; and the Earl of Southampton shoulder by shoulder beside him,' observed Peyton's companion drily.

'That is true, Sir William,' answered Poley readily enough. 'But, as is due to be proclaimed tomorrow, an amnesty will be offered to all those in prison except those held for murder, witchcraft, recusancy or treason. And it is treason, is it not, that the earl was originally charged with? Having stood shoulder to shoulder with a man beheaded for it?'

'Ah, I see,' said Waad. 'Master Secretary Cecil has been active in ensuring the earl is formally released tonight in case of any confusion tomorrow. An astute move. Either by Cecil or King James – or both.'

Sir John broke the seal on the letter which required neither locking nor encoding. 'Very well, he said, having read through the contents. 'Let us go and give the earl the news of his immediate release.'

Peyton and Waad both rose. Poley remained standing, uncertain whether his mission was in fact over. But the Lieutenant of the Tower turned to him. 'You brought the king's directive,' he said. 'It is fitting you should see it enacted. Especially as you, like the earl, stood shoulder to shoulder with Essex at the end.'

'And, indeed,' said Waad, 'stood beside the block as the headsman's axe fell, if my memory served me aright.'

Henry Wriothesley, Earl of Southampton was being held in the White Tower. That is to say, thought Poley who knew both the Tower and its traditions better than most, the rooms he occupied were located there. There were no plebeian niceties such as armed guards or locked doors. No fetters or chains such as Poley had worn when held in the Fleet. The earl had every comfort he would have had at home except for freedom. The three men who had come to restore that last luxury to him knocked at the door of his main chamber and were cordially invited to enter. Southampton was seated in a comfortable chair and did not rise to greet them – not through any sense of superiority, Poley calculated, but because he had a black and white cat curled on his lap. 'Sir John, Sir William,

Master Poley. It is good to see you all. To what do I owe this pleasure?'

'My Lord,' answered Peyton, 'by this letter, signed by the king's own hand and hurried hither by Master Poley, you are free to depart this place, return to Southampton House or any other habitation you list, and to His Majesty's court with all your honours and possessions unsullied and intact.'

'Master Poley, I thank you for your part in this. Sir John, Sir William, you to have my thanks as well. I will send to Southampton House and be out of your care within a day. Then I must go and thank His Majesty.'

'My Lord,' said Poley, 'You should be aware that you need not hurry to return to court unless you burn to do so. The king and his court are currently coming to you and are unlikely to be in place before the end of the month.'

Poley walked back to his lodgings at the Lion along the river. It was a clement evening for early March and he saw no reason to hurry. His route was easy enough – Thames Street ran from the Tower past the north end of London Bridge, past St Peter's Church to Saint Andrews Hill which led up to Blackfriars and Lud Gate in the City wall. Then he went out past Temple Bar, into the Strand past the frontages of Essex House and Durham House to Charing Cross and so to King Street. His mind was so full of the implications arising from tomorrow's proclamation not to mention the further requests Cecil had made of him, that he did not really register the fact that he was being followed – something further concealed by the bustle of the streets along which he was walking.

But his arrival at the Lion only served to add another distraction to his already overcrowded thoughts. 'There's been a woman looking for you,' said Gilbert Gifford. 'Said she'd tried Salisbury House and they said try here. I thought you'd given that sort of thing up after Mistress Yeomans.'

'A woman? What woman?'

'Dunno. Wouldn't leave a message. Said she'd try again. Hard-faced piece, though, with some kind of Scottish accent.'

25

Poley had neither the time nor the desire to speculate about Gifford's hard-faced Scots woman. He was exhausted, aching in every muscle, craving sleep above all and yet poignantly aware of the importance of Cecil's last orders. The list of courtiers, their accommodations, amusements and pleasures might seem a strange request for a spymaster to make of an intelligencer. But it was by no means a strange request from a Cecil. On his journey south, King James planned to stay at Burghley House in Lincolnshire, where the elder Cecil brother, Lord Burghley, would entertain him and his followers. Then, about a week later, the king planned to visit Theobalds House in Hertfordshire, where he would be entertained by the younger Cecil brother – Master Secretary himself. The information in Poley's head might prove vital, therefore. Especially as the Cecils had stirred up local unrest near both great country houses by enclosing common land to add to the flocks of sheep whose wool was the basis of the family fortunes. He was still writing it when he fell asleep and his first task in the morning was to wash the ink off his cheek.

Cecil was unusually indulgent when Poley gave him the annotated list. There were no complaints or cutting comments about the smudges. Instead, Cecil read through what Poley had written with the same focus as he would use on a vital intelligence report.

'Good,' he said at last, looking up. 'As you know, I plan to meet His Majesty in York on the sixteenth. Normally I would set out on the fourteenth, but under the circumstances I think the eleventh or twelfth would be wiser. In that way I can check on the preparations at both Theobalds and Burghley. I want you and Phelippes to remain in London. To begin with, at least. I may have more tasks for you when I have finished going through the correspondence the king has sent to me. And remember, if your see a chance to drive a further wedge between Raleigh and the king, do not hesitate – but do take care. However, if you know my itinerary, you will be able to reach me should some new circumstance demand it.'

'The proclamation due to be published today is likely to stir up some bad feeling,' Poley observed.

'Indeed. Bad feeling amongst hopeful recusants to go with the bad feeling already being generated by His Majesty's over-reliance on his Scottish courtiers. Two dangerous groups indeed – Catholic churchmen, laymen and Jesuits, and the old queen's most powerful courtiers. Raleigh at the head of them, so to speak. You will have to keep your eyes wide until the king is crowned. And after that as well, until all is settled one way or another.'

There was a brief silence, then Poley ventured, 'Lord Kinloss, Master Secretary. I have yet to deliver His Majesty's letter.'

'Ah yes, Sir Edward Bruce as was. I think it would be wise to start keeping eyes on him as well – despite the obvious danger if the king finds out. I have heard it whispered that the king's representatives have been telling our current ambassadors from Europe and beyond that the King James has no time for the old English ways and policies; that he intends to cut down those who have stood against peace with Spain, for instance, or a rapprochement with Italy.'

'And Edward Bruce is one of the men putting these messages about? Lord Kinloss, I should say.'

'Perhaps. And perhaps when you deliver the king's letter to him you might be able to get some idea of the truth. He lodges on Tower Street on the corner of St Dunstan's Hill hard by St Dunstan's in the East. And that is fortuitous because after you have delivered the letter to him I wish you to return to the Tower and inform Sir John Peyton that I wish accommodation to be prepared for the restless Lord Beauchamp.'

The Tower was a half-hour walk from Salisbury House and St Dunstan's in the East was on the way. The morning was clouding over, though it had started chilly, clear and dry. Poley hurried along the bustling streets, therefore, with the hood of his cloak pulled forward. Bustling though the city was, it was not until he came to the crossroads between Lombard Street and Gracechurch Street that it got really busy. And that was because the broad thoroughfare of Gracechurch led down into the narrower New Fish Street which in turn led down to London Bridge. Poley turned right and pushed his way south towards the bridge before he turned left into Little East Cheap and so into Tower Street.

The house Lord Kinloss was renting stood on the corner of St Dunstan's Hill just as Cecil had described, right beside the fine old church. Poley hammered on the door and it was opened at once by a vaguely familiar figure. A tall, powerfully-built man of middle years, straight-backed and square shouldered, wearing a great kilt and a claymore. For an instant Poley could swear there was a glimmer of surprise in the narrow brown eyes staring straight into his own. 'I am Master Secretary Cecil's man, Robert Poley. I have a letter for Lord Kinloss,' said Poley. 'It was given me by King James and I am to place it in no hand other than Lord Kinloss's.'

'Well, come away in Master Poley,' said the stranger speaking with a broad Scottish accent. 'Lord Kinloss is here.'

'What is it, Henderson?' called Kinloss from an inner room, his accent a match for his man's.

'A letter from the king,' answered Henderson. He turned to Poley. 'Follow me.'

Henderson led Poley through into a large room brightly lit by broad windows looking out onto Tower Street. Edward Bruce, Lord Kinloss sat at a table which had a number of open letters scattered across it. He held out his right hand and Poley placed King James's letter into it. Without appearing to do so, he scanned the letters on the table. A glance was hardly enough to make much sense of them, but he recognised several seals and signatures. 'Why is it, do you think, Master Poley, that so many of your countrymen hate so many of mine?' Wondered Kinloss as he broke the seal on James's letter and began to open it.

'Fear, mostly,' answered Poley. 'Fear of strangers. Especially of foreign strangers who have made such a point of befriending our enemies such as France, for instance. Fear that these strangers will take their honours, powers and possessions. Especially as these suddenly frightening foreigners have always been viewed as lesser creatures, hardly more than savages or animals. In the eyes of many, it appears that an army of powerful, acquisitive apes have come streaming across a border which has been sealed against them since the time of the Roman Emperor Hadrian.'

Kinloss gave a shout of laughter. 'Jings, man, I'll be careful what I ask your opinion on in future! Is this the forthright advice you give your Master Secretary?'

'It is, My Lord.'

'Then it is no surprise that you have the reputation you have. King James likes and trusts you.'

'I am honoured and flattered to hear it. He has every reason to do so. Master Secretary has been his friend - whether he knows it or not – since long before the Earl of Essex began working to ensure his succession. And I am Master Secretary's man.'

Kinloss nodded. 'And long may that happy state continue. Now, I have business to attend to.' He turned back to the letters on the table. Dismissed, Poley turned. Kinloss's man Henderson was standing close behind him. There was a moment almost of confusion as Poley waited to step forward and Henderson hesitated to step aside. Then the way was clear and Poley was out in Tower Street. Without a further thought, he turned right and headed for his next destination.

It seemed to him that he was taken to Sir John's quarters by the same yeoman warder as the one who had guided him yesterday. Sir John was once again in close conference with William Waad and, whatever the topic of their conversation, it must have concerned the current unsettled state of the kingdom – neither man was at all amazed at being asked to prepare rooms for the Earl of Beauchamp. Hardly surprisingly, the Lieutenant of the Tower – which was in many ways a mediaeval institution – kept mediaeval habits. Poley had no sooner delivered Master Secretary's message that Sir John's steward announced dinner. When Sir John invited Poley to join them, the intelligencer accepted gladly because he had eaten only the lightest of suppers – cold chicken and winter apples - yesterday and had yet to break his fast today.

But the three men had hardly sat at the dinner table when one of the loudest noises Poley had ever heard shook the Tower to its ancient Norman foundations.

26

From the south-facing curtain walls of the Outer Ward it was possible for the three men to see across the Thames to the southern bank where the hump of Redriffe or Rotherhythe heaved up like the back of some great grey whale contained by a wide northern bend in the river. At the top of this, a column of thick black smoke was rising straight into the windless sky. They looked at each other as the echo of that devastating noise rolled back from the nearest hillsides all around. They had just been discussing restlessness and revolt. And now, right before their very eyes something of incredible violence was taking place. 'Sir John, if you rouse the garrison and make the swiftest arrangements possible to get them across the river, Sir William and I will go and find out what is going on,' said Poley. 'I will need to report to Master Secretary and I might as well do it with first-hand information.'

'Yes, yes of course,' said the lieutenant, almost as badly shaken as the building he was in charge of. 'There is a four-man skiff just inside Traitor's Gate. You and Sir William may take that. It will get you there faster than anything else I have to hand. I'll rouse the garrison commander – though I'd wager he is up and organising his men already. And, of course, the yeoman warders will prepare to defend the Tower itself.'

'Very well,' said Poley. 'Sir William?'

Although in his mid-fifties now, Waad was as fit and healthy in body as he was sharp-witted in mind. He and Poley ran down to the tiny dock within the walls behind Traitor's Gate which opened directly out onto the river. Behind and above them, Sir John was shouting orders and by the time they reached the four-man skiff, the crew was in place and all they had to do was climb aboard, sit in the sleek vessel's lean stern and they were off. 'Could it be some kind of attack?' wondered Waad a little breathlessly. 'One better organised than Beauchamp's attempt on Portsmouth.'

'Unlikely, I'd have thought,' answered Poley. 'Who would want to conquer Redriffe? It has no obvious strategic significance. Indeed, holding it would be difficult and using it to launch attacks on anything other than Wapping and the Tower on the north bank would be near impossible. Now if whatever just happened had occurred downriver at Greenwich, Woolwich or Deptford, I could see the danger. Especially to the royal dockyards or the royal arsenal at Woolwich Warren. But there is nothing at Redriffe worth anyone's time.'

This conversation and the further one that followed it took them downriver and across to the stairs nearest to that threatening column of smoke, but left neither of them any the wiser as to what was going on. As soon as the skiff was nestling up against the bottom of the stairs, Poley led the way onto the shore and up the hill through the modest houses, along part-paved streets strangely empty of people. As they neared the smoke, so the houses through which they were hurrying became more and more seriously damaged. Windows burst, doors a-gape, roof-tiles blown awry, thatch smouldering. The streets were littered with burning debris and dead gulls. Only when they came to the seat of the fire itself did they find people and an explanation.

At the centre of a blackened circle of devastation stood the blazing ruins of a medium-sized building. Nothing above knee-height seemed to be standing, and the earth beneath their feet was littered with bits and pieces of blackened brickwork. All sorts of woodwork from beams to splinters was ablaze as men and women darted in and out of the inferno with buckets of water and makeshift stretchers. It looked to Poley like there were at least ten corpses in various states of disrepair being mourned by an assortment of women and children. A range of wounds that would have done credit to a battlefield were being tended by shocked, black-faced men and women who clearly had little or no idea of how best to go about what they were doing. There was hardly any real organisation, though someone had set up a bucket chain from the nearest water to the fire itself. A long chain, having little effect.

Poley half recognised the figure in charge of this. A man of about thirty, he was directing matters calmly in an authoritative, well-educated voice. Poley crossed over to him, typically focussed on what lay ahead rather than what lay behind. 'I'd suggest you leave the central fire and focus on putting out the smaller ones in nearby houses,' he said. 'Whatever that was, it's beyond saving but some of the houses can still be protected.'

'True,' said the young man. 'I had not thought. He turned to re-direct his bucket-men. 'And there seems to be no-one left to save in there.' He gestured at the blazing building. 'It was a gunpowder mill,' he explained. 'It was designed to supply the Royal Arsenal downriver at Woolwich Warren. I'd have thought you would know that, Master Poley. One wayward spark and it was nothing but a sound, a fury and a memory. The same to be said for the poor souls who were working there or walking nearby.' He surreptitiously crossed himself.

Poley looked more closely at the speaker, and was taken back more than two years. His companion had been one of the men involved on the outskirts of the Essex rebellion. One of the Catholic recusants who had joined in the hope that the new dispensation, which would exist if the rebellion was successful, would be more understanding towards Catholics. Crippled by fines in consequence of the uprising's failure, only recently released from prison too, likely as not judging by the pallor of his skin. And he was right, Poley thought. His assessment of what had happened here was everything that might have been expected of an Oxford scholar who had also studied at the English Catholic college, Douai.

'Catesby, is it not?' said Poley.

The stranger nodded. 'Robert Catesby,' he confirmed.

27

The Scottish intelligencer Sir Anthony Standen was in Brussels. Having passed Poley's message to Udall and started Poley's rumour of an attack on Jersey, he was now settled on the outskirts of the Archduke's court; but he had little intention of remaining here for long. At nearly fifty years old, he was widely experienced. He had been Master of the Horse to Mary Queen of Scots and, after her downfall, had worked for Francis Walsingham, who paid him handsomely despite the fact that he had been involved in a plot to invade England. Or, perhaps, because of it. Now, having worked for Essex's spymaster Anthony Bacon up until both Essex and Bacon were dead, he worked mostly for Poley, turning his coat with ease and regularity; like Poley, wearing his Catholic faith lightly – unless it was a useful cover to hoodwink other, more dangerous Catholics. He was a tall, athletic man with a well-proportioned figure just beginning to run to fat, a full head of fair hair, beginning to silver now, matched by a thick beard. He was a virile lover who had once been thrown out of Antwerp by King Philip of Spain for seducing Don John of Austria's mother. He was more vividly aware than anyone else in Poley's network, of the good use to which pillow-talk could be put. It was almost as effective as the confessional at eliciting guilty revelations.

Standen had established himself on Grand Place, only a short walk from the magnificent warren of the Coudenberg Palace. His espionage technique was simple and he had practised it for years with great success. He gathered in information like a harvester with a scythe. He sifted it carefully, winnowing the wheat of saleable information from the chaff of mere gossip. Then he assessed who would pay the most for each bushel of intelligence he produced. He had travelled widely throughout his long life and harboured ambitions to travel more widely still but at the moment there were only two places a Scotsman or an Englishman in his profession would choose to be found: in Brussels at the court of the Archdukes Albert and Isabella or at Valladolid and the court of Isabella's brother Philip the Third. Those were the two cities where the intelligencers' harvest would be thickest, certainly until King James was settled on the throne of England, and perhaps beyond that time as well. There were numerous men and women, after all, who were finding that the promise of the Scottish King was hollow as far as they were concerned. Men and women who wished to have the promises he had broken fulfilled by someone else. People who would pay handsomely to see their hopes effected. People who would, in fact, pay Sir Anthony Standen for putting them in contact with like-minded strangers. Whose names, of course, were then easily saleable to Poley as well. Men, in fact, like the recently-arrived Englishmen Anthony Dutton and Anthony Rivers together with a French spy called Matthew La Rensy who moved easily between the great houses on the Strand and the outskirts of the Archduke's court for he was the Princely Duke of Aremberg's man.

Sir Anthony's favourite meeting place was one favoured by English wayfarers, especially Catholic ones. It was in Impasse St Nicolas which was a little alleyway off Rue du Marché Aux Herbes, not far from Grand Place. The Scottish intelligencer had annexed a convenient table which he habitually occupied in the early afternoon. He advertised the fact and, even on days where he visited the dazzling court in the magnificent Coudenberg Palace complex, was careful to be at his favourite table, reliably available to anyone wishing to consult him. An increasing number of desperate men carrying a range of messages, pleas and promises were arriving in Brussels only to discover they simply did not know how best to proceed with their missions. Sir Anthony was always there to advise or direct. And, such was his reputation he was regularly consulted.

Today, the first man to sidle nervously up to his table was the newly-arrived Anthony Dutton fresh out of England, less than a week away from London, having arrived via Dover and Calais one hundred and twenty miles due west of the city. Sir Anthony had seen other men in Dutton's situation. He would be carrying a letter from some discontented person or group listing the types and perhaps the names of the most disgruntled factions and their leaders, explaining how a revolt could be raised, if only the Archduke would supply money, men or both. Who in the massive complex of the Coudenberg would it be best to approach? As a matter of fact, Sir Anthony had had that very same conversation with the far more experienced Anthony Rivers only the day before. Like Dutton, Rivers was carrying proof that a Catholic uprising was only weeks away – if the money and support for it could be found.

'Even a promissory note would do,' persisted Dutton now. 'The men I represent are powerful and committed. Thousands would rise under their leadership. They have calculated that six hundred thousand crowns would secure the country and place the Infanta on the English throne. I came via Dover. The money should come back via Jersey and the men I represent would then employ it to raise and arm a force far larger and more effective than those raised by the Earl of Essex and, more lately, by Lord Beauchamp. They would guarantee to open the port, and perhaps four others, to the Spanish fleet and welcome the Spanish army. If I can only reach the Archduke…'

'The Archduke no longer desires a war with England,' said Sir Anthony sadly, as he mentally listed the Governor of Jersey and the Warden of the Cinque Ports among the men who sent the letter. Poley would pay handsomely for that information; it was clearly time to return to London. 'As I explained to Master Rivers yesterday, and indeed the

167

Frenchman La Rensy on a similar mission to yours, all such requests have fallen on deaf ears here in Brussels recently.'

Dutton looked at the Scotsman, stricken.

'Then what am I to do? How am I to proceed?'

'Again, as I suggested to Master Rivers, you must take your message to Valladolid.'

'Take it? To *Valladolid*?' Was it time, distance or expense that so alarmed Dutton wondered Sir Anthony. Not that he actually cared.

'Or you may send it with a trustworthy courier, which is what Master Rivers plans to do. The sum required to do this is paltry - a mere hundred English pounds, which Master Rivers was happy to pay.'

'A courier? Do you know of such a man?' Dutton's face simply shone with relief. Sir Anthony mentally cursed himself for not naming a far higher sum – almost all of which he would keep. A sum augmented in due course when Poley paid him for the names of the couriers, some idea of what their messages contained, and his suspicions about the identities of the men who had sent them in the first place.

'I do,' Sir Anthony beamed. 'An Englishman, from Yorkshire. He has been soldiering in the Low Countries but things have quietened there and he is off to seek his fortune in Spain. He is honest and trustworthy. You may absolutely rely on him to carry your message with Master Rivers's to Valladolid and King Philip's court. I will introduce you in person when we have settled the matter of the coin. His name is Guy Fawkes.'

28

'This man who was murdered in Little Drury Lane, the one whose throat was cut in his mistress's bed. He was Raleigh's man of business you say?'

'He was, Master Secretary. Why do you ask?'

'Mere coincidence. One of the letters you brought gives me authority to assess the worth of Durham House and its interior. Directs that I should do so, in fact.'

'Tobie Matthew, the Bishop of Durham is close to the King at the moment. One of only half a dozen Englishmen with such access.'

'I wonder might he be persuaded to offer the Durham House lease elsewhere. Yes, indeed, the information requested in this letter would be of great interest to me too. But his man of business has been murdered, you say?'

'He has, Master Secretary. Though, because you have been directed and are also interested, I can deal with the matter on your behalf. And I could do so in a manner that would further irritate Sir Walter and, as you have already requested; drive a further wedge between him and the king.'

'You may proceed. And bring a detailed report to me when you are done. I will be at Theobalds or Burghley or York, depending on the time it takes you. Where will you start?'

'At Eltham,' said Poley.

Ingram Frizer, Sir Thomas Walsingham's business manager and occasional undercover courier, lived on Eltham Hill near the Green. He and Poley had known each other for years, even before Frizer was accused of murdering Christopher Marlowe, as witnessed by Poley and Nicholas Skeres. A charge later dismissed by a ruling of self-defence. He was just beginning to settle back into his role as man of business now after Sir Thomas had sent him running to Edinburgh and back a matter of weeks ago. He was therefore not at first best pleased to see his old friend. But when Poley explained what he wanted, Frizer readily agreed. 'I keep current assessments of the worth of buildings and contents for Sir Thomas's great house at Scadbury,' he said. 'And I would be simply fascinated to assess the worth of Durham House and its contents. But has not Sir Walter got a man of business?'

'He had one called Magnall but the man of business is recently deceased and I believe he has yet to employ a replacement. I suppose, if luck was with you, he might even consider employing you.'

'A potent temptation. When has Sir Walter agreed to have the house and contents assessed?'

'He has not yet been informed, but I would be grateful if we could begin immediately.'

'But will not Sir Walter be angered at such an intrusion? Especially if it is unannounced.'

'He will, but we are working under the seal and authority of King James himself and at the prompting of Master Secretary. So, he will have to contain his anger with us and either take his objections to the court of King James or to a court of law.'

Poley and Frizer were greeted at the main door to Durham House by a footman. Who took them to the steward when he saw the King's authority. The steward took them to Sir Walter, who recognised Poley at once. He was in a book-lined study on an upper floor whose windows looked across the river towards the Archbishop's Palace at Lambeth.

'This is Master Secretary's doing!' snapped the angry soldier, throwing the king's letter onto his work-table. 'Why else would you be the one bringing the letter, Poley?'

'No, Sir Walter, it is not,' answered Poley, keeping his tone reasonable in the face of Raleigh's outrage. 'I was given this letter to take to Master Secretary, one among many, by King James himself. If you seek a man to blame, I would suggest you aim your displeasure either at King James or at Tobie

Matthew, Bishop of Durham. He was in close conference with His Majesty not long before the letter was written. Though I believe this letter merely to be one of several which show His Majesty to be exploring what properties he can recover from their current grace and favour tenants and award to his most loyal and trusted followers as a reward for their good service.'

'So, this is Bishop Matthew's doing is it?' sneered Raleigh, clearly unconvinced and simply getting more and more angry.

'I believe so, Sir Walter. I am only involved because Master Secretary is in a hurry to go north and greet the king. Otherwise, I'm sure he would have sent someone else. But as I am here, I will do my best to expedite matters, hence my companion Master Ingram Frizer, Sir Thomas Walsingham's man of business. I believe your man, Magnall is recently deceased?'

'He is.' Raleigh's tone was abrupt, his face suddenly full of suspicion. Poley could almost read his mind – *was Magnall's murder a part of this*?

'Have you had the opportunity to appoint a replacement we can consult?' Poley persisted smoothly.

'I have appointed a man called Dutton.' Raleigh answered thoughtlessly, his mind clearly still wrestling with his suspicions.

'Then we need disturb you no longer,' said Poley, forcing a great deal of relief into his voice. To mask his surprise. If Raleigh had appointed a replacement already, that was fast work indeed! Suspiciously fast work. 'Where is Master Dutton? We will be happy to talk to him.'

'I have sent him abroad on other business.' Raleigh's expression went from suspicion almost to shock. He had clearly said more than he meant to. *Dutton*, thought Poley. I will need to look into Master Dutton.

'That is unfortunate,' Poley said, masking his own suspicion. 'His Majesty does require the information as soon as possible. Would you allow Master Frizer here to do a swift assessment?'

'What choice do I have?' Raleigh was suddenly much more amenable.

'None that I can see, Sir Walter,' Poley's tone and expression oozed regret.

'Very well. But tell Master Secretary I shall not forget this!'

Thus dismissed, the pair went to work. With Frizer in the lead, they started at the top of the house and worked their way down. Poley was certain that Master Secretary and His Majesty alike would be happy with a rough survey of the property but even that took most of the rest of the day to complete.

'Twenty thousand pounds! More! And that's just the most recent improvements!' said Frizer as they walked along the Strand just before sunset. 'Say thirty thousand for the interior fixtures and fittings. To rebuild the house itself would take a fortune that even Master Secretary might balk at.'

'Twenty thousand pounds in recent improvements,' mused Poley. 'And most if not all of that sum paid by Sir Walter himself. You can understand how he might be less than happy at the idea of the bishop reclaiming it or King James letting someone else come to live in it!'

They continued talking as they walked past Essex House and Poley almost automatically glanced up at the windows of the room he had occupied there with Henry Cuffe two years ago, with its corner aspect overlooking the roadway and the courtyard. And as he did so he caught the most fleeting glimpse of a figure turning away and vanishing. The figure of a woman with bright red hair.

29

Tom caught up with King James's massive, itinerant court north of York as it continued to make its dilatory way south. It had stopped in a town that was really too small to contain it. James and his closest courtiers were well accommodated in the houses of the local dignitaries, the mayor and the town council. It seemed to Tom that everyone else had to rely on luck. At first, he thought it must be the cost and frustration of this that explained the striking atmosphere of bitter disappointment that hung in the air like the stench of a dung heap as he arrived. But it was not until he found Udall that he began to understand what was actually going on. As soon as he reached the place, Tom headed for the largest inn in town, the Bell, only to be informed that there was no accommodation to be had there. But by good fortune, Udall was in the tap room and he had secured a room which he was willing to share. Tom saw to the stabling of his horse and went back into the main building to buy Udall dinner in gratitude. As he came into the main room he was struck anew by the anger and tension simmering in the air. 'It is as though we are on the eve of a war,' he said to Udall as they sipped their beer and considered the ordinary, today being Friday and a fish day. There was eel pie, baked sturgeon and trout simmered in milk flavoured with lavender, all served on thick trenchers of wholemeal Yeoman's bread.

'Where to begin?' wondered Udall, keeping his voice low and glancing around as he spoke and ate. 'The Scots. They are arrogant and demanding; they seem to assume that this is the manner in which men of their station should behave. They speak in their heathen brogue and if anyone fails to understand, they repeat themselves louder and louder still. They demand the best but cannot pay for it. Their king has had to declare Scottish coin legal tender here in England, so his followers are not embarrassed by the inability to pay. But the tavern-keepers, shop-keepers, ostlers – everyone the Scots do pay - feel that they are simply being robbed.'

'Well, so they might,' said Tom. 'Is it not the case that an Irish shilling is really only worth nine pence instead of twelve like an English one? So who knows what a Scottish one will really be worth.'

'It will be worth whatever it can purchase I suppose,' shrugged Udall. 'Then, beyond the men disappointed by the Scottish coin, you must consider why a good number of the English have travelled so far to be here, torn between hope and fear. They have come to ask the King for ease and clemency, reduction of the fines for recusants like William Watson who is under my eye. They hope for greater understanding and indulgence for Catholics of all sorts. But even those rare men who have managed to gain an audience – by bribing James's courtiers with English money – have been painfully frustrated by James's will-ye, nill-ye answers. Then, when the proclamation was read out that there was an amnesty allowing the prisons to be open so that everyone within them except witches, traitors, murderers and Catholics could go free, frustration has turned to open rage.'

'Master Poley feared that would be the case,' nodded Tom. 'That is why he has sent me to aid you in keeping Watson under observation. For Watson is a proud man and he has staked his reputation on his ability to convince King James to treat Catholics well – and now the king has done the very opposite! His opponents such as Archpriest Blackwell, and Jesuits Gerard and Garnet must be laughing in their sleeves to see him so struck down.'

'And yet the king himself, walled with his grasping Scottish lords, seems to see nothing of this.' Udall shook his head in apparent despair. 'And in any case his whole approach to kingship is strange and new. I remember the old queen, surrounded by the leeches of her council though she was, declaring that she was a bride eternally married to her people. How it was her privilege and duty to love and serve them. I was at Greenwich in Armada Year and heard her say those very things. But James believes he has been put on the throne by God himself and it is his people who must love and serve him. You have heard how the citizens of Berwick knelt and waited for a word of kindness or gratefulness from him for their welcome, which cost a pretty penny I can tell you. And waited in vain!'

'Is there anyone apart from the Scots who do love and respect him?' asked Tom, nodding in reply.

'The only men I have seen who seem to do so are the local dignitaries, the mayors, law-keepers, sheriffs, judges and such. The men who feel themselves secure in their positions or are desirous of establishing themselves more firmly still in the king's regard.'

Tom shook his head sadly. 'And Watson,' he said. 'Where is he now that he is so disappointed and dangerous?'

'At present he is lodging at The Lamb, a tavern not far from here that seems to be favoured by churchmen and Catholics. William Clark is also there and he is closely associated with Watson. Anthony Copley is there who is friend to them both. But such is the crush in the town here that there are even courtiers and men of substance there. George Brook, the brother of Lord Cobham is there, as is Sir Griffin Markham. All begging to put their cases to the king.'

'Master Poley told me that Sir Griffin Markham paid Watson's passage to Edinburgh so he could put Markham's case to the King along with his own. Apparently, Nick Skeres saw it done. If he is here, then he must be dissatisfied with how things have fallen out.'

'That is not surprising.' Udall shrugged. 'The proclamation demonstrated that Watson had failed to make his case. It must seem that he has also failed to make Markham's therefore!'

They had got this far in their conversation when a commotion began in the street immediately outside. The two intelligencers pushed through the Bell's other clients to observe what was going on. Tom saw a group of men gathered round a single figure who was struggling to escape their clutches and failing to do so. He was young and appeared to be well-dressed. Tom's first impression was that he was a youthful member of King James's court and he was suddenly struck by the suspicion that the townsmen, having had enough of the Scottish arrogance described by Udall, had turned on any courtier they could find.

But no – 'It's a cutpurse,' said Udall, turning back from a hurried conversation with a bystander. 'Caught red-handed.'

'Nothing to worry about then,' shrugged Tom. He was turning to re-enter the tavern when Udall stopped him.

'They're taking the lad to see the king,' he said.

'What! Why?'

'The proclamation! Had the boy already been caught and condemned, he would have been in prison when the proclamation was read out – and would therefore have been released under the king's amnesty.'

'But you can't let cut-purses go running around at liberty, amnesty or no.'

'Precisely. The king has sometimes compared himself to Solomon I hear. Well now let us see him pass judgement!'

King James was easy enough to find; the whole town and no doubt much of the county knew precisely where he was. At this moment he was in the Mayor's house at a formal dinner. Seeing the mob gathered outside he was at first reluctant to come out but then someone suggested they all kneel in supplication and once they had, James grudgingly agreed to see them.

The men holding the still-struggling cutpurse explained the situation.

'And he was taken in the act?' James asked.

'He was, Your Majesty.'

'With witnesses to the event?' The king persisted.

'At least six, Your Majesty. And they would be willing to swear in a court of law…'

'No need for that,' said King James. 'Take him away and hang him.'

As the kneeling crowd realised what the king's judgement had been, a kind of ripple went through them – as though, thought Tom, they were a still pond and the king had dropped a pebble into its midst.

'But Your Majesty,' came an uncertain voice from the group holding the stricken youth. 'Cutting a purse is no hanging offence…' The king looked down, frowning.

'Had he been in prison for it only a day or two since he would have been released at your word, Your Majesty,' persisted another. 'Your amnesty…' The king's frown became thunderous.

Suddenly Sir Robert Carey was at the king's shoulder, the livid bruise on his forehead yellowing as it healed. 'Your Majesty,' he said quietly. 'Perhaps you are as yet unfamiliar with the laws in England. Here no man can be condemned without due process of law. Even the meanest can claim his day in court to be judged by a jury of his peers.'

'Is that so?' answered James, clearly outraged at having been corrected in public. 'Then England had better get used to the fact that from now on the law is in the king's word. What the king says *is* the law. Now take him away and hang him!'

Looking up at the cutpurse's corpse as it swayed in the evening breeze, Udall said, 'That cost the king a good number of the last few Englishmen who would have stood as his friends.'

Tom nodded. 'And has made the list of his enemies all the longer. And has made Master Poley's task and our task to keep him safe – to keep him alive, indeed - all the harder.'

177

30

When Dutton returned to England, he was held up at Dover while the pass Sir Walter had signed for him was checked. Bureaucratic delays were nothing new to the recusant – or to any other Catholic gentleman - and so he thought nothing of it. His ship had docked early, so he was confident that he would return to Durham House before nightfall; though he planned on enjoying the swiftest of dinners on the way. He had never met Nicholas Skeres, so when Skeres appeared as the port authorities finally cleared his papers and fell in behind him as he cantered up the Dover Road towards London, he was none the wiser as to what was going on.

Poley had sent men to all the Cinque ports as soon as Sir Walter unthinkingly revealed that he had sent his new book keeper abroad. It was not so much Dutton they were looking for – none of them knew what he looked like – it was his paperwork, with Raleigh's tell-tale signature. And Poley had sent Skeres to Dover because he was the most experienced agent and as Calais to Dover was the likeliest route for Dutton to return by, no matter where in Europe he had visited. The road between Dover and London was not well-maintained despite its importance. Of the ports it had allowed its original Roman roadbuilders to access, only Dover retained any importance and Dover was nowhere near as important as Portsmouth or Plymouth. But it was still a busy road and the stables that dotted its seventy mile length supplied horses almost as efficiently as those on the Portsmouth Road and the Great North Road, so it was easy enough to get to London in six hours or so. Skeres concealed himself quite efficiently in the bustle of the stable inns as he changed horses – and, indeed, dined - at the same time as Dutton, and so Raleigh's messenger reached London still completely unaware that he was being followed. Indeed, he only discovered what was going on when he dismounted in Southwark and left his horse at the Swan Inn's stables in preparation for walking across London Bridge. He had hardly taken a step into the crowd coming and going there when a blow on the back of his head felled him like a tree.

Dutton woke some uncounted time later in a state of nervous confusion. His first thought was that he had been assaulted by footpads, and this supposition was given weight by the fact that his purse was gone. But other things militated frighteningly against this supposition. He was in utter darkness. And he was in chains. He discovered that he was lying on a floor of stone covered with straw by feeling around with his cuffed hands. He discovered that he was alone by calling out quietly and receiving no answer. It was at this point that he began to call out more loudly. A door opened. Light flooded blindingly into the room, concealing the features of the two men who came in, picked him up and carried him helplessly out, with the chain joining his ankle gyves dragging along the floor behind him. He found himself in a large, bright room which contained a table and several chairs onto one of which he was unceremoniously dumped. The men who had carried him out hesitated until a voice said, 'That will be all, thank you Master Skeres.' Then they went on across the room and left, closing the door behind them. As his head and eyes cleared, he straightened. He was opposite a vaguely familiar man with piercing blue eyes. His missing purse was on the board in front of him with all its contents spread out for inspection.

'Where am I?' He asked. 'Who are you?'

'You are in the Clink prison,' answered the stranger. 'And I am Robert Poley. What happens next lies with me. You can walk free of this place with your property returned and no-one any the wiser. Or you can vanish anonymously into the Bridewell and die quietly. Or you can be taken to the torture chambers in Tower and die screaming.'

Dutton was no fool and he had heard the name Poley before. 'What must I do?' he asked.

'Tell me where Sir Walter sent you and why. In detail, mind. And before you start, I should warn you of two things. First, I know at least part of the answer so I will know if you lie to me. Secondly, the matter you are involved in is treason and will end for some on the block and for others on the gallows.'

Dutton didn't hesitate. He told Poley everything he knew, and in as much detail as he could recall.

'So,' said Poley as the nearest clocks to Salisbury House chimed midnight, 'it is as we suspected. There are at least two letters out there which have passed through Sir Anthony Standen's hands – perhaps directly. There may even be a third carried by this Frenchman La Rensy. If they have, he will have read them unless they are locked or in a cypher Standen cannot decode. I will find out more in due course when he too returns. In the meantime, logic would dictate the following. One of the messages must give details of what Raleigh, Cobham and their friends propose; and, perhaps, whether their plans have any basis in reality. Another one must give another perspective on the relationship between the English and the Scots together with some thoughts on what the increasingly frustrated Catholic priesthood and laity might also be planning. But Master Dutton assures me that although they were both originally sent to Brussels for the attention of Ambassador Aremberg and, ultimately the Archduke, they are now on their way to Valladolid and the court of King Philip. In the hands of this mysterious Yorkshireman who goes by the name of Guy Fawkes.'

'I think it would be wise to warn Master Secretary of the situation,' said Phelippes.

Poley nodded. 'I agree,' he said. 'And he should be warned as soon as possible.'

31

Poley caught up with Cecil at York. He had never seen the city looking so clean and tidy but he had little time to admire it because everyone was just leaving. The king, riding at the front as usual was planning to hunt as much as possible as he continued his journey south past Doncaster and Worksop towards Stamford and Burghley House. But this meant that it was only the younger and fitter of his companions and followers who could get close to him during the day. He was quite capable of covering more than thirty miles in an afternoon and occasionally had to ride back the way he had just come to get to the overnight accommodation that had been prepared for him. Cecil was following in his coach which was not well-adapted to the chase. It was not even very fast, pulled by four horses made fat and lazy by simple inactivity – he rarely left London and the farthest he usually travelled was to his own great house of Theobalds, fifteen miles north of the city. He had arrived late at York, Poley discovered, and had had to bribe Sir George Home with a thousand pounds to gain access to James who was on his way to bed. But, Poley reckoned, setting up a close relationship with Sir George would be as good an investment as cementing his friendship with Lord Kinloss in London – for James trusted both men absolutely.

But if Master Secretary could not keep up with the king in his sluggish coach, he could use it as an office where he could get other work done. It was in the roomy and comfortable conveyance, therefore, that Poley reported the concerns about Sir Walter Raleigh, the letters, the Frenchman La Rensy and the mysterious Yorkshireman, the courier Guy Fawkes, which had brought him hurrying northwards. But Cecil dismissed them at once. He had other priorities he considered more pressing at the moment. 'Leave Raleigh to one side. I want you to contact whoever you have watching Watson,' Cecil ordered. 'He seems to have gone underground since the disappointment of the king's refusal to allow any easement of the recusancy fines. Quite honestly, that is a relief. Any easing of the fines would lead to a disastrous shortfall of much-needed income to the exchequer. Moreover, I believe that Watson presents a far more potent risk than Raleigh or anyone beyond the Channel. And in any case I hear from other sources that Sir Walter is becoming dangerously restive. This may be the very moment to try a little masterly inactivity with him. Especially as I have more personal concerns. Although I have been treated with every courtesy by His Majesty, I fear he is loth to take advice, even from senior and experienced men. Suggestions from the council which I have passed on have managed to put my position at some risk. I am, apparently, Principal Secretary to the Council *for the time-being* according to one of his letters.

'Then there is the fact that we will soon be at Burghley House. My brother is there, arranging everything as best he can – given his responsibilities as Lord of the North, which have already included repairing, staffing and victualling one of the king's overnight resting places which turned out on inspection to be utterly inadequate. And one slip at Burghley, could ruin us both. We grew used to a settled system under Her Majesty but it is seemingly all changed now. Success at court has transformed into a lottery or game of chance.'

Poley, thus dismissed, went about obeying Cecil's instructions immediately but with almost no success. He caught sight of Udall once or twice amongst the hundreds of people milling about but – again – the intelligencer turned away from him and vanished. At last, he managed to find Tom when King James stopped at Worksop. Master Secretary Cecil and his monarch were entertained in Worksop Manor by the Earl of Shrewsbury who was keen to negotiate a release for his cousin the Lady Arbella Stuart from his mother's - her grandmother's - chilly Hardwick Hall. King James happily agreed to her freedom, suggesting that she would be the perfect Mourner in Chief at the old queen's funeral which was still under preparation. Meanwhile, Poley tracked his intelligencers to the Old Ship tavern in the town.

'Watson comes and goes,' admitted Tom as the two of them sat at a secluded table, 'but there's no doubt that he's always close at hand. It seems to Udall and me that he's building a group of like-minded men. Not all recusants – not even all Catholics. An ever-expanding circle of men who have suffered disappointment at the king's hand.'

'You and Udall,' repeated Poley. 'Where is Udall and what is he up to? All I know of him at present is that he is avoiding me.'

'He's keeping clear of me too,' said Tom. 'It's because Watson knows who we are and can recognise us on sight. And I suspect several others in his group would know us as soon as they saw us too. But they don't know Udall.' Tom leaned forward and lowered his voice a little. 'Udall is actually a borderer, from Netherby in the Debatable Lands between England and Scotland. Watson's from Carlisle and that was a bond between them, especially when Udall and he started exchanging tales of the border reivers, the Steel Bonnets as they're called. Udall is pretending to have been one such, fallen on hard times because of King James's actions in the area. Watson, it seems, grew up almost worshiping them. Before he started worshiping his Catholic God.'

'Neither man has a Borders name,' observed Poley, who knew several borderers.

Tom shrugged.

'Get in contact with Udall,' ordered Poley. 'Do it discretely. Tell him I will contact him myself and he can brief me in detail about his discoveries. I will have to think about a suitably secret meeting place, but it will almost certainly be at Burghley House.'

183

True to his passions, James hunted his way south during the next couple of days, overnighting on Good Friday at Belvoir Castle, home of the Earl of Rutland who Poley knew well from his days in Essex's household. Like Southampton, Rutland had paid a high price for his part in Essex's uprising and downfall and had only recently been released from the Tower. Under the same authority, in fact, as that which set Southampton at liberty. Like Southampton, therefore, Rutland was very much in James's favour now. Which, thought the intelligencer, would be something that would stick in Sir Griffin Markham's craw – just as Southampton's release stuck in his longtime enemy Lord Grey de Wilton's. Markham and Rutland had been squabbling over lands and titles for years. It was a plea to support Markham's case against Rutland's that Watson had carried to James for the old soldier. And now, not only was Watson's mission clearly shown to be a failure by the King's proclamation, his indulgent entertainment by Markham's long-time foe made the destruction of his fortune, family and standing plain for all to see. But Poley reckoned that there was little point in setting more eyes on Markham – for Markham was Watson's man and would be unlikely to move without the frustrated, desperate and increasingly dangerous recusant priest. But when would Watson make his move?

In the end, it was not in Burghley House itself that Poley contrived to meet with Udall but in the warm, flame-gold interior of the solid, grey stone inn called the Bull and Swan in Stamford on the evening of Easter Saturday. Burghley House was, in fact, almost large enough to accommodate James, his court and the crowd of hangers-on, and even those unlikely to find shelter there had all gone up in hopes of sharing some of Lord Burghley's bounty. The Bishop of Nottingham stood ready to perform the services on Easter Sunday but the Bishop of Durham was still in King James's train – a circumstance, Poley had discovered, that Cecil was not letting go to waste. If Raleigh, already unsettled by Poley and Frizer's assessment of the worth of Durham House, had known what Master Secretary was up to, he might very well have exploded like the powder mill at Redriffe.

32

'You have to know, Master Poley,' said Udall, 'that they have never all gathered together. Nor have they discussed their plans with me, or indeed vouchsafed any detail of what they mean to do. Watson is friendly enough, with us both being Borders men, but he doesn't trust me. He doesn't trust anyone as far as I can see. Though others may trust in him and rely on him.'

'Very well,' allowed Poley guardedly. 'Tell me what you can.'

Udall paused for a moment, collecting his thoughts, then he began to speak, his voice only a little above a whisper. 'Watson occasionally meets with another lay priest called William. This one is William Clark. It seems that they feel they can rely on raising forty thousand Catholic men if they can find the coin and the leadership.'

'Forty thousand?' Poley didn't know whether to laugh at such a ridiculous number or shiver at such a potent threat. Lord Beauchamp had raised merely a tithe of that number and yet he might have taken Portsmouth.

'It's what they say. But such numbers won't rain down from the Heavens like manna upon the Children of Israel on their way home from Egypt to the Promised Land.'

'Sir Griffin Markham is already involved,' Poley observed. 'We know that. And he's likely to be more so after the king stayed with his enemy Lord Rutland last night. But he could neither raise nor command numbers as vast as those.'

'There's a recently returned recusant exile called Anthony Copley. I have yet to fathom where he fits in. I don't think he's a soldier or a financier either.'

'Copley.' Poley's eyes narrowed. He had met Copley with Watson at the Bishop's Palace in Fulham. So the child-like poet was still in Watson's circle was he? That was information he might well act on later.

'And, though it may be simple chance, Watson has more than once found himself at the same inn as the Reverend George Brooke, Lord Cobham's younger brother.'

'A puritan sheep amongst this recusant flock?' Poley wondered.

'And he's not the only one. Lord Grey de Wilton is sometimes in their company too.'

'Lord Grey is more worrying,' allowed Poley. 'Markham might be a soldier, but he's old and crippled. Lord Grey served with Essex in Ireland and was a cavalry commander of some distinction. Grey could certainly organise a hundred able-bodied men or more to do his will at any time; and lead them well, into the bargain. But forty thousand? I think not.'

'So,' said Udall. 'Does all this add up to a plot solid enough to take to Master Secretary?'

'Not yet,' decided Poley after a moment of reflection. 'I'll need a clearer idea of exactly what they hope to do and when. I would think it highly unlikely they would plan on doing anything tomorrow because it's Easter Sunday and we'll spend a good deal of the day in church listening to not one bishop but two. They are all religious men of one stamp or another and moving against the king when he's at prayer would smack not only of treachery but also blasphemy would it not? I will think over what you have told me and decide the best way forward on Monday.'

But on Monday Poley found that things were moving forward of their own volition.

Lord Burghley planned to follow at Easter a tradition often followed at Christmas – after the holy day itself would come a day of feasting and hunting. The household and its guests rose languidly and partook of little in the way of breakfast, therefore, but at eleven o'clock they were all summoned to the great hall where tables, chairs and benches had been laid out to feast several hundred men and women. The Cecil brothers led the representatives from the English court and Sir George Home, Lord Erskine of Grogar, Captain of King James's Guard and the Earl of Mar, who James had nicknamed Jocky o'Scaitlis led the Scottish court. As host, William Cecil, Lord Burghley, sat at the king's right hand and everyone was then arranged in their degrees all the way down to Robert Poley who only attended because the younger Cecil brother, Master Secretary Robert, demanded it.

The centrepiece of the feast was an entire stag, roasted whole, its antlers silvered and bejewelled, skin replaced prior to serving with fine gold leaf. It was brought in on a wheeled cart and stood before the king as it was stripped of its flesh piece by piece and passed around the guests. There were pies filled with pheasants and prunes, swans, stuffed with larks, the swans' feathers replaced exactly as they had been prior to drawing and roasting, more pies stuffed with fish and fruit, a huge conger eel roasted whole and bursting with preserved greengages, medlars and freshwater elvers. Course after course accompanied by sugared plums, pears poached in sweet wine, candied sweetmeats that James was particularly fond of. All of it stone cold by the time it reached Poley, of course. The point of the food was to flatter the king with its opulence not to be enjoyed in its freshness from the oven; certainly not by those seated below the salt.

The flow of wine was carefully controlled, however, for both the host and his cunning brother were well aware that King James planned on hunting all afternoon. The land belonging to Burghley's neighbour Sir John Harington of Exton had been well stocked with game at Lord Burghley's expense and avenues had been cleared between trees and bushes, through hedges and over the valleys of streams or rivers to facilitate the chase. Even without a great deal of wine having been taken, there was an air of excitement and expectation. Both of the Cecil brothers were positively aglow with relief that everything was going so well.

Sir Walter Raleigh stalked into this scarcely muted hilarity like the wicked witch in a fairy tale. Dressed in black, studded with pearls, erect and square, silver head held high the point of his beard aimed at his monarch like the tip of an arrow, he limped towards the top table, leaving silence to spread behind him like a kind of cloak. When he faced the king, he went down on one knee and lowered his head, fractionally. 'Your Majesty, I have come to request your ear and your signature in the matter of some letters of continuance...'

King James raised his hand. Raleigh stopped speaking. 'Sir Walter, I thought I had made my orders plain to you. You are to remain with the body of the queen until her funeral...'

'Your Majesty, her late Majesty is well-guarded. But there are men here telling lies about me and gaining your trust in despite of me as they do so...'

'You were Captain of the Queen's Guard. It is your duty to guard her, living or dead, as it is Lord Erskine of Grogar's here to guard me as my Captain of the Guard.'

'But, Your Majesty...'

'And when you have guarded your sovereign lady to her final resting place, your duty and your standing will be done. Now stop trying to distract me with letters that hardly need my actual attention at all, let alone my signature and get you back to London and the last of your duties there!'

Raleigh stiffly pulled himself erect, backed away, bowing very slightly, then he turned and limped out of the silent room. Looking at his profile as he passed, Poley thought he had never seen an expression of desperate outrage to match it. Whatever Master Secretary thought, the intelligencer decided, he was going to have to keep the closest watch possible on Sir Walter. For, as long as he remained alive and at liberty, the king would never be safe.

189

33

Although Master Secretary stood no chance of keeping up with King James on horseback, Poley, messenger to the Council, was still the fastest courier between London and Edinburgh by some distance. Given a decent horse, therefore, he could outride any man in the king's court – perhaps in the king's realm. Although Cecil hadn't seen the look on Raleigh's face as he strode out of the great hall, he required little in the way of convincing that his intelligencer should be given the best horse in his brother's stables to keep a close eye on the king for the rest of the day at least. It was a finely-balanced decision, predicated on the belief that if Raleigh had been angered sufficiently to take direct action against the monarch who was seemingly dead-set on ruining him, he probably had neither the strength, the numbers or opportunity to do anything immediately.

Probably; but knowing Raleigh's resourcefulness and rage, by no means certainly.

It seemed best to ensure the king's safety in the immediate future, then to send Poley back to London to set up an even closer watch on Raleigh and his associates once King James was safe in bed tonight. Master Secretary Cecil had been shaken by Raleigh's sudden appearance, however, and he fussed over Poley as they chose his mount in the Burghley House stables. 'You know His Majesty likes to lead the hunt. He will outrun the hounds as often as not if there is a good *view*. So, you will need to stay close to him. But not too close. And you must never get in front of him. And remember, my brother has had the Harington land well stocked and carefully tended so he might well see any game the hounds cause to break cover clearly enough to follow it faster than they can. Last week, I hear, he outran the hounds, caught up with a sizeable doe before anyone else could come near and sent it straight into a bush then he had killed it with that great claymore he wears before the rest of the hunt caught up with him.'

'I will stay close, but not too close, My Lord, I promise. Close enough to watch His Majesty but not to interfere with his pleasure.'

Cecil nodded once and left his intelligencer to his mission.

The first thing Poley did was to select a second horse which was the equal of his, then order the groom to keep an eye on the horses while he sought out Tom, who had also proved himself no mean horseman on the Great North Road. So, when King James mounted up, and cantered off at the head of the hunt, the two intelligencers were the only men following him who sat astride stronger horses than his. Even so, Poley and his young companion kept back, preferring to become lost in the crowd of horsemen following the huntsmen and their hounds. It took almost no time to reach Sir John Harington's well-stocked acres. As the hunters reined in their impatient horses, waiting for the huntsmen, the kennel men and the whippers-in to organise the excited hounds into a tight group, Poley glanced around uneasily. The hounds' excitement was spreading amongst the mounted men and women. Everyone was keen to be off but it seemed to the intelligencer that they were almost spoilt for choice. In his enthusiasm to impress the king, Lord Burghley had overstocked the land. There were more scents than the hounds could handle – one group straining to go one way, another in the opposite direction and a third apparently unable to make up their canine minds. In the meantime, King James, Sir John Harington, Lord Burghley, the senior men of the Scottish court, Sir John Carey and the English hopefuls were presented with an aspect of rolling hills, lightly forested. There were avenues cleared in the undergrowth leading into promising dells and clearings, the whole place alive with game.

'Whit's the matter wi'ye?' bellowed James at last. 'Loose yer hounds, mon!'

And on his word the hunt began.

At first there seemed to be no order. The hounds took the lead eagerly and loudly, barking and baying. The whippers-in rode beside them, trying to keep them in one focussed group. By default, the hunters, led by the king, had to stay behind them. To begin with, they went thundering, whooping and cheering with excitement, over a broad field. But after a few hectic moments, the lightly forested woodland closed around them and the trees acted as whippers-in to make the horsemen gather closer like the dogs. It took all of Poley's considerable skill to place himself close behind the front rank of this group, where he could literally watch the king's back. And it impressed him that Tom was able to do the same.

As the afternoon flashed past, the hounds started hares, foxes and roe deer. The deer they started were hunted to the kill and would provide later feasts. But Lord Burghley had promised James at great red deer stag which had been especially transported down from his highland home. It was not until late in the afternoon that the hounds at last started this magnificent creature. The numbers behind King James had thinned out considerably, horses exhausted by over-enthusiastic riders spurring them on too early, especially as, by Poley's estimation, they must have covered more than twenty miles following one scent after another. Even the hounds were beginning to flag. But King James, Lord Burghley, Sir Robert Carey and several Scottish lords had stayed the pace. Abruptly, Poley found Tom riding close beside him – close enough to put both of their knees at risk of being crushed against each other. 'Do you feel it?' called Tom. 'The sensation that we are being watched?'

'We're with the king, answered Poley breathlessly. 'Of course we're being watched.'

'No! That's not what I meant…'

Tom's words were cut off by an enormous cacophony. Hounds howled, huntsmen bellowed, hunters cheered. The great red deer stag broke cover and flew away like the wind down one of the avenues that had been cleared through the woodland. King James gave a great animal roar of excitement and drove his spurs into the heaving ribs of his tiring horse. The gallant beast galloped off in hot pursuit, its rider leaning forward, his chest low over its withers, the point of his beard aimed at his quarry every bit as fiercely as Raleigh's had been aimed at him earlier. The courtiers gathered in behind, their mounts labouring painfully. Poley and Tom easily overtook them for they were riding the strongest horses. In his excitement and bloodlust, King James rode the hounds down. Most of them leaped nimbly clear of his thundering hooves but one or two were struck and thrown aside, yelping. At least that gave Tom and Poley a clear path to stay close behind their exulting monarch. And, it seemed, James had good reason to exult. The avenue down which the great stag was running so swiftly might have been lengthy but it was arrow-straight, walled on either side by undergrowth between tall tree-trunks, and it was closed off at the far end by a solid-looking hedge. It seemed as though the king's panicked quarry had nowhere to go. Once it reached the end of the avenue it would be trapped.

But then, as the stag and the three closest behind it neared the hedge, Poley saw that what had appeared to be a solid barrier in fact had an opening in it. A gap. Not large by any means, but wide enough to allow one terrified deer a chance of escape. James clearly saw it too, and utterly gripped by the thrill of the chase, he spurred his tired horse to one last great effort. It was not quite enough. The stag threw itself at the opening, leaping upward as well as forward, clearing the gap with one single, elegant bound. The king did not slow. Rather, he drove his spurs into his horse's furrowed flanks once more and charged through the gap hard on the stag's heels. But the horse stumbled. Its forelegs folded, its head

193

went down. James was thrown bodily out of the saddle to crash onto the ground with boneshaking force. Poley and Tom were just able to rein their mounts to a plunging standstill. Then Poley was out of the saddle and pushing through the gap. King James was lying face down on the grass, as still as a statue. Or a corpse, thought Poley grimly. There was something clearly amiss with him. His shoulders no longer matched. Where they had been square, supporting the column of the neck and the great ball of the head, the left now sagged away at a slight angle. It was by no means an acute angle, but it was obvious and it gave the breathless intelligencer the clearest possible impression that King James's neck must be badly broken. Which explained why he was lying there like a dead man.

34

'Did you see that?' demanded Tom, calling Poley out of his momentary stasis.

'No,' he answered as he strode forward. 'What?' as he went down on his knees beside the king.

'There was someone there,' answered Tom. 'I only caught a glimpse of a black cloak. But I'm certain there was someone nearby.' He looked around suspiciously. 'They've gone now.'

Poley leaned forward and placed his hand gently on the royal shoulder. The square one which seemed undamaged. Though he had to reach across that broken neck to do so. Then he stopped, suddenly finding himself at a loss as to what he should do next.

'What has happened here?' demanded a familiar voice. Poley looked up to see Master Secretary's elder brother Lord Burghley with Sir Robert Carey at his shoulder.

'The king has been thrown, My Lord,' he answered as Burghley led the rest of King James's companions through the gap in the hedge, alerted by Tom and Poley's riderless horses to stop and dismount themselves. There was a riot of snarls and yelps from beyond the hedge as the whippers-in stopped the hounds from coming through to investigate as well. In the far distance up ahead, the red stag vanished over the crest of a low hill.

'Is he hurt?' demanded the Earl of Mar.

'I do not know, My Lord...'

'Herries!' called Mar. 'Doctor Herries to the King!'

The gathering group parted and Dr Herries strode through. An instant later he had joined Poley who was still kneeling beside the fallen monarch. 'Help me turn him over,' ordered the doctor. Poley and he gently rolled the king onto his back.

James's face was white, his eyes were closed and he did not seem to be breathing. 'Is His Majesty living?' asked Lord Burghley, his voice shaking with the horror of a host responsible for the death of such a guest as this. His mind filled, no doubt, with visions of the utter ruination of himself, his brother and the entire Cecil clan; wiped out as utterly as the Gowries.

'You'd think his neck was broken, would you not?' asked Herries, showing a simply awe-inspiring lack of tact. 'But it's not. By the grace of God, it's only his shoulder. That's all. There'll be no hunting and indeed precious little horse-riding until it's healed.'

And as he reached this conclusion the royal eyelids flickered and parted. James began to look around, clearly wondering where he was and what had happened to him. Then he flinched as memory returned. And pain.

Tom and Poley were the last to leave the scene of the accident, Poley held back by Tom's silent gesture for him to remain. 'While you were looking to the king,' said the young intelligencer when they were alone at last, 'I looked to his horse which was lucky not to have broken its legs when it stumbled. And, see what I found.' He held up a length of twine. He took both ends and pulled them – the twine seemed almost unbreakable. 'This was wrapped around the horse's forehoof. I'd lay odds it was strung across that gap in the hedge on purpose, perhaps by whoever it was I saw vanishing away. It's what brought the poor beast down and nearly killed the king. I saw the same thing done to Sir Robert Carey on his way to Edinburgh with the ring. I'm told it's an old reiver's trick, popular amongst the Steel Bonnets of the Debateable Lands along the Scottish Borders.'

'You know what you're saying, don't you?' said Poley quietly. 'One man was set on slowing or stopping Carey so he could get to the king with news of the old queen's death first. The same man who has had his own dreams, hopes and reputation destroyed by the king's proclamation. The man

Udall befriended because they are both men born of the Debatable Lands. A man who worshipped the Steel Bonnets before he began to worship his Catholic God. The reverend William Watson.'

'He's vanished,' said Udall, later that evening at a secluded table in the Bull and Swan. 'One moment I knew where he was and the next, he was gone.'

'Hardly surprisingly if he laid the trap that almost killed the king,' said Tom.

'I'd lay odds he'd be hung drawn and quartered like Essex's men Gelly Meyrick and Henry Cuffe,' said Poley. 'Whether or not he chose to plead that he could not be guilty of high treason while the king was not yet enthroned or crowned, as I hear Sir Walter may have argued. Sir Francis Bacon also.'

'Aye,' agreed Udall. 'Watson's a dead man walking without a doubt. So might Sir Walter be, for all I know.'

'And such men are very dangerous so long as they remain alive and at liberty,' Poley observed. There was a brief silence. Then Poley said, 'Will, I want you to find Watson and bring him to me if you can. I'll be at Salisbury House or my lodgings – or word of my whereabouts will have been left there. Tom, you and I will return to London first thing tomorrow. No matter where Watson is or what Raleigh is planning, the king is safe for the time-being. I want you to track down Anthony Copley. I will keep close eyes on Sir Walter.' He took a deep breath. 'It appears we are facing two potent plots to harm the king,' he said. 'But I do not want to bring them to Master Secretary's notice until we have a deal more proof than two pieces of twine and a vague suspicion.'

35

Lady Janet Percy was near exploding with frustration. She herself was confined to Essex House by her cousin the Earl of Northumberland's notions of propriety and each time she sent her servant Agnes out with a message for Poley, the reply was always the same: Poley could not be reached. He was either with the king or carrying vital messages between His Majesty and his Privy Council. In the meantime, already heavy with dangerous knowledge, she took every opportunity she could to add to her deadly store. But in this endeavour also she was frustrated. Cousin Henry still met with Sir Walter Raleigh, Lord Cobham, Sir George Brooke his brother, the Earl of Southampton and a widening circle of malcontents, but they had moved their meetings to Raleigh's Durham House further along the Strand or Southampton's Drury House on Wych Street. It did not occur to her that they began to do this because they were becoming suspicious of her attempts to overhear their planning. However, she found the movement to Drury House particularly unsettling because it was where much of the plotting that led to the fatal Essex revolt had been done. And she had had a hand in frustrating that particular episode, she and Robert Poley. Also unsettling was the fact that Lord Grey had joined them – for it was the fight between Grey and Southampton in the Strand that had set the match to the fuse that caused the Essex plot to explode in the end.

The names of the men who met – and where they did so – were common gossip amongst the Essex House servants. But only Lady Janet had any real knowledge of what they were discussing, motivated, she assumed by the Gowrie plot to kidnap King James which she as a northerner knew all about. They were no doubt continuing to debate the best way to capture the king and make him guarantee their positions, rights and privileges or watch them put the Lady Arbella Stuart or even the Infanta on the throne in his stead.

But Lady Janet was by no means the only player bursting with frustration in this particular game. Poley's game. Sir George Brooke had convinced himself that despite the old queen's promise, the position he coveted at St Cross Hospital at Winchester would be awarded to someone else; to someone Scottish like as not. But, unlike Will Udall, Brooke did know where William Watson could be found.

The pair of them met at The Hand and Heart inn in Peterborough on the road south from Burghley on the afternoon after the king's riding accident. The ultimate plan was for Watson to head west into Wales, but the churchman was determined to try to enact his plot one more time before he cut and ran. In the mean time he admitted to his companion precisely what he had done – and come so close to doing – on the previous afternoon.

'You did what?' demanded Brooke, caught between horror and admiration for what the fellow churchman had dared. 'I thought the king simply fell when his horse stumbled.'

'It's an old reivers' trick,' said Watson. 'And as chance would have it, easy enough to do. I'd been following them, keeping clear and well-hidden when the stag broke cover. There was a long straight run with only one way out for the stag and, therefore for those hunting it. King James always has to lead the pack so I was certain he would be first through the gap. I contrived to get there ahead of him with time in hand to tie my twine across the opening. It was even more certain to succeed than the trap I laid for Sir Robert Carey that let me get to Edinburgh first with news of the old queen's death. Much good that did me. Or Sir Griffin Markham who paid my way there.' His face folded into a thunderous frown, which served to emphasis his fearsome squint.

'They say he was lucky to escape with a broken shoulder instead of a broken neck,' persisted Brooke as he came to terms with what Watson had almost achieved with his simple Border Reivers' trick.

Watson shrugged. 'So all I have contrived in the end is to place the king into even securer safety, walled about with doctors as well as with Scottish and English lords and his guards.'

'But then,' persisted Brooke, continuing despite Watson's depressing observation, 'he would have been succeeded by his son Prince Henry and the men in power would have remained in power despite everything.'

Watson nodded in silent agreement.

'What will you do now?' asked Brooke.

'Seek help for one last attempt. At Theobalds, I think. The king will be there within the week and all the court with him. They should have arrived by the first of May which is the next collar day. Everyone with any position at court will be wearing their chains of office and so they will all be easy to spot and capture. Or to kill should the need arise. We should be able to take the king with only a hundred men or so if they are willing and quick-witted. It is particularly tempting, I must admit – the king was so nearly killed while staying with one Cecil; with the grace of God, we can capture him while he is at the house of the other Cecil. The destruction of the entire grasping and ungodly dynasty – what do they call it? The *Regnum Cecilianum*? The rule of the Cecils would be over, whatever else transpired. There are fifty Jesuits to hand, maybe more. I will see whether I can rouse them to help us. I will approach Persons by letter or, perhaps, Garnet man to man.'

'And there is Lord Grey de Wilton,' added Brooke. 'He is associated with Raleigh and my brother. I believe he can rouse a hundred men to do his bidding. I will be in London tomorrow and I will sound him out. At Theobalds House you say, on May Day.'

'Very well. Look for me at The Black Prince in Waltham Cross from the end of the month. If I'm not there, I will have left word where I can be found.'

And so the two conspirators parted.

The next day found Sir George Brooke not only in London but walking purposefully along Wych Street. The afternoon was overcast, cold and drizzly but Brooke paid no more attention to the weather than he did to the other pedestrians he was pushing past with thoughtless rudeness. He was certain now that his dream of the St Cross Hospital in Winchester was dead and his rage against the man who had killed it knew no bounds, whether he be king or not. Enquiries at Lord Cobham's London address had garnered the information that his Lordship was at Drury House, visiting the Earl of Southampton.

The servants guarding the door to Drury House recognised Sir George and conducted him to the master's study where he found not only his brother Lord Cobham and the Earl of Southampton, but Sir Walter Raleigh and Lord Grey de Wilton. Sir George, frankly was finding it hard to come to terms with this new friendship between Southampton and Grey de Wilton who had been sworn enemies for years. But, he supposed, necessity made strange bedfellows.

It seemed that he had interrupted a heated conversation, but his news gave him license. 'Well, brother George,' said Cobham, 'What brings you in search of me?'

'You know, I suppose, that James Stuart very nearly had his neck broken hunting at Burghley?' In this particular group, Sir George was careful not to call James Stuart King James.

'*Nearly*,' said Sir Walter. 'There's the rub.' His tone was dripping with a bitterness that Sir George had not heard before. He glanced at his brother, eyebrows raised in a silent question, Raleigh saw the gesture and gave the answer, his voice shaking with barely-suppressed outrage. 'I am to relinquish Durham House on James Stuart's word. It is to be returned to the Bishop of Durham until Stuart decides who is to benefit from my eviction! I suspect it will be Cecil, for his creature Poley paid me a visit some time since, soon after the murder of my book keeper Magnall, while Dutton his replacement was still in Brussels.'

'Sir Walter has spent more than twenty thousand pounds renovating the place,' said Cobham, his normally cheery tone sad and sympathetic. 'All to benefit someone else...'

'I have taken the matter to law of course,' added Raleigh. 'But if James Stuart is ever crowned, then his will *becomes* the law and I am ruined.'

'The priest Watson claims that he tripped Stuart's horse by some border reivers' trick in hopes of killing him,' said Sir George. 'But that would only have meant the crown passing to Henry Stuart his son.'

'We would need to kill James Stuart,' spat Raleigh, 'and his wife and all their cubs if the succession is to pass to the Lady Arbella or the Infanta uncontested.'

'But in the meantime, Watson and his associate Clark, hoping to get support from the Jesuits, plan to approach the Jesuit leader Henry Garnet for help...'

'They have already contacted me in a secret note,' said Grey. 'They want a meeting, apparently to ask if I am able or willing to raise a thousand men and be ready to march on Theobalds as soon as James Stuart arrives there. The first of May is the deadline, I believe, for it is the next collar day.'

'Are you committed to them?' demanded Raleigh.

'No. I am considering what best to do,' Grey admitted. 'May Day is fearfully close at hand.'

'And all they plan is to do what the Gowries attempted...'

'Prompted by Sir Griffin Markham,' inserted Sir George.

'To kidnap him at Theobalds, take him to a safe place – the Tower, like as not – and demand that he do their bidding,' Raleigh continued fiercely. 'It is madness. Even if he agrees when under duress, he will surely undo everything once more the instant he is released! Stay well clear of their mad scheme, my Lord Grey.'

'Especially,' added Southampton, 'as I hear the hurts suffered by James Stuart at his accident – whether or not it was Watson's doing – has slowed his progress southward. He will never be at Theobalds by May the first. He may have reached Standen, perhaps even Broxbourne. But never Theobalds. Not now that he is travelling by coach rather than on horseback.'

'And the next collar day after the first of May is in June,' persisted Raleigh, for he could see Lord Grey's jaw setting. The temperamental peer did not like being told what to do. Which lay at the foundation of his war with Southampton of course. 'It is on St John the Baptist's Day on the twenty-fourth of June. Only God knows where he will be then. God and Master Secretary. You had much better join with us, though we cannot be ready as early as May Day.'

'Our letters to Princely Count Aremberg have received a response,' said Cobham, brightening up. 'He has sent our request onwards to King Philip in Valladolid and we have every expectation of a positive outcome there. We plan to send Sir Walter's man Dutton back to Brussels with one final message. To wit that as soon as Her Majesty's funeral is done, I will personally travel post haste to Brussels if I can get a letter of passage from the council. I am assured King Philip has promised six hundred thousand crowns via the Count's good offices. I myself will bring the money back via Jersey…'

'…where I hold the Governorship,' added Raleigh, '…for the time-being at least. So we must not be laggard in the business. Especially of King Philip is actually ready to disburse such a vast sum.'

'…then Raleigh and I will use the money – and your good offices, my Lord Grey – to add to the men you can raise with more men of minds like ours or, indeed, mercenaries. Wherever James Stuart may be, we will strike him there, collar day or no. But our watch word must be *silence*. You all saw how swiftly Master Secretary and his creature Poley reacted when they heard Lord Beauchamp was planning to take action at Portsmouth...'

36

Agnes came into Lady Janet Percy's privy chamber in Essex House carrying a black dress. Janet looked at the garment, her heart quickening. 'Lord Henry wishes a word,' said Agnes. 'And I'm sure you can guess what about.'

'Where is he?'

'In the library.' Agnes' answer made Janet's heart pound faster still. It was the library window she listened at to overhear her cousin's treasonous conversation with his friends and fellow conspirators; so long ago now it almost seemed like weeks. She associated the place with deadly danger still. But, as usual when she found something frightening her, she raised her chin and allowed a little steely resolve to seep into her deceptively gentle eyes. She sped down the stairs and almost ran along the passage leading to the library door.

'Come!' he ordered in answer to her firm knock.

'You wished to see me, My Lord?' she said as she entered. She turned to close the door behind her breathing a sigh of relief she did not want Lord Henry to see. The pair of them were alone in the room. She had for a moment feared she would be confronted by Raleigh, Cobham, Southampton, Grey de Wilton and the rest. When she turned once more, her expression was one of innocent enquiry.

'I wish the women of Essex House to be represented at her late Majesty's funeral,' he said. 'The Lady Lettice will not attend. Queen Elizabeth caused both her husband and her son to be beheaded and, no matter how good the reason the old queen might have had, Lady Lettice cannot forgive her, living or dead. She will attend the coronation of King James, in whose eyes both the Earl of Essex and Sir Charles Blount are martyrs to the cause of his succession. That is the attitude also taken by my wife - the Lady Dorothy Devereux as was - the Earl of Essex's sister.'

'I see,' nodded Lady Janet sympathetically.

'The situation is further complicated by the fact that Lady Arbella Stuart, though released from Hardwick Hall now, steadfastly refuses to act as chief mourner.'

'I believe she feels that, as the queen refused her access to court while she lived,' observed Lady Janet, 'Lady Arbella will not pretend to mourn her now she is dead.'

'That is true. But it also means that the post of chief mourner must now fall upon the wife of Sir Thomas Gorges, who is in her own right the Marchioness of Northampton.'

'The marchioness is the country's senior female aristocrat under Lady Arbella,' nodded Lady Janet. 'She often deputised for Her Majesty towards the end. She was even granted possession of Sheen House with Sir Thomas so they could serve the court in Richmond Palace which is close by.'

'But the point is, I believe, that the Marchioness is Swedish by birth. Helena Snakenbourg as was,' said Lord Henry. 'Master Secretary, who has his fingers in this as he has them in everything, has stipulated that there be ladies of clearly English birth and lineage in attendance as well. And, although you were banished on Her Majesty's whim, you have been, have you not, one of the senior Ladies of the Privy Chamber.'

'I have,' Lady Janet lowered her gaze and set her face in a mournful expression.

'And, I am sure you would wish to mourn your late sovereign with the rest and attend her funeral in consequence.'

'I would,' she said. But her mind was full of exultant thoughts which her downcast gaze concealed: *I would indeed for it may chance that I can see Poley there. Talk to him. Touch his hand, perhaps...* He heart gave yet another leap at the notion.

Someone else keen to talk with Poley – and happy to use the queen's fast-approaching funeral as cover for the meeting if needs-be - was Will Udall. His close eye on Watson had at last paid off. Udall finally caught up with his quarry at Peterborough and contrived to win the increasingly desperate prelate's confidence. Of necessity as far as Watson was concerned, for time was running out and his scheme to kidnap the incumbent king was not making commensurate progress. Was making hardly any progress at all, in fact. Consequently, Udall had managed to work his way into several crucial meetings that Watson had held with men whose support he wished to confirm. The first of these was with Henry Garnet, leader of the Jesuits, fifty of whom Watson hoped would form an important part of his forces when his plan went into action. It was just over thirty miles from Peterborough to Wisbech in the Fen Country where Garnet was. The two men arrived there late on the afternoon of the Tuesday after Easter. Garnet seemed to Udall most unwilling even to see Watson, but at last he grudgingly agreed to an audience. The meeting was formal and stilted. The men clearly did not like each-other or approve of each-others' approach to the problems James's tactics in respect of the recusants was causing. On Garnet's side, his reticence was further strengthened by his distrust of Watson's companion – something which Udall, planning to betray them both, wryly if silently acknowledged to be wise. But the conclusion would have been the same no matter whether Udall had been there or not. 'Brother William,' said Garnet in the end, 'I cannot support your approach or approve your actions. I see in this proposed violence against the royal person of King James – whether he be crowned or not – simply yet another rod which will be used to scourge our Catholic backs. It is a wild scheme with little or no prospect of success. The only certainty I can see about it as I say is the further damage it will do to Mother Church here in England and those poor, suffering, thousands who still seek to follow her dictates in spite of everything.'

And so Watson and Udall were dismissed to spend an extremely uncomfortable night at a nearby inn situated on the border between Deeping Fen and Great Fen that proved almost as damp and featureless as the fenland with which it was surrounded.

The next day, while the king was still slowly recovering, Udall and Watson returned to Peterborough, then rode a little more than thirty miles in the opposite direction to Beskwood, the high, hilly home of Sir Griffin Markham which stood on the outskirts of Sherwood Forest. Udall was well aware that Poley knew it was Sir Griffin who had financed Watson's journey to Edinburgh but now, in the face of that mission's total failure, the two men were willing – keen in fact – to push matters further. Their welcome at Beskwood was the exact opposite to their welcome at Wisbech. Sir Griffin and his brothers Charles and Thomas were clearly pleased to see Watson and keen for him to lead a mass that evening. The three men were also happy to place much more belief in Watson's scheme and over a dinner of paschal lamb, they discussed how best to make Watson's plans a reality. 'I have been discussing matters with George Brooke,' Sir Griffin revealed. 'And he believes both his brother Lord Cobham and Lord Grey de Wilton would be happy to assist. Lord Cobham plans to raise money from Spain. He will do so in person if the council agrees to grant him letters of passage. But Lord Grey de Wilton is a fine soldier. I served with him and respect him. He should be able to raise a hundred men maybe more. Enough to take Theobalds House and hold the king while our downtrodden Catholic gentlemen in their thousands rise in support of our cause. I have heard the figure of forty thousand men for certain sure…'

37

As Udall and Watson rode back towards Peterborough and the Great North Road next morning, Watson said, 'I have approached Lord Grey by secret letter and believe he is willing to meet me. Although he is of the Protestant faith, he has been so badly dealt-with by King James and his followers that he is almost desperate enough to help us. And as Sir Griffin observed, he is an experienced soldier, a fine leader, and in a position to raise an army of one hundred men or more. Let us see whether we can convince him.'

Watson continued, sometime later as the two men approached Lord Grey's temporary lodgings in Buckden near Buckden Palace – taken in hopes that the king might break his journey at the great old building, 'He comes from a line of warlike soldiers. It was his father who oversaw the Siege of Smerwick as Lord Lieutenant of Ireland and who ordered Sir Walter Raleigh in turn to oversee the massacre of the garrison when they surrendered, which he did, with Captain Macworth. I believe the son to be equally ruthless, which in Ireland was a terrible thing but which may serve us better here.'

The two men were shown into Lord Grey's private room and Udall was immediately struck by Grey's demeanour. He was a big, square man, sporting a thick, square-cut beard. His aspect should have been decisive and commanding. From what little Udall knew of the man, he had served against the Great Armada with Howard and Drake, had participated in the Islands Voyage with Essex and Raleigh, then followed Essex into Ireland as colonel in command of a regiment of horse. But Grey had tried to ride astride two very different horses – and he fell out with Essex when he refused to break away from Robert Cecil to whom he stood indebted. From then on, he was Essex's enemy and it was he who sparked Essex's rebellion by attacking the Earl of Southampton in the Strand. All of this should have squared his shoulders, thought Udall, and straightened his spine. And yet despite his physical presence, Lord Grey seemed anything but commanding at the moment. He was clearly in two minds about the wisdom of entertaining Watson and his plans. And yet, he desperately wished to believe those plans could work.

'It depends on timing and the Grace of God, My Lord,' Watson was explaining. 'We believe James Stuart will be at Theobalds by May Day and will be welcomed there by almost the entire court, all in their chains and badges of office, for May Day is a collar day. Sir Griffin Markham and his brothers will lead one contingent and, if you agree, you will lead another. I have approached Garnet the Jesuit and he has promised fifty warrior priests from the Church Militant. We will easily overpower Theobalds House and capture the would-be king. We will then take him to the Tower and hold him there until he has acceded to our demands. We will all be made men, and Mother Church will once again stand tall within the realm.'

'You paint a persuasive picture, Master Watson,' said Lord Grey.

Much of which is wishful thinking, mixed with a little over-exaggeration and several outright lies, thought Udall. Under any other circumstances he would be warning Lord Grey to steer well clear of Watson before he found himself wrecked on the reefs of the churchman's impossible dreams. But protecting Lord Grey from Watson – or indeed from himself – was no part of the intelligencer's mission. So, he noted carefully what was said in the rest of the conversation and got ready to pass it all to Poley at the earliest possible moment.

Sir Anthony Standen stood on the deck of the 5-gun pinnace *Sunne*, which was plying between Calais and Dover carrying passengers and a little freight. Standen himself was freighted with a range of information which he planned to sell to Poley, ultimately for the attention of Master Secretary Cecil and perhaps the king – should James Stuart ever attain the English crown and survive long enough to enjoy it. Standen was particularly well placed to assess these probabilities. His sojourn in Brussels, which had come to an end less than a week ago, had proved even more useful than he had hoped. After passing the letters sent by Raleigh and Cobham and those of the mysterious Frenchman La Rensy to Guy Fawkes for onward transmission to the court of Philip the Third at Valladolid, Standen busied himself around the edges of Count Aremberg's circle, in the lively expectation that Aremberg would be sent to London to congratulate King James on his accession, as he had been sent to Paris to congratulate Henri the Fourth. But the count was growing old and suffering from gout. He had no intention of moving until directly ordered to do so and then in the swiftest, most comfortable manner his various ailments allowed.

Standen was on the point of giving up and going home when Fawkes reappeared with news that the mercenary Yorkshireman found particularly distressing. The soldier's face, with its wide eyes, straight nose and square chin beneath a square-cut beard, looked unaccustomedly troubled as he and Standen discussed his mission to the Spanish court over a bottle of wine in Standen's favourite tavern. 'King Philip works hard to appear inscrutable and unfathomable, particularly when dealing with international matters,' said Fawkes. 'But he seems to have no ready coin for wild schemes and no intention of trying to raise such a vast sum as that suggested in the letters I took to Valladolid.' Fawkes, shook his head sadly.

'No ready money? But that's impossible!' said Standen, shocked.

'It seems that the Spanish treasury never really recovered from the loss of the Great Armada in eighty-eight,' explained Fawkes dully. 'And King Philip the Second's continuing invasion efforts, lesser armadas and of course the wars in the

211

Low Countries and Ireland have never allowed the exchequer to recover; indeed, they have just plunged the country deeper into debt.'

'But the gold of the Indies…'

'Too much of it has been pirated by English privateers like Drake, Hawkins, William Piers. Not enough has ever gotten through to mend matters. And then…'

'Then what?' Standen was simply stunned; his view of Spanish power upended.

'Valladolid itself.' Fawkes glanced around guiltily, afraid that he was being overheard. He pulled his hat even lower over his eyes.

'What about it?' asked Standen, fearing more undreamed-of revelations.

'It seems that King Philip was convinced to move his court there by his advisor the Duke of Lema. But just before the court actually moved, the duke and his associates bought up all the suitable buildings in Valladolid themselves and then charged the court extortionate prices to use them. The current gossip is that King Philip is thinking of moving lock, stock and barrel back to Cadiz – and so Lema and his friends are busily buying up all the property they can lay their hands on there as well. They are coming close to ruining Philip from what I can work out.'

'I have never heard of such a thing!' It was Standen's turn to shake his head in disbelief.

'Nor have I,' admitted Fawkes. 'But the upshot is that King Philip is happier to receive peace overtures from James Stuart than he is to receive pleas for help and coin from Catholic gentlemen in England.' He took a deep breath, clearly trying to control his anger at the situation. Without much success as far as Standen could see. Then, 'If King James is to be removed, then it seems we must somehow find a way to do it ourselves, with no more support from Spain!'

38

Poley had never seen Master Secretary in such a state. Cecil was becoming increasingly convinced that the incumbent monarch was set on governing by whim, and that included appointing advisors and awarding positions and the properties attendant upon them. The fact that he hoped to benefit from this new way of doing things by getting hold of Durham House simply compounded his worries. The accident at Burghley House had put the future of the Cecils very much in question. It was ironic, the intelligencer thought, that the man who had worked so cunningly to ensure the downfall of Walter Raleigh as his rival, should now be fearful of following his victim down into obscurity and pauperhood. Or even, Heaven forefend, into the Tower. Master Secretary spread himself as thin as young ice on a still pond – dancing attendance on the king, trying to ensure the funeral of the queen went well and, most of all, that Theobalds would be ready to dazzle James so much that he would forget Burghley House and his nearly-broken neck. The upshot of all this was that Poley handled almost all of Cecil's communications, sending on for Master Secretary's attention only letters that had been locked, encoded in a manner that even Phelippes could not decipher and those bearing the seals of ambassadors currently in place – like the Frenchman de Beaumont or the Venetian Scaramelli - or those imminently expected like the French ambassador the Marquis de Rosni or the Count of Aremberg.

So it was that the Jesuit Father Garnet's letter arrived on Poley's desk late in the afternoon on the eve of the funeral and, as it was neither locked or sealed with a remarkable seal, Poley opened it. 'What is it?' asked Phelippes, seeing the look on Poley's face as he read the contents.

'The Jesuits are stabbing Watson in the back,' said Poley.

'That's as close as he'll ever come to playing Caesar,' observed Phelippes. 'How so?'

'This letter, over Garnet's signature reveals Watson's plan in some detail. He proposes to strike against the king at Theobalds on the first of May, which is a collar day, because all the officers of the court will make themselves obvious by wearing their chains and badges of office. That is important, it seems because he wishes to add several senior advisors to the list of men he wants in the Tower with the king. He relies upon the fifty Jesuits hidden hereabout, including those held under light guard at Wisbech, he also has hopes of whatever support can be raised by Sir Griffin Markham and his brothers, and he believes he can count on an army of one hundred or so commanded by Lord Grey de Wilton, who apparently remains non-committal, and prays for the forty-thousand stout Catholic gentlemen ready to rise when they see a chance for freedom of worship.'

'We had better take this straight to Master Secretary!' said Phelippes, shaken.

'Not so hasty, Thomas. Think! May Day is three days off. The queen is not yet buried. Lord Grey - at least – must attend the funeral tomorrow. How he will then gather a hundred men by May the first is a matter of some conjecture. Further, we know – as Watson and Garnet apparently do not yet know – that the royal progress has slowed since the king's accident. There is no chance he will be at Theobalds by the first of May. He is more likely to be at Standon, resting in the great house owned by the Sadler family who stood such good guard over his mother the Queen of Scots.'

'So….' Queried Phelippes.

'So, it is a question of logistics and battle-planning is it not? Would they be better to cobble together their forces at such short notice and try to strike at Standon as best they can on May the first. Or should they continue to focus on Theobalds, lay their plans with more time and care, and wait for the king to arrive in a week or so, collar day or no? Especially, now I think of it, that he may be at Standon overnight before moving on to Broxbourne as planned, but once he arrives at Theobalds he will stay there for several days.'

'Still, a finely-balanced problem.'

'Perhaps. Perhaps not. For some of the men associated with Watson have a further agenda, do they not? Markham, Grey – if he is truly with them – George Brooke... All wish to see themselves rise. But, almost as fiercely, they wish to see Master Secretary fall. The accident at Burghley has put the Cecils at risk. One further blow – at Theobalds – and their entire fortune will collapse. The so-called *Regnum Cecilianum* – rule by the Cecils – will be utterly destroyed. Master Secretary sees this. Sees it and fears it.'

'So,' said Phelippes. 'It will be Theobalds whenever the king gets there, perhaps in as much as a week's time.'

'And,' said Poley, unconsciously prophetic, 'we may find out more at the funeral tomorrow.'

39

Despite the fact that Queen Elizabeth had given orders that her corpse should not be disembowelled and embalmed until King James had succeeded her, and Master Secretary had obeyed her wishes until her lead-lined coffin had exploded open to release a cloud of noxious gasses, the queen's body was now lying, securely if clumsily shrouded, in its ceremonial casket. Her successor, as yet uncrowned, lingered in Huntingdon. The casket was topped by a carving of the queen as she had been in life with her hands and face painted youthful pink. The coffin lay on a carriage draped in black velvet and pulled by four black-accoutred horses. The carriage moved at the heart of a great procession that wound its way slowly and sadly from Whitehall Palace to Westminster Abbey. The roads were lined with thousands who had come to see history made and dynasties change. Many were sad to see the end of the Tudors and feared that the arrival of the Stuarts would make their lives no better. Some, indeed, were of the strong opinion that the old queen's final years had been marked by the rise to power of too many grasping men who sought their own good before that of their senile sovereign or her suffering people. Personified, indeed epitomised, by the *Regnum Cecilianum*. And that a gang of heathen Scotsmen were unlikely to do more than add more greedy peers seeking to gouge what good they could from the suffering poor. It was by no means a universally fond farewell despite the weeping and wailing, thought Robert Poley as he walked along the roadside level with the carriage, watching the proceedings and listening to the gossip.

Like everyone else nearby Poley was in black. Too many people knew him as Master Secretary's man for there to be any doubt about his costume. The man and his attire reflected on the master and his standing. He had watched the black-clad women with their black head-dresses and veils lead the parade out of the palace, followed by the first squad of men from the household. Banners of coats-of-arms, glittering and almost gaudy above and against the river of sable were mingled with them and were followed in turn by two horses caparisoned with the arms of England and France to which Elizabeth had laid claim in life – as was the tradition more than the accomplished conquest. These were followed by the arms of the Duchy of Cornwall, the Principality of Wales and the Kingdom of Ireland all carried by senior peers. Master Secretary was there, somewhere amongst the aristocratic crush. The boys of the Chapel Royal were close behind them, singing soft dirges.

Then came the hearse with the coffin topped by the effigy of Elizabeth, crowned, clutching orb and sceptre, and in the robes she habitually wore to Parliament, with which Poley was fighting to keep level. Behind it walked the erect figure of the Marchioness of Northampton as chief mourner, supported by senior members of the council followed in turn by the ladies of the Privy Chamber. Had Poley been less set on looking ahead, he might have glimpsed the Lady Janet Percy restored to her former position amongst them. Janet saw him, however, and – her face hidden by her black veil – she set to calculating the best way to get close enough to talk to him. Though in that desire, she was by no means alone. Behind the Ladies in Waiting came the Guard, led, for the last time, by the Captain of the Guard Sir Walter Raleigh. Who were in turn followed by the yeoman warders of the Tower, their pikes lowered. Poley followed the sombre procession through the ornate, red-brick arch that led into the Abbey precinct, but not into the Abbey itself, preferring to linger outside in Broad Sanctuary. And it was here that both Udall and Standen finally managed to catch up with him. Standen was first. 'I have much to tell you,' he said. 'Where shall we meet?'

'At my lodgings above the Lion on King Street. In an hour.'

'The Lion in an hour,' nodded Standen. 'Bring your purse and a goodly weight of coin.'

No sooner had the elderly knight vanished into the crowd than Udall appeared. As no money was due to be exchanged – merely information – Poley led his associate to a secluded corner where they could talk with no fear of being overheard. Here Udall gave his detailed reports of the meetings between Watson and Garnet, Markham and Lord Grey. He also unburdened himself of his certainty that George Brooke had been in close contact with Watson, as had Anthony Copley and William Clark.

'I see no prospect of them moving by the first of May as they planned,' he concluded. 'Therefore, you had best keep good watch as soon as the king arrives at Theobalds.'

That thought *good watch* filled Poley's head as he pushed his way back through the mass of mourners toward the Great West Door of the Abbey. The most important members of the funeral procession were coming out now and, as opposed to how they went in, there was precious little organisation or order. A wave of black clothed, black-veiled women was flooding onto Broad Sanctuary, most pulling up their veils in order to look for the escorts who had accompanied them here – many of whom, like Poley, were outside awaiting them. But not Lady Janet. She left her black veil in place, keeping her identity concealed for the moment but she could see Poley clearly enough. She pushed her way through the crowd towards him and when she reached him, before it even occurred to her to call his name, she reached out. Their hands met and it was as though a bolt of lightning had passed between them. And he knew her at her touch. It took all his strength not to embrace her there and then but he was strong and so was she. 'I must talk to you,' she breathed.

It did not occur to him to ask what about. It made no difference; whatever she wished to say he wished to hear. But there were proprieties to be observed, perhaps not as strict as those enforced by her cousin Lord Henry, the wizard Earl of Northumberland, but still enough to guard the Lady Janet Percy's reputation. The nearest place he could think to take his importunate lady was to the Lion. His private rooms were out of the question and it was risky enough to be seen with a lady like Lady Janet in the public rooms but he was certain that Gilbert Gifford could find them somewhere they could talk. And then he would escort her back to Essex House and hope no-one would be any the wiser. Certainly, the Lion was no great distance from the Abbey and Poley was certain that he and Lady Janet had reached there unobserved when he ushered her in through the door, still heavily veiled. But the place was packed with men and women of all sorts come to see the funeral who were now desirous of sustenance – solid and liquid. At first Gilbert shook his head at Poley's request for a private, quiet place to talk but then, with a shrug, he offered the barrel store beneath the bar. It was a tiny space piled high with ale and beer casks; so small indeed that Poley and Janet were perforce thrust into unprecedented intimacy, standing almost breast to breast as they faced each other. When she lifted her veil, he found himself gazing deep into her eyes from mere inches away, and when she spoke, the lavender with which she sweetened her breath came near to overwhelming him. 'They have sent to Spain for support,' she said. 'After Raleigh's man Magnall was slaughtered, they sent another man, Dutton…'

'And may send him again,' nodded Poley. 'It seems they all grow desperate. But how do you know this and who do you suspect is involved?'

40

Within ten minutes Lady Janet had told Poley everything she had overheard. He didn't have the heart to tell her that he already knew the most of it, but his pride in her bravery and intrepidity came near to choking him in any case. They were still deep in conversation forty minutes after that when Gifford stuck his head through the door. 'Man here to see you, Poley. Elderly Scot by the name of Standen.'

Sir Anthony Standen, as befitted his social station, had arrived in a privately hired coach and Poley handed Lady Janet up into it and gave the coachman sufficient coin to carry her safely to Essex House before returning to the Lion to await Sir Anthony once more. 'I hope you have a deal more of that to hand,' said Standen as they watched the coach pull away. 'I have information that will be well worth it.'

'Come up to my rooms,' said Poley, 'and we will set to bargaining.'

'A bottle of your finest claret,' ordered Standen as they passed the bar. Gifford grinned and nodded. He only had one type of claret, a dark spiced rose wine imported from Bordeaux – its quality dictated by nothing more than what he charged for it: the more it cost, the better people seemed to like it. Poley with his sweet tooth preferred sack but he wanted to keep a clear head in any case. Twenty minutes of haggling and half of Standen's claret got them to an agreement. Once the coin was piled on the table in front of Sir Anthony, the elderly Scot began to give the detail of what he had learned and what he suspected. 'The group of discontented courtiers and aristocrats who have come to my notice are led by Cobham, with Raleigh at his side. The Reverend George Brooke is also in the centre while Henry

Percy Earl of Northumberland seems to be amongst their outer circle.'

Poley nodded. Lady Janet had told him as much.

Sir Anthony continued, 'I assume that was why you were closeted with that red-head who could only be one of the Percy clan when I arrived. Pretty little thing.' He caught Poley's eye and changed the subject back to his original disclosures. 'Whatever they are plotting looks ambitious – perhaps dangerously so - because it appears to be reliant on raising funds from Spain before they take action. They have sent messages and will in all likelihood send more. They want six hundred thousand crowns. Just think of the damage men like those could do if they ever got a sum like that!'

Sir Anthony paused to take a deep draught of the scented wine before he proceeded, 'But their fund-raising efforts are almost certainly in vain. Spain, it seems, is not in a position to finance any English uprising. The mercenary and messenger Fawkes has convinced me that if the English Catholics and malcontents want anything done, they would have to do it themselves, with no help from abroad.'

'How so?'

Sir Anthony was part-way through an explanation of Fawkes's news about King Philip's finances when a great outroar erupted downstairs. Their interest piqued, the two men ran down to see what was going on; Sir Anthony concerned for his expensive carriage waiting outside the Lion's door once more, and Poley as ever suspicious and curious.

They found themselves confronted by a duel. Well, thought Poley, more of a brawl than a duel. And, it transpired, more of an execution than either. But it involved swords and was clearly going to be fought to the death. Both Standen and he were distracted at first by Sir Anthony's carriage-horse which was badly frightened by what was going on right beneath its nose and the attempts of the carriage driver to back it away to safety – no mean feat given the crowd which had gathered to enjoy the lethal spectacle. Then both men recognised one of the swords at play before Poley realised who was wielding it. 'That's a claymore!' said Sir Anthony, surprise seeming to draw out his Scottish accent. 'And the man it belongs to is wearing a great kilt.'

'That's Henderson,' said Poley. 'He's Lord Kinloss's man. But who is he fighting?' Poley's question hung in the air for a moment as Henderson's claymore clashed against his opponent's rapier. Both men were grunting and snarling with the effort, their blows wide and brutal – no finesse or artistry. Hardly any swordplay, thought Poley who was schooled in Capo Ferro's methods. They might as well have been using clubs.

But then Sir Anthony broke into his thoughts. 'That's Dutton,' he said, gesturing at the man wielding the rapier. 'Raleigh's man Dutton. I last saw him in Brussels when he brought the letters I passed to Fawkes.'

Sir Anthony had only just made that revelation when Gilbert Gifford joined them. 'How did this start?' asked Poley.

'Damned if I know,' answered Gifford. 'It just seemed to explode and it went from words to blades faster than it takes to tell.'

Gifford might have said more but his words were lost. There was a universal groan, as though every spectator had been run through the breast. Just like Dutton had been. As the stricken man sank to his knees, shocked, disbelieving, dying, Henderson tore his claymore blade free and vanished into the crowd which opened almost magically at the sight of his bloodied weapon, his sheer size and his great kilt, but closed again behind him, bystanders straining to witness every detail. Dutton pitched forward onto his face and was dead by the time Poley reached him, a great pool of his blood spreading across King Street, steaming in the cool air.

Poley squatted and rolled the wide-eyed corpse onto its back. 'Did he have a satchel or anything like one?' he asked Gifford.

'Not that I saw.'

'So, anything important would have been carried in his purse here,' said Poley, opening it as he spoke. Then, 'Well, that explains a good deal,' he said, pulling out a carefully folded document and opening it.'

'What is it?' asked Gifford.

'Permission to travel to Brussels. Dated today.'

'He must just have been at Westminster to pick it up,' said Sir Anthony.

'And I'll lay odds Henderson was following him – and then went a little further than merely watching.'

It was a deeply pensive Poley who saw Sir Anthony into his coach and sent him on his way once the body had been moved and the authorities alerted. The pattern was clear in his mind now, perhaps clear enough to take to Master Secretary. But he had better visit Lord Kinloss along the way, he thought; the position of the Scottish intelligencers was something that needed to be clarified. Was Henderson working alone or did Kinloss have an army of such men smoothing King James's path to the throne? But Kinloss was not his top priority. Leaving the enigmatic Scots aside, master Secretary Cecil was too deeply distracted to be disturbed with anything but news of imminent disaster supported by solid proof. And, even though one section of the plotters seemed prepared to attack Theobalds, the more dangerous group for the moment at least seemed to be hesitating. In the mean-time, thought Poley, perhaps he had best take a leaf from the mysterious Guy Fawkes's book – and see what he could organise for himself. He took a horse from the stables behind the Lion and trotted round Dutton's life-blood, out of King Street past Charing Cross into the Strand, up Fleet Street, through Lud Gate, down Ludgate Hill and towards the river through Blackfriars and then along Thames Street to the Tower of London.

223

41

He discovered Sir John Peyton at dinner with Sir William Waad and he accepted a trencher piled with sprats and elvers fresh from the skillet as he talked to them. 'You have, what, fifty yeoman warders in the garrison at present?' he asked.

'Seventy-five in three groups: archers, pikemen and cavalry,' nodded Peyton.

'But you can double that number, or triple it, by calling on the men from Tower Hamlets can you not?'

'Indeed. The Tower is a royal palace as well as a major defence work and a popular prison remember. I can call upon a garrison of as many men as I consider may be needed.'

Poley did a rapid calculation, taking the worst figures he had heard – leaving aside the forty thousand Catholic gentlemen William Watson was dreaming of. Perhaps Grey could recruit one hundred men and Watson raise fifty Jesuits – though Garnet's letter gave plenty of room for doubt. Could Griffin Markham and his brothers raise another fifty? Assume they could. That would mean there was a possibility that two hundred men might be ready willing and able to attack Theobalds almost immediately after King James arrived there. Which would probably be on the third or fourth of May now.

He looked at Sir John Peyton. 'Over and above your yeomen warders,' he said, 'could you raise a further garrison of two-hundred well-armed men? Preferably old soldiers who would need little or no further training?'

'The men would come from the Hamlets,' nodded Peyton. 'And their arms would come from the Tower's armoury. When would you want them ready by?'

On his way back from the Tower, Poley stopped at the corner by St Magnus in the East, dismounted and hitched his horse. Knocked on the nearest door and was admitted.

'I had not realised,' he said to Sir Edward Bruce, the new-made Lord Kinloss, who greeted him in the familiar sitting room, 'that you were so active in guarding your king.'

'In what way?' asked Kinloss.

'In having your man Henderson slaughter anyone Sir Walter Raleigh hoped to send to Brussels in search of finance.'

'We missed Dutton on his first journey,' said Kinloss. 'But I understand that situation had been righted.'

'And Magnall. Was it necessary to kill his mistress too?'

'What's one English whore more or less?' asked Kinloss quietly. Then he continued, as Poley searched for an answer that would properly express his revulsion. 'If I could find a way to unleash Henderson against Cobham or Raleigh in person I would do it. But since I cannot, I work to frustrate their plans.'

'And Watson? What of his plans?'

'Watson is all dreams and lies. He and his plans will come to nothing.'

'Maybe so. But you can hardly rely on it. Especially if it was indeed Watson who used his reivers' trick to trip the king's horse at Burghley.'

'A chance taken but not much harm done. No, Master Poley. In the matter of Watson – and indeed in the matter of Cobham, his brother, Raleigh, Grey and the rest - I rely upon you to keep my king safe if only to keep Master Secretary in power beside him.'

'In that case allow me to advise you against unleashing Henderson against any more of these men's servants – even those sent to Brussels or Valladolid. I have it on very good authority that the Spanish well is dry. They will get neither gold nor much succour from that quarter.'

'Indeed?'

225

'Indeed. Allow me to suggest, further, that now the old queen's funeral is done, most of the court will be heading north to find the king, you and your associates might be well advised to follow them, however many associates besides Henderson dance to your piping. If the king needs guarding, it will be much nearer his person that the job must be done.'

'And you would wish us to augment whatever force you can bring to bear yourself – as you did most effectively against Lord Beauchamp at Portsmouth by all accounts?'

'I cannot rely upon being so fortunate in future.'

'Good fortune? Good planning, rather.'

'And if it was, at least it was against a foe that I was certain of. But I fear planning for the unexpected is much less easy. And I would rather be over-prepared than under-prepared.'

'And your care is all for my king who is also my friend, as I have observed. Of course, I will stand beside you. Look for me at the King James's shoulder when you and your forces arrive to guarantee his safety.'

42

The last link in the chain was Anthony Copley, who Poley had most recently seen with William Watson in the Bishop of London's palace at Fulham. Poley was too busy to search for Copley himself but by good luck he found Tom kicking his heels in the room he shared with Phelippes at Salisbury house when he went there to check Master Secretary's correspondence. 'Watson's disappeared,' said Poley's young brother in law. 'I saw Udall this afternoon and he's gone off in search of him but I have nothing to do unless you have more letters you wish me to carry to Master Secretary at Theobalds.'

'I have something more immediate for you. Find Anthony Copley if you can and bring him to me. He has been seen in London of late and should be easy enough to track down. He will do in place of Watson to tell us how matters stand with the recusants and the malcontents and their fantastical plans to kidnap the king.'

Tom duly departed and Poley returned to his desk opposite Phelippes. He got back to something like his normal work of sifting through Master Secretary's communications and making a pile for Tom to take to Theobalds when his current task was done. This was not as much of a waste of time under the circumstances as it seemed – especially given the possibility that Garnet's letter might be followed by other, more detailed, warnings. But there were no repetitions of the Jesuit's revelations. It was therefore a restless chief intelligencer that Tom found waiting when he returned next day with the news that, like Watson, Copley was nowhere to be found.

'It's just not possible to track him down,' Tom said. Then he began to explain, as though Poley wasn't already well aware of the problem. 'Things are so unsettled at the moment that even moderate Catholic households seem to be willing to take men like Watson or Copley in and hide them, whether they have a priest hole or not.'

'We have lists of the ones with priest holes, proven or suspected,' said Poley. 'The pursuivant priest-hunters share their information with us. But we have neither the time nor the men to search them all, despite the work of the priest-hunters.'

'What you need,' suggested Tom, 'is a way of finding out which Catholic households are truly dangerous and which ones are not.'

'Perhaps,' allowed Poley. 'But we have other more immediate priorities. Where is King James at present?'

'He's arrived at Standon House at last,' answered Phelippes, looking up from the latest report on the royal progress.'

'And tomorrow is the first of May,' said Poley. 'I find it disturbing to say the least of it that the men we have been tracking seem to have vanished on the eve of Watson's original day of action.'

'Could they still be planning to strike tomorrow?' wondered Tom.

'There is only one way we can be certain,' said Poley, coming to his feet, all the frustration he had been feeling abruptly turning to decisive energy. 'In the absence of any reliable intelligence we must go and look for ourselves.' He hesitated for an instant, then turned back to Phelippes. 'If you find anything of concern,' he said, 'send Nick Skeres after me or straight to Theobalds if it calls for Master Secretary's immediate attention.'

'I will,' said Phelippes. 'Ride safely.'

Poley and Tom did not head north at once. The first place they visited on the way was Lord Kinloss's lodging. It was locked up tight and obviously empty. The next place was the Tower. Poley pushed through the bustle of a hundred willing and able volunteers from Tower Hamlets who were arming themselves and being organised into units with a clear command structure. Then Tom waited outside the Queen's House, the Lieutenant's traditional accommodation, while Poley talked to Sir John Peyton. And when the pair of them set out once more, it was at the head of a cavalry troop of twenty yeoman warders, well mounted and very well armed.

Their road north ran parallel to the Great North Road, slightly to the east of it and took them past Finsbury Fields where Londoners were already celebrating the arrival of Spring as they danced around their maypoles. Likewise in Tottenham and Edmonton villages, Waltham Abbey and beyond. They arrived at Standon House a little over two hours after setting out and found the spacious dwelling packed to overflowing. The grounds were also busy with revellers, though the main Spring celebrations would be tomorrow. Which promised to present an interesting contrast, thought Poley. On the one hand the court officials would be in their formal robes and chains of office and on the other the local villagers and the household at Standon would be in such party dresses as they possessed, whirling round maypoles, playing Nine Men's Morris, cavorting with Jack of the Green and the Hobby Horses, selecting, then crowning the May Queen, watching the Morris Dancers and any passing mummers perform their play. *Bringing in the May* as it was called. And, most importantly, consuming as much good ale and spring lamb as their bellies would hold. A scene of merriment and debauchery, thought Poley, that might well provide cover for a serious attempt on the king's liberty; perhaps even on his life.

Poley managed to find Kinloss amongst the more formal element of that merry crowd, however, and Kinloss took him to Thomas Erskine of Gogar, who was Raleigh's opposite number as Captain of the King's guard. The two Scottish lords were happy to accept Poley's beefeaters and subsumed them into the force they already had at their command – thus housing and feeding them. Relieving Poley of those immediate responsibilities. Poley and Tom, too, messed down with the King's Guard which now numbered the better part of forty men. They were lucky to be able to do so. Standon House was stuffed to the rafters with James, his courtiers and hangers-on. The nearest accommodation, the Star at Standon village was packed by all accounts, and the next inn, the White Hart at Puckeridge, seemed equally over-full. Beyond that it was what shelter could be found at Little Hadam or Bishops Stortford.

Even though he was well-housed and well-fed, Poley slept badly. As the hours of darkness passed and May Day approached, he found himself going over and over his calculations, testing the evidence of his intelligencers, their reliability, their hidden agendas. How the May Day celebrations – which he had failed to take fully into account – might help the traitors and slow the king's protectors. He even found himself haunted by the spectre of Watson's fantastical forty-thousand Catholic gentlemen willing to join in the overthrow of the incumbent monarch. Would they really strike here on the morrow, with such courtiers as had arrived in their chains of office and the king protected by only a few good men amongst this wild bacchanalia? Or would they strike at Broxbourne in a couple of days' time when everyone else who had been waiting at their posts until Queen Elizabeth's funeral would come flooding north in greater numbers still. Numbers that might well conceal an army of traitors about their treasonous business if the May Day madness did not. Had he made a fatal miscalculation ordering Sir John Peyton to take his men from Tower Hamlets directly to Theobalds? Was he really seeking to protect the king – or was it actually Master Secretary he was safeguarding? God knew there were enough pamphlets in circulation accusing the Cecils, the *Regnum Cecilianum* of gouging their family fortunes out of the few last possessions still held by their poor tenants and neighbours. In his nightmares it was sometimes difficult to discriminate between the men lining up to attack His Majesty and those waiting to destroy Master Secretary.

Poley pulled himself out of his bed wearily as May Day dawned and went in search of Kinloss and Erskine. They informed him that the king, confined and bored by his slowly-healing shoulder, had every intention of joining in the festivities and making up for his inability to ride by his proclivity for drinking and dancing. But there was one piece of good news. James had been upset by the crowds of his new subjects gathering to see him pass, by their noise, their stench and the amount of dust they kicked up. So he would be dancing round the maypole and cavorting in the traditional English fashions in relative privacy. Well away, they promised, from hidden daggers and secret plotters. Behind, as Poley planned, a circle of well-armed, sharp-eyed guards.

43

And so May Day arrived, then slowly departed. As far as Poley was concerned, each hour passed on leaden feet. Ever vigilant, Poley patrolled the guard points, at first to the amusement of Erskine and Kinloss but eventually to their irritation. The king was in part responsible for this. He was in no mood for formality; he seemed set on enjoying the frivolity despite the strain it put upon those trying to keep him well-guarded and safe. Poley was grudgingly able to see why James was unusually wild today. It was more than simple May Day madness. The court officials who were present – in their robes, chains of office, their collars - waited in lively expectation for the set Collar Day rituals. But those rituals were principally designed to emphasise each courtier's importance. The rituals also clearly confined the king with his inescapable royal duties. And James, Poley saw all too clearly, understood how confined he would soon become. It was not that he begrudged performing his kingly obligations and God-given duties as the price for the almost fairy-tale life it gave him. It was just that this was perhaps, the last truly festive day when those duties could be shrugged off. He was a king, true. But he was also a man approaching his mid-thirties who had been confined by duty and responsibility as interpreted by those harsh Calvinist advisors in Scotland until they felt like the restraints put on madmen.

There was a heady sense of freedom mounting higher and higher the further James came south and the courtiers in Standon with their robes and chains were nowhere near enough to smother the simple enjoyment of eating, drinking and dancing to excess. Pleasures James was egged-on to by the more youthful of his Scottish courtiers such as Sir John Ramsay and Sir Philip Herbert, both beautiful young men in their early twenties, who praised and flattered James almost as though they were courting him, urging him on to excess whenever they could. And today of all days they certainly could. With these two at his side, James was happy to partake of all the informal excesses of the day while the berobed courtiers were almost literally bound in their chains. He danced round maypoles with his beautiful young tempters. There was a Nine Men's Morris board cut into the lawn and James played – and beat – all-comers in the simple game of strategy. He played at bowls and at tennis. He was flattered by the local youth bringing crowns and garlands of bright spring flowers and by the Morris Men dancing for his pleasure. He approved the battle of the hobby horses and was amused by the mummers with their May Day play. He chose and crowned a May Queen, though his eyes lingered on his May Princes. And he ate heartily and drank deeply on every possible occasion. Apart from the increasingly wild indulgences, nothing untoward occurred, and by the time James announced that he would ride to Broxbourne on horseback tomorrow, he was so drunk that Poley reckoned he would have forgotten the decision by morning. And even if he remembered it, he would be too wine-sick to sit safely in a saddle.

But James was made of sterner stuff than Poley realised. He rose the next morning, fresh as a spring flower, ate a swift breakfast and set out for Broxbourne ahead of his far more sluggish courtiers. Even the guards had been sucked into the festivities when it became obvious that the king was in no immediate danger. And the yeoman warders, messed down with their Scottish counterparts, shared their weakness as well as their accommodation. Unlike Poley who remained too tense to eat, let alone to drink – and Tom who refused to do so if Poley was disinclined. The pair of them went to bed hungry and sober – and slept well. So, when James erupted from his privy chamber, snatched his breakfast with Sir John and Sir Philip, his wayward companions from yesterday, then demanded their horses be readied, only Tom and Poley were in a position to follow him immediately.

'This is a bit unexpected,' said Tom as he and Poley tailed the exuberant little group out onto the south-bound road.

'And dangerous,' answered Poley, grimly.

'Still,' said Tom, 'Broxbourne must only be an hour's gallop from here. And it's all downhill once we get up to Colliers End. And most of it is along an old Roman road. Or at least one that is straight enough to be so.'

In spite of his misgivings, Poley could see Tom's point. And, indeed, the king's. It was a beautiful early-spring morning. The sun was getting hotter as it climbed a cloudless sky seemingly chased into the blue by a couple of skylarks. The countryside stretching away on either hand was dressed in Spring green with touches of bright blue and dazzling gold. The horses, as exuberant as their riders, made light work of the uphill slope they were first confronted with. And the road beyond the hillcrest at Colliers End ran arrow straight for more than five miles down the gentle slope into the Lea river-valley and to the bridge at Ware. You didn't have to be king of all you surveyed to be excited at the prospect, Poley grudgingly allowed.

They thundered through the town of Ware as its citizens were still settling into their morning routine. Even those excited at the prospect of seeing their new king were scarcely able to recognise him at the head of the little group of horsemen galloping across the bridge. And if they did recognise him, he was there and gone before they could even raise a cheer. Then the five riders were out in the countryside again, following the river as it ran south towards its distant confluence with the Thames at Bow Creek. Its marshlands spread across the valley to the east and were alive with birds of all sorts. The king and his companions were wise enough to rein back to a canter as they came through the hamlet of Hoddeston, and then Broxbourne lay just ahead hidden behind a stand of trees that were growing close together, almost like walls on each side of the road.

But all of a sudden, the way ahead was no longer empty. A sizeable number of horsemen was riding swiftly northwards, clearly on a collision course unless one group or the other cleared the path. And, with a sinking heart, Poley realised that the king was unlikely to be in a yielding mood. He had two headstrong young attendants beside him both happy to encourage him in his high-handed ways. But there was no guarantee that the men approaching so swiftly would recognise their incumbent king or yield the way to him, even if they did. And, the intelligencer thought with a jolt that robbed him of breath, what if they were part of Watson's traitorous band, actually here to kidnap or to kill King James? Poley pushed his horse into a gallop with Tom at his shoulder so that at least there would be four men supporting James when the confrontation eventually came. As Poley pulled level, James glanced across at him, surprised; then a look of recognition passed across the royal countenance. 'Why, Master Poley, ye're right welcome…'

'Your Majesty, may I take your orders to this oncoming group and demand that they clear your way?'

'In case they do not know their king d'ye mean?'

'Just so, Your Majesty.'

James shot a calculating glance forward, then nodded. 'If ye'd be so kind…'

Poley spurred ahead at once, with Tom close behind. In fact, the oncoming horsemen were approaching so rapidly that it took almost no time to reach them. Poley reined to a halt, his mount sideways across the road and the approaching horsemen had a simple choice – come to a stop or try to ride him down. Fortunately, they chose the former course. And as their leaders came to a halt within a yard of the intelligencer, a shock of mutual recognition passed between them. Just as King James arrived on the other side of Poley's solid horse.

'Majesty,' snapped the newcomer. 'About my monopoly of Cornish tin…'

'Ha, Sir Walter,' said the king interrupting rudely, 'I've heard right rawly of you!' Sir John and Sir Philip chuckled appreciatively. Raleigh's outraged face, however, could have been carved of ice, thought Poley. Or the Cornish tin he had come to discuss.

44

Raleigh and his companions were ordered back to Broxbourne where they were lost amidst the crowd of courtiers who descended on the place now that Elizabeth's funeral was over. Raleigh's concerns about his monopoly on Cornish tin, his last major source of income, were also lost amongst all the competing requests and demands. But that first meeting of the day set the tone. James had started out happy and excited. Raleigh put an end to that. Then Sir Edward Denny, the Sheriff of Hertfordshire, arrived with an escort of one hundred and fifty young men who surrounded the king. All too soon James was overwhelmed not only by his outriders but by the crowds packed along the road, shouting, cheering and throwing their hats in the air as he passed. Which neither the king nor his horse liked at all.

So, observed Poley grimly, James went from feeling gay to out-of-sorts to downright angry by the time he actually arrived at Broxbourne itself. He made it very clear that, no matter what plans had been made by Sir Henry Cock for his entertainment - or at what cost - he was only staying one night and then he was off to Theobalds in the morning. And he did not want hordes of subjects, be they peasants, citizens, courtiers or anyone else, to come crowding around him. Irritating his mouth with their choking dust, his ears with their cheering and bellowing, his nostrils with their foul stench; testing his patience with their never-ending demands and endlessly contriving to come between himself and his desires. The English were all tarred with the same brush. He only wanted his Scottish friends and supporters anywhere near him, Even the ring-bearer Sir Robert Carey was edged out of the inner circle. The latent animosity between the two groups suddenly became more pronounced and was beginning to turn ugly. The only senior courtier who seemed to stay clear of it all was Robert Cecil – and that was simply because Master Secretary had decided to avoid Broxbourne in order to oversee the final preparations to welcome the king at Theobalds in person.

'Master Secretary needs to know about this,' said Poley to Tom. 'King James is likely to be angered and offended by just the sort of welcome is almost certainly planned for him at Theobalds.'

'Theobalds is only another hour's ride,' said Tom. 'Do you think we can risk leaving the king here with Kinloss, Erskine and your yeoman warders to protect him?'

'To protect him from his English courtiers, you mean?' Poley gave a weary chuckle. Then he sobered up. Because Lady Janet and Sir John Standen's warnings slipped into his memory. King James did indeed need protection from courtiers such as Lord Cobham, his brother the Reverend George Brooke, perhaps Janet's relative Henry Percy the Earl of Northumberland, and of course Lord Grey de Wilton. But surely they wouldn't dare take action here and now. No. It was still Watson and his plans that seemed to present the most immediate danger to the king. However, the king's current feelings towards the English might well prove the most potent danger to Master Secretary, no-matter what plots might be afoot. Whatever the risks, he and Tom had better get to Theobalds and report on the current situation festering at Broxbourne.

Poley informed Kinloss of their plans and the Scot nodded. 'In your position I'd probably be doing the same,' he said. 'I'll see you tomorrow, like as not.' The last Poley saw of King James's London representative was Kinloss standing with the figure of Henderson towering at his shoulder. The pair of them deep in conversation.

Tom and Poley had not overtaxed their horses earlier on so they might almost have been riding fresh mounts that afternoon as they cantered out of Broxbourne, following the old Roman road of Ermine Street along the Lea valley. The road led out of Broxbourne and straight down towards the village of Waltham Cross and here they planned to turn towards the great park surrounding Theobalds itself. But before they could do so, a lone rider approached them, heading in the opposite direction – as Sir Walter Raleigh and his companions had done. But as the rider drew nearer, Poley realised that he was a friend rather than an enemy. It was Nicolas Skeres. Who could only be here, reasoned the intelligencer as they approached each other close enough to talk, because Phelippes had freighted him with some important news. And so it proved.

'We've found Udall,' gasped Skeres, turning his mount to ride beside Poley and Tom.

'Where is he?'

'Close-by. He's at the Powder Mill tavern in Waltham Cross, waiting to talk with you. He says he's found Copley and has a deal of news more beside.

The Powder Mill tavern, named for the Royal Powder Mills nearby – whose very existence called Robert Catesby and the great explosion at Redriffe briefly into Poley's memory - was a solid, stone-walled building with a low roof and a sprawling architecture. It offered a great deal of accommodation but even so it was packed with people waiting in anticipation of seeing the king tomorrow or the next day. Poley, Skeres and Tom found a quiet corner to talk with Udall, who was indeed big with news.

'I've tracked Copley,' said Udall. 'I know where he is now and I have a good idea who is with him and what they are discussing – though whether the discussions will become plans and then be put into action I cannot rightly say.'

'Very well,' said Poley. 'Let us start with certainties. Where is Copley now?'

Anthony Copley was in the dining hall of Flamstead End, the home of the recusant Sir John Gage. He and his associates were seated round the great table having just finished their early supper, though they were still partaking of Sir John's good wine; their conversation freer and more enthused because of it. The rambling old building stood in Flamstead Park whose western border almost ran alongside Theobalds Estate. Theobalds House was perhaps a twenty-minute trot on horseback and less than an hour's quick march distant. As matters were coming to a head, the gentleman poet and friend of William Watson who had been so insulted by the Jesuit Robert Persons and who had been so willing to insult him back, was beginning to have second thoughts. The atmosphere in the room was overpowering: a strange mixture of excitement and bitterness. Desperately disappointed men discussed the nearest way to right the wrongs that they believed had been done to them. The amateur revolutionary found himself surrounded by increasingly ruthless plotters actually considering actions and outcomes that had seemed little more than fanciful dreams at the outset.

'There is no doubt,' Watson was saying. 'Word has gone out through all our secret channels including via the Jesuit Henry Garnet himself. We can expect between four hundred and a thousand to arrive here within the next day or two and join the men who are already ready and waiting. They should all be assembled by the end of the first week in May at the latest. Not counting the men who will rise at Lord Grey's command. And Flamstead End is the perfect location to launch an assault on Theobalds.'

'Indeed,' agreed Griffin Markham. 'But there is no need to wait so long as a week, surely. We could move with only four hundred, in expectation of a thousand Catholic gentlemen – and Lord Grey with his thousand into the bargain. I say we strike within days – on the fourth or the fifth at the latest.'

'I can ride to London in less than an hour and have my men ready within a day,' confirmed Grey.

'Then,' continued Markham, nodding at his brothers sitting opposite him, 'It would be child's play to surround Theobalds House with those that are promised to us here. We have the

Gunpowder Mill close by which will supply all our wants and more. We have sufficient guns and ammunition to make good use of all that powder. When everything is well in hand, perhaps as early as tomorrow night or the night after depending on James Stuart's arrival and the numbers of our own men as they amass, we will wait until everyone is tired and getting ready for bed, then we can make our move. Our attack will come as an absolute surprise. Consequently, it will be a matter of ease to overcome the porter or doorkeeper and his men to gain access to the house. I understand James Stuart has some Scottish guards but little more. Erskine of Grogar is his Captain of the Guard but is in no way comparable to Sir Walter Raleigh in regard to experience or ability. Then we will overpower the would-be king and carry him away with us. Sir John has a strong, secure coach which will be perfect for the task. With the James Stuart in the coach, we can be at the Tower in little more than an hour, during which time he will be schooled by me in what he must say if he wishes to stay alive. He must tell the Lieutenant of the Tower that he is under our protection and escaping a murderous treason fomented by the power-hungry grasping lords of his council, led by the Cecil brothers. The so-called *Regnum Cecilianum*.'

'Meanwhile my Lord Grey,' Sir George Brooke bowed towards Grey who was sitting narrow-eyed opposite, 'with his men will take command of all the major roads near the Tower and the east of the City. And access to the river, of course,' he added. 'And we can look for help from my brother Cobham and Sir Walter Raleigh once we have matters in hand. Perhaps even the Earls of Southampton and Northumberland. Then no doubt we will have our forty thousand Catholic gentlemen with us almost at once.'

Copley looked around the grim faces. Griffin Markham's brothers, Watson, the rest. Only Lord Grey seemed less than totally convinced.

'Then what?' asked their host and co-conspirator Sir John Gage.

241

'Why, I will be given the post of Lord Treasurer,' said Sir George Brooke at once.

'And I will be Earl Marshal,' said Sir Griffin.

Grey bestirred himself. 'I will have the post of Captain of the Isle of Wight and all that goes with it,' he said, too full of hatred of Southampton still to see that he was planning to rob one of the other plotters, thought Copley with a chill of concern. Their gaze fell immediately on him and he realised he would have to speak despite his secret misgivings, 'I will prove I am no little *idle-headed boy* in trial by combat against any Jesuit Robert Persons cares to send against me!' he blustered manfully.

Everyone then turned to look at their leader. 'And what about you, Watson?' asked Grey. 'What will you have?'

'I', said Watson, 'Will have the head of every one of James's Privy Councillors. I may even chop them off myself!'

The brutality of his tone as much as the bloodthirstiness of his plan silenced the rest of them. Copley sat, straight-faced, praying that his expression did not betray the revulsion and terror he was beginning to feel being surrounded by such men with such ambitions.

Then, after a moment, Sir John said. 'And we will begin this tomorrow night.'

'Tomorrow,' said Watson. 'Or the night after. Whenever our supporters have assembled and James Stuart has arrived at Theobalds. The sooner he gets here, the sooner we can move against him.'

45

Poley had not expected Master Secretary to be pleased or grateful when he broke the news of the king's dissatisfaction with matters at Broxbourne, his imminent arrival and the state of the plotting against him. But even so he had under-estimated how angry Cecil would be when he heard it all. 'And how do you know all this? All this treasonous plotting?' he demanded, his voice rising an octave – for the first time ever in Poley's experience; a sign of the strain the king's next host was feeling.

'I have some of it from Sir Anthony Standen, recently returned from Brussels and more from Lady Janet Percy who overheard Northumberland talking with Lord Cobham and his brother Sir George Brooke at Essex House…'

'Both of them brothers to my late wife. Brothers-in-law to me!' snapped Cecil. 'I owe great thanks to your light of love for this information do I not?'

'Sir Walter Raleigh, Southampton and Grey were part of the discussion as well…' continued Poley through gritted teeth.

'I had supposed that your main focus at the moment would be Watson and Clark even if Raleigh remains your ultimate goal. We will have to wait a little before dealing with him, especially after the letter from Garnet warning of Watson's plans!' snapped Cecil. 'And you may thank Phelippes for forwarding it to me when I understand you would have kept it secret, together with the seriousness of the position as you now finally explain it to me. At last!'

Poley chose to disregard his friend's treachery for the moment and proceeded, fighting to stay calm in the face of this tirade, 'I hear of them from William Udall who has had eyes on Thomas Copley. Udall, at the moment, is at the Powder Mill tavern in Waltham Cross awaiting my further instructions. And from Nick Skeres who waits there with him, as well as my own brother-in-law Tom here beside me who has in the past watched William Watson. I bring this all to your notice now not only because of his majesty's imminent arrival but because we believe Watson and many of his co-conspirators are at Sir John Gage's house at Flamstead End, whose grounds march with yours to the east.'

'And what do they plan to do there?' demanded Cecil.

'We have no way of knowing at present, and no way of finding out unless we use the men from Tower Hamlets Sir William Waad has brought here to assault the place before they have a chance to do anything.'

'Oh! A fine idea! To have the new king arrive at Theobalds to find a war instead of an entertainment! Especially after what happened to him at Burghley, my brother's estate! Are you mad, Poley?'

It was at this point that Cecil's mistress Lady Catherine Howard entered the room and the discussion. Poley was not surprised to see her. Catherine, Countess of Suffolk, still famously beautiful at thirty-nine, had already prepared her notoriously indulgent husband's London home, the Charterhouse, for James's visit in due course. But then she had yielded to blandishments and bribery from Cecil to oversee the perfection of Theobalds. She was wearing at least part of the bribe, he thought bitterly – a string of pearls that Raleigh would have sold his soul to possess. If Cecil's outrage at the news had been sharp, hers when he repeated it all to her, was cutting. 'After what has happened at Burghley? And, indeed, after what vast sums my Lord Cecil has already committed to this project at Theobalds! It seems to me, Master Poley,' she spat, 'that having brought this matter to Master Secretary's attention so late – a matter you have allowed to grow this dangerous through your own inaction – it should be *you* who assumes responsibility for whatever befalls. And if the king is discomfited in any way, it will mean your head, I assure you! Or, more likely given your station in life, the hanging, drawing and quartering you have caused to be inflicted on so many others unlucky enough to have known and trusted you. Moreover, I would suggest you put little faith in whatever Janet Percy has told you. It was not for nothing she was banned from her late majesty's Ladies of the Privy Chamber – and naming my Lord Cecil's brothers in law is so obviously an act of purest spite!'

'Be about your business, man!' snapped Cecil. 'The Countess and I have work to do, especially if His Majesty is planning to arrive tomorrow as you say!'

'What shall we do friend Robert?' asked Tom as the echoes of the door slammed behind the departing couple faded into silence.

'We will need to keep close watch on Flamstead End,' said Poley.

'Do you suppose the men gathering there suspect how much we know of them and their plots?' said Tom.

Poley shrugged wearily. The reaction of Master Secretary and the Countess had come close to crushing him. Especially the Countess's attitude toward Lady Janet; he could see nothing but sorrow ever coming from that. Sorrow for both of them – for which he felt solely responsible.

'Either way, we would be best not to alert them,' persisted Tom. 'Does the moon shine tonight?' he wondered, apparently oblivious to Poley's grim, defeated silence. 'The sky is clear and if so, it would be easy enough for us to creep close to the house and get some idea of the numbers and sorts of men nearby it.'

Poley nodded, put in mind of the ease with which Lord Beauchamp's fledgling army had been observed at their watch fires and numbered on the eve of Beauchamp's attempt on Portsmouth. The weight he had felt on his shoulders lightened a little. He had done good work at Portsmouth; he would do good work again. Perhaps enough good work to keep Lady Janet well clear of the Countess's spite. 'An excellent thought, lad,' he said.

Rather than risking outright refusal in Theobald's kitchens, they went back and supped at The Powder Mill tavern. Then, as night began to settle, Poley, Tom, Udall and Skeres set out for Flamstead End. The moon was near full and hung low in a sky as liberally bedecked with stars as Walter Raleigh's doublet was hung with pearls. The early sections of their progress were further lit by the flambeaux and lanterns illuminating the work still being done in Theobalds Park as they followed the line dividing the two great estates. Then, as they turned eastwards with the brightness of Theobalds at their back, they found that a wide section of Flamstead Park's western side had been cleared of brush and undergrowth – a fact that abruptly raised Poley's already restive suspicions. It might be that the land was being cleared – as much of Cecil's was, and like the common land nearby – to be turned into grazing for sheep. But on the other hand, the lack of undergrowth might make it a vastly convenient route along which to march an army set on attacking Sir John Gage's courtly neighbour – and any royalty that might happen to be visiting him.

The four spies stuck close together although there seemed to be little to fear. Flamstead Park was silent and still – apart from the rustlings, flutterings, tweets and hoots that might be expected from night creatures on the wing or on the prowl. There certainly seemed to be no other men about, and the four were able to approach the west-facing frontage of the great house quite closely before Poley gestured and they set off southwards, guided by the reflection of the moonlight and starlight in the house's tall windows. Everything within seemed still, and there were no windows lit by candle- or lamp-light. Nor were there any closed off by curtains as far as Poley could tell. It all seemed so innocuous that he found it hard to explain why he felt that he was being watched. No; more than watched – stalked. Had the traitorous plotters set guards after all? he wondered. Was this seemingly innocent silence simply a trap like the twine Watson had used to trip the horses of Sir Robert Carey on the Great North Road and King James himself at Burghley?

With these suspicions still fresh in his mind, Poley led the way round the southern end of the house, to discover that the west-facing elevation they had just followed was the back of the place. Two wings reached eastwards to trap the sunlight in the morning and between them lay the main entrance columned and colonnaded; ahead of that there sloped a great square lawn cleft by a formal avenue leading in from parkland on the east. There were tents and fires here, but it was impossible to estimate how many men they sheltered or warmed. As with the western side, there seemed to be no guards.

'I can't see anyone,' breathed Tom. 'Where are they all?'

'There, answered Udall, gesturing.'

'At chapel,' added Skeres.

And Poley could see the truth of it. Away on the far, northern, side of the fire-dotted lawn there was a sizeable chapel. It was brightly lit and packed with the figures of both men and women which overflowed out on the formal flagstones surrounding it. 'Watson must be holding a mass,' Poley breathed.

'He must be mad to risk it and Sir John must be just as mad to allow it,' said Skeres.

'Or,' said a new voice, in a thick Scottish accent and a faintly mocking tone, 'they dare do it because they know what they are doing will soon be breaking no laws. Because they will have converted or killed the king who makes them.'

Poley swung round, as startled as his three companions. He saw no-one and nothing but shadows. But he recognised the voice and realised who it was must have been stalking them.

Lord Kinloss's murderous Highlander Henderson.

46

'It is a simple enough matter for King James to find out certain things,' said Henderson as he and Poley shared a table in the Powder Mill tavern an hour or so later. A table cleared by a landlord fussing to accommodate a large man wearing bonnet with an eagle's feather, a claymore and plaid belted into a great kilt. A companion of the new king's, therefore, and worthy of the best the tavern could offer in space, service and sustenance. Poley had come to the Powder Mill tavern to further understand Henderson's place in the scheme of things. They had left Tom, Udall and Skeres on watch. If anything important happened, Tom would come hot-footed while the other two assessed events ready to make a report and advise what to do next.

'All the king has to do is ask, and there are men of all sorts and degrees falling over themselves to answer him,' Henderson continued. 'And so, my Lord of Kinloss finds out what the king knows and tells me to act upon it. But...' The big Scot paused, catching Poley's eye, 'there are things you know, Master Poley, that no-one else knows.'

'Exempli gratia?' asked Poley softly.

'For example,' answered Henderson not at all discomfited by the Latin. 'Why there is a small army of men from Tower Hamlets currently camped at Theobalds under the command of Sir William Waad and why a section of Sir John Peyton's yeoman warders has been added to Captain of the Guard Lord Erskine of Grogar's command?'

'Surely that is obvious enough...'

'In general, yes – to add to his majesty's protection. A bairn could see as much. But why so many? Why here? Why *now*? What do you -and presumably Lord Cecil - know that the rest of us don't know?'

Poley hesitated, calculating.

Henderson pushed on. 'That there is a clear and credible threat? That King James is genuinely in immediate and serious danger? Of liberty? Perhaps even of life?'

'No,' lied Poley, hoping he sounded absolutely trustworthy. Reliable. He could not possibly allow Henderson to go telling Kinloss the true situation. Kinloss would tell his sovereign lord the truth at once – he would have no choice. King James's most likely reaction would be to ensure his own immediate safety rather than risking a visit to Theobalds, no matter how much Master Secretary had already spent on his welcome and entertainment. Then he would have with Master Secretary exactly the same conversation Master Secretary and the Countess had just had with Poley himself. And heads might very well roll in consequence. Almost certainly, were Cecil permitted to keep his own head, he would have lost the king's trust and any hope of preferment under the new dispensation. Poley and Master Secretary had played a dangerous enough game in bringing down the Earl of Essex – one whose menaces were still considerable as Essex was now a martyr to the cause of James's succession. But that was nothing to the risks they were running now as they allowed Raleigh sufficient rope to hang himself, especially as that also meant allowing Watson and his Catholic confederates to go about their own version of the Gowrie plot in the meantime. If Poley allowed himself and his master to get tangled in the coils of that particular rope it would be enough to hang them all.

'Perhaps it would be appropriate – politic, even – if you were to join our little band of intelligencers,' suggested Poley. 'That way you can keep Lord Kinloss and Lord Erskine fully apprised of everything that we and Master Secretary know. Until the matter is settled and King James is safely on the throne.'

Henderson's craggy face folded into a slow smile. 'Keep your enemies close,' he suggested, 'but your Scottish friends closer still?' He leaned back and surveyed his new companion. 'I'll gladly stand by any man that will buy me a dram of the usquebaugh,' he announced. And Poley found himself praying that the landlord had been punctilious in preparing for the Scottish invasion the new king was bringing south with him.

James Stuart arrived at Theobalds early the next afternoon with no sense that he was under any sort of threat or standing in any kind of danger. Or that there were eyes upon him, some solicitous of his safety as well as others planning his downfall. With no sense of anything, in fact, except of child-like excitement and a vague feeling that he was somehow coming home. Were there any devious or duplicitous thoughts nearby, in fact, they resided at the back of the young king's own mind. It was love at first sight between him and the great house and he no sooner clapped eyes on it than he began to calculate how he could remove it from Master Secretary Cecil's possession and put it securely into his own. Although he was still at the centre of a group of his most senior Scottish nobles, James had been joined at Broxbourne by many of the Privy Council, including Lord Keeper Edgerton and Lord Admiral Nottingham – who also remained in blissful ignorance of Watson's plans for them and their heads. The arrival of so many senior councillors had simply made Broxbourne even more confining to James, as had their insistence on accompanying him on the next leg of his journey - but his arrival at Theobalds was enhanced by the great contrast it presented to everything that had gone before. True there had been crowds alongside the road as well as stretching along it behind him, but they had been kept well back and as James entered the park itself, he experienced a feeling of space and freedom. A muted fanfare of trumpets rang in golden tones upon the clear, warm Spring air. James's English companions dismounted and his Scots ones fell back. Four lords stepped forward to walk beside James's mount, two at its shoulders and two at its flanks. As they led the king up the long, straight avenue to the great house's forecourt, the crowds who had waited so patiently outside were allowed in to stream across the parkland turf on either side of the avenue behind him. At last, he arrived at the foot of the entrance stair where rank upon rank of beautiful young men waited to greet him. One of these stepped forward and handed the king yet another petition, but it was done so gently and courteously that it hardly caused a ripple on the calm surface of the gilded afternoon. James glanced at it, assured the pretty youth that he would attend to it then dismounted. His host, clad in black and silver, accompanied by his beautiful mistress, all cloth of gold and pearls, stepped forward. Cecil shot a fulminating glance at the young man with the petition and turned to the king, smiling his welcome. As Cecil led the king into his private palace, the crowd outside began to cheer.

With all the pride of a parent showing off a beloved and talented child, Cecil led the king around Theobalds - along galleries and through chambers more fabulously and intricately decorated than anything the young Scot had ever imagined. This was a world so far removed from the dour chambers of the castles of his childhood and young manhood at Stirling and Edinburgh – even of his favourite royal palace at Holyrood – that he might almost have been a spirit transported from Purgatory up past the Celestial Gates. Everywhere he looked there were more wonders, more extravagance, more indisputable proof that he would soon be the ruler of a kingdom whose wealth was more than fabulous; was almost unimaginable. And all his to command. It was, in fact, too much for his reeling mind to grasp and at last he turned to his solicitous host. 'My privy chamber,' he said. 'I must lie down or I will fall.'

The lords of his privy chamber awaited him. After relieving himself and readjusting his clothing, he really did want to lie down, so he dismissed them and fell on his bed. But when he did, his feverish mind would not let him rest and within the hour he was up again. Only to be confronted by Cecil with a humble request that he show himself to his adoring people. So, mind still reeling, he stood in a window and allowed them to cheer and throw their hats in the air while he didn't really look down at them at all. He certainly didn't raise his hand, wave, or show any sign of appreciating their noisy adulation. Truth to tell, he found it quite congenial simply to stand there and try to order his thoughts while his new subjects shouted out their love and duty. But, early May or not, the sun stayed strong and even as evening approached, everything was still as hot as full summer in Scotland. 'Air,' he said as the westering orb cast its red-gold rays directly upon him. 'Give me air.'

Cecil led James out into the garden and the king, his mind beginning to settle, wandered along shady groves walled with bay, brushing up against hardy lavender and rosemary, crushing leaves of early mint between his fingers to let the fragrance help to clear his head. How long he had been wandering there, apparently alone, before he realised he was being watched and followed he had no idea. But when he grasped the truth, he stopped, suddenly nervous. 'Who's there?' he called. 'Show yourself!'

Two men stepped side by side out of the shadows and went down on one knee before him. James recognised Poley at once, with his dark colouring and clothing, pointed beard and piercing eyes. But it was his companion who really claimed James's attention. The huge tartan-clad figure belonged to the man who had refused to kill him at Gowrie House in Perth little more than three years ago. 'I know you,' he said. 'Henderson is it not? You were the Earl of Gowrie's man.'

'I am Lord Kinloss's man nowadays, Your Majesty,' rumbled Henderson. 'And like master Poley here I am employed in preserving your safety.'

'As, it seems, you were in Gowrie House after all,' nodded James.

And he felt very safe indeed.

47

Sir Griffin Markham raked his horse's ribs bloody with brutal spurs as he urged it through The Bishops' Gate into London. It was seven in the evening – an hour since he left Flamstead End and two hours before the city gates were shut for the night. He had much to do and precious little time. His mission was simple but immensely urgent. It was to inform Lord Grey that James Stuart had arrived at Theobalds. Something confirmed by their brave young spy who had even dared hand the would-be king a petition condemning Cecil and his greedy, grasping kind. Now was the time for Lord Grey to fulfil his promise and raise his thousand men. If he had done so already, they could be put in place before the watch went out tonight. If not, tomorrow would have to do. It was growing ever more important that Grey bestirred himself, because the forces promised by Watson were being – at the very least – slow to arrive. The crowds that had assembled to cheer the would-be king, which had been supposed to cover the arrival of some hundreds of recruits to their cause, had largely passed leaving no-one behind. And, the old soldier shrewdly suspected, Watson's men might never actually appear at all despite the wall-eyed priest's vociferous protestations.

The moment Markham arrived at Grey's lodgings he flung himself off his horse and thundered on the door. But the servant who answered it informed him Lord Grey was not at home.

'Not at home?' Markham was stunned. They had agreed Grey would await his word and not stir abroad until he got it. 'I am Sir Griffin Markham and my business is most urgent! Has he left no message for me?'

'None, Sir Griffin, I am sorry.' The man turned, beginning to close the door.

'Wait! If he's away from home, do you know where he actually is?'

'Of course, Sir Griffin. He is visiting the Earl of Southampton in Drury House. Drury House is on Wych…'

'I know where it is damn you!' snarled Markham as he laboured back up into the saddle slowed by the old wounds to his arm and leg; by weariness and – suddenly – by wariness. He was of an age, and indeed of a profession, which did not like sudden changes to plans. Especially not to plans so carefully drawn, fully agreed and deadly serious as these. The servants at the door to Drury House were more forthcoming and accommodating. Lord Grey was with the earl in the library, they said. Sir Griffin was conducted thither and announced. As he was ushered into the smoke-filled room, the two erstwhile enemies glanced up at him. Neither spoke – no welcome; hardly any acknowledgement. Sir Griffin had the feeling that he had interrupted a private conversation. And one whose subject had been himself. The silence hanging heavy in the air was a sign that Grey and Southampton were rapidly trying to come up with some words that would sound innocent and appropriate under the circumstances. They failed.

'Well, Sir Griffin,' said Southampton. 'This is an unexpected pleasure. How goes the world with you and yours?'

'Lord Grey knows the answer to that,' answered the old soldier shortly. 'And my presence should be a pleasure he has been expecting imminently and sharply! My Lord,' Sir Griffin turned to Grey, 'James Stuart is at Theobalds.' He stopped there, uncertain as to how much he should reveal.

'The earl is privy to our plans,' said Grey. 'You may speak freely in front of him.'

Sir Griffin took a deep breath. This was neither the time nor the place to discuss the wisdom of allowing yet more people become privy to what they proposed. But, if the plans were set in motion swiftly enough, no harm would have been done. 'Our forces are assembling at Flamstead End,' Sir Griffin said. 'They are arriving secretly and unsuspected. Even as I speak, Watson should be holding a mass to bless our enterprise and everyone involved in it – such was his intention I know. Our plans are coming to fruition. There is nothing wanting but the men you have promised, my Lord.'

'Ah…' said Lord Grey.

Sir Griffin's heart sank at the sound, even though everything he had experienced since arriving at Grey's door had warned him. Still he persisted. He could see no alternative. 'My Lord, if you act as we have planned it will be a simple thing to snatch the would-be king. If you cannot raise your men today then you must raise them tomorrow and we will make our move tomorrow night. But we must move soon or not at all…'

'Or not at all…' echoed Grey. He and Southampton exchanged a lingering look, puffing thoughtfully on their pipes.

Sir Griffin drew in a desperate breath but the smoke caught in his throat and he started coughing before he could speak. He dashed his hand down his face to wipe away the tears suddenly streaming down his cheeks.

'You see, the problem is this,' said Southampton. 'Once Lord Grey starts raising his men, word will certainly get out - if it has not done so already - and we will all find ourselves in a situation that can only be resolved… *only* be resolved,' he emphasised, 'by the absolute success of the scheme Watson has proposed and you have so enthusiastically joined.'

'Very well,' choked Sir Griffin. 'I see that. And I see every likelihood of success…'

'I'm afraid I do not,' said Grey. 'Even if we manage to wrest James Stuart from the guards at Theobalds – did you know for instance that a hundred men have been raised from Tower Hamlets and dispatched thither by Sir John Peyton…'

'… or that Cecil's intelligencer Poley has caused a further squad of yeoman warders to be added to Erskine of Grogar's royal guard?' added Southampton.

'Even if we wrest him from these protective forces as I say and proceed with Watson's plan to spirit him to the Tower,' Grey continued, 'how are we supposed to convince the Lieutenant of the Tower that we are protecting James Stuart from men he has himself assigned to his protection? It is more likely that the Tower would be shut to us – until it houses us in its dungeons and torture chambers as we await the same fate as the Earl of Essex!'

'And even were all this to go as planned and we convince James Stuart to grant us our wishes, what is to stop him reneging on his promises the moment he is released?' Southampton shook his head at the unworldly naivety of it.

Then Grey concluded, 'When that madman Watson said he wanted the Privy Council's heads I saw how insane the entire scheme had become. The men on James Stuart's Privy Council, Scots or English, are his friends for the most part as well as his advisors. How could Watson even conceive that he would allow them to be beheaded? And, even if he was somehow forced into agreeing, that he would not avenge them, one and all, the moment he got the chance?'

'But… But…' Sir Griffin fought to order his thoughts sufficiently to answer their arguments – indeed, to counter them. But nothing would come. The tears streaming into his grey beard came from more than the tobacco-smoke now. At last he asked, 'Then how will we achieve our aims?'

'Not by controlling James,' said Southampton softly. 'By replacing him.'

'Then we may proceed with Watson's plan, surely,' said Sir Griffin weakly. 'And simply adapt the outcome.'

'No, no. You haven't thought the matter through at all,' said Southampton. 'James is within our reach, I agree. But Queen

Anne is not. Anne with her belly full, we hear, of a second son. Nor is young Prince Henry nor his sister Elizabeth. Even if we remove its head, his line will still stretch out.'

Sir Griffin gulped, looking a little like a frog as the implication of Southampton's words sank in.

'It is as my Lord of Southampton has pointed out,' purred Grey. 'There is no use removing James unless we remove his line of succession into the bargain. So, I fear we will have to wait until Queen Anne and the children come within our reach as well. And you will have to tell friend Watson that, no matter what he plans, it is far too soon to strike.'

48

'He's in a hurry,' said Nick Skeres to his fellow spies as a lone horseman reined to a stop outside the chapel at Flamstead End house, his mount's shoes striking sparks from the flinty flagstones. The service was just ending and the congregations streaming out into the fading moonlight had to leap out of the horse's way. The moon was setting, and Skeres knew moonset would be soon after ten that night. The rider swung out of the saddle and limped into the building, thrusting the worshippers roughly aside. 'Watson?' he bellowed, his voice carrying easily to the watchers on the still night air. 'Where is Watson? Watson, we are undone!'

'Undone are they?' said Udall. 'We need to know who by, how and why. Tom, go fetch Poley and the tartan giant. Skeres and I will try to get closer. When you get back, seek for us down by that chapel. It looks as though that's where the leaders of all this are meeting at the moment…'

As Tom vanished back along the path they had blazed to get here, Skeres and Udall began to creep down the slope, moving across the grass, keeping to the shadows between the fires and ensuring as best they could that their feet were clear of the guy ropes of the tents. As they were not challenged, not even noticed to be strangers, they grew bolder and moved more quickly. 'I guess there are so many men assembling here who are strangers to each-other, two new faces are nothing remarkable,' said Skeres.

'My face might be familiar to a few,' said Udall. 'I've been tracking Watson for long enough. But that might be to our advantage as well.'

'As long as they don't recognise you as an enemy, they will probably assume that you're a friend you mean?'

'Something like that,' nodded Udall.

This conversation covered the final sections of the service after the blessing which had clearly already been given. A young man carried a veiled chalice away into Flamstead House followed by another with wine, water and sacrament and finally a third carrying books – which were probably the Vulgate or the Gospels. All no doubt to be secreted in some priest hole or other – with the priest himself in due course were the pursuivants to pay a visit. It also brought them to the flagstones around the chapel as soon as they were otherwise empty. A fleeting glance through the open door established that the rider's message had indeed been so momentous that it had caused an immediate council among the group's leaders. The empty chapel was a convenient enough meeting place when the congregation and the priest's helpers were gone. And everyone else in and around the great house was about their late-night business or on their way to bed.

Udall had recognised Sir Griffin the moment he saw him limping away from his horse before a groom caught its reins and led it towards the nearby stables. He saw the old soldier clearly now in the candle-light seated, deflated, on a pew with his brothers standing behind his drooping shoulders. It was, thought Udall, typical of the innocent nature of the undertaking, which would have embarrassed the rawest novice intelligencer, that there were no guards and no real attempt by any of the seven outraged men down by the altar to lower their voices or disguise the subject of their angry conversation. Even so, the two spies were careful to step back out of sight behind the north wall, away from the tented lawns and overlooked by nothing other than the stable building which went dark as soon as Sir Griffin's horse was in its stall. When the sleepy stable lad went off in the direction of the north wing, they were confident that there was no-one else there who was likely to discover them as they listened.

'He was a man in whom I placed an absolute trust,' Watson was saying, his voice trembling with outrage.

'We all did,' said Sir Griffin, sounding old and defeated.

'But we were clearly fools to do so,' added George Brooke.

'... spotted and inconstant...' snarled Watson.

'But without Grey and his promised soldiers, can we proceed?' wondered Sir John Gage.

'Should we do so, indeed?' wondered Sir Griffin. 'The point is telling – that we need a new monarch rather than a new mind in the monarch we will soon have.'

'I care not a whit who sits on the throne,' snapped George Brooke, 'so long as he or she grants me the Saint Cross as Queen Elizabeth promised, and considers me for the post of Earl Marshal as I said.'

'But,' said Copley, a voice of reason among the outrage and frustration, 'what does Grey's withdrawal mean here and now? We cannot proceed without him, therefore we cannot proceed at all. Therefore there is no purpose in our gathering here at Flamstead End and nothing likely to arise from it but danger. Especially if Sir Griffin has understood Grey and Southampton aright and Sir John Peyton and Cecil's creature Poley are already moving against us.'

'Not against us, perhaps,' argued George Brooke. 'But in defence of James Stuart against any eventuality – even those as yet unknown.'

'I for one am loth to wager my life on a *perhaps* such as that,' said Copley roundly. 'Master Watson, I believe our enterprise here is dead. Were it a vessel under sail it would never come to safe haven, let alone to home port. It has already foundered on the rocks of circumstance and perhaps upon the reefs of enemy action. I will prepare my own horse if I must, but I am leaving at once. Dawn will find me many miles from Flamstead End and Theobalds. If such a one as I might advise gentlemen such as yourselves, I would urge you in the strongest terms to get as well away from this place and these designs as you are able – and as soon as you may.'

He turned and strode out of the chapel.

'He's going to get his own horse ready,' breathed Skeres as the young man went past them, too self-absorbed to have the slightest inkling of their presence. 'Therefore in that empty, dark stable no doubt. All, all alone...' And with that he was gone.

Udall lingered.

'I cannot just leave,' said Sir John. 'This is my home! My family is here...'

'And I cannot go before morning,' said Watson. 'It may be that scant few have answered my call but those that have done so deserve my blessing and my valediction before they too depart.'

'I and my brothers can take the road to Beskwood,' said Sir Griffin. 'While it still belongs to the Markhams. But I do not care to set out at the mid of the night and after the moon has set.'

'I too will stay 'til morning,' announced George Brook. 'Then I will go to see my brother Cobham when the London gates are opened tomorrow.'

'Well,' said Watson. 'Let us snuff the candles and bustle about. Tomorrow is another day and the Lord may yet provide...'

There was a silent stirring at Udall's shoulder. Poley and Henderson had arrived. The three of them stood, soundless as statues as Gage and Watson led the Markham brothers and George Brooke across to the house, all still deep in conversation, none of them even thinking to look over their shoulders – not that there was much to see except three figures standing almost invisibly in the darkness. Invisibly and noiselessly until the doors to Flamstead End were locked tight and everyone was settled. Then the faintest of clip-clops sounded on the grass and Skeres returned, leading a horse. Over which was draped the figure of a deeply unconscious man.

'Copley?' asked Udall.

'Copley,' confirmed Skeres.

'To the Powder Mill first,' ordered Poley. 'Then to the Waltham Cross gaol, and then to the Tower in the morning.

261

The others will have scattered by then, but we can track them down at our leisure. What we need now is testimony, witnessed recorded and sworn, not bodies. Not at this stage at any rate. We had to start with someone and it might as well be Copley.'

49

Ten o' clock next morning found Poley, not at Sir John Peyton's rooms in the Queen's House at the Tower but in Francis Bacon's rooms at Gray's Inn. The two men were well acquainted – sometime adversaries but currently friendly enough. Sufficiently so, indeed, for Poley to have come to Bacon before proceeding with his plans for Copley. They had talked through the background, what Poley knew – and how he knew it – also what he suspected and why. The manner in which he was proposing to use William Watson's associate to uncover a nest of dangerous plotters would need to stand up in any court of law, from the magistrates' court via the King's Bench to the Star Chamber and the Privy Council or even the House of Lords itself, the highest court in the land; other, perhaps, than the divinely appointed king. And Bacon had been Counsel Extraordinary to the queen until her death – though James had refused to see him so far to discuss whether he would continue to be Counsellor to the King.

In the mean-time, he was Counsellor to Robert Poley.

'Let's go through it, step by step,' said Bacon.

'What we have to do seems clear enough to me,' said Poley. 'I think of us like Theseus in the maze of the Minotaur but instead of following Ariadne's thread to freedom we must lay down a thread of our own. Twist by twist, turn by turn and step by step, our thread must lead to one thing. It must lead to Sir Walter Raleigh's destruction. To his imprisonment at the very least, to his execution possibly. As far as Master Secretary is concerned, Raleigh's downfall is our one true objective.'

'Very well,' said Bacon. 'Explain how your thread will lead from one of William Watson's criminal band of traitors to a well-respected, senior courtier like Sir Walter. And why you need to test it against my knowledge of the law.'

'Because our final objective is not just anybody,' said Poley. 'As you observe, Raleigh is a powerful and popular man, learned and erudite. And we have precious little proof that he has ever done anything wrong. Moreover, even if there is a case to be made against him, we start from a place far removed from anything he has ever been involved in.'

'There's the rub,' said Bacon. 'You say you can build a case against Watson and his associates. But none of them is Sir Walter. On the other hand, you say you have testimony from Lady Janet Percy who overheard the conversation you have described and Sir Anthony Standen who dealt with Dutton and Count Aremberg's contact La Rensy in Brussels, all of which suggests Sir Walter was involved in something. But not in Watson's scheme, though no doubt he will be examined about that as well, whether we may call it the Main plot or the Bye.'

'Lady Janet is well meaning but of little practical help beyond raising our suspicions,' said Poley, refusing to be distracted by thoughts of her. 'The evidence – if it can be called evidence – is that of a woman overhearing parts of a conversation from outside a room she could not see into. How, therefore, can she be certain of the identity of the speakers? Indeed, the true identities of the occupants of the room?'

'Well reasoned,' said Bacon. 'I would demolish her in court and I am gentle as a lamb. Should Sir Edward Coke, or a man of his ruthless and choleric stripe come at her…' he drew a finger across his throat as though it were a blade.

'And, consider,' Poley continued, picking up on the gesture, 'even were she permitted to stand in evidence, who would be standing against her? At least two earls, one of whom is her relative and guardian, a similar number of lords, Master Secretary's brothers in law, a senior courtier, heroic soldier and knight of the realm. Whose word would be believed? Certainly not that of a single woman…'

'And indeed,' said Bacon, 'now I think of it you would need more than one witness in any case. One man's word can never condemn another man to death.'

'Unless it is the word of a king,' said Poley.

'Ah,' said Bacon. 'You heard about the cut-purse in Newark, did you?'

Poley nodded. Then he continued, 'So, Lady Janet is useless to us. More than that, even the faintest hint of her knowledge would place her in the most potent danger of death. I dare not risk it.'

'Well,' said Bacon. 'Sir Anthony Standen then. What of his testimony about what happened in Brussels. The contacts with Dutton and with La Rensy; the evidence of the letter he passed to this man Fawkes. Does that not suggest that Raleigh is or has been involved in something possibly – nay, probably - treasonous?'

'Again, of almost no use. The letter, as you say, was passed to Fawkes. If it still exists, it is in the Spanish court at Valladolid. Did Sir Anthony actually read it? No. Even if he did, was it genuine? From men whose identity could be proved? Was it signed, for instance? Again no. And even had it been signed, who is to say the signatures are real? My friend Phelippes can reproduce the autograph of any member of the council so accurately that even the man whose signature had been forged would swear it was his own. And, further, in his keenness to put an end to Raleigh's correspondence with those who might beat his master to the throne, Lord Kinloss has caused both of Raleigh's couriers Magnall and Dutton to meet brutal and untimely ends at the hand of my new kilted comrade Henderson. So we have lost the only witnesses who could have supported Standen. And of course Lady Janet's evidence – even if we could support it – is too far removed from Standen's in almost every aspect. They could not stand together even were she able to stand in the first place.'

'Other than Fawkes, there is no-one to support Standen.'

'And only the Lord God know what den that particular Fawkes may be hiding in.'

'So,' said Bacon. 'In the face of all these difficulties, tell me more precisely how you are planning to carry the matter forward.'

'I have two possible ways. One requires inactivity and good fortune. The other, which I prefer, is the stratagem of Ariadne's thread in the Minotaur's maze.'

Bacon sat forward and focussed his attention on Poley. 'The first, I assume, is to wait and watch in the hope that Sir Walter and his associates finally do something clearly treasonous. A plan that worked well with the Earl of Essex.'

'Not so, as you know.' Poley shook his head. 'The Earl of Essex was pushed into hasty and unpremeditated action and seen off by a trick.'

'But you are not planning on pushing Sir Walter into hasty action.' Bacon's eyebrows rose, turning the statement into a question.

Poley shook his head once more and shrugged regretfully. 'I cannot get close enough to him for that.'

'Well then. Ariadne's thread it is.' Bacon sat back. 'Though you will have to enlighten me on how you hope to employ whatever testimony you have or might hope for beyond that of Lady Janet and Standen, to use Watson's plot to move against Raleigh who, by your own admission, has had nothing whatsoever to do with it.'

Poley took a deep breath. 'We start with friend Copley, who is currently in the Tower awaiting my presence there. We snatched him from the very heart of Watson's plot when it all came to nothing last night because Lord Grey, who they hoped would lend them his support and a thousand men, very wisely withdrew from the whole mad scheme.'

'You took Copley; well and good. Why did you not arrest all of the conspirators there and then?'

'We have no real evidence against them until Copley furnishes it.'

'But when Copley confesses, your next step must be towards Raleigh as you say. Arresting all the others at this stage would be a distraction I presume.'

'That's right. We plan to question Copley until he gives us names in a full confession, signed and witnessed; a confession that will stand in any court between the magistrates' and the House of Lords with him willing to condemn others as well as himself. Our only problem is that Master Secretary has warned us that the king has forbidden the use of *rigour* in the questioning. So the rack and the thumbscrews are prohibited.'

'As are the strappado, the hot irons and the Little Ease I presume. But the full, detailed confession is crucial,' nodded the Queen's Counsel. 'He must be willing to stand and give evidence under oath – with the written declaration of guilt to back it up. If you do not plan to use it directly against Watson, what then?'

'Even without the use of rigour, we obtain Copley's confession, as I said. Then we examine the list of names he has given us. The roster of his associates. And we select the man or men whose testimony is likely to take us closer to Raleigh. Not to Watson or Gage or Griffin Markham. We take the man whose confession will take us that one vital step nearer to Raleigh. Then we do the same with him, whoever it turns out to be.'

'Question them, you mean, until they too give up a list of names. Which they will swear to in court and so forth...'

'Precisely. Thus we build a strong line of evidence that will stand up in any court. Man after man, moving closer to Sir Walter until someone names him. Names him in such a manner that even were Raleigh as innocent as the day, he would find himself under investigation and hard-put to disprove what is sworn against him...'

267

PETER TONKIN

'Very well. Remember also that treason is of four kinds according to the Treason Act of thirteen fifty one: *treason in corde*, treason in heart; *treason in ore*, treason in mind; *treason in manu*, treason in hand; and *treason in consummatione* treason consummated. In your case against Raleigh you should look for the first three of these; because Raleigh seems to have paused or to have been prevented before the consummation of whatever plan he and his friends are or were considering. But even if prevented, he and his associates are still traitors *in corde, in ore, et in manu*. Even though their practices have been secret, they are still treasons. And remember, since the days of Henry Eight, through his Act of fifteen thirty six, treason begins with the word, not the act.'

'With the word,' said Poley. 'So Raleigh, Cobham and the rest – Watson, Copley and their friends come to that – committed treason when they opened their mouths, long before they took any of the actions they were discussing.'

'Precisely. All you need is a confession that they discussed treasonous plans, laid treasonous plots, discussed how to put them in action – not that they actually did anything at all. Just get them to confess to that.' Bacon paused. Stroked his beard pensively. 'It is a clever stratagem. And do you think you can lay down your thread of allegation and then follow it all the way from Watson via Copley and the men he names all the way up to Sir Walter?'

'I do.'

'And I believe, if properly handled, what you propose would fall within the law while delivering the outcome you and Master Secretary seek. You should go to work with all despatch.'

50

Anthony Copley could not feel his arms. He could feel his shoulders which hurt abominably and his hands which felt as though they were on fire, each digit a fat sausage being caressed by a cooking-flame. But he could feel nothing in between. This was because he was hanging from a hook in the wall of one of the Tower's cells. If he strained on tip-toe he could take some of the weight of his body on his feet, relieve some of the pain in his shoulders at least. But when he did this, his calves cramped agonisingly almost at once because he had been doing the same thing, over and over, for hours.

He had no real idea how long he had been here. Long enough for him to have rendered his throat dust-dry calling for help, he thought. Long enough to have been forced to relive himself into his now-sodden codpiece. He could not remember ever being so terrified and yet no-one had even spoken to him yet. He hadn't actually seen the men who had hung him here and he had certainly seen no-one since they did so. His head still throbbed from the blow that felled him last night in the stables at Flamstead End and several others delivered on the way here. His wrists and ankles were raw from the gyves that had been locked so tightly round them in the Waltham Cross jail. Hurts which were compounded by what was being done to his wrists now, though the chain joining his ankles was an added torment in all sorts of ways. He knew well enough where he was – though how he got here and who had actually brought him was mostly a closed book. He suspected the state of his head went a long way towards explaining that. And the fact that, to top it all off, he felt horribly sick.

When he heard movement outside the cell door, he turned his head. The movement almost made him vomit on the spot and the whole room heaved around him as though the Tower was a ship on a stormy sea. Two men entered. He didn't know either one, but their brief conversation at least gave him some idea of their names.

'Have him taken down, Topcliffe, and brought to the examination room.'

'At once Sir William.'

Sir William turned on his heel and vanished. Topcliffe called a couple of assistants. Copley was lifted non-too gently down. The returning circulation to his hands made him whimper like a whipped child as he was half carried, half dragged out of the cell, along a short corridor and into a larger room. There was a table here. Sir William sat behind it with a second man at his elbow – a secretary or note-taker by the look of things. The note-taker was vaguely familiar but Copley did not really recognise him as Thomas Phelippes, Poley's code-breaking colleague. Copley was dumped on his feet but his legs nearly failed him so Topcliffe's men remained at his shoulders, keeping him upright, much against his will.

'Name?' snapped Sir William.

'Anthony…' Copley's voice gave out on him half way through the word. He tried to clear his throat only to choke on an upwelling of bile and fall to coughing once again.

'His name is Anthony Copley, Sir William. And might I suggest you let him sit and sip some water if you wish him to make a proper answer to any of your questions.'

Copley turned his head carefully. A tall, black-clad, dark-haired figure with piercing blue eyes stood in the doorway. His heart leaped, for he knew the man – it was Robert Poley. Familiarity caused a well-spring of desperate hope.

Poley paused in the doorway for a moment and considered the man he was about to interrogate. Since their last brief meeting in the Bishop of London's palace, Copley appeared to have grown a little fatter. His face was rounder, cheeks bright behind the straggly beard. The wide eyes were brown and bovine above dark bags. The man struck Poley as being weak and easily led. Perhaps he and Sir William Waad had gone too far in preparing him, for their carefully planned, rigour-free, interrogation. But Poley was keen to get things off to the best possible start. So, whether they had done too much to the man already, there was a good deal of softening-up yet to come.

'You are too gentle with these creatures, Poley,' said Sir William angrily.

'Perhaps I am, Sir William. 'And I propose to be more gentle still. With this one at least.' Poley turned to Topcliffe's men. 'One of you two hold him up while the other fetches a stool and a cup of water. I will also have the gyves and chains removed before we proceed I think.'

'Arrant nonsense!' snapped Sir William and stood so abruptly that he almost made his chair tip backwards. He strode out of the room, pushing rudely past Poley, who came fully into the chamber once Sir William was gone.

The stool arrived, Copley collapsed onto it and took the proffered cup of water in both hands. He was still choking the icy liquid down when the locksmith arrived to take off his cuffs and chains. 'Let us begin,' said Poley gently, seating himself casually on the corner of the table. He glanced at Phelippes. 'Write that we are examining Anthony Copley, gentleman, of Roffey near Horsham. A noted poet and scholar. Whose only sin as far as we know at present is that he has made an unfortunate association with the recusant priest William Watson. Is that not so, Master Copley? You know William Watson?'

'You know I do. You talked with us at the Bishop's palace the night the old queen died.'

'So I did! But it is what you and Watson have been doing since that meeting I wish to discuss with you. When you feel strong enough,'

Poley's tone was so easy and understanding, that Copley's courage began to return. The first instance of this was that he felt confident enough to ask to use the nearest jakes. He had already soiled his codpiece and wished to avoid further humiliation. Poley was most accommodating. Topcliffe's men and Poley accompanied Copley to the nearest privy and Poley dismissed the others then waited outside while he relieved both bladder and bowels. It had not occurred to Copley that he might be able to escape from the privy. He had been imprisoned in the Tower before and knew how impregnable it was, from inside as well as outside. He had never been this deep in its cold stone bowels before though. The flaming torches in their wall-sconces threw a weird, restless light which made everything more sinister still. Poley seemed to understand Copley's disorientation as he stiffly made his exit. 'Rather than going straight back,' said Poley easily, 'I thought we might take a short byway through some rooms you may not have visited before.'

Poley set off and, although his legs were still weak and complaining, Copley had no choice but to hobble after him as fast as he could. He was by no means an acute man, but he soon began to understand the dark purpose of what Poley was doing. It was a mute warning against what he might expect if he was less than forthcoming when Sir William questioned him once more. Poley opened the first door into a large room, at whose centre stood a table more than eight feet in length with a wheeled drum at each end. Spokes suck out of the drums' ends and ratchets prevented the drums from loosening once they had been tightened. The ropes reached across the table-top from the drums and ended in manacles. 'This is the realm of Rackmaster Topcliffe,' said Poley, 'and that, of course, is his preferred method of persuasion. We have often discussed, he and I, precisely what part of the anatomy the rack actually breaks. He maintains it is the joints – as for instance the strappado next door, breaks the shoulder joints of anyone hoist and dropped. But I have seen disjointed shoulders popped back in place before the subject was hoist over and over again. It is the jerk at the end of the drop that does the damage in my experience, the way that the jerk at the end of the drop breaks a neck on the gallows at Tyburn, if you're lucky. I maintain that under the steady pressure of the rack, however, it is likely that the joints hold firm and the bones nearest to them break. That was true I remember of Thomas Kyd the playwright and friend of Christopher Marlowe who was with Topcliffe for less than a week and died soon after, a broken man. Literally. Broken.'

Poley paused to let the information sink in. Then he continued, 'This engine hanging on the wall here works in the opposite manner however. Where the rack stretches, the scavenger's daughter contracts. You see how its metal frame is designed to constrict not only the limbs once they are fastened in place, but also the chest. I have even heard of men being smothered to death by it. It must feel a little like the process of squassation where one weight after another is piled upon your chest until you answer our questions or you suffocate. Or your ribs shatter.'

Poley led the way through into the next chamber. A doorway led off this which struck Copley at once as being strangely proportioned. 'Ah,' said Poley, 'I see you have spotted it. Come closer.' He crossed to the door, lifting a flaming torch from the wall nearby as he moved. 'It is called Little Ease. It is a square box less than four feet high, wide or deep. Once locked in there – in absolute darkness – it is impossible to stand, sit or lie down with any comfort whatsoever. Imagine. After an hour or so your limbs begin to cramp. After a few more hours you are desperate for bodily relief such as you have just enjoyed but can you loosen your clothing? If so, can you adjust it again? And is it worth your while to do so for you must inevitably sit or lie in what you have just deposited. After half a day you might feel you will run mad. After one full day, who knows…'

'One full day…' said Copley, horrified but somehow fascinated. 'Has anyone lasted one full day?'

'Some years before Armada year, the Jesuit Edmund Campion was in there for four full days. Only the Good Lord helped him through it, I would guess. But he had to be dragged on a hurdle to Tyburn for his execution because he couldn't move a muscle when they finally pulled him out.'

Copley stepped back in horror, as though the tiny chamber contained some huge venomous creature. He looked round a little wildly. There was a table close by with several sets of thumb-screws upon it, illuminated as Poley replaced the torch in its sconce. The full sets of thumbscrews which were designed to crush every knuckle on each digit of the hands inserted into them. And, beneath the table, the open-topped metal boot with mallet and wedges waiting to be hammered down into it on either side of the unfortunate shin it was designed to contain. Unless it was to be filled with boiling water, boiling oil or boiling lead instead. As he recoiled from this as well, he saw a shadow on the wall. There was something hanging from the ceiling. He looked up and recognised it at once. It was the pulley through which the strappado Poley had mentioned earlier ran. Copley reeled, his imagination suddenly overwhelmed by the realisation of what it must feel like to have your shoulders torn out of their sockets only to have them forced back in then torn out once more, time after time after time.

'Why, Master Copley, you have gone as pale as parchment. I have overtaxed your strength I fear,' said Poley. 'Let us return to Sir William's room at once and proceed with the examination before you faint.'

Copley stumbled in Poley's wake, blearily aware that he had been shown the terrifying instruments of torture as something between a warning and a threat. He had no real notion, however, what the potent mixture of pain, exhaustion and fear was having on his brain and his ability to think and react swiftly or flexibly. It was as though his mind had been locked in the scavenger's daughter and he didn't realise it.

51

'Let us begin again,' said Sir William Waad. 'You are Anthony Copley of Roffey near Horsham.'

'I am.' Copley looked a little drunkenly round the room, head still reeling from his near-faint.

Phelippes the note-taker scribbled industriously.

'And you were arrested by men working for Secretary to the Council Sir Robert Cecil…'

'In that I was hit over the head, slung over a horse and dragged here in chains via the Waltham Cross jail…'

'…at Flamstead End, a house belonging to Sir John Gage, near Waltham Cross in the county of Hertfordshire at about midnight last night.'

'…though I have seen no warrant nor been arraigned before any justice.'

The two men stopped speaking at the same time. Then Poley said sympathetically, 'That is why you are here, Master Copley. To discover whether you should be arraigned as having broken laws of such gravity as might put your life or liberty at hazard.'

'Of course he has!' snapped Sir William. 'His liberty is very much at hazard. And I am here to make a report that will very likely decide about his life. And that report will go first to the council and then to the justices. Especially as it will contain a sworn confession signed as being true by the accused and witnessed as such by both of us.'

'It may well go to King James himself, as it involves His Majesty. But you confess,' probed Poley. 'You were at Flamstead End house last night.'

'I cannot deny it if that is where I was *arrested* as you say,' answered Copley. *His Majesty?* Screamed a tiny part of his mind, simply stunned as he truly began to see the enormity of what he was involved in. Up until now it had all been so vague and theoretical – but now it seemed the king himself was going to read his testimony. And decide how to act upon it – perhaps as he had acted when he had hanged the cutpurse out of hand.

'Very well,' said Poley, glancing at Phelippes. 'That is the first element of your confession recorded. Now, what were you doing there?'

'Visiting friends.' Copley's gaze slid away from his inquisitor's.

'And these friends were Sir John Gage and his family?' asked Poley, who did not seem to notice this.

'Well... yes...'

'You lie!' snarled Sir William. 'You were there to meet William Watson, your co-conspirator and the Lord knows how many more traitors besides!'

'Patience, Sir William; let the poor man finish. So, you were there to meet your friend Sir John and his family. His wife, whose name is...'

'Well...' Copley fought to remember the woman's name. In vain. She and the children had stayed well clear of the meeting in any case.

'And his lovely children called...'

'Ah...' Mary? Elizabeth? He really had no idea.

'Master Copley,' chid Poley sadly. 'You will have to do better than that if you wish to deceive Sir William here.' Copley's heart sank. He was abruptly very scared indeed. His shoulders slumped, making him look as defeated as he felt. 'So Sir William was right.' Poley persisted. 'You were there, not to visit with Sir John but to meet with William Watson.'

'Yes,' said Copley, inwardly cursing himself. How could he have allowed himself to be unmasked so easily? He would have to start thinking a great deal faster if he was to get through this without becoming more closely acquainted with Rackmaster Topcliffe. The thought made his scrotum clench.

He suddenly felt an overwhelming need to relieve himself again.

'And so the second element of your confession is in place. You see how simple it is? What did you and William Watson meet to discuss?' Poley's tone remained one of innocent enquiry. Phelippes' quill pen scratched industriously.

'The succession,' said Copley. 'It is on everyone's lips.' He sat up a little straighter – on firmer ground with that answer. The need to urinate receded.

'How King James will soon succeed the late queen to become not only the Sixth of Scotland but the First of England?' asked Poley, seemingly simply seeking clarification.

Copley sat up straighter still, confident of what his answer would be.

'How best to go about preventing such a succession more likely,' growled Sir William, before Copley could open his mouth - destroying his new-found confidence at once.

'Sir William was right just now, was he not?' prompted Poley. 'Was that what you were discussing?'

'We were discussing whether we could look to King James for easement of the recusancy payments and more recognition of the plight of his Catholic subjects...'

'Matters his majesty has already settled, surely, with his various acts and proclamations since his coming out of Scotland.' Poley observed. 'That's really not good enough, friend Copley.'

'We were discussing whether the king might change his mind...' Copley frowned, trying to cudgel his wits into working more swiftly. With limited success. Even the relentless scratching of the note-taker's pen was an irritating distraction.

'And what was Sir Griffin's opinion?' snapped Sir William.

Copley was still concentrating on trying to think faster. So his tongue went to work all on its own. 'Why, that after a while he might...'

278

'So, Sir Griffin Markham was there too!' Sir William snapped.

'Well…' Copley was simply horrified at how easily he had been outsmarted. Again.

'Come, Master Copley, you have all-but admitted that he was,' said Poley, shaking his head sympathetically.

'Well, it is no great surprise if he was,' said Sir William. 'He has sponsored Watson in the past has ne not? Paid his passage to Edinburgh to be the first with news of the old queen's death in hopes of preferment for both of them. Hopes dashed for them both. I see two bitter men, talking treason within a recusant household.'

'And his brothers?' added Poley. 'Sir Griffin rarely stirs without his brothers?'

'His brothers were there too. But they hardly joined in the conversation…'

'Ah. We are back to the conversation,' said Sir William. 'It was about how to stop the succession of King James, you say?'

'I said nothing of the kind!'

'To change the king, you said. Is that not written down?' Sir William turned to Phelippes.

'To change the king's *mind* I said. Not change the king!'

'And to change the king's mind you needed to assemble…' Sir William paused as though trying to remember the number. 'How many did Watson call for? A thousand?'

'Forty thousand,' said Poley.

'It was a fantasy!' howled Copley. 'Forty thousand. There was no need of so many…'

'To do what?' demanded Sir William. 'How was Watson's army of something less than forty thousand Catholic gentlemen going to change the king's mind there at Theobalds last night, had not something most fortuitously gone amiss?'

'Admit it,' prompted Poley gently. 'Had Watson managed to raise his recusant army, he planned to invade Theobalds

House and kidnap the king. Like the Earl of Gowrie tried to do.'

'No… No…' but even in his own ears Copley's protestation sounded more like *Yes… Yes…*

'So, now we know what was being discussed,' said Sir William with evident satisfaction. 'The third element of your confession is settled. And we have a good idea of who was doing the discussing. Watson, the Markham brothers led by Sir Griffin, Sir John Gage and you, Copley. Who else was there?'

Copley's mind went blank. Naming Watson was one thing. Even naming Sir Griffin and his brothers was simply confirming something made public by the old knight's sponsorship of Watson's journey to Edinburgh. But naming Lord Grey would take him onto an entirely different level of treachery. And as for telling them that Lord Cobham's brother the Reverend George Brooke was also deeply involved could be very dangerous indeed. He had no idea how long it took him to order these thoughts in his battered mind. Or how guilty that long pause was making him look.

52

'But you see,' said Poley gently, 'if Watson's army of forty thousand Catholic gentlemen was nothing more than a fantasy, as you have already admitted that it was, then how were you hoping to gather enough men to your cause to effect the outcome you planned and change the king's mind – as you have confessed was your objective?'

'Did the men who arrested Copley estimate how many others were already there?' asked Sir William.

'They did,' answered Poley. 'Perhaps fifty, they thought.'

'So, your plan stood in urgent need of further support, did it not, Copley?' demanded Sir William.

'… not *my* plan…'

'Your confession will make such minor details clear I assure you,' snapped Sir William, his tone making the words a threat. 'But to return to the question: Where were the men you needed going to come from if not from Watson?'

Copley looked at the three faces opposite, his mouth open. Just at the very moment when he needed his wits to be most nimble, they were failing him utterly. He could think of nothing to say – except for the unsettlingly dangerous truth.

'Perhaps Sir Griffin's wild ride to London yesterday afternoon had something to do with it,' suggested Poley. 'Who did Sir Griffin plan to see?'

'You would have to ask Sir Griffin…'

'Come come, Copley,' purred Poley. 'You can see as well as we can that Sir Griffin is not here. You are. We cannot ask him. Therefore we are asking you.'

'Who did Sir Griffin come to London to see?' shouted Sir William. Copley flinched.

'You need not fear to name him,' said Poley. 'For he must be innocent of any wrongdoing must he not?'

'What do you mean?' Copley shook his head. Regretted it. Fought to understand this shift in perspective. Failed.

'It is so simple,' said Poley. 'My logic suggests the following. By yesterday afternoon King James was at Theobalds. Your plan to kidnap him like the Gowries did some two years ago was nearing fruition. All it needed was more men. Watson's promised Catholic gentlemen had not appeared, so Sir Griffin came to London to beg for support from someone you had hoped might be sympathetic. But this man refused to help. This is not treason, it is patriotism. Surely you must see that? By failing to name the man who disappointed Sir Griffin, stopped your plot in its tracks and thus probably saved the king, you are simply robbing him of a well-deserved reward.'

Copley gaped at Poley.

'Were I this man,' said Sir William abruptly, 'and it came to my notice that you could have revealed my great patriotism and refused, I would make it my business to destroy you utterly. You and yours.'

'Let us hope that this patriotic gentleman is not too well connected or powerful, then,' said Poley. 'Or poor Copley here might just as well cut his own throat as wait for some assassin employed to do it for him…'

'Grey,' gasped Copley. 'It was Lord Grey de Wilton!' But the moment he spoke he knew he had been tricked again. Tears welled in his wide eyes. His nose began to run. He sniffed, then rubbed the sleeve of his doublet across it.

'Lord Grey? Indeed? But he is no recusant. He's not even Catholic. Why does he seek to change the king's mind about the standing of Catholics in the kingdom?'

'You would have to ask him!'

'Oh,' said Sir William, 'we certainly will.'

'But if there were protestant plotters amongst you,' said Poley, 'the Catholic question cannot be the only one you wished the king to settle. What was it each of you truly wished for - and hoped the king would grant alongside more understanding of the Catholic position?'

'For myself it was a mere nothing, and Sir John, likewise had no strong desires. Sir Griffin wished to retain Beskwood and his rights to the forest and – so he said – the post of Earl Marshal. Lord Grey, I recall, wished to be granted some rights currently held by the Earl of Southampton...'

'Oh, if only I had realised it was Lord Grey you were about to name,' said Poley, his voice heavy with regret. 'Lord Grey is notorious for his fiery temper and his unforgiving nature. Why, it was Lord Grey was it not, who supplied the spark that ignited the Earl of Essex's uprising when he attacked the Earl of Southampton on the Strand and killed his page stone dead. Oh, I do fear you may have made an implacable enemy by naming Lord Grey...'

'But you said... You said...'

'But surely, if you had been making plans with Watson and Grey amongst others, you must have seen Grey's true nature yourself? Did you not realise the risk you were running in naming him?'

'We will arrest him for questioning next,' decided Sir William. 'And we will release you.'

'We will even let it be widely known how much you have aided our enquiries,' said Poley.

'No!' Copley was simply horrified at the thought. Grey looming in his imagination like a murderous monster. Like Sir Walter Raleigh, leader of the slaughter at Smerwick – an act ordered by Lord Grey's father.

'You are married are you not? With a promising family?' asked Sir William.

'More throats for Lord Grey to cut!' Poley shook his head sadly. But then he suddenly brightened. 'However,' he said, 'I see a way forward which might preserve all. Is there anyone else involved? Anyone we might find more interesting to examine than Grey? Sir William, were Master Copley to name someone of greater interest to us, might we not leave

Lord Grey and, indeed, Master Copley and his family out of the matter altogether?'

'Why yes,' said Sir William. 'Were there someone as yet unnamed who might be of greater interest to us, then yes indeed, I would see that as an excellent way forward.'

'So,' Poley turned to Copley. 'Can you think of anyone else whose involvement in this might serve to distract our investigators from Lord Grey?'

'Yes!' said Copley, swept away on a great wave of relief. 'Oh yes!'

An hour later, the examination was over and Phelippes cleared his throat to read out the confession he had been writing as Copley answered Poley and Sir William's questions. 'When you have heard it, you must agree it and then sign it,' Sir William told him. 'And, in the unlikely event you are ever called as witness, you must stand up in court and swear to the truth of it.'

'Do you understand?' asked Poley.

'Yes,' said Copley. 'Yes, I understand.'

'Very well,' said Sir William. 'Read on, master Phelippes.'

'I, Anthony Copley of Roffey near Horsham, being of sound mind, do freely and fully confess the following,' said Phelippes, reading slowly and clearly.

'Item. That on or about the third of May in this year of grace sixteen hundred and three I met together with several others at Flamstead End in Hertfordshire, the home of Sir John Gage.

'Item. That my main purpose in going to Flamstead End was not to visit Sir John but to meet with the recusant and traitorous outlaw William Watson and the like-minded men he had assembled there.

'Item. That our purpose in so meeting was to discuss how to change the king's mind with regard to recusancy charges and to the recognition of the Catholic faith in his realm.

'Item. That it was decided, at Watson's suggestion and under his leadership, that the most effective way to do this

284

would be to kidnap the king who was at that time a guest of Secretary to the Council Sir Robert Cecil at his nearby house of Theobalds, also in Hertfordshire.

'Item. That the following men were involved in planning and preparing this kidnapping under Watson's direction at that place and at that time. William Watson, myself, Sir John Gage, Sir Griffin Markham of Beskwood Park in Nottinghamshire, his brothers Sir Thomas Markham and Sir William Markham, Sir Thomas Grey Lord Grey de Wilton and the Reverend George Brooke, Prebendary of York.

'Item. That a wider list of requirements was to be demanded other than Catholic emancipation when the king was successfully in our hands and presented with the alternatives of acquiescence or death – to wit Sir Griffin Markham's rights to Beskwood Park and the forest nearby as well as the post of Earl Marshal. To wit Lord Grey's demand for the governorship of the Isle of Wight as currently held by the Earl of Southampton. Item, Sir George Brooke's desire to be granted the living of Saint Cross in Winchester as promised to him by the late Queen. To wit William Watson's desire to behead the entire Privy Council.

'Item that Lord Grey had promised to raise a thousand men in support of this enterprise but when approached by Sir Griffin Markham he refused, causing the entire plot to come to nothing.

'Item. That I have no doubt that, had Lord Grey supplied the men as promised, the kidnapping of the king would have proceeded with the full involvement and co-operation of everyone named above – and a great number more besides, committed through the treasonous work of recusant priest William Watson.

'Item, that upon the failure of Lord Grey to supply the men as promised, the enterprise was forthwith abandoned but not by all. Sir Griffin Markham and his brothers returned to Beskwood Park, defeated. Sir John Gage withdrew absolutely. Lord Grey de Wilton had clearly already done so.

But Watson vowed he would proceed as best he could and went to contact his co-conspirator William Clark. And Sir George Brooke declared that he would go to his brother Lord Cobham in hopes of recruiting either Cobham or Sir Walter Raleigh or both to the scheme.

'To this I set my hand, this fourth day of May, sixteen hundred and three, Anthony Copley

'As Witnessed, William Waad, Robert Poley.'

53

'So,' said Poley after Copley had left the interrogation chamber to take up residence - temporary as he hoped - in that section of the building they were already calling the Devereux Tower after its most famous recent occupant, 'our thread leading from Watson to Sir Walter is shorter than we might have supposed.'

'We obviously question George Brooke next,' said Sir William. 'Perhaps tomorrow if we can move things along so quickly. His involvement in Watson's plot is plain. As is his relationship with Lord Cobham.'

'We must ensure that he leads us to Cobham,' nodded Poley.

'And Cobham in turn will lead to Sir Walter Raleigh. And then all he has to do is name Raleigh in a questionable context as part of his confession as witnessed by ourselves. Even if neither of them has been involved in anything to do with Watson's plot.' Sir William narrowed his eyes and shook his head dubiously, clearly not convinced of their ability to close the final link in the chain of evidence they were following.

'They have been involved in something, though,' said Poley. 'That's where Lady Janet's and Sir Anthony Standen's information has proved invaluable, though it would be useless as evidence in court as we have established. Whatever they have been up to may not have been anything much, especially compared with Watson's plot, and it may not have proceeded beyond some discussions and a letter or two – all of which came to nothing. But it seems that there was an enterprise of some sort. And starting it is where the treason lies – no matter where or how it ended. Remember, the old king's Treason Act still stands nearly seventy years after it was passed. Treason is to be found in the words long before the act…'

'Very well. So, we send for the Reverend Prebendary George Brooke and in due course confront him with Copley's confession.'

'Sir George Brooke. That's where we go next.'

54

The Reverend George Brooke, Prebendary of York Cathedral, the next turn in the thread joining Watson to Raleigh, was the exact opposite of Copley. He was all supercilious bluster from the very moment he arrived the next day. Poley and Sir William Waad immediately decided they would save Copley's confession to confront Brooke with later, as they both wished to break down the wall of arrogance first. They had no chance to tire him out or disorientate him as they had with their first subject. And showing him round Topcliffe's realm was unlikely to have much of an effect on him for one simple reason – and that reason was the first thing out of his mouth even before they began their interrogation.

'You'll regret this!' he snarled as he was shown into Sir William's interview room and limped across to the chair that awaited him. 'My brother Lord Cobham has many powerful friends. The moment you do or say anything to discomfit me he will be certain to destroy you both!'

'You had best take care, Sir George, that you do or say nothing that will damage *him*!' snapped Sir William. 'No man is above the law.'

Sir George had the grace to look a little shifty as the implications of Waad's words hit him. He made a great play of sitting down and stretching out his bad leg. He had been born lame and never failed to play on the affliction.

Poley narrowed his eyes and examined his adversary. Sir George was the youngest of the four Brooke brothers. Poley did not come from a large family but he knew how such things often worked – even with only four rather than eight or ten. The youngest was either the bullied butt of his elder siblings or was indulged and spoiled until he came to believe that his merest whim had the force of a natural law. George

Brooke was of the latter variety, despite the rumours that he had fallen out with his elder brother recently. This was seemingly compounded by simple physiognomy. His eyes were close set, bulbous and bovine. His straggling beard could not disguise the weakness of his chin. Below each feature, a nose and an Adam's apple jutted strikingly. And, as Poley had observed, George Brooke was lame, and possessed of a character which demanded sympathy and support for his affliction alongside everything else.

And yet behind it all there was a brain. Brooke was no amiable buffoon like his brother Lord Cobham was reputed to be. He was a graduate of King's College, Cambridge with both Batchelor's and Master's degrees. The Master's was in Divinity. He was currently the holder of the post of Prebendary of York's Anglican Cathedral which he rarely visited but which provided a steady income from the Cathedral funds. An income that was not sufficient for the young man's needs – hence his begging the Mastership of the rich St Cross Hospital near Winchester. A post that had been promised him by the indulgent old queen but lost to him now with her death. He was not a man who took such reverses gracefully, Poley silently observed. Hence his part in the Watson plot. Hence his presence here.

'What were you doing at Flamstead End two nights ago?' demanded Sir William, angered by Brooke's attitude and demeanour. Even though Brooke was thirty five now, thought Poley, he still behaved like a spoiled child. Nothing could be more precisely designed to get under William Waad's skin. Waad and Phelippes exchanged glances and the note-taking began.

'That's none of your concern,' Brooke sneered now. 'It was a private matter and nothing to do with you or your master that crookback spider Robert Cecil.'

'It became our business when you started plotting with those other churchmen, William Watson and William Clark.' Sir William spat.

'Was Watson there? I did not see him,' shrugged Brooke.

'Did you see Sir Griffin Markham and his brothers?' wondered Poley.

'Sir Griffin? Of course. We are old friends.'

'The same Sir Griffin as paid Watson's passage to Edinburgh the night the old queen died?' Poley persisted.

'Did he so? I had no idea! I am shocked if that is true. Deeply shocked!' Brooke tried to look shocked. Without much success.

'And Lord Grey de Wilton? Did you see him there?' asked Sir William.

'Not two nights ago, no. He had returned to his London home.' Brooke smirked, clearly believing he had scored a point. But this was no game, Poley knew; and he had done the opposite.

'Did Lord Grey return to London for any particular reason? On any specific mission?' demanded Sir William.

'What reason or mission could he have? He is a senior peer of the realm, a member of Her Majesty's Council...'

'Of *Her* Majesty's Council perhaps; of Her *late* Majesty's in fact. But not, it seems of *His* Majesty's,' Poley pointed out.

'A detail, nothing more. A detail I am certain that time will rectify.'

'Time perhaps. Or Watson's plots. A man of uncertain standing – a bitterly disappointed man – might well wish to move matters forward using Watson's method,' Poley answered.

'Disappointed?' Brooke paled a little. Then began to bluster once more. 'Who do you say is disappointed? Not Lord Grey, surely.'

'We will ask him,' said Sir William. 'We are due to see him next. In the expectation that he might well have seen Watson before he left Flamstead End for London. And seen who was actually talking to him into the bargain.'

'Well,' said Brooke, raising his chin to stare at them down the considerable beak of his nose, a gesture he had clearly found in the past to be effective in quelling importunate inferiors and troublesome authorities, 'if Watson was at the dinner table, he might have been in my presence without my noticing him at all.'

'Of course, of course,' nodded Poley understandingly. 'And it was a large party, was it? All assembled there?'

'Well yes, Sir John Gage our host of course. Lady Gage. The children…'

'There, but too young to be at table, surely? And taken to bed by their mother, so I hear?'

'Yes, Yes of course.' Brooke shrugged as though being caught in a lie was of no consequence. 'Sir Griffin was there as we have discussed. His brothers Thomas and William were with him as usual. Lord Grey…'

'Who departed for London that afternoon and so was not at table on the evening of the third?'

'I have already said so.' Another shrug. 'Anthony Copley was there…'

'A close friend of Watson's. How could you have noticed Copley and not Watson? They would have been seated side by side, surely. And this is not a very great gathering after all, is it?'

'Copley remembers you very clearly,' said Sir William abruptly. 'And he remembers your conversation with Watson. Word for word.'

Brooke seemed to freeze. Then, 'You have already talked to Copley,' whispered Brooke.

'At length,' said Sir William.

'And in great detail,' added Poley.

'And what did he tell you?'

'The truth,' said Sir William.

'At least he said it was the truth,' added Poley. 'He swore to the truth of it, signed at the foot of it and was witnessed in doing so by Sir William and myself. He has declared, indeed, that he will stand up in any court in the land and witness or confess as appropriate to the specific details of it.'

'Let me see it!' snarled Brooke. 'Let me see this *truth*!'

'In due time,' said Sir William. 'When you have told us the truth as you remember it.'

'You will need to be careful,' warned Poley. 'And very precise. We are, after all, dealing with high treason here.'

'Ha!' sneered Brooke. 'It cannot be high treason! James Stuart is no king in England. There is no high treason to be done against him here until he is crowned and throned.'

'So,' said Poley, 'Simple treason it is, then. And you have thereby exchanged one stroke of the headsman's axe for the rather more lingering departure by hanging, drawing and quartering. You have made a fine bargain for yourself and your associates there, have you not?'

'You would not dare…'

Sir William ran out of patience. 'That is what the Earl of Essex thought!' he snapped. 'And his stepfather Sir Christopher Blount! And his secretary Sir Henry Cuffe. And his Steward Sir Gelly Meyrick…'

'Enough!' commanded Brooke, visibly shaken.

'You dare to command me?' snarled Waad, coming to his feet and leaning across the table separating them. 'Why you insolent…'

'Perhaps, Sir William,' suggested Poley gently, 'now is the time to allow the Reverend Prebendary here to understand the danger he is in.'

Sir William took a deep breath. As he sat down again, Poley had leisure to wonder how much of Sir William's outrage was play-acting and how much was genuine. A fine line between them perhaps. But even his outraged movement had come nowhere near disturbing Phelippes and his note-taking. 'Very well,' grated Waad. 'Secretary…' He turned to Phelippes and dropped his voice. What the two men discussed was lost beneath the rustling of papers.

'I believe Sir William wants you to know in a little more detail what Anthony Copley has sworn against the men who plotted with Watson on the third of May at Flamstead End.

Those plotters, he is willing to name and swear on oath were present and involved. And the men named include yourself.'

'I was there! I admit it! I have never hidden it!'

'But so far you have only admitted to taking dinner and have refused to confirm whether or not you were party to any discussions, plots or plans. You cannot even remember, for instance, whether you actually saw Watson there – let alone conversed with him. I believe Sir William thinks Copley's confession may refresh your memory somewhat.'

55

'Copley!' sneered George Brooke. 'And what makes you think his recollections will prompt my own? What is there anything to say that he will be believed above me, even should our recollections differ?'

'He has sworn to the truth of his words,' explained Poley patiently, as though talking to a student slow to understand a simple lesson. 'Sworn an oath before God, the force of which you of all people should understand.'

'If you swear to something different, then naturally it will be up to the court to decide between you,' explained Sir William mimicking Poley's tone. This made Brooke's patrician nostrils flare with outrage but his mouth remained tightly closed – a thin line downturned at each end.

'Of course,' added Poley, 'you may, if you wish, lie with impunity for if the court chooses to believe Copley rather than you and thus catch you in a falsehood, then your sentence for perjury will be subsumed in any case into your sentence for treason.'

'Have you witnessed a hanging, drawing and quartering?' asked Sir William.

'Of course, who has not attended one?' demanded Brooke before he realised the implication of Sir William's words.

Which Sir William was happy to drive home. 'Consider then,' he observed, 'that you might view the next one you attend from an entirely new perspective. A more participatory perspective, shall we say.'

'So,' said Poley as Brooke gaped, fighting to find the words he wanted. 'Let us proceed. Do you swear before God that your testimony will be the truth?'

Brooke blinked, almost as though he was waking up. Out of a nightmare? Wondered Poley. Or into one? 'Of course…' whispered the Reverend Prebendary of York.

'Note that,' said Sir William, glancing at Phelippes. 'The Reverend Brooke has sworn before God to tell the truth and nothing but the truth.'

Poley turned to Brooke, suddenly all formality, as though the Tower's interrogation room had become a court of law. 'Please listen to the evidence as presented by Copley and read by our scribe, Reverend Brooke. You will no doubt wish to rebut it, perhaps in detail. Master Phelippes, we will take things slowly. Read the evidence you recorded yesterday and get ready to record the Reverend Brooke's reactions.'

Phelippes nodded, rearranged his papers, put his pen, inkwell and sand shaker close at hand and began to read. 'This is the testimony of Anthony Copley, gentleman, given before Sir William Waad and Master Robert Poley on the fourth of May in the year of grace sixteen hundred and three. "Item. That my main purpose in going to Flamstead End was not to visit Sir John but to meet with the recusant and traitorous outlaw William Watson and the like-minded men he had assembled there."'

'Copley may have had such a purpose,' blustered Brooke. 'But that is no evidence I shared that purpose!' Phelippes reached for his pen.

'But you were, were you not, one of the group he calls the "like minded men"?' probed Sir William.

'I was not "like minded" and you cannot prove that I was!' The pen scratched industriously.

'Why were you there, then?' asked Poley. 'One of a small group, housed by Sir John Gage but led by William Watson? What purpose could you have had other than to talk to him?'

Brooke's eyes swivelled from side to side so swiftly as his mind raced that he looked a lot like his wall-eyed leader. 'Why, to talk to him, yes, but to talk him *out of his madness*!'

'What madness?' demanded Sir William at once.

'Why, his plan to kidnap…'

'So you admit that you knew the plan, then,' said Poley. 'How else could it be that you were trying to stop it?'

'Make sure you have noted that clearly, Master Phelippes,' ordered Sir William, 'The Reverend Brooke knew of Watson's plan to kidnap the king. Then you may read the next two items of Copley's confession.'

Brooke sat silently. But he was gasping for breath like a man on the verge of drowning. There was perspiration on his forehead, noted Poley, and tears in his wide brown eyes.

After a moment more, Phelippes put his pen back in its inkwell, took up Copley's confession and did as he was told. '"Item. That our purpose in so meeting was to discuss how to change the king's mind with regard to recusancy charges and to the recognition of the Catholic faith in his realm. Item. That it was decided, at Watson's suggestion and under his leadership, that the most effective way to do this would be to kidnap the king who was at that time a guest of Secretary to the Council Sir Robert Cecil at his nearby house of Theobalds, also in Hertfordshire."'

'I *knew of it*,' howled Brooke. 'I have admitted as much. But I was there to put a stop to it, I swear!'

'Indeed?' said Sir William. 'That was not the impression Anthony Copley gained. Quite the reverse, in fact. Phelippes, the next paragraph if you please.'

'"Item. That the following men were involved in planning and preparing this kidnapping under Watson's direction at that place and at that time. William Watson, myself, Sir John Gage, Sir Griffin Markham of Beskwood Park in Nottinghamshire, his brothers Sir Thomas Markham and Sir William Markham, Sir Thomas Grey Lord Grey de Wilton and the Reverend George Brooke."'

'No! As God is my witness…'

'God *is* your witness is He not, Reverend Brooke?' demanded Poley. 'But so are Sir William and I - and I fear we have caught you in a barefaced lie.'

297

'And on your scared oath,' emphasised Sir William brutally. 'You know the executioner at Tyburn will first cut off your privities but perhaps he ought to cut out your tongue as well!'

'Did not Copley say I was arguing against such action?' There was a tone of supplication, almost of begging in Brooke's words. 'Did he not say it was clearly my intention to put a stop to the whole thing? For I swear before God and on my life that this was my purpose. My only purpose in attending. Why else would I, an Anglican clergyman, become involved with a Catholic plot?'

Poley's eyebrows rose in disbelief. Could the man be so self-absorbed and spoiled that he really supposed his wishes could alter the past and change the truth? It was almost incomprehensible.

Sir William shook his head sadly. 'Read the next item of Copley's confession Master Phelippes,' he ordered.

'"Item. That a wider list of requirements was to be demanded other than Catholic emancipation when the king was successfully in our hands and presented with the alternatives of acquiescence or death – to wit Sir Griffin Markham's rights to Beskwood Park and the forest nearby as well as the post of Earl Marshal. To wit Lord Grey's demand for the governorship of the Isle of Wight as currently held by the Earl of Southampton. Item, Sir George Brooke's desire to be granted the living of Saint Cross in Winchester as promised to him by the late queen. To wit William Watson's desire to behead the entire Privy Council."'

'No!' Brooke's tone shook with earnestness. 'It was not like that. Copley is mistaken…'

'That's not how it sounds to me,' said Sir William.

'That's not how it will sound to a court preparing to condemn you for your part in this…' added Poley.

'My brother,' said Brooke desperately, the tears at last cascading down his face.

'Your brother cannot help you escape the weight of the law in this,' said Sir William, 'Powerful and well-respected though he is.'

Neither he nor Poley dared exchange even the briefest glance with the other. Brooke had put Lord Cobham on their hook. Now they had to reel him in, and Raleigh along with him.

'No! No!' Brooke was almost falling over himself as he tried to explain. 'I asked for his advice in this matter and he told me to take the greatest care. Moreover, he knows of a far more dangerous plot which may still be in motion! Forget about me, I am nothing compared to this. Watson and Clark are nothing compared to this! Ask him!'

Sir William was simply disbelieving. 'Lord Cobham? Knew of the Watson treason but he was and is also aware of some other plot besides? Impossible. He would have reported such knowledge to the appropriate authorities at once. You are either mistaken or you are lying to throw us off your track.'

'No! I swear on my life. We talked. I shared my devastation of spirit that the king's agent Hudson had sold the St Cross to one James Lake to the ruination of my hopes. Cobham knew of Watson's purposes as well as I do myself – but Cobham also knows of a far more deadly plot put in motion by men immeasurably more important and powerful than I am; than any of us associated with Watson. Its outcome deigned to be far worse than merely kidnapping the king.'

'I do not believe a word of this,' said Sir William. 'Master Poley? Have you or any of your intelligencers heard anything of such a plot?'

'Nothing, Sir William…'

'There you are then.' He turned to Brooke. 'Tyburn awaits. The hangman stands ready. His brazier for your manhood. His knives for the opening of your belly and the drawing of your guts. His axes and choppers for the removal of your head and the quartering of your corpse…'

299

'... but,' continued Poley, the voice of quiet reason pulling Brooke back out of the nightmare vision Waad had conjured, 'perhaps we should listen to the detail of what the Reverend Brooke has to tell us about this second plot before we condemn him out of hand.'

56

'And,' said Cecil, 'George Brook will stand by this?' He shook his head in simple disbelief.

'As you see, Master Secretary, he has signed it to the effect that he gave the evidence of his own free will and under oath. It was recorded verbatim by Thomas Phelippes. It has been witnessed by myself and by Sir William. The Reverend Brooke will stand up in any court in the land and give this in evidence.'

'I can scarce believe it. Read it again. The final section. Read it again.'

It was the morning of a day early in the following week. The king had left Theobalds some time ago in a mood of joyous generosity. He had never rested in such a wonderful house, hunted in such a well-stocked park or enjoyed such entertainment. Cecil was certain to keep his post of Secretary to the Council and could well look for further honours still. And soon by all accounts. Poley had never seen Master Secretary so happy as he took his ease in his office in Theobalds all aglow with a sense of having overcome an almost insurmountable hurdle. He would be chasing the king south as soon as he had finished overseeing Theobalds' recovery from the royal visit. But, all that aside, at this moment, Poley had never seen him look so surprised or, indeed, so shocked.

'"Item,"' read Poley clearly, an easy task given Phelippes unrivalled penmanship. '"That in my dealings with William Watson. Sir Griffin Markham, his brothers, Lord Grey de Wilton and the rest, I opened my mind to my brother Lord Cobham and became aware that he had his suspicions about another, deeper and more secret plot. This second plot to my certain knowledge, involves men of the highest elevation, reputation and power. Its purpose is not to kidnap the king but to remove him altogether and replace him with an alternative monarch more amenable to mending their situations and willing to meet their demands. I do not know who they are planning on putting on the throne. Nor do I know the names of the men involved. I know they have been in contact with the Princely Count of Aremburg by English and French messengers and have been seeking funding through his good offices from the Spanish Court. That is the limit of my knowledge in the matter but I swear that my brother Lord Cobham is also aware of it and may be privy to more details than I have managed to learn. To this I set my hand… and so-on and so-forth.... As witnessed by Sir William Waad…" And so-forth…' Poley looked up from George Brooke's confession and fell silent.

Cecil's long, pale face was locked in a pensive frown. 'He has offered this as a distraction from his own treasonable doings proven and confessed,' said Master Secretary. Poley forbore to remark that this much was obvious. 'And perhaps to spite his brother with whom he is currently at odds, I understand. You have eyes on Cobham?' asked Cecil.

'My best. Nick Skeres. Also, since our interview with George Brooke, Udall and Tom Watson as well.'

'And the Reverend George is…?

'Like Copley, in some of the more salubrious rooms in the Flint Tower. Not really under arrest, but…'

'Unable to warn his brother of his treacherous confession.'

'Just so, Master Secretary.'

'And what news of the innocently ignorant Cobham?'

'He flits between Essex House, Drury House and Durham House. I do not believe he realises we have eyes on him. He is not as insightful or as observant as his brother or his associates.'

'Northumberland and Southampton are distractions. Raleigh remains the main object of your work, though if what George Brooke says is true – as your informers seem to suggest most strongly – then whatever is going on involves them all in some measure at least.'

'Even if nothing is going on now, something certainly has been afoot. George Brooke's testimony proves that. But Sir William and I strained our authority to the limit in bringing George Brooke before us. We need much more power if we are to arraign members of the Privy Council such as Cobham and Raleigh.'

'I will discuss matters with Sir John Herbert as my fellow Secretary of State. Lord High Admiral Effingham, Attorney General Popham and one or two other senior men.'

Men who neither like nor trust the arrogant upstart Raleigh, Poley thought. 'And, perhaps, Sir John Peyton,' he suggested. 'Not even Raleigh could stand against the yeoman warders; while he and Cobham will end up being examined by Sir William Waad in the Tower, will they not?'

'And the king, of course,' continued Cecil as though he had not heard Poley at all. 'His Majesty might wish to have his Captain of the Guard arrange a detail of men to perform the arrest on her late Majesty's Captain of the Guard. Or Lord Kinloss...'

Poley had an instantaneous mental vision of Raleigh and Henderson confronting each other like a couple of fighting cocks in the cock-pit. Or would Raleigh at bay be more like a bear chained to the stake in the bear-baiting pit beside the Globe, unable to fight or flee?

Cecil broke into Poley's chain of thought at that point. 'You have done well,' he said. 'Go back to London now and inform both Sir John Peyton and Sir William Waad that they can expect Raleigh and Cobham at the Tower within a week or so. I will return to London soon myself. It would not do to leave His Majesty unattended for too long.'

As Poley rose to leave, Cecil added, 'Where are you lodging at the moment?'

'Above the Lion in King Street hard by Whitehall Palace, Master Secretary,' answered Poley.

'Tell Peyton to give you decent rooms, bed and board in the Tower too. I want you on hand when Raleigh and Cobham arrive. They will be held there in separate accommodation and forbidden to communicate with each-other until I am satisfied we have the story we need from each of them before the full council steps in. And it would be as well to get you clear of the city. I understand the plague is rampant there – and High Summer not yet upon us. The council will be meeting at Windsor until things in the city improve.'

'Very good, Master Secretary, and my thanks.'

'But I think the council will not examine them at the Tower. Not formally. You and Sir William may do so to establish the grounds of our further questions, but the council is at Windsor as I say and we will perform our formal interviews there, I think.'

But as he rode south towards the city, Poley's mind was taken up with the best way to ensure the various elements of his network could contact him at his new address should anything unforeseen arise now that the net was closing around Cobham and Raleigh.

57

But as things turned out, the net did not close as quickly as Poley might have hoped. While he was making arrangements to move his possessions from the Lion Tavern to his new rooms, Master Secretary, on behalf of the council, informed Sir Thomas Gerard and Sir Thomas Vavasour that they would soon be despatched to summon Cobham and Raleigh for questioning. But almost immediately this process was frustrated as Raleigh was first summoned to the Charterhouse, where James was temporarily in residence, to be officially relieved of his post as Captain of the Guard, which resulted in him angrily retiring to Durham House, which he refused to leave for fear the Bishop of Durham might repossess it behind his back. At least the pause gave Poley a chance to leave messages at the Lion and at Salisbury House as to where he might be found in an emergency – a necessary action made more important by the fact that Phelippes was also to be housed in the Tower.

In the mean-time also, Poley's and Waad's plans were further thwarted by the king himself. James came downriver by barge from the Charterhouse to enjoy his first formal visit to the Tower, where he was greeted by one of the loudest and longest gun-salutes that anyone could remember. Meanwhile, Poley's removal to his new quarters was paused and Waad's duties became ceremonial rather than investigatory. Until the royal visit was completed, at least.

King James was conducted round the great old fortress by Sir John Peyton, Sir William Waad and a range of other men responsible for the upkeep, smooth running and security of the building - or buildings rather, for there were within the castle's curtain walls nearly twenty individual towers as well as a great range of other structures in various states of repair and security. Peyton affirmed its antiquity, telling James that the foundations of its central edifices were believed to have been laid by Julius Caesar but modified and modernised by William the Conqueror and many of the kings who succeeded him. King James saw not only the jewel house, the armoury, the gunpowder store, the mint and the menagerie but the rooms he was due to occupy when preparing for his coronation. In celebration of his visit, almost everyone imprisoned there was released, except for those held at Master Secretary's pleasure accused of involvement in treasonous Catholic plots – a relief to Sir John Peyton who was well aware that Master Secretary, William Waad and Robert Poley had every intention of filling the newly-vacant accommodation as soon as possible with yet more men involved in one plot or another.

When the king at last left and Poley was able to complete his move, he found himself above the armoury in the White Tower, the Tower's original Keep and its central fortification. His rooms above the armoury were also immediately above the great gunpowder store, something that, after the explosion of the powder mill at Redriffe, gave him the occasional sleepless night. Now, however, the planned arrests could proceed, so Gerard and Vavasour were despatched. But it was typical of the arrogant Sir Walter, thought Poley, that he refused to obey the council's summons until Master Secretary went to fetch him himself. He did this, as he had been handling all his interactions with Sir Walter, under the cloak of concerned friendship. A friendship and a concern of which Raleigh must eventually discover the true nature.

Sir Thomas Gerard and Lord Cobham arrived in Gerard's coach, entering through the main gate at the Middle Tower, across the bridge over the moat, between the curtain walls, past the Byward Tower and the Bell Tower before turning left to enter past the Wakefield Tower and the Bloody Tower into The Green. Then the coach stopped beside the spot where the block had stood and the Earl of Essex had lost his head a little over two years earlier. Cobham, alighting nervously, was greeted by a welcoming committee that comprised Sir John Peyton, Sir William Waad and a squad of yeoman warders. Poley stood well back, observing his man and his demeanour.

Master Secretary on the other hand, collected Sir Walter from Durham House Steps the better part of a week later still and carried him down river in his barge, all courtesy and concern, before bringing him in from the River into the Tower through Traitor's Gate. Poley watched them arrive from a window high in St Thomas's Tower, well aware that a man of Raleigh's acuity would not miss Master Secretary's point; though he may have misinterpreted it as a friendly warning of difficulties soon to come.

Then, as Poley was finally making his accommodation above the gunpowder store truly his own, Cobham was settling reluctantly into the Wakefield Tower and Raleigh, quivering with righteous outrage at his ill-usage by this Scottish upstart, into two rooms in the Bloody Tower close by. It suited Poley well enough to take a little more time still before he and Waad began questioning the new arrivals. Poley had practical things to learn and re-learn. He had stayed at the Tower before, both as part of the complement and as an apparent prisoner listening out for other men's unwise words. But now he had to settle into the yeoman warders' mess, for he and Phelippes were to eat and drink with them. He was fortunate to have ready coin about him and easy access to outside victuallers, he realised, for the food in the warders' mess was meagre and the pay of his red-coated colleagues hardly kept them from starvation. It was a long time since they had been awarded a pay rise despite the fact that the price of food and drink had risen steeply of late on the back of one drowned harvest after another and the visitations of the plague. On occasion, however, he was to be invited to dine with Sir John Peyton, who six years after being appointed to the post of Lieutenant, was still listing all the parts of his command that stood in urgent need of refurbishment and repair, prompted to renewed activity by King James's observations when he visited.

But by the time the king was safely settled in Whitehall Palace well clear of the plague-ridden city and waiting for the rest of his family to join him, Poley and William Waad were starting to plan their crucial assault on the men at the heart of what, following Bacon's suggestion, they were now beginning to call the Plot of the Main to discriminate it from Watson's Plot or the Plot of the Bye, also known within their secret circle as the Surprising Plot and the Plot of the Priests. The arrival of Queen Anne and the children added to the urgency. Poley for one was well aware that by joining the king they were very likely adding themselves to the fate the plotters were planning for him.

'Our task and our situation seem to me to be different with regard to Raleigh and Cobham,' said Waad at the beginning of their first planning meeting.

'How so?' asked Poley.

'Surely,' answered Waad pensively, 'it is not up to us to break them ourselves but to ensure that the council are armed with sufficient information to break them when they hold the formal interrogations at Windsor.'

'The council's interrogations are certainly crucial,' agreed Poley. 'And of course Master Secretary's orders that Raleigh be destroyed will be all the more effectively achieved if it is done in front of the council and apparently *by* the council with Master Secretary still his seeming friend.'

'My immediate concern is that these are men of pith and moment – powerful and well-friended,' said Waad.

'I agree, we cannot bully or brow-beat them; or indeed frighten them with the machines in Rackmaster Topcliffe's domain.'

'Or, I suspect, outfox them quite as easily as the two we have interrogated so far.'

'Again, I agree,' Poley nodded. 'Certainly, Sir Walter is notoriously quick-witted; though I doubt the same could be said of Lord Cobham. But I should point out that we are not coming to this fight completely unarmed. These two men – no matter how powerful or popular among even more powerful friends – do not completely trust each other. They certainly do not like each other. As long as we keep them from communicating with each-other, each of them will sit day-in day-out wondering what the other has revealed about him under interrogation.'

'That would be true were they sitting idly,' said Waad. 'But I understand from Sir John Peyton that Raleigh's secretary Hancock has already organised for him a goodly supply of law-books.'

'That fact alone might strengthen our hand,' suggested Poley. 'For Raleigh only needs law books if he is considering conducting his own defence. And he can only study his defence effectively if he has a good idea what he is to be charged with. And that of course means he guesses what we suspect him to be guilty of. Perhaps because he knows himself to be guilty of it too.'

'I see your reasoning. The law books may be the sign of a guilty conscience.'

'*Treason in corde*, perhaps.' Poley quoted Sir Francis Bacon. 'Maybe even *Treason in ore*, treason in heart and mind as our friend the Queen's Counsellor would have it. And, were we to start with Cobham – and start there by mentioning Raleigh's law books, we might well drive a further wedge between the two of them.'

'Unless Cobham believes Raleigh is preparing a defence for both of them,' suggested Waad warily.

'I suggest, Sir William, that pigs might fly before he would think that!'

Waad was silent for a moment, then he continued, 'And if we can foster this air of mutual distrust…'

'We could, perhaps, make one man believe that the other has betrayed him in an attempt to save his own head – which might well lead to much more detailed revelations in return.

309

More detailed than we might otherwise have hoped to gain,'
nodded Poley.

'Which we can pass to Master Secretary so that the council
can be guided by sworn testimony when they come to the
formal interrogation at Windsor and, indeed, to trial -
whenever that can be arranged.'

'Who would you think it best to see first, Cobham or
Raleigh?'

'Cobham,' said Sir William without a moment's hesitation.

'Very well then,' said Poley. 'Let it be Cobham!'

58

Sir Henry Brooke Lord Cobham entered the interrogation room slowly, his eyes cast down and his expression guarded. The guards Topcliffe had supplied to supplement the yeoman warders in bringing him here stood outside. One of them leaned in and closed the nail-studded black oak door firmly behind Cobham's back. Cobham jumped a little at the sound and paused as though waiting for permission to sit. Although he was nearing forty years of age, he struck Poley as being like a schoolboy caught about some mischief called upon to explain himself to an angry parent. There was something almost endearing about him. He was plump, with a round, good-natured face, which a gossamer beard matched by thinning hair did nothing to conceal. His eyes were hazel and wide, his nose – in contrast to his young brother's – was short and snub. His lips were full, but he was unfortunate in sharing with Sir George that weak chin which was doubled – almost trebled - by the time it reached his ruff.

'I really have no idea why I am here,' he said as he took a seat. 'Either in the Tower or in this room. Or before the three of you.'

Sir William smiled – like the tiger in the Tower's menagerie, thought Poley. 'I'm sure you will find yourself enlightened before you leave,' he said. 'With regard to all three situations. Let us begin with the easiest to resolve. I am William Waad. This is Robert Poley. We have been commissioned by the Privy Council under orders of King James, to establish certain facts with regard to some plot or plots currently being hatched against the king, his throne and his family. Our colleague Master Phelippes there is making a detailed record of everything we say. And we will be requested to sign it at the end of the session as being the whole truth.'

'I'm not signing anything!' snapped Cobham.

'Well, well,' said Sir William. 'We will see what we will see.''

Cobham's gaze flashed up then down again.

'Do you have much commerce with the Reverend George, your brother?' asked Poley.

'Not recently.' Cobham appeared surprised by this line of questioning. 'Why?' The thoughtless enquiry betrayed his innocence, thought Poley – not innocence of treason; innocence and inexperience in situations like this.

Waad leaped on the opening the unconsidered query offered. 'Because your brother seems to have had a good deal of contact with you, recently. Or so he has sworn in evidence recorded verbatim by Master Phelippes there, witnessed and signed by your brother, Master Poley here and myself.

'Perhaps you should think again,' suggested Poley.

'Clarify your memory,' suggested Sir William. 'At the moment it seems that either you are mistaken or the Reverend George is committing perjury.'

'Let us not put too much faith in the evidence of one brother who is at odds with another.' Poley suggested. 'Pay too much attention to Abel in the matter of the sins of Cain.'

'But surely we have more evidence than merely the Reverend George's,' observed Waad.

'Ah, you mean Raleigh's? But that was not under oath and his library of law-books will no doubt guide him further in understanding his legal rights. Besides I believe Sir Walter and Lord Cobham here are also at odds are they not?'

'Raleigh?' Cobham sat up straight, his gaze at last focussed on his interrogators and his usually placid countenance folding into a mask of outrage. 'What does Raleigh know of me? What law books does he have? What does he say that is to the purpose?'

'Nothing,' placated Poley. 'It was a passing remark. We have not even recorded it. All is well, Your Lordship.'

312

'Well, well, let us put Raleigh and his books aside then,' allowed Waad. 'But there is still the matter of your brother, My Lord, for he gave his evidence under oath, as we have witnessed, and swore that he would stand up in court…'

'… in any court in the land be it never so elevated…' added Poley.

'…to support it with his spoken evidence. So,' continued Waad, 'let us begin again. The first thing we must establish, My Lord, is that you too are speaking under oath. A formality, of course, with a man such as yourself for I am certain you would never deal in untruths and your simple word is as good as any other man's sworn oath, but it is best that we are all aware…'

'In case there is any dispute later on,' explained Poley.

'I'm still not signing anything,' said Cobham. His expression set mulishly.

Waad smiled his tiger-smile. 'After we ask, Master Secretary will ask. After Master Secretary asks, King James will ask. And after the king, perhaps Saint Peter will ask, as you carry your head through Heaven's gate.'

'But let us leave all that aside, with Raleigh and his law books,' said Poley. 'The first question we must clear up is this: when did your brother tell you about William Watson and his plan to kidnap the king?'

'Tell me *what*? He never told me anything! Why should he?'

Once more with the unwise question, thought Poley as Waad leaped upon it once again. 'Because the Revered George was part of Watson's plot and told Watson – and, indeed, Master Poley and myself – that when that plot failed to move forward as speedily as he would have wished, he planned to approach you.'

'He may have said he planned to. I say he never did!'

'So, you had no knowledge of your brother's association with William Watson, Sir Griffin Markham and his brothers, Sir John Gage or Lord Grey de Wilton?' probed Poley.

313

'I knew he was friends with some of the men you have named. Perhaps he was acquainted with the others. We have only spoken rarely of late. I do not move in his circles nor he in mine.'

'And you have no memory of him coming to you for advice in the matter of Watson's plot?' Poley emphasised.

'None.'

'Nor telling him that you knew of a far more puissant and dangerous plot being prepared by men of standing, power and moment?' Waad continued.

'A puissant plot? Certainly not. Why should I have any knowledge of such a thing?'

'Because you are part of it, perhaps.' Waad jumped on the thoughtless comment. 'You and Sir Walter Raleigh.'

'More than a part of it – a leading mover.' Poley leaned forward, eyes narrow.

'This is arrant nonsense…'

'Sir Walter does not seem to think so,' snapped Waad. 'He has demanded law books, therefore he wishes to prepare some sort of a defence does he not?'

'And therefore he fears he will be accused of something,' added Poley. 'Perhaps we should supply you with law-books too.'

'What would be the point? I am innocent of any wrongdoing. I have no need to prepare my defence, whatever Raleigh might choose to do. I do not like the man and have never confederated with him in any enterprise, legal or otherwise.'

'That is not quite what your brother has led us to believe,' said Poley. 'And I am by no means convinced that it will be what Sir Walter will wish us to believe.'

'After all, as your brother has probably known since childhood, the most effective defence against any charge is often to blame someone else…'

314

59

'Named me?' said Sir Walter Raleigh. 'Cobham named me how? In what context?'

'Both brothers have named you now, indeed,' explained Poley. 'And in more than one context. More than one plot.'

'I do not believe you. I do not know George Brooke and although I know Henry, Lord Cobham, a little better, we have had precious little to do with each other. We have hardly talked of late, let alone plotted!'

Whereas both Brooke brothers had appeared strained, perhaps guilt-ridden under interrogation, Raleigh sat at ease, unruffled, answering in measured tones. The very picture of a reasonable man safe in the knowledge of his innocence. Willing to answer reasonable questions in a reasonable manner. Indeed, willing to answer unreasonable questions reasonably. Even under oath – which he had agreed to apparently without a second thought, just as he had shrugged equably when informed that Phelippes would be recording verbatim everything that was about to be said.

The man was extraordinary thought Poley, looking down at his hands lying clasped on the table as he considered his opponent. Even coming down here from his two scantly furnished rooms in the Bloody Tower, across the Green and past the place he had watched his enemy the Earl of Essex lose his head twenty-six months ago, and on a wet morning into the bargain, Raleigh looked as though he had just stepped out of Her Majesty's privy chamber. Not one steel-grey hair appeared to be out of place on head, lip or chin. His sea-blue eyes looked directly at whoever he was conversing with – nothing nervous or shuffling in them. The expression on his angular, aristocratic countenance, indeed seemed relaxed and faintly amused. How he could still afford to dress himself in pearls now that so much of his income had been stopped, the intelligencer could not begin to guess. Poley glanced up, to find Raleigh's calm gaze resting thoughtfully upon him. The shock of that cool scrutiny was almost like a blow. I will have to take care, he thought, that Sir Walter does not turn the tables on us and begin to interrogate Sir William and me.

'Let us begin with the first plot described by the Reverend George Brooke,' Poley began – as much for something to say as for any other reason. 'When was the first time you met William Watson?'

'William Watson? I have never met William Watson. Nor heard of the man as far as I can recall,' answered Raleigh calmly.

'Well, then, Watson's co-conspirator William Clark?'

Raleigh shrugged and shook his head.

'You mean to say you have never met William Clark?' said Waad, for Phelippes's benefit.

'Or ever heard of him as far as I recall,' added Raleigh helpfully.

'Sir John Gage?' probed Waad.

'Of some great house near to Robert Cecil's palace at Theobalds? Perhaps. But I have no idea when or where – or why come to that.'

'Sir Griffin Markham?' said Poley.

'Oh yes indeed. I know Sir Griffin and his brothers. I fought alongside Sir Griffin in the Low Countries when we were both much younger and before he was wounded and retired from active service to run his estate at Beskwood. But, again, I have had no contact with the Markhams for many years past, unless we met at some unremembered occasion at the old queen's court.' Again, Sir Walter shrugged easily.

'Lord Grey de Wilton?' asked Waad.

'Oh, who does not know Thomas Grey? He's a good soldier, excellent cavalry commander but, as Plutarch describes Mark Anthony I seem to recall, hot-headed and prone to acting outside his orders. Or even to acting before those orders are given – as the Earl of Southampton discovered to his cost in Ireland, so I'm told. It cost Grey his commission and led to his humiliation in front of Essex and his army. A slight for which he blamed Southampton and which he could never forgive. It was in the Strand outside my Durham House that Grey attacked Southampton in revenge for the insult and killed his page. Which some say started the Essex rebellion. But you know all about that, Poley, for you were in Essex's household at the time, though I believe you were secretly working for Master Secretary even then, were you not? As you and Ingram Frizer were working for Master Secretary when you came to value Durham house and its contents. A slight that I shall not forget or easily forgive.'

Unlike Cobham's unconsidered questions and afterthoughts which only betrayed his weakness, Raleigh's question and the observation following it were carefully calculated. I will certainly have to keep my guard up, thought Poley.

'And Anthony Copley?' he asked.

'Ah. Copley. Now there's another familiar name. When I was on the council, before the old queen died, there was occasional talk of Master Copley. A recusant willing to work with the pursuivants. A double agent, happy to sell information to each side against the other. Started his career under Sir Francis Walsingham if I remember aright. I'm surprised you were not running him, Poley, by the time Sir Francis died. Or, if he was mixed up with all the other men you have just named, perhaps you have been running him after all.'

'Copley's confession chimes with that of Sir George Brooke,' warned Sir William, as much to cover Poley's momentary discomfiture as for any other reason. But that was a mistake.

'So,' said Raleigh from the height of his new legal expertise, 'you have the word of a paid informer which you used, no doubt, to coerce the confession of George Brooke who has now made some mention of his brother within a context that

317

you wish to extend to cover the possibility that poor old
Cobham might be involved in something treasonous. You are
stretching this far too thin to bear any legal weight. It will
never stand. Even the magistrates would laugh it out of court,
and as for the council...' Again that eloquent shrug. 'I seem
to remember that the elements of treason – inevitably enough
– have prompted some ancient lawyer to compare the whole
thing to a tree – root, branch, flower and fruit. Well, I would
suggest to you, gentlemen, that if you hope to use evidence
that begins with any statement sworn to by Copley, you are
dealing with poisoned fruit as surely as was Adam in the
Garden of Eden.'

60

'Poisoned fruit,' said Sir Francis Bacon. 'A neat analogy. But I fear if Raleigh relies on it, he will find himself outmatched, especially if Chief Justice Sir Edward Coke is leading the prosecution. Coke looks like the truest gentleman of the royal circle but he fights like the veriest swashbuckler straight out of the gutter. Though I must observe that the outcome will also depend on who defends Raleigh in court.'

'His acquisition of so many law books makes Sir William and me suspect that he plans to defend himself,' said Poley.

'A highly dangerous course of action if true. To my mind, a man who is his own lawyer has a fool for a client.'

'But Raleigh may see it as the action of an innocent man; or an action designed to present an appearance of innocence before the jury if not the judges.'

'Remember, this is no Ancient Rome with Marcus Tullius Cicero here to plead his case. There is no supposition of innocence until proof of guilt in our current legal system. He is only innocent if the court declares him to be so – and that will depend on the strength of his defence rather than the actual truth of his blamelessness. Which defence an advocate can build as high as the walls of Troy but which an amateur can scarcely construct, one brick upon another.'

'Should we lay aside Copley's evidence, though?' wondered Poley. 'Now that Raleigh has called it into question so effectively?'

'Surely that depends on what further evidence you find,' said Bacon. 'In any case, Copley does not mention Raleigh. Neither – to any real effect – does George Brooke. You will in their stead have to rely on what evidence Lord Cobham can supply. Though even that might stand on a slightly shaky foundation. One that you will have to ensure that the prosecuting authorities are willing to put aside.'

'What is that?'

'One that I'm sure the law books you say Raleigh is studying are bound to mention, and one I myself touched upon at our last meeting. It is this: that in a capital trial, one man's evidence is never counted as sufficient to condemn another man to death. I mentioned that, I think when we were discussing Lady Janet Percy's evidence.'

'I remember,' said Poley, less than truthfully. His head had been full of Lady Janet at the time – not of law and Bacon's interpretations of it. 'So, Cobham's evidence might not be sufficient on its own?'

'It depends,' Bacon answered, 'on the willingness of the court to overlook the rule, which I admit is an extremely ancient one. And that in turn might well depend on how powerful Cobham's evidence is. And on your ability to adduce information that you have gathered, from Standen and Lady Janet. Such evidence might not be strong enough to stand in court. But you may wish to present it off the record as a persuasive background in any case. Persuasive enough to sway the judges, perhaps. And the judges, of course, can direct the jury if they choose to do so.'

'I can certainly try that.'

'A wise move. But I should emphasise that such manoeuvrings, sub-rosa if not sub-judice so to speak, are nowhere near as useful to your cause as ensuring that Lord Cobham's condemnation of Raleigh is detailed and effectively irrefutable.'

With Sir Francis Bacon's advice rattling around in his head like a small nut in a great shell, Poley went back from Grey's Inn along Holborn and Moorgate outside the pestilential city's wall then down to the Tower's postern gate, staying as clear of plague-riven London town as he could. Then, still in a brown study, he went through the Tower grounds to Tower

Wharf and summoned a wherry to take him upriver to Salisbury House steps.

Master Secretary had become only an occasional visitor to his own London house. Like all the rest of London who could afford to, he was staying well clear of the city the numbers of whose plague-dead were mounting inexorably even though it was not yet full summer. He was lodging close to Attorney General Popham in Richmond and working further upriver in Windsor like the rest of the council. Salisbury House's front gates were locked tight on the city side with no-one coming or going. What necessary movement in and out of the great house was conducted along the garden and down the steps to the river. And movement there had been – not only by the master of the house coming back and forth on his occasional visits from Richmond or Windsor but also by messengers, many of whom were working for Poley and his network.

While Poley had been with Sir Francis Bacon, therefore, and Sir William Waad had been in discussion with Sir John Peyton – while Cobham had been growing ever more worried and Raleigh had been studying his law-books, Phelippes had come to the office he shared with Poley to go through the secret correspondence waiting there. Neither man had been to the office lately and so there were a number of reports to be studied. But Phelippes put them all aside except the ones that were apparently pertinent to the Bye Plot and the Main Plot. Then he and Poley began to go through them as carefully as the urgency of the situation allowed as soon as Poley returned.

They had hardly begun when Phelippes said, 'When was the last time you saw Standen?'

'On the day of the old queen's funeral.'

'That's a fair time ago now.'

'It is. Why?'

'I have a letter here written apparently that same evening, soon after he left you. Sent immediately and marked urgent.'

Poley frowned. An urgent letter should have come to him at once but clearly this one had slipped through the net. 'And what does it say?'

'That Standen chanced upon Count Aremberg's man La Rensy in Westminster soon after you had parted. La Rensy who he had last seen in Brussels and whom he knew had carried letters from Cobham to the Count. He followed him to lodgings in St Mary Saviours in Southwark. He made enquiries of course and is fairly certain La Rensy has been in residence there for some time. He feels you should keep eyes on La Rensy, especially as the Count is due to arrive in England soon as the Archduke's ambassador.'

'So, La Rensy was in the country before we were keeping close watch on Cobham. Or Raleigh for that matter.'

The conversation had reached that point when Master Secretary himself arrived, in an unusually good mood. 'Well done, Poley,' he said. 'You and Sir William appear to have shaken Raleigh.'

'Have we so?' asked Poley, surprised. 'We saw precious little sign of it, Master Secretary.'

Cecil flourished a letter. 'This proves you have done it, whether you knew it or not! He held it close to his short-sighted eyes and began to read.

' "I write to you, my Lord Cecil because, despite what I have said under examination so far, I suspect that Lord Cobham has had intelligence with Count Aremberg in the matter of removing the king and replacing him with the Lady Arbella Stuart. My reason for suspecting him is that long since, in the late Queen's time, I knew that he had corresponded with the Count in the Low Countries, as was well known also to Sir Thomas Sackville, the Lord Treasurer and to you, my Lord Cecil. Besides, I suspected his continuing contact with Count Aremberg from these further facts. At our last meeting at dinner, after Cobham departed from me at Durham House shortly before we were taken up for examination in the matters of the Bye and the Main, I saw him pass by his own stairs and go over to St. Mary Saviours. I now know that La Rensy lay in lodgings there, who was a follower of Count Aremberg. Wherefore I write to you, Lord Cecil, that if La Rensy is not secured swiftly the matter will not be discovered, for he will fly; yet if he is apprehended, it will give matter of great suspicion to Lord Cobham for being involved both in the Bye with his brother George, and in the Main with La Rensy, the Count Aremberg and King Phillip of Spain as well as with the Lady Arbella Stuart with whom I understand he has been in lengthy correspondence."'

'Excellent,' said Poley. 'We will be able to move forward with that, especially if your Lordship is happy to lend the letter to Phelippes for as long as it takes him to copy it. Then we will consider whether we need to amend it to any degree before we show it to Cobham. Though, from the sound of it, it will start him as it stands. Start him like a stag to run from hound and hunter in the chase.'

'You may have it for as long as you need it, Phelippes,' said Cecil. 'But I will need it back to show to the council before we start our formal interrogation of Cobham and Raleigh at Windsor. Meantime, Poley, you and I need to complete another matter of business.'

'What is that, Master Secretary?'

'You told me, I believe, that Cobham refuses to sign the first part of his evidence.'

'That's true. He insists that the word of a peer needs no subscription to be believed in court.'

'Hmmm. I doubt that. Therefore, I have asked Lord Popham the Attorney General, to come to the Tower and explain to the reluctant lord the importance of a signature and the weakness of his position in standing against giving it.'

There was a moment's silence, then Poley said, 'And if the Attorney General can be sufficiently forceful, especially with regard to the weakness – indeed the mortal danger – of Cobham's position, then Raleigh's letter should be more than enough to elicit a lengthy and detailed submission when we next interrogate him.'

61

Attorney General Popham's visit left Cobham badly shaken, for it undermined many of the assumption on which he had stood in refusing to sign his submission so far, though of course he signed it before Lord Popham left. While he was still in this shaken state, Poley and Waad invited him back into their interrogation room. As they were waiting for him to arrive, Poley observed, 'Popham's visit has served several ends. Raleigh saw him come and go – a hidden benefit, perhaps, of placing him in the Bloody Tower past which everyone must come and go. So now it is not only Cobham who is discomfited but also Raleigh. And Raleigh must also be wondering how wide a circle Master Secretary has shared his letter with, especially as the Attorney General has come a'visiting.'

'Imagine his discomfiture when he realises it has been shared with Cobham,' said Waad. 'Not that it has been. Yet.'

It was a cowed Cobham who came into the interrogation room. But, observed Poley, by no means a defeated one. 'Let us start where we left off,' he suggested. 'You believed that here was no plot toward - other, perhaps, than the Plot of the Bye in which your brother George was involved, with William Watson, Griffin Markham, Lord Grey and the others.'

'But if there was,' said Waad, 'then perhaps Sir Walter Raleigh might know about it – but you certainly do not. Is that what you told us?'

'That is the case. That is what I signed,' allowed Cobham.

'But that was all. As far as you are aware there was no substance to what we call the Plot of the Main. You were never involved in any aspect of it or contacted anyone who might have anything to do with it.'

'Correct. And I hope your note-taker is recording all this as I give it in evidence.'

'On your word.'

'On my word as a peer of the realm. Let us not begin that game all over again. You may record what I say now but be aware that I shall not demean myself or my standing by signing it like some commoner under oath, though you bring an army of Pophams to the Tower.'

'Very well then, let us start once more,' said Waad. 'However, not with the Plot of the Bye but with the Main. You confirm that you were never confederated with anyone in a plot to remove the king and replace him with the Lady Arbella Stuart.'

'The notion is ridiculous.'

'And yet you have been in correspondence with the Lady Arbella,' Poley reminded him.

'I have, when she was like a poor bird caged in Hardwick Hall under the strict tutelage of her grandmother the Countess of Shrewsbury, Lady Bess of Hardwick.'

'But not since the king released her to fly free?' Poley asked.

'A letter or two of congratulation and advice, nothing more.' Cobham shrugged dismissively.

'I see,' said Poley. 'But, talking of correspondence, what contact have you had in recent times with the Princely Count Aremberg?'

'Why, none. What should I do holding correspondence with the Archduke's ambassador?'

'We will come to that,' said Waad. 'But yet I must press the point. Have you had recent contact either with the Count direct or via his man La Rensy?'

'Of course not! To what end would I do so?'

That fatal extra question, thought Poley. He almost felt sorry for Cobham. Almost.

'To answer your question directly,' said Waad, smiling his dangerous smile, 'to the end of removing the king,

326

slaughtering all who stand in his succession and handing his throne to Arbella Stuart.'

Cobham reacted as though Waad had slapped him in the face. He was instantly all outrage. 'How dare you!' he shouted. 'What proof have you to support such an allegation?'

'The submission of your co-conspirator,' answered Waad.

Cobham gaped like the veriest booby, thought Poley. He watched Cobham fighting to come to terms with what he had just heard. 'You lie!' was the best he could come up with. 'You lie in your teeth like the most arrant knave.'

Waad just looked at him, eyebrows raised.

Cobham's assurance began to crumble at once. 'You lie…' His tone of voice made the statement sounds more like a question, thought Poley. And he knew they had won.

Waad observed this, as did Poley, with an almost weary sense of inevitability. 'Master Phelippes,' said Waad. 'Please read aloud to Lord Cobham the letter that Sir Walter has just sent to Master Secretary.'

Phelippes picked up the copy he had made of Raleigh's letter. 'Gladly, Sir William. "I write to you, my Lord Cecil because, despite what I have said under examination so far, I suspect the Lord Cobham has had intelligence with Count Aremberg in the matter of removing the king and replacing him with the Lady Arbella Stuart…"'

By the time Phelippes had finished reading, Cobham was bone-white and shaking like a man with the Plague. His countenance looked more like a skull than a face, thought Poley. Even his eyes seemed to have sunk into dark-ringed pits. For a moment Poley was reminded of what the old queen looked like on her death bed. As Phelippes finished, he put the paper with its damning testimony down. Poley continued to watch his victim, secretly marvelling at how effective Raleigh's betrayal had been.

'Oh, the caitiff traitor,' whispered Cobham into the cavernous silence of the room. 'The turncoat. The veriest Judas!'

'If he is Judas indeed,' said Poley, 'I suggest, My Lord, that now is the time to tell us the truth of the matter before his betrayal carries you to a personal Calvary and your own crucifixion.'

'What do you want to know?' whispered Cobham, his resolve utterly broken.

'Tell us all you know,' said Poley simply.

'Well,' Cobham paused, clearly ordering his thoughts – honing the edge of his revenge. Like Cassius sharpening his dagger for Caesar's back. Then he began to speak so rapidly that Phelippes was hard-put to keep up with him. 'The plot you call the Bye had as its main objective kidnapping the king and forcing him to change his mind. It centred round Watson but involved several others including my youngest brother George - from whom I had the details - Griffin Markham, his brothers, Anthony Copley and Lord Grey.'

'Indeed,' said Waad. 'But putting that to one side, for we have as much evidence about the Bye as we need...'

'The plot of the Main as you call it had as its objective the removal of King James altogether, along with his family, and his replacement on the throne by the Lady Arbella Stuart.'

'And the king? Removed, you say?' probed Waad.

'Raleigh wanted them all killed, to clear the line of succession; the king, the queen with her unborn child, the prince and the princess. All at one fell swoop.'

'So, despite the fact that Raleigh has in his letter to Master Secretary accused you of being the man at the heart of this – the one in contact with Lady Arbella on the one hand and via La Rensy with the Count of Aremberg on the other - you now contend that it was Raleigh himself who was the prime mover behind the plot.'

'I do. It was Raleigh; all Raleigh.'

62

'I swear it,' said Cobham, sitting up straight and meeting their gazes - to Poley's mind suddenly self-confident and decisive; a petty man set on revenge. 'It was Raleigh who was the original of the scheme you now call the Plot of the Main and, through his promises, pulled in not only myself but my brother George and Lord Grey both of whom were uncertain that their hopes and plans would be met by the Bye. But he and he alone was the *primum mobile* or main mover of the scheme. In order to effect the destruction of James Stuart and his heirs in succession and the enthronement of Lady Arbella Stuart, Raleigh formulated a plan. He sent messengers to approach the Princely Count of Aremberg in Brussels via whose good offices he hoped to get aid and support from the King of Spain.'

'We know that one of you did and you say it was Raleigh; Raleigh alone. You are under oath, remember.'

'He planned to send his man of business Magnall with a message to be passed on by the Count's man La Rensy, but when he was murdered, Raleigh replaced him with the recusant book-keeper Dutton.'

'We have evidence from Sir Anthony Standen whom Dutton and La Rensy both met in Brussels in an attempt to enlist Count Aremberg's aid. And it was Raleigh who sent Dutton, you say?'

'He did. But only to open negotiations you understand. Raleigh planned that I would travel to Europe and use the Count's good offices in furtherance of the Main plot. I was in contact with the Count some years ago in the Low Countries. Both he and his man La Rensy know me. But they do not know Raleigh – hence his decision that I should go.'

'And what was the point of this visit to the Count if you finally made it?'

'I was to collect all the coin needed to finance Raleigh's scheme, some five or six hundred thousand crowns.'

'And the Count could get such a vast sum from King Philip of Spain, you say?' Waad shook his head. 'It almost beggars belief! Well, then what?'

'I was to return with the money from either Brussels or Valladolid via Jersey. I was to come that way, of course, because Raleigh is governor of Jersey. I was afraid of lingering on the island, however, for fear Raleigh would have me in his power and might reveal my actions to the king and the council to my ruin and his own benefit.'

'And this was the level of trust between you?' asked Poley. 'That you feared he would hand you over to the authorities for his own benefit?'

'If I returned without the money, certainly!' said Cobham bitterly. 'But think. Is that not what he has just done in any case?

Cobham's acrimonious question stopped the interrogation for a moment as they all considered Raleigh's perfidy.

Then Cobham continued, intensely, 'But howsoever, I freely attest Raleigh planned the following. That once he had the money safe, he would share it out amongst his friends and co-conspirators including my brother, Lord Grey and, perhaps the Earl of Northumberland in order to raise an army puissant or powerful enough to take the king and his family. And to deal with them on the manner I have mentioned.'

Poley nodded. Cobham had just named all the men Lady Janet overheard in her Cousin Henry Percy's rooms in Essex House. 'And yet the plot of the Main has not proceeded as yet,' he observed.

'It was to a certain extent slowed by the Bye, for some of the participants in both gave their immediate attention to the one that seemed most likely to proceed the soonest. The Bye went forward, so the Main did not. Nor is it likely to do so now.'

'Why is that?'

'The principal part of the plot – getting the money from King Phillip of Spain via La Rensy and Count Aremberg - was thwarted by my horror at seeing the sum above Raleigh's signature and therefore my reluctance to travel under Raleigh's orders. I strongly doubted that King Philip would have six hundred thousand crowns readily to hand, so if I went as Raleigh planned, I would almost certainly return empty-handed. I had a potent fear as I have already described, of falling into his power in Jersey on my return, especially if I had failed to get the money. And in any case my travels were curtailed by the refusal of the council to grant safe passage to go abroad. In the meantime, without my knowledge Raleigh was in contact with La Rensy himself, preparing the ground for him to take the letters I should have carried to the Count were I to balk at his order. In the end, of course, he sent Dutton after Magnall's murder. But nothing came of that as far as I know.'

Poley and Waad exchanged a glance. Something might indeed have come of Raleigh's messages to King Philip, for they had gone to Valladolid after all according to Standen, carried by the Catholic mercenary from Yorkshire, Guy Fawkes.

'That was not the end of the matter, however? probed Poley. 'Raleigh's plans were not frustrated by these setbacks?'

'No. Raleigh still proceeded nevertheless. He continued to draw his plans in hopes that he would find an alternative to my embassy either in person or via La Rensy once more to Count Aremberg. I believe brother George, Lord Grey and the Earl of Northumberland, were of no use to him because they were all under observation for one reason or another. And so he considered making use of Lords Westmoreland or Bothwell who, while not being privy to the plot and therefore not being watched, were nevertheless desperate for funds.'

331

'Westmoreland and Bothwell, you say. But they were not privy to the Main Plot.'

'That is so, but things moved on and Count Aremberg prepared to come to England as the Archduke's representative at King James's coronation. He sent La Rensy on before him, who I visited occasionally at his lodgings at St Mary Saviours, for we are old friends as I have said. So, as things transpired, Raleigh's new plan was to proceed by sending me to the Count the moment the Count's embassy arrived in England. I was to meet him at Dover, the principal of the Cinque Ports of which I am still Warden. He would disburse the money and the plot would proceed. Once the king was "safe" by which Raleigh meant "dead", forces from the Low Countries in Europe would be invited to enter England through the Cinque Ports, using Jersey as a staging-post, if necessary, in order to ensure the succession of the Lady Arbella Stuart, with whom, at Raleigh's direction, I was already in correspondence. Indeed, I had already passed her a book of Raleigh's writing proving her succession superior to that of James Stuart. But - see the man's cunning in this - he planned that King James's death would be blamed on Master Secretary and the Council. It would be his reason for having them all executed. But also, it could be used as a potent motive to stir unrest in Scotland and an invasion of the northern counties – leading to the destruction of Lord Burghley, Lord of the North. And the Scots, too, would support him in replacing their dead king with his nearest Stuart relative – the Lady Arbella!'

'So, the plan was also to cause the Scots to rise and invade, as well as the French or Spanish armies from the Low Countries.' said Waad. 'I had not realised.'

'Once Lady Arbella's coronation had been achieved, Raleigh planned to reward the men who were willing to support him and had proved their worth through their actions, seemingly in one plot or the other. In the place of Sir Thomas Edgerton, Lord Chancellor, Raleigh planned to appoint

William Watson, the recusant priest. The Reverend George Brooke was to be Lord Treasurer in place of Sir Thomas Sackville; Sir Griffin Markham, Principal Secretary in place of Sir Robert Cecil your master. Lord Grey de Wilton must be Earl Marshall and Master of the Horse, both posts having been left vacant by the Earl of Essex's death.'

'But these are men who were involved with the Bye or with both the Bye and the Main. What did you who were solely involved in the Main hope to achieve?'

'Why, we would reserve tens of thousands of crowns to our own personal use and then replace the *Regnum Cecilianum* with the rule of Raleigh and myself. Like Master Secretary, his father and his brother, we would be the powers behind Queen Arbella's throne; the effective rulers of the land.'

63

Sir John Peyton had a son, also called John, who lived, for the moment, with the rest of Peyton's family in the Tower – which was currently a stout bulwark against the rising tide of plague victims flooding the city. Young John was an intelligent lad with an enquiring mind and a thirst for knowledge which could never be quenched. He was also lonely and bored, with time weighing heavy on his hands and nothing much to do. Raleigh had only been in the Bloody Tower for a matter of days before John Peyton junior contrived to visit him. In the two cramped rooms that housed Raleigh, he also met Edward Hancock, Raleigh's secretary, who was only a year or so older than John and also recently down from Cambridge. The two young men formed an instant friendship. The three of them shared a pipe of tobacco and a glass or two of wine while they discussed Raleigh's experiences and the knowledge that grew out of them. Furthermore, young John – like Edward - had ambitions to follow the law but neither student had yet been awarded a place at one of the Inns of Court. However, Raleigh was not only well-supplied with law books, but demonstrated a ready understanding of their contents, which he was happy to share. The visits became so regular that young John effectively joined Edward Hancock and the team of yeoman warders in charge of supplying Raleigh's food and drink – a responsibility he was content to undertake. After a while it was no surprise to see him carrying trays in and out of Raleigh's rooms – though he and what he carried were always subject to close scrutiny. This was, perhaps, fortunate, for while John Peyton was all wide-eyed innocence; Raleigh was all desperation, cunning and calculation.

As time dragged on, and no-one summoned him back for further interrogation, Raleigh became convinced that Cobham must be undergoing lengthy examination; something he was able to confirm simply by asking his would-be student, who revealed that Cobham was in the interrogation room more often than not. But that knowledge proved to be double-edged. Raleigh had no real confidence that Cobham was being questioned at length because he was steadfast in his refusal to answer Waad and Poley's inquiries. It seemed much more likely to Sir Walter that Cobham was simply giving his two interrogators more and more detail. Detail that would damn Sir Walter while allowing Cobham to walk free. John, however, could not confirm or deny Raleigh's greatest fear – that his letter to Cecil might have been shared with the voluble Cobham. If that had happened, there was no way to assess how his co-conspirator was reacting and what he was saying by way of revenge.

Raleigh was a man of action. Faced with this conundrum, he decided to take the initiative. He wrote another letter, this time to Cobham himself.

'Can you deliver a letter to Lord Cobham for me?' he asked John, one evening in mid-July. 'Edward here would do it but he is of course strictly forbidden to go anywhere near Lord Cobham, his rooms or his attendants.'

'It would be difficult,' warned John. 'I am searched upon entering and leaving your rooms and again before entering or leaving Lord Cobham's. My father is set upon ensuring you do not communicate with each-other.

'One letter could do no harm, surely, if we could hit upon a stratagem that allows you to deliver it for me.'

'Surely, Sir Walter,' said John, instantly caught up in the problem and seeking a solution as eagerly as Raleigh, 'that depends on the length of the letter, the size of the paper and the method of concealment'

'Well thought on, lad. I will keep it as short as possible and Edward will use the smallest script he can on the thinnest piece of paper we can get hold of. Then we will see what we will see…'

So Raleigh whispered his dictation and Edward his secretary set to writing:

My Lord Cobham, I fear it is the plan of Lord Cecil and his minions to drive a wedge betwixt we two and by the word of one, destroy the other. Therefore I have this day written to My Lord Cecil to make clear the following: That it is very strange that I should be supposed to have plotted a civil uprising with you, my Lord, knowing you to be someone who has no following of men under arms in England, as for instance, Sir Grenville Markham and my Lord Grey of Wilton do. What would we plan together then? To beg a sum of money from the King of Spain amounting to hundreds of thousands of crowns? I am not such a madman as to make myself a Robin Hood in such a hopeless cause. I know the state of Spain as well as you do my Lord; its weakness, and poorness, and humbleness at this time. I know that King Philip stands discouraged and dishonoured. I know that of five-and-twenty millions he had from his Indies, he has scarcely any left. Then, was it ever read or heard-of that any prince should disburse so much money without sufficient assurance or property held in pawn? And anyone who knows what great assurances the king of Spain insists upon with other states for smaller sums, will not think that he would so freely disburse to you, my Lord Cobham the hundreds of thousands of crowns already mentioned. And if I had minded to set you to work in this case, I should surely have given you some more detailed instructions how you should persuade the king of Spain and answer his objections. For I know you my Lord Cobham to be no such minion as could persuade a king, who is already in want, to disburse so great a sum without great reason and some assurance for his money. In short, my Lord, I have further assured my Lord Cecil that there could never have been any such stratagem planned between us, and whatever I stand accused of, you are as innocent as a new-born babe. Your Faithful Friend and Servant, Walter Raleigh, Knight.

The letter was longer than Raleigh intended, but Edward had found a piece of parchment that was very thin and they were able to fold it into a spill about the same size as Raleigh's smallest finger. It was John who hit upon the idea of hiding it inside a hollowed-out apple. They worked on the fruit with care and saved the top and bottom of the core to plug the holes they had made, leaving the apple apparently whole and untouched. John had no trouble smuggling it out of Raleigh's room with the left-overs and he claimed it for himself before any hungry beefeaters could get their hands on it.

He was walking back out of the Bloody Tower towards St Thomas' Tower and Traitor's Gate, past Wakefield Tower, wondering how best to proceed, when he looked up to see Cobham himself leaning on the sill of a window he had opened in search of a cool evening breeze. The window and its occupant were on the first floor of the tower, not too far above John's head. 'My Lord!' called the young man without a second thought, 'Catch!' And he threw the apple upward.

The act of catching the apple dislodged the top and bottom of the core so that, moments later, Cobham was reading Raleigh's letter.

That night, Cobham, overcome with remorse, wrote a letter of his own, which he sent back via John to Raleigh next morning, concealed in another apple:

Now that the arraignment draws near, not knowing which should be first, I or you, to clear my conscience, satisfy the world with truth, and free myself from the cry of blood, I protest upon my soul and before God and his angels, I never had conference with you in any treason, nor was ever moved by you to the things I heretofore accused you of; and for any thing I know, you are as innocent and as clear from any treasons against the king as is any subject living. Therefore I wash my hands, and pronounce with Daniel, 'Purus sum a sanguine hujus' I am cleansed of this blood; and God so deal with me and have mercy on my soul, as this is true!

64

Master Secretary looked down at Cobham's letter to Raleigh, frowning. Then he glanced up at Waad and Poley. 'It appears that all your hard work is undone by this,' he said grimly. 'I ordered Sir John Peyton to ensure there was no communication between Cobham and Raleigh and yet this proves that he has failed utterly! Were the king not due here within the week to start preparing for his coronation, I would have Sir John replaced and move him and his family out of the Tower forthwith. But the king *is* coming and I dare not have someone unfamiliar with the Tower in charge until after the coronation.'

'But Cobham's letter, Master Secretary,' said Waad. 'What are we to do with it?'

'Perhaps we can turn to Sir Francis Bacon for guidance,' suggested Poley, 'I know you, Sir William and you Master Secretary, are both learned in the law but it is some years since you studied at the Inns and you have been involved in many distractions since. Sir Francis is Counsellor Extraordinary and may see more alternatives than we can readily call to mind.'

Sir Robert Cecil gave a grunt of amusement, 'You are the very essence of tact, Poley. Very well, let us by all means call on this younger and more lively head than ours which are clearly entering our dotage! We have time in any case, for we have what we want from Cobham and just need guidance on how best to employ it despite the later retraction. There will be no further interrogation until the king has come to the Tower and gone to his coronation. In the mean-time, while you consult Francis Bacon, I will put in hand warrants to take up the men named in Cobham's evidence, and in such evidence as we have had from other sources. It is as well the king released so many prisoners on his first visit here or we would have to hold our suspects in the Royal Apartments for lack of secure space.'

Young John Peyton found himself banned from visiting any prisoners as part of a further tightening of restrictions; even his new friend Edward Hancock was forbidden - so Poley asked his father's permission to employ the lad in carrying a request that Sir Francis Bacon visit the Tower. The young man returned with the Counsel Extraordinary but, despite the fact that Bacon had taken a shine to him and John was eager to extend their acquaintance, he was banned from hearing the legal discussion Bacon, Waad and Poley undertook. As the three of them sat at the long table in the interrogation room, Bacon read Cobham's confession carefully and at some length. Then he read the letter to Raleigh which retracted it. 'I believe you place too much weight upon Cobham's retraction,' he said at last. 'To begin with, it is sufficiently self- serving to undermine itself in great degree.'

'How so?' asked Waad.

'I'm sure a moment's thought will make it clear to you, Sir William. But look: the original confession, while blaming Raleigh as instigator and *primum mobile* in the Plot of the Main nevertheless confesses that Cobham was intimately involved in the treason himself.'

'I see that,' nodded Waad.

'The retraction, however, says that nothing in the confession is true. That it was all designed to cause the innocent Raleigh to be charged with a capital offence. In revenge, one assumes, for the letter Raleigh sent to Master Secretary suggesting Cobham was holding secret assignations with La Rensy. But in making that retraction about Raleigh, see how it absolves Cobham as well? "I never had conference with you in any treason, nor was ever moved by you to the things I heretofore accused you of ". You see how that clears Cobham as well as Raleigh? Our Daniel is not only washing his hands clean of blood, he is trying his best to get out of the lions' den into

340

which he put himself with his ill-considered confession. It is a commonplace that men who have pled guilty to some crime will in the end declare themselves innocent after all. Especially in cases such as this where the sentence is likely to waver between beheading and hanging, drawing and quartering!'

'So,' said Poley, 'we can even advise Master Secretary that he would be safe to allow the retraction to appear when Raleigh eventually faces his full, formal trial by the council? It poses no threat to his case because it can be explained away in these terms?'

'Yes. But there is a further element you should bear in mind. The council will be providing prosecutors. Attorney General Sir Edward Coke and Lord Chief Justice Sir John Popham almost certainly be there as well as a panel of judges, including Master Secretary Cecil himself I would hazard. But in the final analysis, guilt or innocence will be decided not by the prosecution or the judges but by a jury of Raleigh's peers. And it is those twelve good men and true who must be convinced either way, beyond a reasonable doubt. But remember, there is no automatic assumption that the accused is innocent until proved otherwise. Like Caesar's wife, the accused must not only be innocent, he must be seen to be innocent. And it is often the case that the slightest thing can destroy that appearance in the jury's eyes. No matter what the prosecution are given to work with beyond Cobham's confession plain and simple, they only need to convince the jury that the confession was given in good faith and is true while the retraction was the action of a man whose nerve was failing him at the last moment and is therefore deeply suspect.'

'So, we proceed,' said Poley.

'You do. And as far as I can see, you only have one more step to take, and that is the formal indictment. Which I will be happy to draft for you, based upon Cobham's full confession. Having drafted it, I will take it to Sir Edward

Coke as King's Counsel and Attorney General and to Lord
Chief Justice Popham to see which of them wishes to start the
process by presenting Raleigh with the formal charges he will
have to face when the matter goes to formal examination
before the council and, if they so decide, to trial, whenever
that will be.

So, as the last week in July approached – as did King James,
Queen Anne and their households – Poley found himself in
company with chief investigator Sir William Waad,
Lieutenant of the Tower Sir John Peyton, Sir John Popham
Lord Chief Justice and King's Counsel, Attorney General Sir
Edward Coke, all seated behind the long table in the
interrogation room. Facing them, with a guard at each
shoulder, stood Sir Walter Raleigh. Raleigh stood erect, silent
and unmoving as Coke read out the charge he would have to
face before the Council for further questioning and at his
formal trial in due course:

'That you, Sir Walter Raleigh, with other persons, have
conspired to kill the king, to raise a rebellion, with intent to
change religion and subvert the government, and, for that
purpose, to encourage and incite the king's enemies to invade
the realm.

'The overt acts charged are as follows:

'Item: that you, Sir Walter Raleigh have conferred with
Lord Cobham about advancing Arbella Stuart to the Crown
of England, and dispossessing the king;

'Item: that it was arranged by you that Lord Cobham should
go to the king of Spain and the archduke of Austria to obtain
from them six hundred thousand crowns for the purpose of
supporting Arbella Stuart's claim to the throne.

'The indictment further charges the following:

'Item: that it was also agreed by you that Cobham should
return by the Isle of Jersey, and there meet you, Sir Walter
Raleigh, as Governor of the island, to consult further of the
plot and the distribution of the six hundred thousand crowns;

'Item: that Lord Cobham communicated this agreement to George Brooke, who assented to it; that Cobham and Brooke said that 'there never would be a good world in England till the King and his cubs were taken away', as you Sir Walter Raleigh had first observed;

'Item: that, in furtherance of the above confederacy, you, Sir Walter Raleigh delivered to Cobham a book written against the king's title to the crown, which Cobham afterwards delivered to Brooke for the purpose of confirming him in his treasons;

'Item: that Cobham, by the instigation of you, Sir Walter Raleigh, persuaded Brooke to urge Arbella Stuart to write letters to Count Aremberg and the king of Spain, which Brooke undertook to do; that Cobham also wrote letters to Count Aremberg for the advance of six hundred thousand crowns, and sent the letters by one Dutton, a recusant in the employ of you, Sir Walter Raleigh, and also by Matthew La Rensy, the Count of Aremberg's man;

'Item: that, by letter received by Lord Cobham, Count Aremberg promised the money and that Cobham then promised you, Sir Walter Raleigh, that on the receipt of the money he would give you eight thousand crowns for your personal use, the rest to be used in pursuance of the plot to kill the king and to raise a rebellion, with intent to change religion and subvert the government as aforesaid, and, for that purpose, to encourage and incite the king's enemies to invade the realm.'

'This is the charge is it?' demanded Raleigh.

'It is,' answered Coke.

'But it turns upon the evidence of one accuser – and that evidence has since been retracted!'

'Points you may raise during your formal examination in Windsor,' snapped Coke. 'Points which you may raise again at your trial. For you will go to trial, Sir Walter, be in no doubt about that. And upon the charges I have just read to you.'

'You will be held here until an occasion can be arranged for you to appear before the Privy Council,' said Popham. 'Which may take some time, given the importance of our attending His Majesty's coronation.'

'And,' added Peyton, 'because we expect His Majesty, the Royal Family and their household almost hour by hour now, you will be held under close confinement until the coronation ceremony has been completed.'

65

Now that his principal assignment was successfully concluded, Poley expected to be ejected from the Tower, especially as the royal household was due at almost any moment. He was well aware that other responsibilities awaited him at Salisbury House to where Phelippes had already gone. But a kind of lethargy overtook him and so he was content to await a summons or an eviction. But it seemed that, now he and Sir William Waad had established the facts and the guilt appertaining to the Plot of the Bye and the Plot of the Main, everyone simply forgot about him.

'Or,' suggested young John Peyton, cheerfully unaware of the damage he had done to his father's career by smuggling Raleigh's letter or that he and his family were facing imminent eviction themselves, 'nobody else wants to bed down in rooms immediately above so much gunpowder. Did you hear about the powder mill that exploded across the river at Redriffe?'

At first, Poley counted himself fortunate to remain in the Tower clear of the plague but all too soon the sickness breached the curtain walls and the place became a trap for him almost as confining as it was for Raleigh and Cobham. This feeling was compounded by the arrival of Tom one afternoon a few days later with an urgent summons from Lady Janet. It was contained in a note sent via Janet's maid Agnes to Salisbury House and then by Phelippes via Tom to Poley himself. The message which Tom delivered after gaining entrance through the main gateway from the city requested Poley to come to Essex House at once. But there was no date on the note that Tom handed over, and Phelippes had not added any indication of when it had arrived at Salisbury House.

Frowning with concern, Poley was in action at once, only to find his plans frustrated almost instantly. With Tom at his shoulder, he hurried down to Tower wharf, planning to take a wherry upriver to the Essex House steps. But the entire riverside was closed to him – King James, Queen Anne and their attendant households were just arriving. Their barges jostled for limited space on the waterfront, the wharves themselves were packed with men and women whose bags and baggage made things even more congested and whose excitement at arriving here was rapidly turning to irritation. There were only two realistic options open to the impatient intelligencer – to wait for the royal parties to finally come ashore and clear their luggage or to retrace the steps Tom had taken in coming here.

Poley decided on the latter course and the pair of them set off side by side back up from the wharf, in through the outer curtain wall then left, past the Cradle Tower on their left and the Lanthorn Tower on their right, walking as fast as they could past the Wakefield Tower on their right and St Thomas's Tower above Traitor's Gate on their left, past the main entrance onto The Green beyond the Bloody Tower, then onward past the Bell Tower and the Byward Tower, over the bridge across the moat to the Middle Tower, and out onto Tower Green.

Here they turned left once more and almost ran down Petty Wales to the eastern end of Thames Street. The first building they came to on the corner there was the Dragon Inn, which boasted a stable and not many customers, given the number of potential patrons fleeing the plague-smitten city, despite the counter-pull of a coronation in prospect after a few more days at most. Within a very few minutes, they were both mounted and cantering down Thames Street, westward towards the distant Strand. Thames Street was unusually empty, something explained by the mounting fury of the plague which was itself emphasised by the constant clangour of the church bells as they rode past belltower after steeple

346

after spire, all, it seemed, tolling out the nine tailors for a dead man or six tailors for a dead woman in the parish. There was little opportunity for conversation and no point in it either, so Poley was left to his own thoughts which were soon as dark as the gathering shadows.

Poley's concern for Lady Janet and the reason for her uncharacteristic summons was slowly subsumed by more immediate impressions. Night was falling and the city through which he and Tom were riding was rapidly becoming a strange, almost alien place. It was some while now since Poley first took up residence in the Tower and in that time London seemed to have changed. Its very life-breath and its urgent civic pulse both appeared to be faltering. The bustle he was used to in the early evening had slowed – almost ceased. Streets he had last seen filled with golden brightness from numberless flambeaux and lanterns lit against nightfall, were now cavernous with shadows; their eerie darkness emphasised by one or two distant flickers of sepulchral lamplight. Even London Bridge, when they crossed Fish Street and could look down at it down the hill beyond St Magnus' church, was a depressingly dim reflection of its usual self. The further they went the worse things became. Increasingly, the shadows on their right, which hid the bulk of the city, were filled with ghostly cries of inarticulate agony and distress. Such light as there was showed door after door marked with the hay-bales and crosses that warned of sickness and death within. The only movement in some areas seemed to be the plague carts collecting the recently deceased, under the guidance of the local Searchers, and carrying them to the plague pits for burial. The only audible words that made any sense amid the clamour of the bells and the howls of distress were, 'Bring out your dead. Bring out your dead…'

But then, as Poley and Tom reached the western end of the city, the grim atmosphere was weirdly compounded by the preparations the Lord Mayor and the London guilds had made

347

to welcome their new king before the proclamations that announced he was not coming into the city after all. There were wooden arches straddling the road King James and Queen Anne were no longer going to follow. They were hung with decorations of all sorts. But these had been left to decay, in the knowledge that the royal procession would never be passing this way. Not until the plague died down, at any rate, thought Poley. And the plague was unlikely to loosen its grip until the autumn – and even then only if the weather became cool and dry. In the last few years, autumns had been stifling, hot and humid so the plague had stayed rampant for another month and more. The sodden decorations drooped, flags and banners dangled like wet rags, the garlands of flowers hung bedraggled and rotting into fetid slime. The arches themselves were swollen, splintering, coming apart at the joints. The gaudy paint with which they had been decorated was blistered and oozing – as though the constructions had caught the plague themselves and were covered with lethal buboes like the citizens dying nearby.

66

At last Poley and Tom passed St Peter's Church and the Barklay Inn, then they swung right up Addle Hill and into Blackfriars. They trotted out through Lud Gate just before it was closed for the night and cantered down to Essex House. They stopped here, shocked and concerned. For Essex House was shut up tight. The gates into the Strand were closed; the great house they protected was dark and clearly empty. Essex's mother Lady Lettice had clearly gone to one of her other houses. And so had her tenant Henry Percy, Earl of Northumberland, together with his household. Which included Lady Janet.

'They should all still be here,' said Poley, trying to order his thoughts. 'At the very least, Earl Henry must have some sort of duty in the coronation ceremony.'

'Do you think that's why she wrote you that note?' asked Tom after a few moments, as the pair of them sat, looking up at the deserted mansion while their horses snorted and shook their heads, impatient to be gone. 'Because the Earl has moved them all somewhere else as he gets ready?'

'I don't know,' answered Poley. 'I hope it was only something as unimportant as that. But I somehow doubt it.' He shook his head, consumed with deep foreboding.

'Where shall we go now?' asked Tom, almost as shaken as Poley.

'Home,' said the intelligencer. 'Home to the Lion.'

'I can let you have one of your old rooms,' said Gilbert Gifford as the stable lad was seeing to their horses in the stables behind the Lion tavern. 'You'll have to share with young Tom here. I've given your other room – the one with the bed in it – to Sir Anthony Standen. But I warned him the outer room would probably go too. I'm packed to the rafters.

But I can let you have a couple of mattresses and some bedding – and it won't be for long. The coronation's on St James's Day and that's hardly any time at all. Only the Good Lord knows how many have come to see it. And they're all down this end of town because the king and queen will have to process to Westminster Abbey from Whitehall Palace I would guess for the ceremony, even if they're not coming through the city from the Tower as is traditional.'

This conversation was taking place in the tap room which – like the tavern itself - was heaving. Poley scanned it and was aware of Tom doing the same at his side.

'Needs must…' shrugged Poley, glancing back from the bustling barroom and turning towards Gifford once again. 'But I have more important things on my mind at the moment. Do you have any news of the Earl of Northumberland?'

'Of Lady Janet Percy, you mean…' Gifford gave a knowing wink. 'Nothing in particular, why?'

'Essex House is shut up tight and obviously empty. Does anyone know where they've all gone?'

'Fled, mayhap,' suggested Gifford. 'The Earl has been mentioned on the outskirts of a plot to kill the king from what I hear. And there's men held in prison awaiting formal examination and trial.'

'I know,' said Poley shortly, surprised that the information, which he had supposed to be secret until all the suspects were taken up, was current already.

'They say Sir Walter Raleigh is taken. And Lord Cobham,' said a familiar voice behind Poley. He turned and found himself face to face with Sir Anthony Standen. 'As you of all people should know…'

Poley met his intelligencer's quizzical gaze and kept his own mouth firmly closed. He glanced at Tom to make sure he was being equally tight-lipped.

'The importance of the plotters seems to have been emphasised by His Majesty himself – in the latest proclamation,' Sir Anthony continued, amused by the dogged silence from his two colleagues. 'At the coronation, as is traditional, the king will offer a general pardon to everyone still held in jail for any offence. Except for Catholics, those accused of witchcraft and those being held on suspicion of involvement in the two plots known as the Bye and the Main.'

'Any particular names?' wondered Poley.

It was Tom who spoke next. 'I see Nick Skeres and Will Udall over there,' he said. 'Perhaps we should ask them.'

Ten minutes later, Poley's team of intelligencers was gathered in the outer of the two rooms he usually occupied. They were grouped round a table, some sitting, some standing. The little room was crowded even though the mattresses and bedding had yet to arrive.

Udall reported first. 'Watson and Clark are still at liberty,' he said. 'They are by far the most dangerous. Apparently, they're running from one recusant house to another, priest-hole after priest-hole. There are too many like Sir John Gage around the city and the country for such men to be easily found. Even with the priest hunters after them. Sir John Gage is taken up, though. As is Sir Griffin Markham and his brothers, I understand.'

'Word is that Sir George Brooke is being held,' added Nick Skeres. 'And so is Lord Grey de Wilton, though no-one is quite sure where. And with them under lock and key Anthony Copley is undergoing questioning as well – and it was probably his evidence that has condemned them.'

'Once Watson and Clark are taken, the backbone of the Bye Plot will be broken,' said Poley. The others nodded their agreement. 'But we do need to find them as soon as possible...'

Poley had reached this point when Gifford himself knocked on the door and thrust his head round the edge at once. 'Poley,' he said. 'You're summoned.'

'At this hour?' said Poley. 'Where to?'

'Richmond. There's a barge waiting at Westminster stairs.'

351

Phelippes was waiting in the barge, gazing up at the fresh decorations that had been placed there in preparation for the coronation. The fact that Phelippes was there told Poley who had summoned him, not that there had been much doubt. But, 'How did Master Secretary know where I was?' he asked as the vessel pulled out into the stream.

'He didn't,' answered Phelippes. 'The barge has been at the Tower and at Salisbury House. That's where I was picked up.'

'So, we're off to Richmond.'

'Apparently Sir Francis Bacon is currying favour,' said Phelippes. 'A wise enough move in the circumstances. He's staying in his rooms at Grey's Inn so that Master Secretary can have the loan of his house across the river from Richmond Palace. Well clear of the city and the plague. And better lodged than even Lord Justice Popham.'

'That's all well and good,' said Poley. 'But why does he want to see us all of a sudden?'

The answer to that was simple enough and had Poley been less concerned about Lady Janet he could have worked it out for himself. Most of it at any rate.

'There are still too many of them out there,' said Master Secretary as the three of them sat in the main reception room of Bacon's Richmond house. 'And both Watson and Clark represent a potent danger.' They were seated on comfortable chairs grouped around a table whose only contents was a large carved wooden box. There had been no offer of refreshment either from Master Secretary or from his mistress Lady Catherine Howard who had vanished as soon as Poley and Phelippes appeared. Poley had stayed here before and had to concentrate on what Cecil was saying as the familiarity of the location brought back more distracting memories. 'If they are convinced by the argument that Watson amongst others has used,' continued Master Secretary, 'then the coronation is the last moment they have to kill James before he becomes king of England and the act therefore becomes

352

High Treason. And, if His Majesty is correct in his beliefs about kingship, it also comes close to blasphemy, for he considers himself to be God-appointed.'

'God-appointed?' queried Phelippes, who had clearly never heard the phrase before.

Master Secretary looked at his senior intelligencers, his face absolutely expressionless. 'I have heard him say, in conversation, as I believe he is preparing to repeat to Parliament in due course, that the state of monarchy is the highest thing upon earth. Kings are not only God's lieutenants, and sit upon God's throne, but even God himself calls them gods. That's what King James believes and it was, I believe, ideas such as this which first put the notion of limiting royal power through a kind of commonwealth into Sir Walter Raleigh's head.'

'So,' said Poley, 'the coronation might well be the most dangerous time of all unless God Himself is willing to take a hand and protect his earthly equivalent. Something that history suggests that He is very loth to do.'

'What do you wish us to do about this?' asked Phelippes.

'Godless though we are,' added Poley quietly.

'You and the men you have been working with are the only ones who have seen Watson, Clark and a number of their associates,' said Master Secretary with a frown at Poley. 'You would recognise them at once were they to hide themselves amongst the crowds who have come to see the king crowned. Under normal circumstances, the old queen's guard could be counted upon to augment and advise the new king's guard. But the old Captain of the Guard is in the Tower and his men are scattered. The new Captain of the Guard, Lord Erskine of Grogar, has found it hard enough to assemble a full-strength detachment and both he and the king are set on using them to make the ceremonial more impressive. So, in many ways the king and queen will be unguarded as they process towards Westminster and enter the Abbey. His Majesty is not unaware of the danger, of course. It is little more than thirty years since the Earl of Moray, was shot dead as he rode through Linlithgow. And the assassination of William the Silent took place only twenty years since, in Delft. The two deaths stand as paradigms for any malcontent who can get his hands on a gun and find a place close enough to shoot the king with it.'

'I see,' said Poley. 'You wish to use us as a last line of defence. But how are we to be employed? Deployed, rather? Made effective against men with pistols, should they suddenly appear?'

'By these,' said Master Secretary. 'They are by Balthazar Dressler of Dresden and I am assured they are the best that money can buy.' As he spoke, he stood, leaned over and opened the box on the table. As the lid was raised, a hinged section of the front swung down to reveal a matched set of six of the most elegantly lethal wheellock pistols that Poley had ever seen.

67

'You'd better be absolutely certain about whoever you give one of these things to,' said Phelippes next morning as a wherry rowed them downstream after a night grudgingly allowed by Master Secretary bedded down in Francis Bacon's servants' quarters.

'I see two main problems,' said Poley. 'Other, that is, than carrying these about but keeping them hidden. They are nearly two feet long and they must weigh a couple of pounds each; they are soldiers' weapons after all, designed for cavalry rather than infantry by the look of them. Then, I have to be certain that whoever has one knows how to use it and can fire it with reliable accuracy.'

'I hadn't thought of that,' said Phelippes. 'But it only makes my point even more vital. You had better be equally certain that your extra-accurate gun-men aren't going to be shooting these things at the king as opposed to his enemies.'

'Yes, I know. I've been going through everybody in case we have a turncoat in our midst. But no-one comes readily to mind.'

'Well, who have we got?' Phelippes extended Poley's thoughts and started counting on his fingers. 'There's you and me – we're pretty trustworthy. Then who? Your brother-in-law Tom. He's new to us. Do we trust him?' Phelippes shrugged when Poley said nothing, then continued. 'Nick Skeres? He'd swindle your grandam out of her last farthing but at least we've known him for years. And Ingram Frizer if we can get him up from Eltham in time. We know he doesn't flinch at killing.'

'Udall and Standen are unknown elements,' said Poley. 'But let's not rule them out. We have a day in hand to get ready and at least they are both close by.'

'Good,' said Phelippes. 'If we don't count Frizer, that's six of us true enough. What's the plan?'

'I'm confident I can handle a wheellock pistol with ease and accuracy; what about you?'

'The same.'

'So, we can rely on ourselves whether we get any practise or not. What I plan to do is to give the guns to the others and see how they handle them. We are fortunate in that the box here not only contains wheellocks but enough powder and shot to arm a regiment of musketeers.'

'So that's it?' asked Phelippes. 'Find a field and blaze away until everyone can load, prepare and fire in a reasonable time. Then shoot accurately enough to hit something – preferably something they were aiming at?'

'And not one of the others.' Poley gave a wry smile. 'No, that's only one element. I'll have to walk the new coronation route and look out for obvious places an assassin could use as a vantage point. Thank the Lord it's a short route and one we're already pretty familiar with. The Earl of Moray was shot from an upper-storey window. That's where we'll focus our energies. William the Silent was shot in his house. We can't get close enough to the royal party to cover that. If someone manages to smuggle a pistol into the Abbey, we'll be lucky to stop him.'

'So…' said Phelippes. 'What? If there are windows that offer a good clear shot…'

'One of our men should be at them. That should stop anyone else from using them.'

'Good. But to be fair, a man guarding a window doesn't need a wheellock. A dagger would do just as well. Or a club, come to that. And, now I think of it, I can't begin to calculate how many windows there actually are overlooking the route – short though it is. Windows within the range of a pistol or even a carbine, remember. Moray was shot with a carbine.'

'Right,' said Poley. 'We clearly need more men to stand guard. I'll see if Gifford knows any reliable associates who can help us.'

'So, you want the men with the guns in the crowd.'

'In the crowd but unobtrusive,' confirmed Poley. 'And moving to stay in contact with the king and queen as they process to the Abbey.'

'But not into the Abbey.'

'Let's pray that there's no need for anyone to be in the Abbey,' said Poley.

'I'd have thought,' said Phelippes grimly, 'that we'll need to pray for a good deal more than that.'

King James's Coronation Day dawned overcast, dull and damp. A fine drizzle fell relentlessly from a low grey sky and soaked everyone standing out of doors as effectively as the heaviest downpour. On the previous day, which had been bright and sunny, the royal party returned from the Tower wharf to Westminster stairs while Poley and his team were practising their marksmanship in St Martin's Fields at the end of Cockspur Street and Hedge Lane. Despite those doing the target-practice being inexperienced with the weapons and in some cases being worryingly maladroit, none of the local washerwomen laying out their sheets to dry, the local herdsmen or their cattle sustained any real damage. By the end of a long day, Tom was loading, priming and firing with some speed and accuracy. Sir Anthony was loudly upset at having to demean himself with a commoners' weapon that stank worse than Raleigh's foul tobacco; however only Poley himself was faster and more accurate with Master Secretary's Saxon weapons.

The weather on St James' Day, carefully chosen for King James's coronation, at least meant that Poley and the five of his intelligencers armed with Cecil's two-foot wheellocks could use their cloaks to conceal the weapons and to keep their powder dry. Poley fought to see this as a positive thing, though he was also well aware that it afforded any would-be

357

assassins the same anonymity and security. He was hopeful, however, that the modern and expensive guns he and his men were carrying had one advantage over any that Watson, Clark or their confederates could get their hands on – they had tight-fitting pan covers which slid forward to protect and secure the powder in the pan itself and only slid back at the instant the gun was fired. It was possible, therefore, to carry the wheellocks already loaded, primed and ready to fire at an instant's notice.

Other than that, it was difficult to see anything positive in the situation or the approaching ceremony. Rather, it was the stuff of Poley's nightmares. The royal couple would walk from Westminster's Privy Stairs, past the Star Chamber and Westminster Hall through New Palace Yard where the rest of the procession would fall into place around them. Then out into King Street where the house-fronts had all been hung with white cloth. Then they would turn, pass through a sizeable, brick-built arch, which was buttressed and adorned with various religious decorations, into Broad Sanctuary and the Abbey's precinct. They would then cross the precinct passing the entire length of the Abbey and enter through the Great West Door. The Abbey would already be filled with the great and the good called hither to witness the ceremony, places reserved for those taking part in the procession.

Just as the main path of the procession's route had been hung with white fabrics, all the side-streets reaching off the route to one side or the other were festooned with violet cloth. Poley and Phelippes had watched it all being hung as they walked the route the previous evening after target practise was complete. 'Do they not realise,' said Poley softly but bitterly, 'that their pretty decorations are simply offering cover to anyone wishing to complete Watson's plans?'

'Gifford can raise an army of window-watchers,' said Phelippes bracingly. 'He says he can place them at any windows we wish – local folk are likely offering view-points, wherever they have them, to any that will pay.'

'If we offer sufficient coin, then, we can perhaps secure the king and queen,' said Poley more loudly but no less bitterly.

'Needs must,' said Phelippes with a shrug.

And so it had been agreed.

68

Putting the windows and the cost of stationing Gifford's men at them out of his mind, Poley began to place his guards amongst the gathering crowds in the first grey light after the dull, drizzling dawn next morning. Nick Skeres was stationed near the Westminster Privy Stairs with a good view up and down the river as well as into New Palace Yard outside Westminster Hall. Standen was stationed at the corner where the procession would exit New Palace Yard into King Street. They were Poley's most reliable men and they needed to be: the Yard was a point of potent danger. For a start, it would be filled with the members of the procession who would only move when the king and queen arrived. There was little room for the crowds of well-wishers who wanted to see the royal barge dock so only the most desperate would force their way in. The most desperate and the most calculating, for the river offered a tempting escape route to a successful assassin after the fatal deed was done. The king had ordered a proclamation read throughout the city and nearby locations on the Southwark side as far downriver as Redriffe and upriver as far as Lambeth warning that anyone crowding the water with unauthorised vessels would face arrest. But Poley was well aware that few watermen would obey this once they too were offered enough coin by the crowds of eager spectators. Moreover, during the Essex uprising, several shots had been fired at Sir Walter Raleigh when he approached the north bank in a small wherry. The king and queen would likely be even more exposed in an open barge. Poley had his work cut out ensuring the king's safety on the streets of Whitehall and Westminster. He could no more control what happened on the river than he could control what happened in the Abbey.

Once the royal couple came ashore and the procession started, Nick would move as unobtrusively as possible keeping as close to the king as he could. And so would Standen once the procession came out onto the public roads. Tom was stationed at the arch which opened into the Abbey precinct but by the time the royal pair reached him, Skeres and Standen would be close at hand, able to support the lad if need-be. Those three would follow the king and queen for as long as they could. Poley, Phelippes and Udall, on the other hand, had a less structured but equally vital mission.

Poley and his two companions started at the Lion after they agreed with Gifford where his team of watchers would stand and how much they would cost to deploy. Then the three of them exited, joining the excited crowd choking King Street as far back as Charing Cross and Cockspur Street, all a-buzz with excitement. Separating but maintaining eye-contact, they moved through the close-packed bodies. Poley at first pulled his hood up but almost immediately discovered that it restricted his vision far too much to be risked. He pushed it back, therefore, and tried to concentrate on the men and women surrounding him, though he could not help but glance up at the windows overlooking the end of the street. All of them, stood wide, almost all packed with animated faces. Each also, thank the Lord, seemed to contain one face frowning with concentration as he watched for trouble below him and, Poley hoped, behind him too.

Yesterday had demonstrated that Master Secretary's weapons had a range of fifty paces, though the accuracy at that distance was by no means reliable. Height and luck, however, might well put the king in danger as much as eighty paces away. And one of Gifford's watchers had served as a musketeer and warned that if anyone got a carbine up to one of the windows overlooking the king's route, the royal couple would be in danger at a range of one hundred and twenty paces, perhaps one hundred and forty. It all depended,

everyone agreed, on how good a target King James and
Queen Anne presented.

A few minutes after ten, although he had no real idea of the
time, Poley was alerted by the sound of cheering and the
sudden movement of the crowd in front of him, as though a
new current had swept into the side of this river of humanity.
Clearly the royal barge was approaching the Westminster
Privy Stairs. The intelligencer glanced towards his two
nearest colleagues and redoubled his efforts to move forward.
He joined Standen at the exit from New Palace Yard as
twelve men dressed in gold tabards marched out, formally,
shoulder to shoulder. The crowd parted in front of them and
they processed into the open road, turned left and continued
towards the Abbey through the heart of the cheering throng.
Poley got the briefest sight down to the water and saw the
king and queen being handed up out of their gilded barge. It
was the merest glimpse, hardly a heartbeat long and then the
next section of the coronation parade obscured his view.
Representatives of the merchant guilds, city officers and Lord
Mayor Sir Thomas Bennet formed up in a walking wall of
damp red broadcloth that followed their gold-clad leaders out
onto the street. No sooner had they reached Standen and
Poley than the martial beat of drums began and a blast of
trumpet call rang out. A parliament of judges followed by
Lord Chief Justice Popham, all in their robes and chains of
office appeared, all of them completely dry. 'Waiting in the
Star Chamber building,' said Standen. Poley only just heard
him over the clamour.

'The others will be in Westminster Hall I should hazard,'
Poley shouted in answer, but his thoughts, like his eyes, were
elsewhere. He had nothing to fear from the justices, nor from
the knights of bath and garter who followed them. The more
such dignitaries that were in the parade, in fact, the more
likely it was that the king and queen might be all-but invisible
amongst them. But still he swung his gaze restlessly up across
the high windows, and down among the cheering faces at

street level. Then his focus switched back again as the barons and earls – some of whom he did not trust at all – came striding out of the Yard and turned down towards the Abbey and its precinct, passing Tom Watson standing guard at the arch. A poor showing of ambassadors joined the parade, many staying away in protest at the form of service James had announced he would be using, but the Princely Count Aremberg was there - like some of the earls, high on Poley's list of suspects. Elderly now, and by no means well, limping forward on gouty feet. But still wielding enormous power. Poley eased back from Standen, his eyes sweeping the nearby faces.

'Look!' spat Standen.

With a shock of recognition Poley saw Matthew La Rensy, who had played go-between carrying letters from Cobham and Raleigh to Aremberg. The two of them exchanged a long look, which struck Poley as being unsettlingly sinister. A hidden message was being passed and he had no idea what it might be.

But then another distraction called for his attention. The heart of the procession arrived. Three earls carrying ceremonial swords: Lord Edward Somerset, the Earl of Worcester was the Lord High Constable and the Earl Marshal; George Carey, a relative of Sir Robert Carey who took the ring to Edinburgh, was Lord Chamberlain. Behind them came Lord Buckhurst, carrying the crown. Behind Buckhurst came the king and queen. Both were dressed in bright red. Both wore golden coronets and Queen Anne had let her fair hair down. It clothed her breast, shoulders and back. It was a sign of purity if not quite chastity, thought Poley. Not given her current gravid state. But, together with the golden headgear and the red robes, that dazzling hair made an absolutely excellent target. But then, he thought with a cynicism that came close to blasphemy, perhaps God was looking after his divinely appointed deity-on-earth after all. The piercing drizzle had prompted whoever was in charge of the arrangements – Master Secretary as like as not – to have a cloth of gold awning held above the regal heads, supported by four long poles, each held by the barons of the Cinque Ports, even though their superior, Lord Cobham, was currently locked away safely in the Tower. It would take the eyes of a cat, the steadiest of hands and the luck of the Devil to send a shot through that into either of the prospective targets. Policing the windows had been a waste of time and money after all. Poley breathed a sigh of relief as Nick Skeres joined Standen at his shoulder. He glanced back again just in time to see Lady Arbella Stuart joining the procession, also shielded by cloth of gold. Then Standen, Skeres and he took their next steps forward towards the sanctuary of the Abbey.

'Poley!' snapped Skeres. 'It's Watson!'

69

'*Where*?'

'There!' Skeres gestured and Poley saw his worst nightmare coming true before his waking eyes. Watson hadn't bothered with a cloak, in spite of the rain but for obvious reasons. Despite his recusant beliefs, he was disguised as a Puritan. He was wearing a wide-brimmed *capotain* hat which seemed to be jammed on tight despite the wind and Watson's position, a black broadcloth doublet reaching almost to his knees, with breeches, stockings and stout shoes. He had managed to climb the buttresses and decorations on the arch that led into the Abbey precinct. His back was pressed to the brickwork but his foothold was steady. Under any other circumstances he would have stood out. But today, of course, every vantage point was swarming with onlookers hoping to catch a glimpse of their new king and queen. No-one gave yet another sight-seer a second look. And, had Skeres not recognised him, Poley would hardly have looked twice either. In a moment that had Poley teetering on the edge of madness, he realised that Watson was actually just behind Tom, who was stationed there but whose attention was focussed exclusively on the gaudy fascination of the procession with not the faintest inkling of what was going on. Not only behind him but also above him. Watson had placed himself just, calculated Poley, five feet above the roadway, his shoes level with Tom's shoulders, with his gun – if he had one - at the perfect angle to shoot below the leading edge of the canopy with the golden crowns, the flaxen hair and the bright red breasts as perfect targets.

Poley pushed wildly forward, only to find himself trapped on the wrong side of the road, with a solid wall of courtiers followed by the scarlet-clad halberdiers of Captain of the

Guard Lord Erskine of Grogar's command. It must be strange for the Scottish soldiers, thought Poley, side-tracked for a heartbeat, to be wearing English ceremonial dress instead of their native Scottish uniform. Or, like Henderson, the tartan of the Highlanders' great kilt. But in the blink of an eye he was back in the immediate present. It would be useless to shout – the air was ringing thunderously with cheering and cries of, 'God bless the Queen! Welcome to England and long may you reign!' He felt Standen stirring and caught his arm just as he went to raise his wheellock. 'If they see that we'll be dead before you can take aim, let alone pull the trigger,' he shouted into Sir Anthony's ear as he gestured at the halberdiers, each with his great axe on its long pole lowered but still lethal.

The instant he turned back, Poley saw something that gave him a flash of hope. Udall was pushing through the crush toward Tom. But then he realised the agent, like his young colleague, was too fascinated by the procession to look up or back. A moment later, Udall was standing beside Tom. Both of them watching, rapt, as king and queen approached, beneath their golden awning, with Lady Arbella close behind. There was no sign of Phelippes at all.

Watson wrestled with the silver buttons on his black doublet, reached under it for something concealed at his waist. After an instant clearly spent wrestling something free of his belt, he pulled out a wheellock pistol. It was half the size and appeared to be twice the age of the ones Master Secretary supplied. But it looked every bit as lethal.

'It won't fire,' said a deep voice behind Poley. 'Dinna fash yersel.' He and the others swung round and found Henderson behind them, still in his great kilt and bonnet with its eagle feather, his left fist resting easily on the hilt of his claymore. Poley paid no attention to the big Scotsman's airy assurance. Instead, he dived desperately forward into the red ranks of the halberdiers. At least they were carrying their fearsome weapons reversed, he thought, with the deadly spiked axe heads down by their ankles. Poley reckoned this fact, and a great deal of luck, might give him a chance to get through. That chance was enhanced at once by the fact that Henderson came hard on his heels and the other two followed the pair of them, spreading confusion left and right amongst the red-clad ranks. As Poley had hoped, the long poleaxes were clumsy weapons at the best of times, and anyone trying to lift his into battle-readiness in the confusion caused by their four bodies, soon found one end of the pole or the other tangled up with his neighbours to either side, in front or behind. There was little chance that the men immediately around Poley and his followers would have room or time to stop them after all. There were some quicker-thinking soldiers two ranks back from all the disorder, however. They stopped, gave themselves room and swung their axes up. 'The king!' bellowed Poley desperately. 'Guard the king!'

He burst through the far side of the procession and swung round at once, fighting to untangle his wheellock from the folds of his cloak. Just in time to see that he was too late. Watson had taken aim and now he pulled the trigger. The doghead hammer, loaded with iron pyrites designed to cause a shower of sparks swung down. The pyrites hit the spinning wheel and did indeed give off a cascade of sparks. But that was all. The powder in the pan was either wet or had been blown away. As Henderson predicted, the gun misfired. With desperate haste, Watson pulled out a tiny powder horn and reprimed the mechanism. But he would have to wind it once more as well, calculated Poley, and take aim all over again – with his target still marching towards him all unaware of the danger. The king stiff-backed, and limping; the queen almost dancing with excitement, waving and nodding to the ecstatic crowd.

Poley pulled his pistol free, but as he did so, there was an explosion close enough to deafen him. He saw the brick-work above Watson's head explode into red splinters. The would-be assassin flinched with shock at the near-miss, lost his footing and vanished behind Tom and Udall who were swinging round, their faces frozen with amazement. Skeres and Standen collided with Poley's back, causing him to step further forward, still disorientated, ears ringing, eyes streaming from the cloud of acrid smoke that suddenly enveloped him. He just managed to stop, rising on tip-toe as he did so. Phelippes was almost beneath the intelligencer's feet, curled around his still-smoking pistol, knocked to the ground by the crowd during Poley's moment of blindness. Flattened by outraged citizens who believed he was trying to kill the king and were ready to kill him now.

Then Henderson was standing over him, his great claymore angled across his broad breast. 'I'll watch your wee man here. You gang after yon murderous priest,' he said. His accent and his tartan were enough to call Lord Erskine's Scottish halberdiers to his side and by the time Poley turned with Skeres and Standen to push through towards the red brick arch, they were already forming a protective ring round the fallen man and his huge Highland protector.

70

Poley, Skeres and Standen were all carrying dangerous-looking wheellocks nearly two feet long. The crowd before them parted like the Red Sea before Moses. They ran towards the arch unhindered, Poley, in the lead, just able to see the king and queen pass safely into the Abbey's precincts. Then they swung right as they reached the arch itself. In the middle-distance Tom and Udall were visible with Watson's black-clad figure just ahead of them, hat gone, arms pumping, pistol in his right fist, seemingly forgotten in his panic to escape. There was no wall encircling the precinct on this side and a road – little more than a track after the last of the house-fronts – led down a slight slope past some more distant alms houses and a hospital towards the muddy expanse of Tothill Fields where the Horse Ferry docked on the north bank.

The soggy Fields, little more than a mud-bath after the rain of the last few weeks boasted only one notable feature apart from the ferry dock. This was the arena erected for trial by combat which could in very rare cases still be used to settle legal disputes. There was a gallery for the Lord Mayor and his panel of judges on one side and seating for spectators on the other. Needless to say, it was absolutely empty today. Watson ran through the midst of this at full tilt with Tom and Udall hard on his heels, Poley and Skeres hard on theirs with the more elderly Standen beginning to flag and fall behind. But the truth of the matter was that Watson had nowhere to go.

At the far end of Tothill Fields, a road ran from side to side from Finsbury Fields in the east to Poulteney Park in the west. Beyond it, reared a wall that stretched away on either hand. It marked the limit of the hunting grounds the old queen's father had created from the combined holdings of Eton

College and St James Hospital for female lepers whose burial pit lay in the Poulteney Park. St James's Park, as it was becoming known, was lower still, its grassed and bushy slopes leading down to a lake that was so full of aquatic birdlife that the Park was a favourite place for hawking as well as hunting, and the old queen had from time to time considered erecting an aviary there.

Seeing his escape cut off and clearly running out of breath, Watson hunched over, obviously trying to bring his wheellock back into commission. And, by the time he crossed the road and turned, with the wall at his back, he felt confident enough to raise it once again. 'Stop!' he shouted. Neither Tom nor Udall paid him any attention but continued their charge towards him, so he pulled the trigger.

This time the gun worked. The hammer drove the pyrites down against the spinning wheel. The result was a bright shower of sparks. The powder in the pan ignited, shooting flames through the touch hole and into the barrel where the main charge was rammed tight with its bullet safely secured by yet more wadding. The charge exploded with a great cloud of yellowish smoke and the bullet took Tom full in the chest, just below the pit of his throat and it killed him stone dead at once. He crashed face down in the mud and lay still. Udall hurled himself aside as though he feared the gun was just about to fire again. Poley threw himself down on one knee beside his brother-in-law. He turned the boy over to reveal the gaping wound at the top of his breast; a black hole large enough to have taken Poley's finger, like Doubting Thomas's thrust into the wounds of the resurrected Christ. He realised with a lurch that brought tears to his eyes that the young man's face, still and pale in death, looked exactly like the face of his elder sister, Poley's dead wife. The intelligencer saw this in a heartbeat, gasped with shock as though he had been struck and looked up once more. He had seen in that glance that there was nothing he could do for the boy. He began to pull himself to his feet looking for Skeres. Skeres had carried on at full tilt without the slightest hesitation but as he neared the wall and the terrified murderer, Watson threw his gun at his lone pursuer with all his strength, hitting him full in the face. The force of the impact was augmented by the speed of Skeres's charge and it knocked him off his feet. By the time any of them pulled themselves up and began to move forward once more, Watson had managed to scramble over the wall and had taken off across St James's Park as though he was a deer being hunted by the king.

In the Abbey, Master Secretary Cecil was seated comfortably observing the service as it got fully under way. The king of Scotland and his Danish queen sat on the lower step of a dais, on seats facing back towards the altar. In front of them, at a higher level were the thrones on which they would be seated as king and queen of England. Between the thrones, stood the ancient ceremonial throne of Edward the Confessor, whose seat was the Scottish Stone of Scone. James would be formally crowned King of England on this throne, though Cecil knew he wished to dispense with the divisive names England, Scotland, Wales and Ireland in favour of the universal name Britain. Beyond the thrones stood the altar covered in cloth of gold and laid out with cups and basins in the Protestant fashion. Part of the reason so many Catholic ambassadors had regretfully declined their invitations to attend.

Even so, Robert Cecil allowed himself a secret smile of success. Nothing could possibly go wrong now. Watson, Raleigh and all the rest had failed. He had outmanoeuvred them at every turn. James of Scotland would be king of England at last. And king of Britain as soon as he could have the name changed. Robert Cecil's position at the king's right hand was secure; his star was on the rise and likely to rise further and further still.

The Bishop of London, Richard Bancroft, whose church this was, had guided the king and queen to their places with the assistance of Tobie Matthew, Bishop of Durham, soon to be

371

back in possession of Durham House. The very reverend John Whitgift, Archbishop of Canterbury stood nearest to Edward the Confessor's throne as he prepared to place the crown on his sovereign's head. He, the Chancellor the Lord High Admiral and the Earl Marshal stood at the four corners of the raised platform. An expectant hush fell on the congregation. The ceremony began.

'Hear ye, Hear ye, Hear ye,' called the chief Herald. 'Gentles, you see before you James, the Sixth of that name King of Scotland, come here with due right of succession to be King of England. If any man have any reason to deny that King James the Sixth of Scotland is King James the First of England, let him speak now or forever after be held guilty of High Treason...'

Cecil choked on a laugh of amused surprise at this departure from the usual coronation service, swiftly turning the chuckle into a cough. So, Watson and his recusant friends, Raleigh and his law-books and Francis Bacon, were right all along, he thought. Killing James would not have been High Treason after all.

Until now.

71

Preparing Tom for burial opened a great well of sorrow and guilt in Poley. The need for a Crowner's Quest by the Coroner Royal, required by law because the lad had died violently within The Verge, a circle thirteen miles from the king, took him back ten clear years to the Quest on Kit Marlowe's violent death – a death in which he had been intimately involved. Further, the arrangements he had to make as Tom's only living relative emphasised to the intelligencer how terribly he had let down Tom's sister, his wife. There was no grave for her or her parents. They lay namelessly bundled in some anonymous plague pit, out of sight and out of mind. Not only had they no memorial, their memory had hardly disturbed the unruffled calm of his consciousness ion the years since their passing. He saw all too clearly how he had filled his mind with other distractions. As his wife lay dying, he had been working undercover far from home, mounting Joan Yeomans as his all-too-willing mistress. And after Joan's husband had taken his revenge, sent him to the Fleet prison and put the lickerish Joan far beyond his reach, Poley had packed his head instead with the fantasy of the unattainable Lady Janet Percy. Misinterpreting – no doubt – simple kindness and courtesy on her part as something so much more. The lapsed Catholic in Poley castigated himself with that notion, as he found it particularly painful. Often enough during the last few weeks he had bemoaned the lack of confession and absolution, both now closed to him. But he was not above engineering for himself the most powerful penance in the meantime. Not that he had any hope that the penitential agonies would cleanse his soul and give him any sort of a chance of Heaven when he stood

PETER TONKIN

naked before the Eternal Judge on Doomsday, with his heart
at last open and all his sins known.

So it was that he did not return to the Tower for another two
days, planning to remove his possessions from the room
above the powder store in the White Tower. There was not
much to collect, nor time to collect it in, unless he wished to
find himself benighted here. Consequently, he was just about
to hurry back down to Tower wharf when young John Peyton
appeared in his doorway. The lad looked as hangdog and
depressed as Poley felt. 'We are leaving the Tower too,' he
told Poley, looking around the bare room. 'My father has
found the last weeks too much of a strain to bear.
Furthermore, the fact that he failed to stop Raleigh and
Cobham communicating with each-other has angered Master
Secretary. Were Father not resigning the post of Lieutenant,
he would no doubt have been dismissed forthwith. And that
is my fault. How apt that it was an apple which caused our
downfall and expulsion. Though you could hardly call the
Tower any kind of Eden.'

'Well, it is done now,' sympathised Poley. 'And no real
harm – you have only ensured that your father gets what he
really wants – freedom from this place and the
responsibilities of being Lieutenant in these restless times and
dangerous days.'

'There is talk that Sir William Waad will succeed him,' said
John.

'He would be a good choice,' said Poley. 'But the king and
Master Secretary will wish to discuss the matter I have no
doubt.'

'Master Secretary is here,' said John.

'Here?' Poley was taken aback. 'In the Tower?'

'Yes. There have been new inmates brought in during the
two days since the coronation. He is interviewing them in
person. I'm surprised he has not told you.'

'I have been busy on other matters,' said Poley to cover the
fact that he too was surprised. 'Who is he questioning now?'

374

'I believe he is still with the Earl of Northumberland who was brought in with some of his close family today.'

'Northumberland you say? Sir Henry Percy?'

'I believe he was one of Sir Walter's circle and so he is now subject to the same accusations of treason as Sir Walter and Lord Cobham.'

'And the Earl's family, you said? Is Lady Janet Percy amongst them?'

'She is. I believe she is accused of withholding vital knowledge of plotting that she overheard at Essex House…'

Poley stood, irresolute, his mind racing. Then, 'Where is Master Secretary?' he demanded.

Henry Percy, Earl of Northumberland was in the relatively pleasant accommodation that had been occupied until recently by the Earl of Southampton, who had been a beneficiary of the change in monarch; though by no means a grateful or quiescent one, thought Poley. He found Sir Henry and Master Secretary sitting comfortably near the window and sharing a glass of wine, more like friends discussing the matters of the day than interrogator and subject.

'Ah, Poley,' said Cecil. 'Moving out? I hazard His Lordship here would be envious of you, had we not just come to an agreement.'

'Master Secretary,' said Poley. 'I would be grateful if we could discuss…'

'…Lady Janet,' Cecil completed the sentence for him. 'For an intelligencer, you are unsettlingly transparent, Master Poley. As it happens His Lordship and I were discussing that very matter. He is understandably disappointed that she eavesdropped on a private conversation between himself and some intimate friends. I on the other hand am disappointed that she did not report what she had heard much more swiftly than she did.'

'She reported to me, Master Secretary,' said Poley a little desperately. 'The delay was mine.'

375

'I suppose I should not look for truth either from an intelligencer or from a man in love, but I am further disappointed to find that you are lying to me, Poley. Phelippes has kept clear records which Lord Henry here has been happy to confirm. I'm afraid your russet song-thrush must stay caged for a little longer. Count yourself lucky – as she does – that she will remain here in relative comfort rather than in the Fleet, the Counter or the Clink. Now, be on your way before you join her.'

Thus dismissed, Poley was on his way towards the Tower wharf once more. He had just crossed Tower Green and was approaching the Bloody Tower when young John Peyton reappeared, ghost-like amongst the shadows. He was white with shock, shaking so much that he grabbed Poley's arm to steady himself. And when he spoke, his breath smelt of vomit. 'Hancock!' blurted the young man, as though the name of Raleigh's secretary was yet more vomit. 'Poor Edward Hancock!'

'What about him?' demanded Poley.

'Dead!' gasped John. 'Hanged himself!'

'How? Did Sir Walter not prevent such a desperate act?'

'He's not there. He's at dinner with Father. They are bidding each-other a final farewell.'

That phrase *a final farewell* struck a chord deep in Poley. He turned, his mind full of foreboding and, with John at his shoulder he ran back towards the Lieutenant's quarters. They crossed the lower end of Tower Green and pounded towards the Queen's House, where the Peyton family lived, as did every other Lieutenant and their families. John pushed the front door open and the two men hurried along the wood-panelled corridor to the dining room. John reached the door first and opened this one too. Then he hesitated. Poley pushed past him into the room. Sir John and Sir Walter were alone, seated on opposite sides of a modest dining table. On the board between them stood the remains of a supper – a loaf of bread, a plate of salad and a roast capon with a knife large enough to carve the carcase beside it on the platter. Both men looked up, surprised at the tumultuous entrance which had clearly interrupted an intense conversation.

Sir John's face folded into a frown. 'John!' he said, addressing his son as though Poley wasn't there at all. 'What…'

Young John looked from his father to Sir Walter, his mouth moving soundlessly.

'Well?' snapped Sir John.

The young man's gaze settled on Sir Walter. 'Hancock…' he said.

Sir Walter reacted with astonishing speed. He leaned forward, half rising out of his chair, reaching across the table. His fist closed round the handle of the carving knife and he snatched it off the platter, sending the carcase of the capon rolling onto the floor. His left fist joined his right on the handle and as he straightened, he turned the point against himself. He drove it with all his strength into his chest.

Quick as he was. Poley was quicker still. He flung himself forward, reaching for the knife. The steel point and the reaching hand arrived at Sir Walter's breast at the same time. The power of his thrust sent the blade through the middle of Poley's hand, but the intelligencer's wild lunge turned the knife's planned path. Instead of driving straight through Raleigh's heart, it skidded off a rib and opened a long gash in his side, tearing wide the cloth of his doublet, and the shirt beneath. Both men shouted with agony, but it seemed to Poley that Sir Walter's bellow also contained something of disappointment and frustration. The instant he realised his suicide attempt had failed, Raleigh let go of the handle and Poley staggered back, lifting his knife-skewered hand which seemed almost to have been cut in half.

The blade had pierced the back of Poley's hand, just missing the vein that ran down it and the point now stood out of the centre of his palm. The sharp edge was down towards the wrist and the blunt spine was towards the two central fingers, the blade separating the bones that led up to them. Blood was flowing copiously down front and back, though Poley, light-headed with shock and pain, nevertheless calculated that a good deal of the blood on the palm belonged to Sir Walter, who was slumped back in his chair, dazedly watching the great red stain on his side spreading down towards his right hip.

'John!' snapped Sir John. 'Get help!'

John vanished through the dining room door shouting, 'Help! Help! Sir Walter is sorely wounded.'

The lieutenant's household exploded into action. John's mother came rushing in, but staggered back when she saw the bloodstain on Sir Walter's side and Poley thought she was actually going to faint when she saw the state of his hand. The alarm was spreading out of the Queen's House and across Tower Green now. The sounds of yeoman warders shouting orders to one another was unmistakable. But it was the least likely respondents who were actually first to arrive and the most help. Master Secretary rushed into the room with Lady Janet close behind. 'I have brought Lady Janet Percy as Earl Henry assures me she has enjoyed wide experience treating wounds in her home beside the Debatable Lands,' he said, taking charge at once. 'We will see to Sir Walter first.'

'Lady Peyton, we will require hot water and cloth for cleaning, packing and bandaging wounds,' said Lady Janet, not at all disturbed by the state of either man. 'Perhaps the kitchen staff can supply our immediate needs if your water is clear and clean. And if you have any sage or witch hazel to hand, put them in the water as it boils. By the look of things, I will also require a needle and some thread.'

She joined Master Secretary at Raleigh's side. 'Sir John, could you aid us in tearing Sir Walter's doublet wide?' said Cecil. 'Lady Janet will need to get at the wound and any attempt to take off the doublet or the shirt beneath will simply make matters worse.'

Sir John obeyed and the sounds of ripping cloth almost drowned out the arrival of a squad of beefeaters. Poley, unbidden, apparently unremarked, seemingly forgotten, sank into a chair. He held up his stricken hand surprised to feel, all of a sudden, that it was growing strangely heavy; as though he was wearing a leaden gauntlet. Dreamily he thought of the iron boot he had shown Copley in the chambers below. That too could be filled with lead. Perhaps the pain of that would be worse. Perhaps not. He placed his riven hand in his lap as gently as though it were a sleeping babe and looked down at it, wonderstruck. Wave after wave of pain washed over him. He felt sick and wondered whether he should send for a bowl. Still in an almost dream-like state, he took the handle of the knife in his left fist and was just about to pull the blade free. 'Don't!' snapped Lady Janet. 'Poley! Leave it alone. You will only make the wound bleed more.' Her tone softened. 'I will attend to it in a moment. Be patient.' So, she's watching me after all, he thought. And the notion filled him with happiness.

As it became clear that Sir Walter's suicide attempt had failed, the tension eased and matters returned towards normal in the Tower – or as normal as could be expected with one wounded man one attempted suicide and one successful suicide. The dining room slowly emptied. Lady Peyton recovered sufficiently to oversee the removal of the food and the tidying of the room, though there was no real attempt to clean the blood until Sir Walter was helped away. Master Secretary, walking alongside the wounded man, was speaking softly but clearly enough for Poley to hear the first few sentences at least. 'Do not despair, Sir Walter. Yes, had you achieved self-slaughter before your trial you might have protected your family's assets from confiscation. But you might still be found not guilty by a jury of your peers. And even in the case of a guilty verdict, your wife and family's fate will be in the hands of King James and I'm sure we can

379

persuade him towards a merciful outcome. Take heart, I am by no means the only one who wishes you well…'

Outside, the yeoman warders assisted in the disposal of Hancock's body and sent word to the King's Crowner who was in for a busy few days. Sir John and Master Secretary sought alternative accommodation for Sir Walter and arranged that anything which might be used for self-harm be removed while a regular watch would be kept on him.

As soon as Raleigh was gone, Lady Janet crossed to Poley, bringing her bowl of hot, herb-filled water and her bandages. She had required minimal help in tending Sir Walter and that had been supplied by Master Secretary, Sir John and a couple of serving girls with strong stomachs. These had been a decided asset when Lady Janet began to stitch Sir Walter's wound closed.

Lady Janet dismissed them now, pulled up a stool, sat on it at Poley's side, his knees by her hips and hers beside his, the bowl placed carefully in her lap. She took his wounded hand, still skewered with the knife, and looked at it, tutting gently, like a mother tending a hurt child. She dipped a clean cloth in the steaming water then wiped the back of the hand and the palm, squeezing the hot liquid into the junction of skin and steel. Then with delicacy and gentleness – combined with smooth force – she pulled the blade out in one swift, sure motion. As soon as the blade come free, she pushed Poley's fist into the water with one hand while she laid the knife aside with the other. He gasped, fearing himself scalded. 'Hush,' she said. 'The heat will be of great benefit, as will the herbs. Open your fist. Let the water do its work.'

She pulled the hand out again after a moment and examined it as it dripped water and blood back into the bowl. 'You have stigmata,' she said. 'The wounds Our Lord suffered when he was nailed to the cross.' She glanced up at him almost roguishly from beneath the red curls of her fringe. 'You will be taken for a very holy man.'

'I doubt that, My Lady,' he said.

380

'Did my message reach you?' she wondered and she dabbed the bleeding wound in his palm.

'It did, but too late, alas. By the time I reached Essex House you were gone.'

'To house arrest in St James's Palace – and not the royal suite either. But you came? As soon as you received my note?'

'I did.'

'Well then, I thank you for that, kind sir.' She fell silent, busily packing front and back of his hand with wads of cloth to soak up any blood the bandaging failed to stanch. Then, as he watched her, wide-eyed with wonder, she took one long piece of linen and bound it tightly round and round his hand, leaving only the tips of his fingers and his thumb free. Finally, she tore the last six inches or so into two sections long enough to bind the whole thing securely in place.

She sat for a few more moments, holding his hand as though it was some sort of flower. Then, abruptly she leaned down and pressed her lips to it.

Poley caught his breath. It was as though he could feel the kiss, even through the layers of bandaging. Without a second thought, he too leaned down, sliding his left arm round her shoulder and pressing his own lips to the crown of her head. His nostrils filled with the heady scent of her perfume. Almost beyond his control, his arms tightened further still until she called gently, 'Robert! Robert my love, take care; you will spill the bloody water all over me!'

AFTERWORD

The only characters in this story who are not historical figures are Lady Janet Percy, Agnes, her maid, Kinborough, Magnall, Dutton and Tom Watson. Everyone named in the Bye Plot and the Main Plot is part of the historical record and acted in the manner described (though I have departed from the historical time-line on several occasions), as did the various members of the Privy Council. Poley, Skeres, Frizer, Udall, Standen, Rivers, Robert Catesby, Guy Fawkes and Matthew La Rensy not only lived but also served as secret agents; however, making them witnesses to and/or participants in the downfall of Sir Walter Raleigh is where the fiction begins. Any reader wishing to check the historical facts is warmly recommended to consult Leanda De Lisle's brilliant *After Elizabeth*.

SOURCES & AUTHORITIES
The Reckoning Charles Nicholl,
Elizabeth and Essex Steven Veerapen,
The Winding Stair Daphne DuMaurier,
The A – Z of Elizabethan London Adrian Procter and Robert Taylor,
Shakespeare's England R E Pritchard,
Elizabeth's London Liza Picard,
The Time Traveller's Guide to Elizabethan England Ian Mortimer,
The Elizabethan Underworld Gamini Salgado,
Hung, Drawn and Quartered Jonathan J Moore,
The Elizabethan Secret Service Alan Haynes,
Elizabeth's Spymaster Robert Hutchinson,
The Thames Peter Ackroyd,
Shakespeare The Biography Peter Ackroyd.

Most important, however, were the following crucial texts:

After Elizabeth Leanda De Lisle,

That Great Lucifer Margaret Irwin,

The Tower of London The Biography Stephen Porter,

Several internet sites were consulted, particularly: *The trial of Sir Walter Ralegh: a transcript* Mathew Lyons.

Any reader wishing to see how Simeon Foxe locked his letters should watch:

https://www.youtube.com/watch?v=16GAIaYN_Gk

I must also thank my wife Charmaine who is prime editrix on all my manuscripts, Angela, Librarian at Castletown library on the Isle of Man, and Dr Steven Veerapen for his excellent book, his help and advice.

Peter Tonkin, Hurghada, Castletown and Tunbridge Wells, 2022

Printed in Great Britain
by Amazon

17946238R00222